# A WOMAN OF TEXAS

*by Robert Tyler Stevens*

A WOMAN OF TEXAS
MY ENEMY, MY LOVE
FLIGHT FROM BUCHAREST
THE SUMMER DAY IS DONE

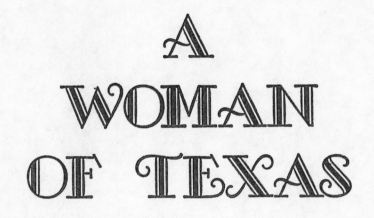

# A WOMAN OF TEXAS

**R. T. Stevens**

DOUBLEDAY & COMPANY, INC.

GARDEN CITY, NEW YORK

1980

ISBN: 0-385-15325-2
Library of Congress Catalog Card Number 79-7212

# A WOMAN OF TEXAS

# BOOK ONE

# CORDOVA

# 1

"*Amigo mío?*"

The white-clad Mexican brought his buggy to a halt on the dusty dirt road and glanced up at the man on a black horse. The horse was old but looked as if it still had as many active years ahead as others half its age. Its rider was of an indeterminate age, perhaps in his early thirties. His features, though finely drawn, were pleasant and gave him the personable quality of a man of good nature. But his blue eyes were hard and searching, so much so that the Mexican felt here was one who had known only maturity, who had been denied the irresponsible and carefree years of youth. He looked weathered from travel and lean from hardship. Around his cheekbones he did not have an ounce of flesh to spare. The sun and wind had burned him a deep, dry brown despite the shade given by the wide brim of his round black hat. His buckskin shirt showed dark patches of sweat, his pack sat solidly behind him. From the belt of his corded breeches hung a black scabbard, the hilt of an English cavalry sabre protruding. He smiled at the Mexican, his teeth gleaming below his dark moustache.

"Señor?" said the Mexican politely.

"My friend, what is this place?" The man's voice was clipped.

The Mexican turned to look back at the small town he had just left.

"Once it was called San Carlos, señor, now it is known as West-boro."

"Westboro." The man seemed satisfied. "What does it offer?"

"Americans, señor. They are everywhere in Texas now. They multiply. You are one of them?"

"A distant cousin, perhaps. English."

"So?" The Mexican thought about that. *Inglés. Americanos.* Was one any better than the other? "Is there a difference, señor?"

The black horse, which had known the heat of India, tossed its head. It might, during its years of listening to human tongues, have heard that question before. It might, in its gesture, have been offering an answer.

"A difference, my friend?" The man smiled again. "Well, we are old. The Americans are young." He seemed disposed to linger, sitting on his horse in the relaxed fashion of a rider who knew his mount's every sinew. "It's an attitude of mind."

"Ah," said the Mexican. He was given to lingering himself. For unless one's house was on fire, what did hurrying do for a man except to blur his pictures of life? "I have heard it said that a hundred men can look at the same mountain and each see it differently. You are saying, señor, that although the English and Americans speak the same tongue they see many things differently."

"True. We are hidebound by conventions and traditions, while the Americans subscribe only to the principles of being free. So they soar like birds."

"Señor," said the Mexican, "if I may say so, they come to ground very heavily at times. Nor do they always care whose ground it is."

"Well, we have done our share of that," said the man. Beneath the wide brim of his black hat his searching blue eyes glinted a little. He looked around. The sun, as fiery hot as brass, covered the land with bright, scorching heat. He thought about cool rain and wet grass. "What is there to do here?"

"If you do not have a land grant, or a rich American to work for, nothing," said the Mexican. "Do you have a land grant?" The enquiry was courteous.

"I only have my horse, my pack, and a few silver dollars," said the man, his eyes lined from so much peering into the sun. "What is your name, my friend?"

"José Ferrara."

"Are you a poor man, José?"

"Señor," said the Mexican gravely, "I have a fine wife, three children, and a place with Señorita Isabella Cordova. Therefore, I am neither poor nor rich. I am fortunate."

"Who is Señorita Isabella Cordova?"

To José the stranger was formidable enough to be suspect. Was he English, as he said? True, he did not talk like most Americans. But might he not be a representative of the new overlords of Texas? If so, perhaps that was why he was asking questions and why his eyes were so searching. It was a bewildering fact that Americans who had taken up residence in Texas had, after only a few years, claimed that the country was now theirs. An American called Houston said Santa Anna from the government in Mexico City had given it to them. But he, José, had not, nor had any of his family or friends, nor had the Comanches or Pueblos. Nor had Señorita Isabella. She was still angry about it. The man Houston said the people owned Texas now. Ah, but which people? The Mexican government had treated everyone as equal despite being imperfect, while the Americans, according to Señorita Isabella, had curious ideas about who were people and who were equal. Blacks, for example, were not people to them, so they did not qualify for being equal.

It was possible, thought José, that this man who said he was English had come from Houston to ask questions. Perhaps even to ask why the Cordova family had more land here than the Americans. He had just asked who Señorita Isabella was. That was strange in itself. She was the Cordova, everyone knew that.

"Señor," replied the Mexican eventually, "the señorita of whom I speak is the land, the river, and the hills."

"That," said the man, "is a little too cryptic for me, José."

"Then look." José took off his straw sombrero and described an arc with it. The man turned in his saddle and took in the panoramic vista embraced by the gesture. Every color devised by nature lay glimmering under the hot sun. In the distance rose a range of hills, barren, glinting and burning. The horizon danced in the heat. Yellow grasses created magnificent images of moving gold. Valleys dipped and shelved, and the cedar brakes stood in darkly massive possession of the southern acres. "That is Cordova, señor," continued José, "and though you might ride far in a day, you would touch but few of its boundary markers."

"God's life," said the stranger, "that is land enough for the King of Prussia himself. It all belongs to Señorita Cordova?"

"That is so, señor. And before her, to her grandfather, Don Carlos Cordova. It is good land, which is why the Cordova family bought it a hundred years ago when Spain ruled Texas. But some

Americans are saying it is not right for one family to own so much."

"It's not a modest estate, certainly. But if the family holds the deeds to all of it, there's nothing the Americans can do." The man sounded friendly, but José thought his eyes had not warmed to people for years. "Land titles and deeds are respected by every government."

"Perhaps you know about these things, señor. Look," said José, once again describing an informative arc, this time towards the town, "that is where the Americans have land. It meets Cordova land in many places. There is an argument now about part of Cordova land."

"The Cordova grant was made by the old Spanish provincial government?"

"So I believe, señor."

"Then that is good enough, José."

José made up his mind that the stranger, for all his questions, was an honest man. "Ah, señor," he said, "but they say there is someone who claims he was given part of the river land by Señorita Isabella's grandfather many years ago. The señorita disputes this and says that if any man sets foot on such land she will either shoot him or hang him."

"Personally?" Again a glint seemed to touch the hard blue eyes.

"It is not wise for any man to regard her too casually, señor."

"Is there temporary work I might do for Señorita Isabella Cordova? I'm short of funds, *amigo*. I must either gamble for a night or work for a while. And if I gamble I may lose."

"The señorita hires no hands, señor," said José. "She has us, her people. All who live on Cordova land and work for her are her people."

"A gentleman's work, then?" The man looked as if he had taken a liking to José. "I can speak and write Spanish, and could put her accounts in order in a week."

"You are an agreeable man, señor, but I doubt if there is anything not in order at Cordova."

"Well, I will take your word for it. Is there an hotel in the town?"

"There is a place where you can drink, señor," said José. "A place with rooms above it. I would not call it a hotel, although I believe it to be clean and comfortable. *Adiós*, señor."

"One moment." The blue eyes detained the Mexican. "Do you know of a man called Sylvestre?"

José smiled.

"Ah, señor," he said, "is that the last of your many questions or the first?"

"It's a question. Do you have an answer?"

"Señor, the full name of the Cordova family is Sylvestre y Cordova. That is the only Sylvestre I know of."

"Ah." It was almost a sigh. "It's the name of the señorita?"

"And of her father."

The shaded blue eyes flickered.

"*Gracias*, José. *Adiós*."

"*Adiós*, señor."

He rode slowly into the town. It was dry, dusty. Texas was a land of fierce beauty, variable enormities, and summer dust. It was the dust that invaded the towns, and drought that parched timber buildings.

The flies buzzed and bit. Scaffolding sprouted on developing sites. Westboro had a look of impermanence, as if it was there only out of temporary necessity. It was a deceptive look, for every solid town and village in America had grown out of pine or oak or cedar or other woods. And it was Americans who were making their mark here. Immigrants from the United States had built this particular town close to a Mexican-Indian village of tiny proportions called San Carlos. But most of the Indians had long since gone, squeezed out by the influx of rambunctious pioneering Americans.

The gringos had come to make of Texas what others had made of Arkansas and Kansas. They were big men or wiry men, and rarely without their long muskets. Neither, for that matter, had any sandalled Mexican or moccasined Indian ever seen an American pioneer with his boots off. Yankees were people who were either roaringly jovial or mutteringly terse: they spoke either to make the heavens quake or in elusive monosyllables that crept into whiskers or beards and were lost there. Many of them had been to places where the stillness of petrified forests or the echoing vastness of stone canyons appeared never before to have known the presence of man. And yet, finally, they had decided that Texas, above all places, offered God's greatest challenges and richest rewards to God's own men.

Those who had women took them on their wanderings. Gaunt women, strong women: women who had married them and followed them, and women who had been born of them. Women as leathery as any man. Women ruddy of face, or chapped brick-brown; women whose skin was honey-gold and women with thrusting cheekbones. And women, who for all the rigors, were handsome and shapely. As hardy pioneers as the men, they rarely lost sight of what they were striving for—the end of the wagon trail and a homestead of simple comfort. A homestead and a community, with children, a school, a church, and neighbors. A porch and just a little time to sit at evening's end, to watch the red sun slashing the sky, and the wild duck winging in from the Gulf. And sometimes even to catch the piping of the mockingbird.

It was an ever-receding dream for some, an ever-approaching dream for many, and a realised dream for those who had settled in the area of San Carlos, east of Cordova.

The boarded walks on either side of the street kept one's feet out of the mud when it rained; they were a civilised requirement for women at all times. One crossed the street when one had to—one did not actually use it. The man on the black horse ambled down this thoroughfare; coming to a halt halfway to look around. The sun was torrid; the shadows of buildings lay black over the pale dust. The rider heard the ring of cold iron striking hot from the forge. Nearby, a knot of tethered horses beat away at the flies with whisking tails. He saw a sign indicating that Elmer Harrison was the Prop. of the general store. Outside the store was a four-wheel carriage with a fringed top, brass hubs gleaming dully through a covering of dust. An Indian sat on the driving board, the reins lax in his hands. A small group of Americans stood on the boardwalk. All wore the flop-brimmed hats that looked like reductions of the Mexican sombrero. They were muscular, rangy men, with huge drooping moustaches and bristly chins. Theirs were the tethered horses, theirs were the muskets rammed into the leather holds on the saddles. As cheerful and amiable as they were in their exchange of talk, physically they seemed solidly entrenched in a space close to the door of the store.

A girl came out, a girl in a blue and white bonnet and full-skirted, flowered dress of India muslin. She was accompanied by her duenna, a buxom Mexican woman. Following them was an Indian, a tall slim Navaho, with sleek black hair banded. A long necklace of beads dangled against his shiny-buttoned jacket; under one arm he carried a musket.

One of the Americans spoke up.

"Now, ain't that like I said? An Injun with a gun. You all see that?"

"Sure I see it," said another.

A third man said good-temperedly, "Well, it ain't hardly pointing at me."

The girl, coming up against them, said with a lilting accent, "May we pass?"

But resolute, they stood in her way.

The first man said, "Now, Miss Luisa, you know it ain't right, your Navaho carryin' a musket."

The girl's light olive skin flushed. Her Navaho servant stood impassively at her back.

"Señores, you will let us pass, please," she said.

"Ain't gonna let no Injun pass till he hands over that musket," said the first man. The man on the black horse looked on silently.

"Señor Braddock," said the girl, "Apulca is our servant. The law has always been that our servants may carry muskets for our protection."

"That ain't Texas law, that's Cordova law."

"You have a new law, a different law?" said the girl. Though she looked no more than eighteen, she held herself with pride and courage.

"It ain't no use bein' uppity, Miss Luisa," said Ed Braddock, tall and broad-shouldered. "I'm sayin' there ain't no law permittin' no Injun to carry a gun."

She looked him up and down. The big man grinned at her challenging air.

~ 9 ~

"Who has changed the old law?" she asked. "You, Señor Braddock?"

Braddock's grin spread and a couple of the Americans acknowledged her spunkiness with winks that encouraged her to keep right on.

"You all is a sassy one, Miss Luisa," said Braddock, "an' you got yourself a sassy Injun too. He's carryin' a gun and it ain't allowed."

"Does the law say Texans may carry guns?" asked the girl.

"Ain't ever been no law to say Texans can't."

"Apulca is a Texan," said the girl.

This last brought momentary shock, and then an explosive roar of derisive laughter.

"You all hear that?" he said to the other men.

"I heard it," said one, "and I figure she ain't all wrong."

"You been eating locoweed, Charley," said Braddock.

"Let it ride, Ed," said the man, "the girl ain't full-growed yet."

"That ain't the point," said Braddock, no longer amiable. He turned to the girl again. "Now see here, Miss Luisa. You go tell your sister Miss Isabella Almighty she ain't God no more. She ain't no more account than anyone and that goes for you too. Your Injun—he's less'n anybody—he ain't no Texan."

"Apulca was born here in Texas," said the girl. "Or is it more important to *arrive* in Texas?"

"Guns ain't for Injuns," said Braddock stubbornly.

"Please let us pass," she repeated. Her duenna fluttered nervously. The Navaho remained impassive.

"I'm warranted to uphold the law," said Braddock.

"You are warranted by Colonel Hendricks," said the girl, "and *he* is not the law."

The horse man edged forward his mount.

"Gentlemen," he began. They looked round and peered up at him. "And Señorita Cordova," he added. He raised his hat to the girl and inclined his head, his dark hair moist at the temples. The girl looked curiously. The reflection of the sun made his eyes seem as bright as polished stones. They darkened as he replaced his hat. He smiled down at her. "I'm in luck, I believe. I've business with Señorita Isabella Cordova. May I ride along with you?"

Luisa Cordova, dark-lashed and pretty, recognised the offer of help.

"You are most welcome, señor," she said.

She moved forward. Braddock refused to yield but the others made way for her. She stopped, turned, and spoke to the Navaho, who placed the musket in her white-gloved hands. She looked up at the man on the horse.

"I am satisfying a new law, señor," she said.

"Hold on, mister," interrupted Braddock, with the forthrightness of his kind, "who are you?" He had fought a good fight with a band of American sharpshooters against the Mexicans, and believed, like Sam Houston, in the Americanisation of Texas.

"I'm a lawyer from Washington," said the newcomer.

"Washington ain't here," said Braddock, "we'll tend our own patch."

"You asked, sir. I can't give you a different answer."

Braddock's eyes narrowed. "You sound like a fancy mouth," he said.

"That's common to most lawyers."

Braddock grinned. "Ain't it, though?" He stood aside, for Washington was Washington after all, though most lawyers were smart alecks. Luisa Cordova and her duenna boarded the carriage. The Navaho got up beside the driver, who shook the reins. They moved away down the street, the man on the horse riding alongside. The Americans watched them go.

"Them Cordovas and their Injuns," said Braddock. "They got to change their ways."

"Maybe so," said the man called Charley, "but I ain't too keen on crowdin' 'em. I go along with tellin' 'em, but they got rights too."

"Just as long as they know who's runnin' things," said Braddock.

Once out of town, Luisa spoke to the man on the horse. "Is it true, señor, that you have business with my sister?"

"Not true," he said.

She cast him a little smile. "It was a lie?" she said.

"A small one," he said.

"But you are a lawyer from Washington?"

"That," he replied, "was a slightly bigger one."

Luisa's smile had all the charm of the young. Though her duenna muttered, Luisa ignored her.

"You think those men are afraid of lawyers from Washington?" she asked.

"No. Only of how a lawyer might argue, even a lawyer from another country. I felt the large gentleman wasn't too sure whether the old law permitting your servants to carry weapons was still good or not. I was prepared to try to make a case for you, though without knowing anything about it."

"That was kind of you, señor." Luisa shrugged off the cautionary hand of her chaperone, who was none too happy with her talking to a man who had not observed the courtesy of introducing himself, despite his timely appearance. "But there is no old law," Luisa went on, "it has just been a custom with us."

"Then together, it seems," he said, "we have been responsible for one small lie, one not so small, and one tactical evasion."

"Then is it possible, señor, that between us we left them scratching their heads?"

He smiled, leaving unspoken the fact that his action had not been motivated entirely by chivalry. The carriage rolled on, he cantering beside it. The distant hills had become a smoky blue streaked with ridged light. To the left the high yellow grasses stretched away until they lost ground to a pine belt. Far to the right the sun clamped its fiery hold over the immensity of valleys sheltering the river. There wild, lushly blooming magnolias grew huge and unchecked.

"Is there a law which will now force you to change your custom?" he asked.

"Who knows?" said Luisa. "But if the Houston government does not provide enough convenient laws, the Americans here will make some of their own. Or so my sister Isabella says. Señor, although you do not have business with her, you are being kind enough to escort me home—and therefore I shall be glad to have you meet her."

It was obvious to anyone who had the smallest understanding of civilities that she was asking him to introduce himself. Either he missed her hint or he was disinclined to give his name, for he only said, "Is your father at home that I may meet him too?"

"My father was home, señor, after a long absence. But has gone again, visiting Austin for a little while."

"Austin, I see." A small grimace touched his mouth. "Well

then, señorita, permit me to introduce myself. I am Jason Rawlings."

"And I am Luisa Cordova," she said, not without pride. Luisa affected deafness to her duenna's whisperings, and continued, "Now we may converse, señor, even though you are not a lawyer. But you are from Washington?"

"No, from England." Seeing she was a little taken aback, he added, "Some other birthplace would be preferable, señorita?"

Luisa, blushing, said, "Oh, no."

"If you wish to be frank, señorita, I shall not be offended."

"Señor, I do not say it myself, you understand, but I have heard others declare the English are worse than Americans for taking other people's land."

"And the Spanish, what is said about them?" he asked. The carriage wheels trailed dust and the duenna had her parasol up under the fringed top.

"Señor, the Spanish have devoted themselves to spreading the word of God."

"The English, perhaps, are simply acquisitive?"

"Do you confess so?" she asked, her colouring soft with youth.

"I confess to helping the cause of acquisition in India," he said.

"Señor," she said with interest, "you have been as far as India?"

"With the Queen's 7th Lancers," he said.

Luisa was impressed. He looked, she thought, as a cavalryman should, as if he had led a hundred charges against an enemy under a burning sun.

"Perhaps, señor, we should not mention this to my sister Isabella. Between you and me," said Luisa with infectious charm, "she has only one word for the English. Pirates."

He laughed and said, "And what word does she have for the Americans?"

"Robbers," said Luisa with a demure smile.

"That seems consistent at least," he returned. He supposed her sister thought that the Spanish conquistadores who carried the word of God to the conquered were more nobly motivated than adventurers who did not.

"Señor, you are the only *Inglés* I have met," said Luisa, "and you spoke up for us. I would not have taken the musket from Apulca otherwise." The Navaho now had the weapon back. It lay across his knees as he sat with eyes on the land which once had known only his people. "I knew you were for us, so it was easier for me to be wise instead of proud. The Americans squeeze people: always they want more land. I do not understand them. They do not think we or the Mexicans or Indians deserve to own land because we do not use it as they do. When Mexicans only grow enough for their families, the Americans say, 'What are you doing? That is no way to work your land. Fill it with cotton and become rich, or give the land to us.' But it is good to have time to sit in the sun, and to sing, and if sometimes there is not as much corn in a larder as some would like, they do not complain. At Cordova, we cannot grow cotton as Americans do, by using slaves. Free men work for us, not slaves, so we cannot grow cotton as cheaply as the Americans. So they would like to have our land too, to use it in their way, but even the land, señor, has some right to be free."

Jason, riding loosely under the heat of the sun, said, "A fine point, señorita, and well made on behalf of the land."

"Today in San Carlos," she went on, "which they now call Westboro, the storekeeper said Indians were no longer allowed in shops when ladies were present, or even to enter with ladies. I said I thought it very strange that people born in the country could be forbidden to enter shops by people who had not long arrived. The storekeeper said he did not know what I was talking about, that he was informing me of the law. Do you believe that, señor?"

"I don't believe your new government would make that kind of law," he said. "It's more than likely local prejudice. We exercise a little of that in India."

"Cordova now belongs to my sister Isabella," Luisa ran on loquaciously. "My father did not want it, for he prefers towns and cities. So my grandfather gave him money, and left the hacienda to Isabella, who loves it. Now there is a man called Sancho López, who says my grandfather made him a grant of part of our land, and that he has a document to prove it. My sister refuses to believe this, and so Sancho López has said he will sell this grant to the Americans. And here, señor, is our hacienda."

The carriage forked off the dirt road, ran in under a stone arch emblazoned with the name "Cordova," and entered a long winding drive. On either side within were arboreous borders of longleaf pines, red oaks, and massive magnolias. Within a few minutes the house appeared, rising out of the ground and shrubbery in dazzling white Spanish-style symmetry. A red-tiled roof capped the building with sun-splashed colour.

"That is your home?" said Jason.

"That is Cordova, Señor Rawlings," said Luisa. "And you will do us the honour, will you not, of coming in?"

"Indeed," he said, "I had hoped I might step inside your home."

They reached the arched entrance in the high white wall that surrounded the house. The gate was open and they passed through. The Indian drove the carriage over a huge paved frontage to pull up outside the ironbound, citadel-like oak door. Jason dismounted. Apulca the Navaho took charge of his horse as he gave his hand to Luisa and then to her duenna. As she alighted, the plump Mexican woman peered shrewdly but not unkindly at him. Inside the house Luisa sped to find her sister. Jason looked around the tiled hall, which soared to the highest of ceilings. A solid, finely carved staircase led to a galleried landing. There were doors on either side of the hall and on each side of the staircase at the rear. On the walls hung paintings, religious in the main. The colours were sombre, as if the artists had felt they could not achieve the right note of reverence except by use of the darker oils, although wherever the Virgin Mary and the saints were depicted the haloes shone like bright rings of gold. Worn and pitted in parts, the floor tiles looked very much as if they had endured the endless comings and goings of booted feet. All the woodwork was of red oak.

He heard voices. Luisa appeared as the door to the left of the staircase opened. He glimpsed a passage beyond and a shaft of light from the patio. Accompanying her was a woman in a black riding habit, carrying a white stock. Taller than Luisa, she was slender of waist, superb of figure, and warmly beautiful. Greeks who had crossed the "wine-dark" seas for Helen of Troy might have sailed all the oceans for this woman of Cordova. A classically oval face, with the rich Spanish colouring of her ancestors, was crowned with black hair glinting with the night blue of a raven's wing, dressed to form clusters of curls and ringlets. Her eyes were as dark and glossy as chestnuts newly sprung from their husks. In all, she was as elegantly turned out as an English duchess ready for the hunt. Beside her, Luisa's prettiness had the pink bloom of youth. This woman, her sister, was four years older. She swept animatedly towards Jason, carrying herself with the pride of old Castile, but for all her pride her eyes were warm and glowing, and the smile that parted her wide, shapely mouth was one that was born of exuberant vitality and the pleasure of the moment.

"Señor Rawlings?" Her voice had the same Spanish lilt as Luisa's, but was more resonant. She extended her hand. An American would have forthrightly taken it and shaken it, but Jason suspected she would rather he did not treat her as a man. He brought her fingers lightly up to his lips.

"Señorita, a privilege," he said.

She liked the courtesy. Her warm smile became vivid, her eyes danced, and her white teeth were a brightness that lingered. She regarded him with interest, for he was a visitor whose intriguing qualities had preceded him—Luisa had already made sure of that. The brilliant brown eyes held his. Jason, who had not come looking for a woman, not even a woman as richly beautiful as this one, smiled politely.

The faintest flush tinted her. She dragged her eyes from those that were starkly blue.

"I am Isabella Cordova," she said, "and am told by my sister that you are a man of splendid expediency. Welcome to my house, Señor Rawlings. Is it true you are English?"

"Quite true," he said, neither in chauvinism nor in apology—he was long past taking on nationalistic attitudes. Every country, when looking critically at another, seemed to him to be guilty of sweeping generalisations. The imperfection of all peoples was the only true generalisation. The holiest accuser could not look too long into his own mirror.

"Your country and mine are old enemies," said Isabella.

"Well, we're over that now, aren't we?" he said.

She smiled appreciatively.

"We are a forgiving people, señor," she said, "but oh, that Drake of yours, that most thieving of pirates, and so many others like him, all plundering the treasures of Spain."

"That is a fact, señorita?" said Jason in mild irony. Isabella Cordova obviously closed her eyes to what was well known: those treasures had previously been plundered by Spain during her conquest of the Americas.

"What does it matter now?" Isabella laughed. "Señor, have you

~ 16 ~

not made up for all your pirates by taking such good care of my little sister today?"

"Little? Who is little?" Luisa was on her mettle. Although young, she was not without her share of grace, form, and height. She conceded Isabella's rich beauty, but was not dissatisfied with the reflections in her own mirror.

"I assure you, señorita," said Jason, "your sister was taking very good care of herself. Mine was only moral support. However, if it made up a little for my country's taking ways, then we've no need to dig up too many old bones."

Isabella's smile was teasing as she said, "Señor, you must not take me too seriously."

"Señor," said Luisa, "I must warn you that my sister would not thank any man who took her too lightly."

"Shoo, little squirrel," said Isabella. "But there, perhaps it is better if no one mentions Drake, for although I am a woman of sweet charity, I am inclined at the merest whisper of that pirate's name to become almost fretful."

"Señorita," said Jason, "if I might mention it, Drake has been dead for two centuries and more. Has no one told you?"

That delighted Luisa. It made Isabella quite put her chin up. She was not too used to having a man sharpen his wit on her. However, since she had the slenderest of necks no one could have said proud reaction did not suit her. But she could not sustain it for long. Laughter began in her eyes and trembled on her lips.

"Señor Rawlings," she said, "even if you had not taken such good care of Luisa today, you would still be very welcome, for you have given me the happiest piece of news. So, the pirate is dead. Bueno! May he rest in peace, for all his acquisitive ways. We will drink to that. In any event, Luisa and I do not intend to let you go without taking wine with us. So come, please."

She led the way towards a door.

Jason said, "I'm very dusty."

"Señor?" Her smile was a soft reproach. It let him know that the hospitality of Cordova was not withheld simply because a man had just got off his horse.

"I am in your house, señorita," he said, "and am honoured."

"As we are too, by your presence. So come, please." Her warmth was irresistible.

With the sisters he entered a large room that was a haven of coolness. Its thick walls defied the intrusion of heat, and its shuttered windows kept out the sun. Only a few streaks of light filtered through. The polished oak floor shone. The leather upholstery of the mahogany furniture was edged with brass binding studs, and they too had a lustre to them. The stone fireplace was huge, the mantelshelf high. Isabella pulled on a bell rope. The summons brought a servant clad in a white shirt, white trousers gathered at the ankles, and a blue sash cummerbund. Isabella asked him to bring wine, while Luisa entreated Jason to sit. It was rather nice to entertain a visitor from the Old World, reflected the elder of the two sisters, even if he was an Anglo-Saxon, a race on whom she did not exactly dote. Actually, while always faultlessly hospitable to any guest, she did not pine if men were few and far between. That was because Cordova meant more to her than any man. There was only one who had ever brought a heady flush of excitement to her. That was Philip de Ravero, kin to the Alba family, which owned a ranch three hundred miles west of Cordova.

"Señor Rawlings, please do sit," insisted Luisa.

"I'm quite comfortable," said Jason, disinclined to leave a layer of dust on any piece of this well-kept furniture. Moreover, he was interested in the portraits on the walls. One, that of a handsome man, particularly caught his eye.

"But, señor—"

"I really am very dusty," said Jason.

"Señor Rawlings," said Isabella, "how long have you been in Texas?"

"Oh, some weeks," said Jason, "no more."

"Señor," said Luisa, "Isabella is now going to tell you that although we are reasonably civilised, we are not quite as daintily fastidious as they are in London and Madrid. Our furniture is to be sat on at all times. Isabella is going to ride out later, and when she returns she will be as dusty as you. But she will still sink into a chair, kick her boots off—"

"Little squirrel, you are chattering," said Isabella. "I will do no such thing. Señor Rawlings, please sit down."

Jason took a chair. The smooth leather of the chair was comfortable, and the shaded coolness of the room welcome, after the fierce light Texas sun. Luisa without her bonnet showed a wealth of shining black hair whose ringlets danced with every turn of her head. She was a girl born to be liked, with an engaging personality and just enough spirit to resist the constraint imposed by a strict Spanish upbringing. And she had all the charm of her eighteen bright years. Isabella, at twenty-two, was a woman, undeniably so in line, form, and the maturity of her self-assurance. She had been her grandfather's pride and joy—the confidante of the old eagle, as his people had called him, from the age of seventeen. His death a year ago had brought her into possession of Cordova. Her widowed father loved the excitements of life, though not its responsibilities. He had been quite happy to let his elder daughter have the ranch in return for a handsome financial settlement. When the money was given to him four years ago he had headed at once for the civilised fleshpots of the East and of Europe.

Isabella had taken her grandfather's death sadly, but she took over Cordova without hesitation. She was a woman to whom life was a challenge, a joy, to whom laughter came far in advance of tears. "It is permissible to weep for a loved one," her grandfather had once said, "but it is an indulgence to weep over disappointments."

For more than a hundred years the family had been established at Cordova, breeding horses and raising cattle, first for the Spanish civil and military authorities, and then for the Mexicans after they had won Texas back from Spain. That lasted until Sam Houston and the American immigrants, risen to a strength of twenty thousand, decided Mexican rule was not for them. After a series of battles that left the Americans victorious, an independent Texas Republic, with Houston as its first President, was proclaimed.

The legend now was that the Mexicans had been the villains, as the British had been in the previous century. Isabella watched the newcomers with suspicion. Warmhearted and generous, she was also temperamental and could be headstrong. The knowledge of these attributes did not discomfit her. She regarded such fine Spanish traits as assets rather than liabilities. Her mother had been placid, her grandmother fiery, and there was no doubt in Isabella's mind which of the two had lived the more appealing life. A woman without spirit was a woman without spice. From her grandmother she learned that no woman should practise meek acceptance, for in all loomed the dictates of men. Life's rewards for women came from adapting to those dictates, or foiling them.

Every woman had it in her to cajole a man, outwit him, or bemuse him. No woman, therefore, should set aside her superior subtleties.

The servant reappeared, bringing a bottle of wine and three slender-stemmed glasses on a silver tray. The imported wine was light, dry, and cool on the palate. Its coolness came from a lengthy sojourn in one of the cellars. It eased a parched tongue and lightly drowned the dust. Luisa drank hers with relish. Isabella sipped hers, letting it linger. Jason took a mouthful, thought about foaming Dorset ale, felt the wine tempt his thirst, and drained his glass. Isabella said to the servant, "For the señor, Manuel." Manuel moved a small table within Jason's reach, set down the tray and its bottle, then retired.

"I'm much obliged," said Jason, and refilled his glass. "Your health, señoritas."

Because he was so dark from the sun and wind, Isabella thought his eyes almost disconcertingly blue, and even abrasive in the way they went in search of everything, the room and its corners, walls and pictures, and not stopping at Luisa and herself. They passed without a flicker over her habited form. She wanted to smile, thinking to herself: There is a typical Anglo-Saxon for you. They never make their surveys caressingly, as a Latin does. They are far more deliberate. But how interesting his features were, how masculine in their hard lines, and yet containing a certain implicit good humour. A hint of this lurked around the mouth.

Luisa, for her part, wanted to know more about him. He looked as if he could tell a hundred absorbing stories about life and people. But it would not do to ask inquisitive questions, especially of a stranger. So she avoided the crime of impertinent curiosity simply by asking him what he thought of Texas. Jason said Texas had drowned him and scorched him. He understood that in the far north it might even snow on him. Therefore he thought in Texas the variability of the elements was impressive. Fortunately, he was used to the four seasons in Britain, making it possible for him to endure anything other countries could throw at him.

"If you have been drowned," said Isabella, "you have almost certainly entered Texas from Louisiana. But scorched? Señor, that is a question of learning to live with the sun. What else have you observed about our country?"

"That it's extremely large, señorita," said Jason. He poured himself more wine.

Large, thought Luisa, was certainly an observation. It was also uninformative.

"*Grande, mismo grande,*" said Isabella.

"*Mismo,*" agreed Jason.

"You speak Spanish?" said Luisa.

"Passably," said Jason.

"Then you are a civilised man," said Isabella. She moved about the room, her riding skirt softly swishing, the underskirt caressing her legs. "Yes, Texas is very large, which is why the Americans want it. They must come from small European countries, I think, because whatever is huge is intoxicating to them. In the United States they will not be satisfied until they have claimed all the land from the Atlantic to the Pacific. Señor, are you not concerned that they are flooding Oregon with immigrants so that they can take it over completely from the British? They also have their eyes on New Mexico and California, which belong to Spain. The scorn the builders of empires, yet they are building one of their own."

"We all have ambitions, señorita," said Jason, "and not many of us walk the path of purity in pursuit of them."

"I am boring you, señor?" said Isabella with a sweet smile.

"Not at all," he said, eyeing the portrait of the handsome man again.

"The Americans looked north not long ago, but the British Canadians would not have it," she said.

"Well," said Jason, "many of them come from the old Loyalist stock, I believe."

"In Texas," said Isabella, warmly earnest, "they mean to eat us up, if they can. Their President Monroe declared that the American continents were no longer in part to be acquired and settled by European powers. Which meant, of course, that only the United States was to have a free hand. Was that not both hypocritical and greedy, señor?"

"That," said Jason, "was an attitude that comes easily to all politicians, señorita." He finished his third glass of wine. "One might say you have acquired a large amount of South America yourself. Was not Cordova once the hunting ground of Indians?"

Oh, thought Isabella, here is more than an Anglo-Saxon, here is a Tartar.

"It still is, señor," she said. "The Indians come and go on our land. We neither shoot them nor sell them bad whisky. You are speaking up for the Americans? Of course, the English and Americans have much in common—"

"Isabella," said Luisa, "you are not to make speeches, or Señor Rawlings will go away with a buzzing in his head."

"A buzzing?" Isabella laughed. "Señor Rawlings is a man who has stood up to being drowned and scorched. Do you think he would rather listen to small chatterings than honest opinions?"

"I would rather keep the peace," said Jason.

"That is not always easy in Texas, señor," said Isabella. "If you will allow me?" She stepped forward, took up the bottle and filled his glass again, bringing to Jason an awareness of her physical warmth. "Do you know about Indians, Señor Rawlings?"

"I've done my best to avoid them while in Texas, God's life I have," said Jason, "but I'm in your hands now, and you are filling me with wine."

"Indeed, you are trapped," smiled Isabella, and Luisa laughed softly. "Señor, nearly all Indians are *errante*. I think you would say nomadic. Yes? Good. In the United States the Indians move from here to there, from there to here, and so on. They think that the lands they roam belong to no particular man, but are free to all. They do not understand Americans who arrive with pieces of paper and claim this piece of land or that. The Indians do not understand land transactions at all. Only the Pueblo Indians set up permanent homes. Most others follow the buffalo herds and rarely plant their corn in the same place each year. To an Indian a fence is a mystery he will never comprehend. The Comanches never stay still. The land is there for them, they think, as it always has been. You will find some of them on Cordova land at times. They will stay for the winter, perhaps, but by the spring will be gone. Perhaps the same ones will return next winter, perhaps not. We have never denied them access, never told them they could not hunt without our permission. Señor, you have been in India, Luisa says. Did you drive the Indians there from their lands, from their homes, did you compel them in their millions to go and live elsewhere, where there are no buffalo?"

"In building an empire, señorita, the best policy is to use the people," said Jason, not without a little cynicism. "It would be very shortsighted to empty India of Indians."

Isabella's delight evinced itself in an impulsive swing of her body.

"Bravo, señor," she cried, "and how good it would be to hear you tell that to your American friends."

"I am not here, señorita, to get my head cracked."

"So?" said Isabella, and eyed him enquiringly.

He smiled. "We're all on uncertain ground," he said.

"Ah, there is a look in your eyes," said Isabella, "and I have seen such a look in other eyes."

"It's the wine," he said.

"Luisa," said Isabella, "he is thinking things about Spain."

"Isabella," said Luisa, "that is not something forbidden, is it?"

Isabella swished her skirt at her sister.

"Señor Rawlings," she said, "it is true, yes, that Spain has things on her conscience too, even on the conscience of her priests. But this is because of misguided policies, not hypocrisy. From Washington, and now from Houston, come the cries that all people must be free and equal. Señor, Americans not only eat all other people, they also eat each other."

"Well, let us look at it philosophically," said Jason, "and wish them *bon appétit.*"

"*Bon appétit?* Oh, Señor Rawlings!" Isabella, never a woman to hide what she felt, burst into delighted laughter. "Luisa, did you hear that? Here is a man with sweet vinegar on his tongue."

"Sweet vinegar?" said Luisa, smiling.

"But yes," enthused Isabella, "for although his words bite, they do so deliciously. Already I bear my own marks, and now he has put out his tongue at the Americans. You must bring him again, sweet sister. Señor, when Americans come to live in Texas they call themselves Texans. In five minutes they are Texans. But to them no one else is. The Mexicans are mostly called, let me see—yes, 'Hey, you.' Luisa, that is right? I am not making a big fish of a little one?"

"That is right, Isabella," said Luisa, "and you are not making a big fish of a little one."

"Señorita," said Jason to Isabella, "are you Spanish or Texan? That is, how do you regard yourself?"

Isabella was too much a Cordova to wriggle out of that one.

"Our culture is still Spanish," she said. "So is our language, but for over one hundred years the Cordovas have been Texans. We did not return to Spain as some did when Spain relinquished Texas to Mexico, for in Spain we might have walked as strangers. But that is not to say we have no pride in our blood and history."

"Sometimes we are very proud," said Luisa with the demurest of smiles.

"We are the Cordovas of Texas," said Isabella, "and will not sell any part of our land to American planters, nor will we let them take it from us. You may carry that message, señor, to any Americans you meet in San Carlos, which they now call Westboro."

"Señorita." Jason, rising, made Isabella a small bow. "Thank you for your hospitality." He smiled at Luisa, who returned his smile. She had really wanted to listen to him, not to Isabella, whose natural animation had taken wings, rather as if she had enjoyed her audience. "And thank you for the wine," added Jason. "I must be on my way now."

"There, Isabella," said Luisa, "you have added to his drowning and scorching with a smother of words, and he is going before an avalanche descends on him."

"Luisa, I have only said a little," protested Isabella. She looked at Jason, just a hint of confusion in her brown eyes in case he thought her tongue had run away with her. "Señor, you must forgive me—"

"I enjoyed every word," said Jason.

Her smile came back. She said, "Señor, you are more than welcome to call again. You will, please? Luisa and I are always at home to you, and I must thank you again for the protection you gave her."

"I'm obliged," said Jason, "and thank you. Among other things, I'd like to meet your father."

"My father?" said Isabella.

"He is Don Esteban Sylvestre y Cordova?"

"Yes. Do you know him, then?" Isabella was curious. Señor Rawlings, she thought, was not her father's kind. Dilettantes were her father's kind.

"No, I've never met him," said Jason evenly, "but I'd like to."

"Has my father achieved some kind of fame, that you should wish this?"

"He has fathered you and your sister," said Jason, "which is not a bad achievement for any man."

The warm laughter danced in Isabella's eyes.

"I will tell him that," she said, "but unfortunately he is in Austin at the moment."

"So your sister said."

"He will not be back for two weeks."

"I'm in no hurry," said Jason, "it's only a pleasure deferred. That is your father?" He indicated the portrait which had caught his eye. It depicted a handsome man in his late thirties, with dark hair arranged in a modishly careless way. The artist had caught an expression of faint amusement rather than Cordova pride.

"Yes, that is Father," said Luisa, "though the painting is ten years old. Are we as handsome as he is that you should recognise him so easily?"

"He is not quite as pretty as either of you," said Jason.

Isabella, her curiosity consuming, said, "I wish you would tell us why you are so set on meeting him."

"Señorita," said Jason, "I simply heard on the way here that he was worth meeting in a land full of Americans."

Luisa laughed.

"Señor, I am very pleased to have met you," she said.

"May I ask if you have come to Texas to buy land?" said Isabella.

"I am only wandering about," said Jason. "Señoritas, *adiós*."

When he had gone, Luisa said, "You were very oratorical, Isabella."

"But, Luisa," said Isabella, "it isn't often one has the chance to engage in words with a compatriot of Francis Drake."

"Oh, you and your pirates. You get it all from Grandfather. I think Señor Rawlings a most interesting and likeable man."

"You are taken with him?" smiled Isabella.

"From the way you monopolised him," said Luisa sweetly, "I was under the impression that you were."

"I?" Isabella coloured just a little. "Oh, shoo, little peahen."

"Oh, quack, quack, big duck," said Luisa.

Jason rode back to Westboro. A man passed him on the way. It was Ed Braddock. The big American pulled up, turned, and looked at Jason with a grin that was like that of an amiable bear.

"Hey, Mr. Lawman," he said.

"I think we've met," said Jason.

"Ain't we, then? I'm Braddock, Colonel Hendriks' overseer, an' I got me a warrant to represent the county sheriff in Wes'boro."

"You're a lawman too?"

"I ain't no attorney," said Braddock, "I jest see that wrongdoers face up to the like. Like Injuns carryin' muskets that shouldn't."

"I'm Jason Rawlings. You're about to call on Cordova?"

Braddock took a folded paper from his pocket.

"I'm deputed to hand 'em a mite of Texas law."

"Concerning muskets?" said Jason.

"Nope." Braddock held up the paper. It looked stiffly official. "Land dispute."

"That's a court order you're serving?"

"Isabella Cordova, she got served it last week," said Braddock. "In the store. But she didn't take hold of it—left it on the counter. She's nervy, I'll give her that." He grinned again, quite affably. "I'm deliverin' it personally today. Judge Conner's sittin' tomorrow. She's holdin' land she ain't entitled to, and she's gotta come to court. It's gonna make her madder'n a wet hen."

"You think so?" said Jason. He understood then why there was a bitter edge to Isabella Cordova's opinion of Americans. Braddock was waving the court order as if it represented some kind of ethnic superiority.

"She'll scratch more'n some, I'll lay yer."

"I'd not lay wagers myself," said Jason, and rode on. Whatever the nature of the fight between Isabella Cordova and the Americans of Westboro, he doubted if she would run around like a scratching chicken.

Entering Westboro, he looked for the saloon, which according to José Ferrara combined drinking with sleeping. There it was, farther up the street. "Saloon—Sam Purdy, Prop." Two ladies on the planked sidewalk glanced at him from under poke bonnets as he tethered his horse. He lifted his hat to them with a smile that startled them into blushes.

"Well, ain't he fetchin'?" said one.

"Sassy, more like," said the other, "an' him an uppity Mex an' all."

"You sure he's Mex, Miz Patchett?" They talked with barely a whisper between them.

"I ain't ever seen one more like."

They eyed him as he mounted the sidewalk. Jason, impervious to all things that were unimportant—and all things were except one—let his right eye close and open in a slow wink. The women blushed scarlet—a mixture of indignation and confusion. Jason passed by, entering the dim saloon. There were tables and chairs, a long bar, a bartender, and two men sitting at one of the tables.

"Mister?" said the bartender.

"A shot," said Jason, who knew Americans liked to deal in their own lingo and thought anything outside of that was fancy talk. The bartender, a rugged and expressionless man, poured him a small glass of corn whisky. Jason downed it, and the last of the wine, sleep-inducing at this time of the day, died in the fire.

"Ten cents," said the bartender.

"Five too many," said Jason.

"Ten cents."

"You're calling," said Jason. He had a few coins besides his American silver dollars and parted with one. Another coin beside the first entitled him to help himself. Two corn whiskies represented his maximum intake at any one sitting—a little fire was a temporary indulgence. Anything more was slow poison. Strangely, many Americans regarded the steady progress of man's advance towards delirium tremens as a sign of virility: only real men could tread that kind of path. Jason had listened to Americans recounting folk-hero fables of men clasped permanently to the stone bottle, men who had rotted themselves into early graves and so earned themselves a curious kind of fame. They represented folk-lore at its most incomprehensible.

Jason, with the second whisky turning him, more or less, into a customer (rather than a stranger), said to the bartender, "You're Sam Purdy?"

"Yep."

"A friend recommended you."

"Who?"

"José Ferrara."

"He's a Mex," said Sam Purdy.

"One of God's better creatures," said Jason. "Do you have a room?"

"Nope."

Jason recognised what he had come up against before, the habitual negative of the mulish pioneer stock.

"Sure?" he said.

Sam Purdy, about to be positively negative, was suddenly aware that the look in the blue eyes and the mild friendliness of the smile were distinctly divisible.

"Yuh a Mex?" he said.

"I'm one of God's other kind. Do you have a room?"

"Maybe. But yuh got Mex friends?"

"I'm not looking for friends, only a room."

"Maybe we got one," said Sam.

"I'll take it. How much?"

"Dollar a night. Thought you was a Mex. So you ain't. But you talk kinda funny."

"So do you," said Jason.

"Hell, I ain't no talker," said Sam.

"You're doing all right," said Jason.

Sam's face creased for a moment.

"Say, mister." One of the seated men hailed Jason and pointed to the scabbard, black with age and soil. "That your cutlery?"

"In a way," said Jason.

"It ain't no jackknife," said the man, swarthy and bristly.

"A sabre," said Jason.

"Mister?"

"Cavalry sword."

"You a Mex?" said the second man, not so swarthy but just as bristly.

"You drinkin'?" Sam cut in with his question to both men.

"Ain't got a nickel," said the first. "You offerin'?"

"Nope," said Sam.

"He a Mex?" persisted the second man, nodding at Jason.

"Nope," said Sam.

The men got up. They took a blunt and uninvited close look at the sabre's hilt.

"We run all the Mex cavalry outa Texas," said the first.

"Personally?" said Jason.

"Looks dandy," said the second man, and placed a hand on the hilt of the sabre, about to draw it. Jason put his own hand around the man's wrist and squeezed. The bristly face contorted and the man let go.

"It's my hardware," said Jason, "you know the rules."

"He ain't no Mex," said the first man.

"He ain't nothing but a mite touchy," said the second. "God-damnit, mister, you near broke my arm."

"No fightin', yellin', or carryin' on," said Sam, pointing to a notice. "You drinkin'?" he said again.

"You settin' 'em up?" suggested the second man.

"Git," said Sam.

The men returned to their table and put their boots up.

"Card games?" said Jason.

"This evenin', maybe," said Sam.

"I'll be here for two weeks or so and need to eat and sleep."

"Countin' on winnin' your keep?"

"Or working," said Jason. "Change these, will you, my friend?" He put three silver American dollars on the counter.

Sam bit them, and then gave Jason ten Texas dollar bills.

"Ten? You mean fifteen," said Jason.

"You do, I don't," said Sam.

"I'll take twenty," said Jason.

"You're uppin'," said Sam.

"Fifteen, then. That splits the difference."

"You're still uppin'. But I'm still callin'."

"I know that," said Jason pleasantly, "so I'll be happy just to take fifteen. That's a fair rate. Economically you're tottering a little in Texas. Those are silver American dollars I've given you."

Sam pushed across another five Texas dollars. Once again he smiled.

"You're meaner'n a polecat," he said.

The doors swung apart. A tall man, black-hatted and brown-coated, walked in. He was middle-aged but sleekly vigourous, and by Westboro standards, distinctively well dressed. An iron-grey moustache matched his sideburns. The only faint mar was the onset of pouchiness beneath the grey eyes. He glanced at the seated men and stopped.

"Colonel Hendriks?" said one.

"You addressing me?"

"We—"

"On your feet."

They swung their boots down and got to their feet. The Colonel looked prosperous as well as commanding. The men, drifters, were broke. It made the difference between sitting and standing.

"Heard you was lookin' for riders, Colonel."

"Boundary riders. So you're the men." The Colonel looked them over. "See my overseer, Ed Braddock. Wait at the law office. He'll be there in a while, he'll bring you out."

"You hirin' us, Colonel?"

"I'm not. Braddock might, if you satisfy him. You can go." The Colonel walked to the bar as the men left, and placed his hat on the counter. His iron-grey hair was well brushed and lightly dressed with bay rum. "Riffraff," he said.

"Colonel?" said Sam with a touch of deference.

"The usual," said the Colonel. His handsomeness was slightly dissolute, his eyes faintly flecked by the tiny red veins of the hard drinker. Sam took a bottle down from the top shelf; it flashed in the mirror. The Colonel filled his own glass to the top, glancing over at Jason. The younger man, matching him for height, nodded.

"Cotton comin' on, Colonel?" asked Sam.

"What's that?" said the Colonel, and drank half the whisky.

"Cotton comin' on?"

Jason had the feeling that the taciturn Sam felt he had to be sociable.

"Damn me," said Colonel Hendriks, "are you being talkative?"

"Askin' ain't talkin'," said Sam. "You stayin' a while, Colonel?"

"Staying?"

"Gennleman here's lookin' for a card game."

~ 30 ~

"That's talking, by God," said the Colonel.

"Sayin' ain't talkin' neither, Colonel."

The Colonel finished his drink, drew out a silk square, and wiped his lips.

"This gentleman?" he said, looking at Jason. His accent was Virginian, drawling and fruity.

"Ain't give his name yet," said Sam.

"Rawlings, sir, at your service," said Jason.

"Hendriks, Colonel J. B. Hendriks. You a gentleman, sir?"

"I have the honour, sir, of never having quit a card game while winning, or having failed to pay when losing."

"That don't necessarily make you a gentleman, sir." The Colonel helped himself to a second glass of his special. He saw the dollar bills that still lay in front of Jason. They represented less than a fistful of small change to him, but his eyes flickered nonetheless. Whatever the stake, a challenge stirred his blood. "I'll cover that for a single cut," he said, "it's all I've time for."

"My pleasure," said Jason.

Sam produced a pack. They cut for shuffle. Jason won. He split the pack, rejoined it, shuffled, and laid it down. The Colonel sliced off the top dozen cards and turned up a nine. Jason cut and showed a queen. The Colonel tossed down his second whisky; Jason finished his own. The Colonel pulled out a large English hunter watch and checked the time, and eyed Jason. The man could have been riffraff, but wasn't. Instinct told him so.

"Give you ten minutes," he said, "half a dozen hands."

"I'm obliged," said Jason.

"Sam, one from the wood," said the Colonel. "You, sir?" he said to Jason.

"You're very kind, Colonel," said Jason.

Sam filled two beer glasses from a barrel. The beer gushed ripely. The Colonel used half of his to chase and drown the two whiskies, then took his glass to a table. Jason joined him and they sat down. He took a mouthful of the beer and set the glass aside. The Colonel settled what he had lost with the cut, and Jason found himself with thirty Texas dollars. He watched as the Colonel shuffled the cards. The long-fingered, well-kept brown hands were dexterous.

"Well, sir?" said the Colonel.

"It's your choice, I think," said Jason.

"Between gentlemen there's only poker."

"That's the new rage, I believe."

"New, sir?" The Colonel looked down his nose. "Gentlemen were playing it in Venice two hundred years ago."

"Do you say so?" Jason smiled. He could afford to be agreeable in his mood. The day had been a satisfying one so far. "Then it seems to have come to life again among gentlemen in Texas, although in New Orleans they're still playing *vingt-et-un*."

"Not a city I admire," said Colonel Hendriks, dealing.

Jason, picking up his hand, found he had two kings and three non-runners. He disliked discarding three cards in a situation where it was all or nothing. Discarding three told the opposition he had a pair. He kept the two kings and a ten. He drew two. The Colonel drew one. That meant, thought Jason, that the man held two pairs, almost certainly. The starting price was five dollars. Jason put in another five to commence the play. The Colonel covered that and raised by ten. Jason, beginning with thirty dollars, had twenty left. He covered the raise and put in his last ten to see the Colonel. That surprised the Colonel, who was still debating whether Jason's original holding was three of a kind.

"There, sir, a middling beginning," he said, and turned up two solid pairs, jacks and nines.

"As with me, sir, but slightly more middling," said Jason, countering with his two kings and a backup of a drawn ten allied to his original ten.

"By God," said the Colonel, eyes sharp, "that's a staying hand, sir."

Jason, not wishing to disclose that he had been limited by his resources, said, "I'm a keen player, Colonel, but a modest performer. I have the nervous gambler's instinct for avoiding the long drop from a great height."

"I will not be bluffed by that, sir. Deal."

Jason won steadily, for he made no attempt to raise on moderate hands, and threw in on obvious losers. He stayed with his good hands, which came along at a satisfying rate, if not a spectacular one. The obviousness of his system would have been quickly seen by a professional, and the system itself been made unprofitable by an experienced opponent ready to devote an hour or more to the play. But it was a mere interlude for the Colonel, who chose to give it a fillip by fighting every hand. It resulted, after a while, in Jason showing a profit of seventy-five dollars. At this stage, the Colonel dug in hard with a full house, noting with satisfaction that for once his man had neither thrown in nor called him, and that the ante of five dollars had grown to a combined stake of ninety. Relatively, the Colonel was still playing for loose change—but it did not diminish the enjoyment of the cards.

Sam Purdy had gone to the doors. They heard him raise his voice a little.

"Now you know better, Miss Lisbet, it's for gennlemen only."

A girl's voice responded crossly. "Since when did more than one gentleman a year enter this royal palace? Sam Purdy, you go play in your trash can, you hear?"

The Colonel stayed his raise to consult his watch again.

"My daughter, sir," he said, "but we'll play the hand through."

The girl swung in. She was no pioneer female: hers was a complexion that had sheltered for years under the parasols of Virginia; a mass of dark auburn hair sprang from a moist, healthy scalp. Her hazel eyes looked hot, her rose-white complexion flushed. A soft leather riding skirt with a fringed hem frisked around her ankles; high-heeled brown boots, spinning spurs, brown gloves, and a waistcoat-style jacket topping a white blouse completed her outfit. A green ribbon held her hair at the neck, and she carried a wide-brimmed hat in her hand. She had the shape and vitality of any girl of twenty.

Seeing her father, she stopped in the middle of the saloon, put her hands on her hips, and said, "Pa, I'm waiting."

"A moment, Lisbet," said the Colonel, and had another look at his three eights and two aces. What had his man drawn? Two, yes, two.

"I've been fretting for twenty minutes." The girl's Virginian drawl matched her father's. She came closer, stood at the Colonel's elbow, and looked at his cards. "See him, Pa."

"Not yet," said the Colonel. He pushed bills into the pile. "Cover you, sir, and raise you twenty."

Jason, aware that his profit and his original sum were close to the brink, sat back and reflected. The Colonel's daughter glanced up from her father's cards and said again, "See him, Pa." She looked impatiently at Jason. He came out of his reflections, rose to his feet, and gave her a bow. That brought Virginia back to her, for in that state there still were social niceties. She regarded Jason less impatiently, more interestingly. Her eyes made a lazy meal of him.

"Colonel," said Jason, "for the sake of the young lady, I'll see you." For the sake of honour he had to. He was too close to forfeiture if the Colonel raised again. He covered and he paid to see. The Colonel turned up his full house. "That's a great pity, when it's your best hand yet," said Jason, and spread his own hand. Three jacks and two sixes.

"Damned if I like that, sir," said the Colonel, an edge to his voice and his eyes sharper.

"Colonel?" Jason made the enquiry politely. The Colonel looked up and met eyes gone steely. Abruptly he thrust cards, money, and pack into a heap in front of Jason. His distinguished Virginian look seemed ugly for a moment, then he tossed in a concessionary note.

"I mean I don't like losing on such a hand, sir."

"A chastening moment, Colonel," said Jason, "and I should not have loved it myself."

His clipped voice came pleasantly to Lisbet Hendriks' ears.

"Pa," she said, "who is this gentleman?"

"I can only say he's a little richer than he was," said her father.

"My pleasure, sir," said Jason, tidily stacking the bills. He was less in danger of being in want now. There was enough to see him through two weeks in Westboro.

Lisbet was still studying him. Texas had its share of hard-bitten, hard-living men. Planters for the most part in this region, but cattle farmers and horse breeders too. This one did not seem like most of the others, even though life had pared him down to muscle and bone. Nor did he talk like any of the others. Vexed that her father had still not introduced him, she said again, but with more deliberation, "Who is this gentleman?"

"Did I get your name, sir?" asked the Colonel, with the growl of a dissatisfied loser.

"You did, sir. Jason Rawlings."

The Colonel eased himself off his chair. He stood up, straightening his brown coat.

"Mr. Rawlings, my daughter Elisabeth May," he said.

"Your servant, Miss Hendriks," said Jason, and gave her another bow.

"Well, I do declare, sir, I surely do," said Lisbet with mischievous extravagance, and followed this with a sweeping curtsey. One spur jingled.

"You, sir, I hazard, are from the old country," said Colonel Hendriks, who had met a native Briton or two in Richmond.

"I am, Colonel," said Jason.

"You're from England?" said Lisbet.

"I left almost three years ago."

"You're a planter now?" She smiled.

Since he had already introduced himself to some citizens of Westboro as a lawyer Jason decided to be consistent; the deception was of no importance.

"A lawyer, Miss Hendriks."

"A lawyer?" Lisbet thought that the last kind of calling to fit him. Lawyers, to her, were pale people surrounded by dusty files and other lawyers. "Sir, you'll not find rich pastures in Westboro."

"Fortunately," said Jason, "I can escape that disappointment. I travel, Miss Hendriks. I come and go. That too isn't a lucrative way of following one's profession, travelling in search of clients, but at least it ensures I don't have to spend ten hours a day in an office shut off from light and life. And here and there I turn out to be the one person a harassed citizen is looking for."

"You go looking for clients?" said Lisbet.

"For the last few years I've been engaged in the most meticulous search," said Jason.

A little fascinated, Lisbet said, "It's a waste, sir."

"A waste?"

"I declare quite positively, Mr. Rawlings, you are fitted for better than that. So is any man who can best my father when he's holding a full house." Her smile was innocent. "Yours was remarkably well endowed, sir."

"Miss Hendriks?" Jason was again very polite.

"Oh, by no other means than the luck of the draw," she said, pinking a little.

"Mr. Rawlings," said the Colonel, good humour returning,

"whatever you find in Westboro, I hope it will include the time and opportunity for you to give me my revenge."

"No gentleman would plan to depart immediately," said Jason.

Lisbet, with a satisfied air, said, "Then you may rely on me, Pa, to arrange such an opportunity."

"You are a minx, young lady," said her father. "Now, where's those damn niggers?"

"They're loaded up and waiting," said Lisbet.

Jason accompanied them from the saloon. Outside stood a plantation waggon piled with goods from the store, and atop the goods sat three straw-hatted Negroes.

"You all can get now," said Lisbet.

"Yes'm," said one Negro. He climbed into the seat and shook up the horse. The waggon trundled off. Lisbet slapped on her hat and drew the holding cord under her chin. She untethered her horse, a peaceful but fine-running roan gelding. She put a foot into the lower stirrup. For a Virginian lady—for almost any lady —it was the wrong foot. The Colonel's brows drew grimly together.

"Missy," he said, "I'll tan your hide."

Lisbet, tempted to show off because of Jason watching from the sidewalk, thought better of it. There were folks about; and her father, for all that he indulged her, did not care too much for public exhibitions. She changed feet, and in no need of a hand, eased herself up on to the lady's saddle. The Colonel swung himself up on his own horse, a hunter brought from Virginia. In the eyes of a mature lady or two, he cut an extremely fine figure. And a younger woman, pretty and quite cuddlesome of shape, glanced up at him as she approached. The Colonel lifted his hat to her.

"Howdy do, Miz Purdy, ma'am," he said, and Jason saw his features shed a few years under the gallantry of his smile. Mrs. Purdy coloured, murmured a shy and inaudible response, hurried on, and turned into the passage leading to the rear of the saloon.

"Shame on you, Pa, to make her blush so," laughed Lisbet. She waved to Jason and cantered off, her father following.

The Hendriks plantation, mostly turned over to countless acres of soft, fluffy cotton, was three miles out of town. The large, sprawling house had the size but not the grace and grandeur of the Colonial-style houses of Virginia. But then it had been built by the elder brother of the Colonel, a man with a practical rather than an imaginative outlook. George Hendriks had invested the money his prosperous father had left him twelve years ago in Texas land which had never known cultivation. It burst into prolific life at the first planting. And he, married to the soil, was a good husband to it. He had bedded mulatto women and saved himself the expense, responsibility, and peevishness of a wife; he was not a man who looked beyond the horizon of his own stay on earth. He indulged in growing cotton, French wine at the table, whisky in the evenings, and promiscuity in bed, unconcerned with what happened after his departure from this earth. And he had, three years ago, dropped dead from hard work, too many evening tots, and too many voluptuous brown-skinned women.

The Hendriks plantation was left to his brother, Colonel John B., a man who liked wealth and power. Unfortunately, in Richmond, with avid help from his wife, his money had flowed away. Their father had been a merchant, not a landowner. With the Colonel's affluence weakened by profligacy, and his standing in Richmond devalued by his appetite for women—and his wife's appetite for men—he was more than ready to leave Virginia. There in Texas, before he was too old, he could make a fresh start. His wife had declined to go: not a hundred wild horses could drag her into the uncivilised horrors of any territory west of Virginia. She remained, therefore, in the arms of her various Richmond paramours; with their kind and amorous help she could be safely left to her own ruin. Without her, Colonel Hendriks was a relatively free man, and determined not to repeat his mistakes. A small fortune had come to him again, but he knew that only when money was made to work could a man acquire power.

In less than two years, Hendriks owned most of the new town, Westboro, and most of its people. His only rival as far as position and influence was concerned had been old Carlos Cordova, who, Spanish to the core, remained finely aloof from what he obviously considered the petty machinations of one more small and unlovely American-style town. Don Cordova watched the rise of wooden Westboro with contempt. He saw it smother old San Carlos, built by the first Cordovas for the little community of Mexicans and Indians, and he refused to have anything to do with the new town. Dying at the ripe old age of seventy-seven, he may have been mourned by all who worked for him—but not by the Americans, who frankly felt that no feudal Spanish grandee belonged in Texas. Cordova's death left Colonel Hendriks with no rival. The lands and holdings passed to the elder granddaughter, Isabella. Adjacent to the Hendriks plantation was a tract of Cordova land the Colonel wanted. He had not thought it would be difficult to charm Isabella into selling it. He had charmed more than a few proud Virginian ladies into parting with what most of them considered was dearer than land. But Isabella Cordova could not be charmed: she would sell no part of Cordova to anyone.

Lisbet Hendriks enjoyed Texas in respect of the freedom it seemed to offer her. In Virginia the proprieties that ordered a young lady's conduct, and those of a married woman, were rooted and fixed. Dos and don'ts assailed one's daily life. She began to resist at the age of thirteen. Her mother, a Virginian belle in the traditional mould—flawless of skin, posturing of manner, flirtatious of behaviour, and extremely expensive to keep—noted with alarm the possibility of being rivalled by her daughter and packed her off to an academy in Charleston. There Lisbet profited minimally in a scholastic sense but learned a great deal about the more interesting facts of life from her sister boarders.

Nevertheless, at seventeen she emerged a fairly intelligent, strong-willed lady. She was determined not to be drawn into the limitations of conventional wifehood, which her mother was keen to impose on her, and which other young ladies eagerly sought. At some time in the future she might be a man's joy; she would not be a mere appendage. And it was most unfair of her mother to try to push her into a state of dull wifehood, for her mother played life fast and loose. Richmond society gradually ostracised Mrs. Hendriks and turned blank eyes on her. She refused to grow old or placid, burning herself out in her constant pursuit of ever-re-treating youth; the last person Mrs. Hendriks wanted by her side was her seventeen-year-old daughter. Having loaded her husband with debts, she loaded him with Lisbet too when he left Richmond for his new life in Texas. And Lisbet went willingly. Her father had always spoiled her.

So it was that, less than a mile from the house, Lisbet parted company from her cantering father to gallop the rest of the way. With only the heavens as witness, she rode astride, despite the design of the saddle. True, she began to pass Negro workers in the fields, but they could not be said to be responsible enough to bear witness. Her fringed skirt and cream underskirt flew back, the underskirt fluttering. Boots and pantalooned knees showed as she raced pell-mell towards the long drive that led to the house.

Not far away a boss Negro field worker stared.

"That Miss Lisbet," he said, "sho' as the good Lord made me, never seen her like. Her mammy gonna cuss her all the way to perdition if she see her come home like that."

"White folks got no respect," said another. "They cuss and carry on. She ain't got no notion 'bout respect. The Colonel, he be madder'n the devil if he catch her."

The Colonel, in fact, thundered by right then in the wake of his erring daughter. The dust flew and the cotton fluff danced. He did not catch her until he came up with her on the verandah overlooking the massed fields of swimming white. She lay in a long cane chair, letting the heat of her body ease away in the shade.

"Ah see yuh, miss," he said, and sat down in his own chair. He called for Joe, his senior house servant and butler. Joe arrived, black face shiny.

"Yessuh?"

"Break a bottle, Joe."

"Yessuh. Yes'm?"

"Bring two glasses," said Lisbet, "sugar rim on mine."

"Yes'm." Joe departed.

"You damn well shock those field niggers," said the Colonel.

"I never even notice them," said Lisbet.

"Well, they notice you."

"They complain, do they, that I act disrespectful?"

"You do. The Richmond ladies would skin you."

"You might just be right, Pa, having firsthand knowledge." Lisbet smiled. "You and Mama were skinned seven times a week by looks alone."

"Don't concern yourself with how your mama and I observed the rules of Richmond, miss. In front of the niggers your mama never put a foot out of place; neither did I. Neither will you."

"Don't scowl so, Pa." With the flush of exercise cooling, Lisbet stretched. The bees hummed in the sun. "What did you think of Mr. Rawlings?"

"Sneaky poker player, by God." The Colonel fingered his moustache. "I haven't given any other thought to him."

Lisbet mused.

"I thought him gallantly polite, Pa. But his eyes, they look through you. I declare, there's a devil waiting to get out of that man."

"It's the same devil that gets into you at times."

"But a lawyer on horseback, Pa, that's no way for a man like him to carry on. Travelling preachers, yes, but I surely never did hear of travelling lawyers. That's not worth two cents. You could do with a lawyer. Why don't you hire him?"

"I don't need to. There's Herman Schumaker."

"Oh, Pa." Lisbet wrinkled her nose. The clumps of bluebonnet patterned the fallow fields lying beyond the corral. They were almost brilliantly glossy.

"I'd let Herman Schumaker draw up a document for me if I had to sell a dead horse, but I wouldn't take him into a courtroom to handle a real case for me. I do swear, Pa, that if you made a hole in him he'd spill dust."

The Colonel smiled. Lisbet was his one weakness—his one present weakness. Putting too tight a rein on her would do nothing for her, though the occasional curb was necessary.

"Herman Schumaker can do all that I need him to. Meanwhile, missy, I'll not have you riding wild and showing the niggers your limbs."

"Legs, Pa," she said with her lazy smile. "I surely do find it refreshing that in Texas they accept a woman has legs."

He laughed. Joe came, bringing a brassbound oak bucket, half full of icy-cold water from the well. In it reposed a bottle of champagne. With it came two tall glasses on a tray. The rim of one was sugar-coated, first moistened with a slice of orange, then dusted with sugar. Other folks had their own traditional hot-weather aperitifs—the Hendriks clan favoured champagne. It had begun with the Colonel's bubbly wife, a custom now regarded almost as a legacy. The filled glasses sparkled. Joe, the napkinned bottle in his hands, stood by while the glasses were slowly and appreciatively drained. He refilled them before returning the bottle to the bucket. The waiting and refilling were part of the custom too. The rest of the bottle was the Colonel's responsibility, and now Joe could retire. Before doing so he bowed, according the bottle due reverence. That was another part of the ritual.

The champagne ran sweetly for Lisbet over the sugared rim.

"I surely do declare this to be mortally addictive," she sighed.

"Death could come in no more civilised way," said the Colonel sonorously. His eyes darkened. "I rightly guess there are exceptions."

"Pa, do you think you'll get the land you want?" asked Lisbet. She looked languid but felt vitally alive. Her mind reviewed the day's events: That man—Jason Rawlings—he was different, exciting.

The Colonel leaned back, his eyes on the endless fields of cotton: they'd had a damn fine year.

"By tomorrow that parcel of land will be ours," he said. "Judge Conner will find in favor of that half-witted old drunk, Sancho López, and we'll then exercise our option to purchase. He's in our pockets."

"Judge Conner? Or that old Mexican drunk?"

"You're pert, miss. I'll have you know there are always questions which shouldn't be asked, and a mite more which won't be answered."

"Pa," said Lisbet, tongue in her cheek, "you mean they're both in our pockets?"

"Button your lip, miss." But the Colonel smiled again. "I'll tell you, Lisbet, the acquisition of that Cordova land will treble our holdings."

"And take that snooty Isabella off her high horse." Lisbet contemplated that picture with pleasure. There were occasions in the town when the Cordova and Hendriks carriages passed each other. The Colonel always raised his hat, while Lisbet sweetly showed her teeth. In return Isabella unfailingly produced a light but grandiloquent gesture of her hand, accompanied by a smile of regal condescension usually found in empresses. And all without really looking at the Hendrikses though her sister Luisa usually did give a shy nod. Lisbet knew her father had done all he could to be neighbourly but Isabella Cordova could have been her grandfather all over again for all the response she showed.

Three times the Colonel asked her to receive him so that he might discuss with her the prospects of buying from her the piece of land he had in mind. The tract to which the man Sancho López claimed title roughly paralleled that area, and would do very nicely. It was a courtesy, not a necessity, for the Colonel to offer to discuss its purchase with Isabella. She responded to the first two requests with brief, negative notes. To the third and final request, which concerned the tract claimed by López, she couched her reply in the coolest terms. No part of Cordova land was for sale, nor in her lifetime would it be. Therefore, any suggestions that they might meet for a discussion were an unfortunate waste of time. She would be glad to hear he fully understood her so that she might know he would not raise the subject again; and he was also asked to understand that Sancho López was an irrelevance.

Once Lisbet came face to face with the sisters in the store. Isabella and Luisa were waiting to be served, Elmer Harrison being busy with another customer. Looking up from some material they were examining, they saw Lisbet. She, refusing to be stared out of countenance, said very cheerfully, "Good morning."

"Ah," said Isabella in a way that made Lisbet feel she was being addressed from the most regal heights of the Spanish throne, "are you the assistant here?" It took the Colonel's daughter only a moment or two to deliver her riposte. "I confess I can't claim that honour," she said sweetly, "nor did I know that Mr. Harrison was looking for an assistant. In any case, you are first in the queue for the post and must be considered in front of anyone else."

Lisbet was not quite sure who had won that little social fracas, but felt she had hardly lost.

She let the champagne caress her tongue. Though it was hot here in Texas, it was a drier and less humid heat than that which sometimes afflicted America's southern states.

"We'll have to buy more slaves," said the Colonel. "Costly, by God, but worth it. You can't find better cotton pickers." He fished the bottle from the bucket and did the honours. The glasses sparkled again with the purity of pale, living gold. "In addition, Lisbet, I intend to rebuild the house."

"You said that before, Pa. You surely mean to live in style. And you really do know how. Some folks call this area Cordova, some still call it San Carlos, and most call it Westboro. But I vow, Pa, one day nobody's going to call it anything but Hendriks County. They say the time's going to come when Texas will be in the United States."

"It's only those damn northern abolitionists who are keeping us out now," said the Colonel. "But they can't keep Texas out forever, any more than Isabella Cordova can keep the Hendrikses out forever. I guess I'm due to consider divorcing your mother. I'm not too old to get married again and bring a wife home to the new Hendriks mansion."

Lisbet vibrated.

"I shouldn't like that, Pa, so don't do it." She would hate it; she enjoyed her relationship with her influential father, loved the feeling of sharing the power he had. She wasn't about to be displaced by a critical stepmother. "I swear, Pa, I'd act up so bad she'd spend her days screaming her head off."

Her father sat up and glared at her. Blood rushed to the tiny veins in his eyes.

"By God," he said, "I won't have you getting mean and uppity, Lisbet, do you hear me? Niggers and trash get mean and uppity, not ladies. Ladies have style—*Hendriks* ladies have style. I allow you to run a mite wild now and then; you're the kind of gal who has to have her head once in a while. But if I ever hear folks whisper you've got no style, that they don't regard you as a lady, I'll shut you up in your room with your mammy Meralda until you are eating out of her hand. If it takes years, hear me?"

"Then don't you go getting married again," said Lisbet in

flushed defiance. "I won't have you slighting Mama by talking about putting someone in her place."

"And I won't have that talk from you." The Colonel's face darkened. "By God, you and your mama never met that you didn't spit at each other."

"How you can say such things about my dear mama and me, I just don't know," said Lisbet. "You should go down on your knees and beg forgiveness."

"Of whom, eh? Eh?"

Lisbet saw the danger signals in his reddened eyes. He spoiled her up to a point, but when she passed that point the choleric nature of his temper flared. Her smile, innocence itself, sought to sweeten him.

"Why, how you do take on, Pa. And you making eyes at Miz Purdy the way you do, with Sam Purdy not being able to say a word because he owes you for most of what he's got." Lisbet followed her smile with a laugh, sure from the way the dark blood was receding that she should whimsy her father back into good humour. "I see her blush pinker than a rose when you pass. I do declare you've waisted her and bussed her, Pa. You're still the prettiest gentleman with the ladies."

"Hush now, missy." The Colonel's teeth gleamed.

"Not another word, I promise," said Lisbet, "except to say that if Uncle George felt no need to get married here, why do you?"

He frowned. His own daughter was telling him he could bed whatever women he liked, as long as he refrained from divorcing his wife and taking another. She was a precocious girl. His frown changed to a laugh, and he turned his head as Esmeralda appeared. Lisbet's mammy, thin and bony, grey-headed and severe, had been in charge of Lisbet in Virginia, and kept a sharper eye on her now than she ever had in Virginia. To Esmeralda, Texas was a land where white folks were so busy making a living that they gave no time to learning how to live. White folks in Virginia had dignity, they knew about respect. In Virginia, Colonel Hendriks had been a gentleman, Esmeralda recalled. He gave handsome balls in his house, which he said he never knew how to pay for, which was just how a real gentleman talked. Miz Hendriks might act up a bit, but only in the way of a fine spirited lady. Why Colonel Hendriks had to come to Texas was a mystery.

"Meralda?" said the Colonel.

"Massuh Colonel, I'm goin' to speak my mind to Miss Lisbet," said Esmeralda determinedly. "I declare—just look at her."

The offending Lisbet, relaxed in her long chair, showed booted legs emerging from peeping underskirt.

"Meralda, you may speak," said the Colonel.

"I can't," complained Esmeralda, "not when you're here, suh. It wouldn't be fittin', it just wouldn't."

"Then I'll leave you," said the Colonel, and took his glass and the bottle elsewhere.

Esmeralda advanced grimly on Lisbet, whose look of defiance lay thinly over the champagne-induced mellowness. She had escaped Esmeralda's vigilance for four short years only, during her time at the Charleston academy.

"Meralda, don't you make faces at me," began Lisbet.

Esmeralda, fists on hips, said crossly, "How you ain't blushin' fit to take fire, I don't know. I brung you up to be a lady like your mama. How come you don't behave? Them field niggers, they seen you—Ol' Elijah Jones hisself done told me you come ridin' like the daughter of the devil, ridin' like a man. I'm fair dyin' with shame."

"Meralda, don't you go on at me like that." Lisbet sat up. Esmeralda glowered at the visible shamelessness of booted legs and ruffled underskirt. Lisbet tucked up her legs and hid them. "Meralda, you speak to me like that and I'll have Pa sell you down the river."

Esmeralda gave a scornful sniff.

"Your pa ain't goin' sell me down no river," she said. "You is just sayin' that to scare me, and I ain't scarin' none. I'm mighty put out, Miss Lisbet. How you figger to catch a fine gennleman when you don't act like no lady? No gennleman goin' marry no gal rides like a man. I don't stop you, no gennleman'll have you."

"Meralda, you just stop getting after me," said Lisbet, "it's not as if I ride around town showing my legs—"

"Don' you dare say that word!" Esmeralda shook an angry finger. "I never did hear the like! Your mama, she'd git your pa to take the strap to you if she hear tell you talk that way."

"My mama kicked her legs up more than once," said Lisbet.

She remembered an incident when she was nearing her twelfth

birthday, the noise of music and laughter that woke her in her bed, kept her awake. Venturing from her room and along to the landing, she peeped over the staircase at the scene below. She saw her mother on a table, dancing to fiddles. Laughing men and women were clustered around the table. Her father was there too, and he was also laughing. Her mother held her crinoline skirt and petticoats high, white, lace-hemmed pantaloons showing, and whirled to fall backwards off the table and be caught by the men. They took her slippers off and poured wine into them; the men drank from the elegant pumps, the wine slopping. Lisbet crept back to her bed and lay sleepless for a long while.

"That ain't so," said Esmeralda stoutly, "your mama she just gay sometimes."

"So am I," said Lisbet.

"That give you no right to sit on that hoss with your limbs showin'. Those field men, when they tole me, I nearly died. How you think it make me look, them comin' an' tellin' me you got no respect? It make me look bad. You got to stop, you hear, Miss Lisbet? Or you goin' end up an ol' maid for sure."

"Meralda, you know very well I don't wish to catch any man in the way you mean," said Lisbet. "I don't ever incline to sit playing pretty-pretty behind my fan—especially in Texas. Mr. Rawlings, I'm sure, would consider it laughable."

"Mr. Rawlings? Where you find him?" Esmeralda peered suspiciously. "He ain't no gennleman I ever heard of."

Lisbet's confident smile wooed her mammy.

"I too was ignorant of his existence until today," she said, "but I vow and declare, Meralda, I'd no sooner laid eyes on him than I felt he might be the one man to match up to what I'd demand in a husband. I surely do consider him a possibility. What I'm saying," said Lisbet, sweet as wildflower honey, "is that I just might advertise my eligibility."

The room above the saloon was surprisingly neat and clean, the brass on the iron bedstead polished, the bed itself covered with a colourful patchwork quilt. The pitcher that stood in the bowl on the washtable was full of clear water on which showed not a speck of dust. And Mrs. Laura Purdy herself was neat and clean. She was standing inside the door in her plain, sweeping brown skirt and roundly filled white front, looking prettily cuddlesome for all her air of modesty.

"I'm downright regretful, Mr. Rawlings," she said, "but we only let rooms." Jason had enquired about food. "We'd serve meals if we could, but it's not allowed."

"Not allowed?" Jason poured water into the bowl.

Mrs. Purdy's prettiness took on a shy deference.

"Colonel Hendriks, he kind of built the best part of Westboro," she said.

"Colonel Hendriks?"

His cool enquiry tinted her shyness with a faint blush.

"He says trade has to be shared—so we do rooms and drinks, and Mary Lou, she does food. She's further down the street." Mrs. Purdy spoke in the soft, pleasant way of a homey woman who found satisfaction in providing. She looked as if the denying of food to room guests was a little upsetting to her.

"Does that make sense?" asked Jason.

"It does to Mary Lou," said Mrs. Purdy.

"And to Colonel Hendriks?"

The faint blush came again.

"The Colonel, he's been good to Sam," she said. "Loaned him money to get this place built and started two years ago. He says maybe in two more years there'll be call for a hotel, which is what me and Sam would like."

"An eating hotel?" said Jason with a smile. Mrs. Purdy thought he looked a hard and weathered man, yet he spoke like a gentleman, with an accent unfamiliar to her, and he could smile at people. Which was nice.

"That's what we'd like," she said, "a hotel. Sam's working hard an' only using one black to help out. He's no talker, he don't rightly say more than ten words a day, but he knows folks, he knows them that are worth a word or two and them that ain't—aren't." She blushed again, self-consciously. She wanted to be a ladylike hotelkeeper and speak decently, not like a cotton picker: she knew when she made the obvious mistakes. "Colonel Hendriks, when he builds his hotel, Sam and me would like it if he kept us in mind, so though we'd like to do food we go along with the Colonel and let Mary Lou provide."

"It's the Colonel's town, is it?" Jason was not particularly interested, but realised this pretty woman was pleased to have someone to talk to.

"Oh, it surely is, Mr. Rawlings. A few years ago it wasn't hardly nothing—anything—but then he came along and told folks something better had got to be made of it, 'specially if we wanted to get more people here. So he lent everyone money to help put places up. Folks come to a place where there's a good store, and two years back that Elmer Harrison's store was so poky—you never saw any store so poky. Now it's four times the size and stocks most everything. The Colonel helped Mr. Harrison to build big and to buy lots of stock."

"I'm pleased for you, Mrs. Purdy," said Jason without a flicker of an eyelash, "and for Mr. Harrison too."

She took that at face value and said, "That's right nice of you, Mr. Rawlings. Is your room kind of satisfactory enough?"

"Better than I've had for weeks," said Jason. "You'll run a very comfortable hotel. Is this place yours yet?"

"Not yet. Sam's still paying off and it takes time," she said. "And the Colonel also has a stake in the business, so he gets a third of what Sam makes. Sam don't—doesn't—make a right fortune, and the Colonel says he ought to have girls."

"Saloon girls?" Jason wanted to strip and wash, but decided an uncovered chest might be more likely to embarrass the good lady than encourage her to pass the soap.

"Sam's not keen. on that." Mrs. Purdy was obviously not keen on it either. "He says it runs a place down, that we'd get more customers in to look at the girls than buy drinks. And Sam also says where could you find girls when you reckon there's no more than one of that kind every thousand square miles in Texas."

"Perhaps Colonel Hendriks can find them for you? He seems a man with a prolific touch."

Without knowing what "prolific" meant, Mrs. Purdy said, "Oh, no, the Colonel wouldn't do that. Anyway, Sam says saloon girls —well, he says having them would make folks pass us by in the street 'stead of stopping to talk with us."

"But they'd help to increase the takings, I assume," said Jason, "and the Colonel's share of the profits."

"Oh, I don't think he'd look at it like that, Mr. Rawlings."

"A financier of such integrity is very uncommon, Mrs. Purdy. Westboro is graced with a boon."

"Oh, he surely has been very good to us," she said, "but I'm keeping you talking like a homebody."

"There's nothing special claiming my attention," said Jason, "except my stomach."

"Mary Lou does good food," she said.

"Then I shall track Mary Lou down," he said.

She went downstairs. Jason stripped and washed and brushed his hair. Mrs. Purdy returned to say that someone wanted to see him.

"Who is someone?"

"People," she said.

What were people? She, like everyone else, always talked of folks. So who and what were people?

"An assembly?" he ventured.

"Assembly?" Mrs. Purdy looked puzzled.

"A deputation?"

She gave up trying to interpret and said, "It's a Navaho and a Mexican."

"I see," he said, "people. Can you send them up?"

Mrs. Purdy looked uncomfortable, even hurt.

"Mr. Rawlings, you know those sort of people aren't allowed into places," she said.

"Do they set fire to them?" he asked. But his teasing was only confusing her, so he smiled and said, "I'll come down."

"They're waiting in the street," said Mrs. Purdy.

And indeed they were, in a dusty buggy: José Ferrara and Apulca the Navaho.

"Señor," said José, "I am asked to give you this personally. I am also to take back your reply."

He handed Jason a letter. Jason broke the stiff envelope and took out a penned note.

*Señor Rawlings. Forgive me my many words of this morning. Be so kind as to come and see me as soon as you can. I wish the goodness of your help. Isabella Cordova.*

It was, he thought, not far short of a royal command.

"José, why am I wanted, do you know?" he asked.

"I am not in her confidence, señor, but you are a man who seems better than others and it is possible Señorita Isabella has observed this. Therefore, if she needs to consult with someone she has perhaps decided she would prefer you."

Jason's look was ironic.

"In what way do I look better?" he asked.

"Señor, who can say?" José shrugged; the Navaho sat impassively. "It is not something one wears like a coat, visible to every eye. To some it is there, to others, not. Perhaps it was seen by Señorita Luisa, who I am told you helped this morning."

"And Señorita Isabella wishes help of the indefinable?"

"Who knows, señor? Not I." José was smiling. The afternoon sun was hot and burning, reducing the timbered town to inertia. Save for themselves, the street was empty. Westboro had elbowed aside old Spanish-built San Carlos, but wisely seemed to have taken on the custom of the siesta—or at least committed itself to a minimum of afternoon activity.

"Tell the señorita I'll ride out later, when it's cooler," said Jason.

"Señor, it is not for me to advise you," said José, "but I think you are expected earlier than later."

"Sometimes, *amigo*, a man must make up his own mind about when to arrive."

José smiled again, and even the grave countenance of Apulca seemed to yield for a moment.

"True, señor, true," said José, "but for what it is worth, while you are making up your mind do not set aside the fact that the señorita is not a woman who likes to play games."

"Myself," said Jason, "I have given up all games."

"*Sí*, so?" José lifted an eyebrow. "But however serious life is, there should always be some time to play. *Adiós*, señor."

Mary Lou's was a small diner with six tables, all laid with green and white check cloths. Mary Lou herself was large and round, her face rather like a flushed and tender dumpling. Jason was greeted like a friend, although she did tell him to take his hat off.

"Ain't havin' no man sittin' an' eatin' with his hat on," she said. "It ain't mannerly. An' it don't look right, 'specially if we got ladies in. Oh, an' no spittin'. Ain't no cuspidors. If we had them things there'd be more spittin' than eatin'. House rules. You ain't offended, mister?"

"I'm extremely impressed," said Jason, and handed her his hat.

"What's this?" she said.

"My hat."

Mary Lou gave it back.

"You been in fancy eatin' places maybe," she said. "Well, we surely do have rules here but we ain't fancy. You can sit on it or put it on a chair, but I ain't holdin' it or hangin' it."

"No cuspidors, that's understandable," said Jason, "but no pegs?"

Mary Lou guffawed, her dumpling opening wide.

"I can't see none," she said.

Jason sat down and put his hat on the chair beside him; he was the only customer.

"Is anybody eating today?" he asked.

"It ain't eatin' time right now, 'cept for you. It's ham an' eggs."

"Might I ask what's on during regular eating times?"

"Ham an' eggs."

"I'll have ham and eggs," said Jason reasonably.

"Well, ain't that nice," said Mary Lou to a paw-licking cat on her way to the kitchen, "the gent and me coincidin'."

While he waited, Jason thought about a man called Sylvestre.

When he rode out to the Cordova hacienda the sun was on its way down. It burned the horizon, which lay over the earth like a fiery rim. Red and purple flushed the silent sky and shot Texas with flame. The cedar brakes glowed, and to the east the pine belts were tipped with the wildness of untamed colour. A thousand whispers stirred the mesquite as the nocturnal creatures

~ 51 ~

rustled into awakening. He thought again about cool rain and lush green grass. Yielding grass and air fragrant with moistness, and fields spangled with white and yellow and gold.

It was José who opened the door to him.

"Ah, señor," he said, with relief, "welcome. I have had my ears pulled."

"I'll try to take care of mine," said Jason.

"This way, señor," said José. He led Jason into the presence of the sisters, into the presence, thought Jason, of demure young loveliness (represented by Luisa) and richly warm beauty (which was Isabella). A lighted crystal lamp glowed with prismatic reflections. Luisa and Isabella rose to their feet, petticoats stiffly rustling. They may have considered themselves Texans, but they looked as if they belonged irrefutably to old Castile. Luisa's dress of deep maroon was tiny-waisted, the skirt billowing over the starched petticoats, the bodice exposing slim neck, bare shoulders, and youthful curves. Isabella was superbly Spanish in patterned black and white. Her shoulders were smooth with the sheen of a honeyed skin—skin which the sun would gladly have kissed to the colour of deep gold; her bosom was a softly clefted shadow. Her feet were clad in narrow white shoes with a satin finish. Her smile was a little nervous coming and going, and her brown eyes flickered with their rediscovery of him.

"Señoritas," said Jason and bowed. José left, closing the door quietly. The duenna hovered in the hall. José pointed her in the direction of the kitchen. She frowned, then giggled; and she waddled off in search of kitchen titbits.

Luisa smiled at Jason, but waited for her sister to speak first. The room, lit by a single lamp, was soft with colour.

"Thank you for coming, Señor Rawlings," said Isabella. "I began to think you would not."

"I told José I would."

"It is just that I expected you much earlier," said Isabella. For all the warmth with which she dealt with those she liked, she was not precisely glowing at the moment. She was not used to people who did not come at once, or almost at once, when she issued a request.

"Myself," said Luisa, "I decided to expect you when you arrived. I did not suppose you were doing nothing when you received my sister's note."

"I am here," said Jason. He regarded them. "The welcome is dazzling."

"Oh, we have done our best to impress you," confessed Luisa, "we did not want you to think we do not dress in Texas."

"Please sit down, Señor Rawlings," said Isabella, her slightly dissatisfied mood evaporating.

Jason chose a straight-backed chair with a firm leather seat; such a chair kept a man alert: There was no knowing what warm beauty and demure youth had in store for him.

As the sisters seated themselves on a sofa, Luisa said, "Isabella will do the talking. I am only present, señor, to listen and to nod or shake my head."

"I am expected, I presume," said Jason, "to do somewhat more than that."

"Señor Rawlings," said Isabella, "please let me thank you for coming. Although I have only just made your acquaintance, I wish to ask a favour of you. I would very much like you to act for us."

"Represent you, you mean?" Jason looked at her. She smiled, a glow of beguilement swimming in her eyes. "In what way, señorita?"

"As our lawyer. Do you think you could do it, please? Luisa has told me how you presented yourself as a lawyer to the Americans."

"But surely your sister also told you this was a bluff?"

"So you are not officially a lawyer?" Isabella smiled again. "Señor, what does that matter? There is only one lawyer practising in Westboro, and we do not care to engage him. There is no time to bring our own lawyer from San Antonio. Señor?"

"Señorita?" Jason was cool, wary.

"We are up against people intent on robbing us. You are a man of clever expediency." Isabella's voice was as warm and velvety as she appeared. "Luisa and I have also decided you are a man of integrity."

"We also decided," said Luisa, "that we like you. Isabella, it is only fair to say that."

"Well, you have said it," smiled Isabella. "Señor, the fact that you are not a genuine lawyer is not a disappointment to me, for I do not consider lawyers the most admirable of people. They have a miserable facility for standing the innocent on their heads and setting the guilty on their feet."

"A little sweeping," said Jason.

"But you will allow it? *Bueno*. Señor, although you are not a lawyer, I do not see why you cannot act for us. It will be another bluff, yes? No one will question it unless you become tongue-tied, and Luisa and I both feel you will not let that affliction overtake you."

"I am happy, naturally, with that opinion," said Jason drily.

Isabella, finding him still cool, said more firmly, "I will tell you what we wish you to do."

But Luisa, thinking that it sounded as if her sister had made a unilateral decision, said, "Isabella, should we not wait for Señor Rawlings to say yes or no?"

Isabella turned a look of surprise on Luisa, then glanced at Jason.

"Señor Rawlings, you will say yes, won't you?" She did not lack faith in the justice of her cause—nor, in all modesty, in her looks. She had attired herself with care for the interview; and Luisa, telling her she looked beautiful, had asked whether she intended to impress the visitor or sweep him off his feet. "Señor Rawlings?"

A warm witch of a woman, thought Jason. There was even a hint of laughter in her eyes.

"I'd not write myself down as a cautious man, señorita," he said, shifting his gaze to the silken-clad ankles visible above the satin slippers, "but I rarely risk a leap into the unknown. Second thoughts can be mortifying when one is already on the slippery slope leading to the abyss. Is it impertinent to suggest you first disclose what is expected of me?"

Isabella in all fairness could not quarrel with that, yet there was a little disappointment that he had not given an unconditional yes. She let a small sigh escape. It made Luisa smile. Isabella had the gift of beguilement; but Señor Rawlings, it seemed, had a way of resisting it.

"Oh, señor," said Isabella, shaking her head, "it is not at all impertinent, of course it isn't. But it *is* a little disappointing. Not so long ago, when the world was more gracious than it is now, any woman needing help would only have had to ask a man. He would have responded without hesitation and without question."

"I've no doubt, señorita, that it was just as you say," said Jason, "but as you point out, things are not the same today. We're all more cautious about what is in front of us."

"In any event, Isabella," said Luisa, "you must not look at it so. What would be the good of Señor Rawlings saying yes if, when he knew what was required of him, he then had to turn yes into no? It is not what a gentleman likes to do, and we are not presuming Señor Rawlings to be a magician, are we? After all, how can he know what is required of him before he is told?"

"Oh," said Isabella, laughing, "is this how you merely nod your head or shake it?"

Luisa faced up brightly to her sister and said, "I was not to know you would try to confuse Señor Rawlings by making little speeches and being mysterious. Isabella, may we offer him a cigar? They are said to please a guest and mellow the company."

Isabella rose and swept gracefully across the room to the fireplace. From the high mantelpiece she took down a chased silver casket, offered it and its contents to Jason.

"Señor Rawlings, do you care for a cigar? They are Cuban."

"Thank you, señorita," he said, "but not now. Perhaps when we have finished talking. Please continue."

He was not busy; he had little to do except wait. Isabella cast a grand look at her sister, who evaded it. She was contemplating a portrait of her fiercely moustached grandfather. Isabella remained standing, the prismed light playing over her carefully coiffured curls.

"Señor Rawlings, although you are not a lawyer, you have publicly claimed to be one—and in consequence some people in Westboro believe this. I have received an order to attend a court hearing tomorrow. It concerns a ridiculous claim made by a man— one Sancho López—on part of our land. This order was served on me by an American who declared himself a representative of the law. I know that he works for Colonel Hendriks, however. I have mislaid his name."

"Señor Braddock," said Luisa.

"Yes, it is something or other," said Isabella with an air of inconsequence. "But much more important than his name is the fact that he presumed the reason for your visit to me was because you were my lawyer."

"And you told him?" said Jason.

"Señor, was I to throw away a heaven-sent opportunity?"

"I am heaven-sent?" asked Jason.

Luisa laughed, and Isabella looked at Jason with new delight.

"There, señor, you see," she said, "you have just the tongue we need. So now people think you a lawyer, yes? It is always more commanding in a courtroom to be a lawyer, not simply a mouthpiece. At first I had no intention of attending the hearing, for I did not wish to stand up in an American courtroom—"

"Texan, surely," said Jason.

"Yes, but everything else will be American—the judge, the rules, and the interests. However, my sister and I thought perhaps you might stand up in court and speak for us. I should not be able to speak myself without becoming angry, and I know that would not do. If we were opposing this claim in a court governed by the old Spanish or Mexican laws, I should not be afraid to speak for myself. But now we shall be fighting laws made by the Americans of Texas."

"Señorita," said Jason, "your Houston government wouldn't make laws that would give you less protection than other citizens. There's no reputation among American legislatures, is there, for producing unfair or discriminatory laws?"

Isabella's smile was a little scornful.

"I am afraid, señor, that you have believed too much of what you have heard Americans say about themselves," she said. "Tomorrow, Colonel Hendriks will use an American lawyer to try to prove that Sancho López holds genuine title to a part of Cordova land, which he intends to purchase from Señor López the moment the court pronounces in favour."

"Señorita." Jason spoke calmly, for Isabella was becoming a little overwrought. "Señorita, I imagine the Americanised laws of Texas compare favourably, say, with the laws of Spain. You may be up against local prejudices and interests, but I don't think any judge will be influenced by this. You do own an immense piece of Texas. Is one part of it so important?"

"Señor," said Luisa, "what is that to do with it?"

"I agree," he said, "it's the principle."

"Yes, señor, that is just what it is," smiled Luisa.

"But if the claim of this man López is genuine?"

"Never," said Isabella. "Why, señor, the piece of land in question is as valuable as any we have. The soil is good, the river deep, and the grass grows thick and high. Do you think my grandfather would have given away such land as this? Señor, Cordova is being squeezed. We breed horses and raise cattle, and have done so since the first Cordovas settled here. We have lost stock during the last year: there is a saying among cattle thieves that they always have too little and the owners too much. The theft of horses and cattle is a growing trade in Texas, señor—were it not for our vaqueros, Cordova would be stripped of its herds in months."

"What is it you expect of me?" asked Jason.

"To be on our side," said Isabella. "Señor, act for us tomorrow, speak for us at the hearing, be our lawyer and win the case for us. Sancho López says his document of ownership came from my grandfather, that it was effective on the day my grandfather died. But my grandfather would never have made over any Cordova land to someone outside the family and not a word of it was mentioned in his will. Therefore the document is a forgery; it must be. You must prove it so."

She was not simply asking for his help; she was commanding civil law valour and victory of him.

"How am I to do this?" he asked, and she could not have known the irony of the situation.

Isabella looked surprised.

"But, Señor Rawlings," she said, "if I knew that, I should not need you." She gave him a persuasive smile. "I am relying on your resourcefulness. You will come face to face with Sancho López. You will see the document, and either expose it as a forgery or as something quite worthless."

He did not seem impressed by her confidence in him.

"As your sister has already said, I am not a magician, señorita. I presume you've seen the document yourself?"

"I have not." Isabella was lightly dismissive. "I have never considered it necessary to see something that cannot possibly be what it is claimed to be."

"That was your pride again," said Luisa. She said to Jason, "No one should be too humble. But no one should be too proud either, should they?"

"I'm on the fence," said Jason.

"Luisa," protested Isabella, "am I at fault in fighting for Cordova?"

"But you should have seen the document and examined it,"

said Luisa. "It would have been of some help. As it is, we are asking Señor Rawlings to go into court quite unprepared."

Isabella thought about that, frowning a little before smiling. "But you see, Luisa, Señor Rawlings is not like Herman Schumaker. Herman Schumaker is only a clerk. Do you think I would command the services of Señor Rawlings if he were only a clerk too?"

"Isabella," said Luisa, shaking her head, "you should not speak of commanding Señor Rawlings."

"That was not quite what I said and, certainly not what I meant," said Isabella. "No, not at all. Oh, I should mortify myself with fire and water if Señor Rawlings thought me overbearing. I simply wish him to act for us because I think he will do as well for us in court tomorrow as he did for you in town this morning."

"You shouldn't make so much of that," said Jason.

"Señor, I was very glad you were there," said Luisa with charming candour, "and if you stood up for us in court tomorrow, I should be very grateful."

He considered. With a smile that was faintly ironic he said, "Well, I do have time on my hands, for I'm merely sitting and waiting. So I must think about what I might do for you. Who is this man Sancho López?"

"Señor, you will think hard, won't you?" said Isabella. "Sancho López is a very simple Mexican. He worked for my grandfather, and retired when my grandfather died about a year ago. Cordova was left to me, not my father, which was agreeable to everyone. Not long ago I received a visit from Señora López, Sancho's mother. She is old, but still alert. She informed me that my grandfather had bequeathed land to her son, but that her son did not wish the responsibility of it and was prepared to return it to Cordova on payment of two thousand American dollars. I refused. Why should I buy something I already own?" Isabella made her appeal with her warmest smile. "So the land was offered to Colonel Hendriks, who tried to arrange a meeting with me concerning its purchase—"

"Which suggests he might have doubts himself about the document?" said Jason.

Isabella clapped her hands impulsively in happy appreciation.

"There, señor, see how clever you are?" she said. "I did not think of that. I advised Colonel Hendriks I would not discuss the matter, no, not at all, never. So he decided that Sancho López should take his claim before a judge. I think from what you have just said, Señor Rawlings, that Colonel Hendriks does not wish to purchase from Sancho López and risk a counterclaim from me—or to have his workers thrown into the river if they set foot on my land. So tomorrow a visiting judge is to hear the case. I am angry, señor, I am angry with the López family, for never would I have believed they would contrive to sell the smallest part of Texas to Americans. I had always thought that Señora López likes them no more than I do."

"She makes the decisions?" said Jason.

"Because Sancho is a simple man, señor, his mother has always ordered his life for him."

Jason thought.

"Señorita," he said, "if this document is a forgery, and if Señora López normally would not want her son to sell to Americans, who is behind it all, who is responsible for such a forgery?"

"That is something else I have not thought of," said Isabella, and regarded him with the delighted satisfaction of a woman who had chosen well.

"Nor I," said Luisa. "It is interesting, isn't it, Isabella, to remark how the arrival of a fresh mind opens up our own?"

"I have already said that Señor Rawlings is not just a clerk," smiled Isabella.

"Nor is he a practised advocate," said Jason. "If there is a forgery to contend with, we must find a way of bringing the unknown into the open. May I have that cigar now?"

"Señor, does that mean you are agreeing to represent us?" asked Isabella.

"As long as you understand I'm far more likely to lose the case for you than win it," said Jason, and wondered why the devil he had let himself be persuaded.

"Oh, señor, I am so grateful," said Isabella with a warm rush of feeling, "and no one is to think in terms of losing. I shall not, not now. Señor?" She opened up the casket of cigars again, and Jason took one. Luisa lit a taper from the lamp and brought it to him. Isabella handed him a little silver-handled knife and he neatly prepared the cigar. Luisa passed the flame around its tip while Jason drew until it glowed; she sniffed the aroma and sighed blissfully.

"Oh, it is always such a good smell," she said.

"It comes from a good cigar," said Jason. "Now, basing our hopes on a forgery, we'll need one or two documents bearing your grandfather's signature. And we also ought to take a look at the kind of paper he used for documents. There may be a weak link in the other side's case there. And do you have some reference books? Encyclopaedias?"

"Señor, all that shall be laid at your feet," said Isabella, theatrical in her animation. "I shall now attend the hearing with a brave heart. And you must have brandy as well as a cigar—I will find Manuel—and the best brandy—Manuel?—Manuel?" She was already across the room, sailing exhilaratedly out of the door. Her exit left Luisa smiling and Jason amused.

"I must tell you, señor," confided Luisa, "it is not that my sister is afraid, only very proud. She would have had to stand up in the courtroom if she wished to dispute the claim. She would have had to confront Herman Schumaker, whom she dislikes. He would have put questions to her, questions she has no wish whatsoever to answer; he would have said to her that surely Sancho López was an old and trusted servant of her family—how could such a man possibly lodge a false claim? He would have asked her how old she was, and whether or not she was married—and then asked her why she was *not* married. Questions designed purely to humiliate her, because she is the Cordova and looked upon by the people who work for us as their patroness, provider, and guardian. It is tradition, señor, that in the bad times as well as the good the people of Cordova do not starve. Did you see how happy Isabella was that you will represent her and protect her in court tomorrow?"

"Candidly," said Jason, "I'd have thought her courageous enough to stand up for herself."

"Normally she would," said Luisa, "but I will tell you she thinks that by herself she will be humiliated, outwitted, and beaten and in public."

"God's life, is she counting on me to save her from defeat?"

"Señor, as you will have observed," said Luisa with demure precision, "she has much confidence in you."

"She knows nothing about me," said Jason.

"Nevertheless, you have impressed her," said Luisa.

"You mentioned that she might be asked why she wasn't married. I might ask that myself, or do none of the Spanish landowners in Texas have eyes?"

"Oh, she is quite beautiful, yes," said Luisa, "but in our family we do not marry until we fall in love."

With a smile Jason said, "That, señorita, is a good answer to an inquisitive question."

"Yes? I too suffer from inquisitiveness," she said ingenuously, "but I suffer even more from not being able to satisfy it. I am not, perhaps, the most estimable of young ladies, as I find it very frustrating to ask only polite questions of interesting visitors."

"I fancy that inquisitive young ladies who manage to ask only polite questions are at least never told to mind their own business."

Luisa laughed.

"Señor, if I may say so, you are very agreeable," she said.

"Señorita, you are distinctly so," he said, "and also much prettier."

Isabella returned, along with Manuel and the brandy, to find Luisa full of laughter.

# 6

"Therefore," droned Herman Schumaker, wiry, stooping, and birdlike, "it don't behoove my client to say much himself, especially as he can't speak the language—"

"Not so fast," said Judge Conner. He was silver-haired, with a great beak of a nose, gaunt features, and alert, youthful eyes. "Do you mean you don't speak your client's language?"

"Oh, so-so," said Schumaker, "but I disclaim competence to address the court in it."

"Disgraceful," said Judge Conner.

"Anyway," said Schumaker, a third-generation American from

Pomerania, "seems to me it just wouldn't be right using a lingo most folks here wouldn't understand."

The schoolroom, which doubled as a courthouse when required, was fairly crowded. Someone had scrawled on the blackboard; and someone else had given it a hasty wipe, and "Ambrose Franks wets his pants" was only faintly visible through the dusty white smears. There was an air of expectancy among the Americans present. It was based on their belief that Isabella Cordova would receive her comeuppance, which, in the opinion of most of Westboro folk, would be high time: she always looked as if she were Castile's most priceless gift to Spanish America, as if only Castilian could reach the ears of the Lord. The Cordovas only got their land by sneaking into Texas a little ahead of other folks, thought more than one onlooker. She could make do with less than half of what she had. If she sold some of those acres to American planters and homesteaders, a mighty fine crop of things could be raised. Trouble was, those Cordovas didn't rate Americans very high.

"Mr. Schumaker," said Judge Conner, leaning over, "this hearing is not a performance put on for the benefit of onlookers. It concerns only the plaintiff and the defendant directly. Never have I heard such an unethical admission. A case in Texas involving Spanish-speaking citizens, and the lawyer for the plaintiff not competent to make his submission in his client's language? Spanish has been the official language of Texas for centuries."

"Hardly so now, Judge," said Schumaker.

"Irrelevant. Proceed."

Schumaker explained that the document he held, together with two letters, were in submission of his client's claim. The document, belonging to his client, emanated from the late Don Carlos Sylvestre y Cordova. It made over to the client, Sancho López, a delineated tract of Cordova land. Mr. López was entitled to ownership of the said area on the death of said Cordova. The letters before the court had been written by said Cordova, and been loaned by the addressees so that the signature on each could be compared with that on the document.

Monotonously he droned on. The flies buzzed as the schoolroom warmed up. Jason, sitting between the sisters, studied his feet. On the other side of the room sat Lisbet Hendriks, covertly studying Jason. He looked very much the gentleman today, in a bottle-green coat, buff breeches, and polished boots. That, she supposed, was his professional garb. So he was representing the Cordovas. That prickled her a little; but it also intrigued her. Didn't he realise the Cordova family would not advance him? They'd use him, pay him, and do no more. He wasn't one of them; he wasn't Spanish. He was—wait, he was English. That just might make those Cordova sisters look at him differently. They disliked Americans, but they might consider the English their aristocratic equals, even if they were old rivals. Isabella was putting on her most self-satisfied airs today, knowing she was in possession of the most interesting man in the place.

A sleepy hum invaded the court.

"Hold on," said Judge Conner, well aware that Herman Schumaker was the cause of it. He peered down his hook of a nose. "It's my opinion you've made a submission and a half already, Mr. Attorney. Identify the exhibits."

"The document which we lay before your honour constitutes a title to the land in question," said Schumaker, and placed the exhibit before the judge. "And how about these for corroborative signatures?" He handed up the two letters.

"How about them nothing," said Judge Conner. "I don't recognise that terminology." He handed the letters back.

"Askin' the court's pardon," said Schumaker, "we submit them as being corroborative."

Judge Conner finally accepted them. He studied the document, taking his time. Jason continued his survey of his booted feet. Isabella sat straight-backed and composed. Luisa was faintly flushed from inner excitement. Judge Conner turned to the letters.

"Who declares ownership of these letters?" he asked. Two elderly men stood up and affirmed they had received the letters from the late Carlos Cordova some years ago. Judge Conner returned to the missives, comparing the signatures they bore with that on the document.

Sancho López, a grey-moustached Mexican, sat by himself. He was stout, sparse of hair, and given to sweating most of the wine he so frequently drank. He wiped his face every few minutes with a large cotton square. He chewed on his lip. He was a simple man, asking little from life except few responsibilities, a quiet place in the sun and a bottle. The constitutional gravity of the court sat heavily on him. He plainly looked as if he would have preferred not to be there.

"Judge," said Schumaker, "since the death of Don Carlos a year ago, precisely on—"

"Irrelevant. Who challenges the legitimacy of the document?"

Jason rose. The great beak thrust at him, the youthful eyes glittering as they glanced at a slip of paper on the table.

"Ah, Mr. Rawlings." The judge's smile was bleak. "Your fame has preceded you. Washington, I believe?"

"I have been in Washington, sir. Also in London and New Orleans."

Oh, such a perfect response, thought Isabella. Not the smallest suspicion of an untruth. He has been in those cities, been heard in them. Though he had not claimed that he had been heard in their law courts.

"Your client contests the validity of this document?" said Judge Conner.

"Señorita Isabella Cordova, the present owner of Cordova, questions it," said Jason.

"Has she seen it?"

"I haven't," said Jason. "May I, your honour?"

Judge Conner handed the document over, and regarded Jason unblinkingly as he perused it.

"I will tell you now, sir, I am satisfied the signature is genuine," commented the judge.

"We may make our own comparisons?" asked Jason politely.

"You may."

The courtroom was sitting up. Isabella extracted documents from a leather bag and gave them to Jason. He made his comparisons and returned the documents to her, she casting him a quick glance. He was quite expressionless. He held Sancho's document up to the light. It was yellowing, its creases worn. He rustled it and held it higher.

"Are you about to make it fly off, Mr. Rawlings?" asked Judge Conner drily. That drew a little laughter.

"That might be one way of solving things for my client," said Jason.

Oh, the sardonic beast, thought Lisbet. But he is formidable, I know he is. And he looks as if he could split rocks. He must know that in acting for the Cordovas he's opposing Pa and Westboro. But I do believe Judge Conner looks more favourably on him than on that owl-faced Herman Schumaker—who wouldn't? And what is he doing, squinting at the deed like that?

"Well, sir?" said Judge Conner.

"May I ask Señor López some questions, your honour?"

"Thank you for asking me first," said the judge, "but it's your privilege."

"Señor López," said Jason, "the date on this document is the seventh of September 1790. How old were you then?"

Another bleak smile flitted over the face of Judge Conner, for Jason had put the question in Spanish. Sancho López wiped his face and blinked and thought, while Herman Schumaker raised an objection to the Spanish language.

"You object, Mr. Schumaker, to the Spanish language?" The beak pointed enquiringly at the lawyer. "Are you sure?"

"I'm objecting, Judge, to the use of it."

"Are you objecting in behalf of your client, or the onlookers? We have a learned counsellor speaking, sir, a Daniel perhaps."

"I'm just objecting," said Schumaker.

"There's no one on trial, Mr. Attorney. This is a hearing before me in civil law. There's no jury. It's my case. The plaintiff and the defendant are Spanish-speaking. The courtesy of this court is theirs. You understand the language yourself—"

"Just so-so," said Schumaker.

"And I understand it," continued the judge. "Your objection can't stand. Put your question again, Mr. Rawlings, if you wish."

Jason repeated his question. In Spanish again.

"Señor," said Sancho uneasily, "I cannot remember how old I was then."

"How old are you now?"

Sancho fumbled with his fingers and said, "Fifty-four, señor."

"Then in 1790 you were five."

"Ah, you have worked it out for me. *Gracias*, señor." And Sancho looked sincerely indebted.

"Señor López," said Jason with a friendly smile, "do you say that the late Don Carlos Cordova made you this grant of land when you were five?"

Judge Conner's beaked nose twitched.

"Mmm," he said.

"It ain't relevant," grumbled Schumaker, in slight mental stress

~ 65 ~

from having to concentrate on catching the gist of questions and answers.

Luisa was utterly absorbed; Isabella had a warm light in her eyes. Lisbet, not understanding a word of the dialogue, was beginning to fume. Colonel Hendriks sat with his arms folded, his irritation mounting.

"Señor, was I five?" asked Sancho.

"If you are fifty-four now, Señor López," said Jason, "the immutable laws of subtraction cannot make you other than five in 1790."

"It is an age of childish ignorance and bliss, señor," said Sancho, hoping that would be the end of it.

Jason then said, "Why did Señor Carlos Cordova, your future employer at the time, decide then, when you were only five, to make you a beneficiary on his death?"

"He was a generous man, señor." Sancho wiped his face again, but Schumaker allowed himself a smirk.

"I have heard he was an admirable patron," said Jason, "but hardly as generous to his other employees as he was to you. Come, Señor López, there must be a reason why he decided, when you were only five, that you should eventually benefit to a far greater extent than all the others who worked for him."

"Judge, now that ain't relevant, you know it ain't," said Schumaker, who had gotten the unpalatable gist of the intimidating suggestiveness.

"Mr. Rawlings," said Judge Conner, "you are advancing into a wall, sir. The age of the beneficiary has no bearing on the case, even had he been a babe in arms at the time the grant was made. Retreat from the wall."

"I bow to you, sir," said Jason, and turned again to Sancho. "Señor López, do you know anything about paper?"

"Paper?" said Sancho in honest bewilderment.

Jason turned back to the judge.

"Your honour," he said, "I submit the possibility that we have here a grant made in September 1790, but written down on paper not manufactured until 1814 at the earliest."

The courtroom buzzed. Colonel Hendriks drew his brows sharply together. Lisbet wondered what that cold-eyed British devil was up to. Judge Conner pointed his nose in all directions before aiming it straight at Jason.

"Mr. Rawlings," he said, "be so good as to repeat that in Spanish for the benefit of Señor López." Jason did so. It laid the sweat of unhappiness over Sancho's bewilderment, the unhappiness of discomfort. He shook his head.

"I do not understand, señor," he said.

"Nor I," said Jason.

"Mr. Rawlings," said the judge, "a possibility, you said? You aren't making a positive declaration?"

"A conclusion?" suggested Jason.

"You must enlighten me, sir," said Judge Conner. "I'm not so learned as you on the significances that point to the age of a sheet of paper. I hope, sir, I shall not find myself following a red herring."

Schumaker got to his feet and said, "It don't signify and I object."

"Sit down," said Judge Conner, and Schumaker subsided peevishly.

"Documents of every kind, your honour," said Jason, "find their way into courts of law all over the world." He might have said his experience of the law extended only as far as two courts-martial, but wisely refrained. "Forgeries slip in, and sometimes slip by. Occasionally the age of a document can help to determine for or against. The age of a document can be related to the age of the paper. Paper-mill experts are able to determine when a particular paper was manufactured. But watermarks can help the layman. I've made a study of watermarks." He had—the previous evening in an encyclopaedia from the Cordova library. "This document, sir." He held it high. "The watermark is an ibex. This shows the paper to be from the Spanish mill in Barcelona, for the ibex is their watermark."

Judge Conner examined the document for himself. The watermark was visible against the light.

"Very pretty," he said, but his scepticism was evident. "Yet it tells me nothing relevant. You are coming to the relevancy, counsellor?"

"I hope so," said Jason.

"Proceed."

"You'll note the ibex has a crown."

"I concur," said the judge after another survey, "the ibex has a crown."

Schumaker sat fidgeting and muttering. Isabella was almost in danger of letting a delighted smile show.

Jason went on. "The Barcelona mill did not crown their watermark ibex until 1814, when they added it to celebrate the release of King Ferdinand by Napoleon, who had tried to place his own brother Joseph on the Spanish throne. Therefore, sir, it seems that in September 1790 the late Don Carlos Cordova wrote out this grant of land to Señor López on a sheet of paper containing a watermark which only came into being by 1814 at the earliest."

"The court is confounded," said Judge Conner with a smile. "How do you feel, Mr. Schumaker?"

Schumaker got up and tugged at the revers of his coat.

"It don't signify, Judge," he said. "It don't do anything except abuse my client. It's an attempt to get him indicted for forgery—"

"I'm sure that Señor López is incapable of forgery," said Jason. "I'm sure that he has neither the gift for it nor the instinct."

Judge Conner's bright eyes glinted.

"You wish to enlarge on that, Mr. Rawlings?" he said.

The courtroom was buzzing.

Jason said, "Only to say that in coming face to face with Señor López, it's my opinion he's an honest man. Nevertheless, I submit that the watermark makes the document questionable."

"The document can't be questionable," said Judge Conner. "It is there, sir, it exists. A small point you'll allow, but a fact."

"I stand corrected," said Jason. "I should have said the validity of its content is questionable."

"If you're right about the watermark," observed the judge.

Colonel Hendriks stood up.

"I hope, Judge, the court isn't—"

"Who are you?" the judge interrupted coldly.

"You know me, sir, I'm Colonel Hendriks—"

"Have you been called, sir?" asked the judge.

"I exercise my right to—"

"Your right in my court, sir, is at my discretion, and dependent on observance of the due processes of the court. Mr. Schumaker, Mr. Rawlings, do either of you have any objection to hearing Colonel Hendriks?"

"I declare my client and self in favour," said Schumaker.

"I've no objection," said Jason, and so unconcernedly that Lisbet did not know, given the opportunity, whether she would rather bite him than kiss him.

Judge Conner nodded at the Colonel.

"You may speak, sir."

"I'm obliged," said the Colonel heavily. "I wish to say that document was drawn up and signed by the deceased. I've—"

"You'll pardon me a moment," said Judge Conner. "How is it, Mr. Schumaker, that the witnesses to the signature have not been produced?"

"Been dead and gone these last few years," said Schumaker moodily. "Seems like they were old family retainers."

"A pity," said Judge Conner. "Please continue, Colonel Hendriks."

"I've seen that document, sir," said the Colonel, "and I know it. The handwriting and signature are open to comparison. I've not seen any irregularities in the comparisons I've made. The grant of land can't be disclaimed, and it's my opinion that the watermark theory has been tossed into this court like an open sack of dust."

"Thank you," said Judge Conner, "you have spoken, sir. You've done more than that. You've made a judgement. I thought I was here to do that."

The Colonel's eyes darkened.

"I've no wish to usurp your position—"

"I'm relieved, sir, relieved," said Judge Conner. "Do you have evidence to submit?"

"My opinions, Judge, are based—"

"Irrelevant. Sit down, sir."

The Colonel remained on his feet and said, "Is the court to consider an opinion on watermarks relevant?"

"Sit down," said the judge, his beak thrusting. The Colonel, mottled, resumed his seat; and Lisbet whispered to him that she was fretting hot at things.

"Mr. Rawlings," continued the judge, "how do you propose to set before this court evidence constituting proof of your watermark claim?"

Isabella opened up the leather bag again, and extracted a black-bound tome whose pages were edged with glittering gilt. Jason took the volume, opened it up, and requested the judge to note that the inscribed year of publication was 1830. He then turned to a page indicated by a marker, and placed the book on the table in front of the judge.

"Do you also read Spanish, your honour?"

"I'm a little more competent than Mr. Schumaker," said Judge Conner, and began to peruse the long paragraph indicated by Jason.

The talking ceased; the room became quiet, except for the hum of the flies. Luisa looked at Jason. He seemed unperturbed and quite relaxed. She could not share his apparent ease. She was in nervous tension. But she knew, at least, that this judge was going to make a fair and unbiased decision. He was going to consider only the facts. He was going to have nothing to do with local politics, with what some people wanted and some did not. Nor, she thought, was he going to be influenced by Spanish-American hostility; he was going to make up his own mind. Isabella had been wrong in thinking otherwise.

Isabella at the moment was only thinking that Señor Rawlings had the whole court by its coattails. She could forgive him all his piratical ancestors.

"Mr. Schumaker?" Judge Conner looked up. "Do you wish to read this?"

"I can't rightly say I could make it out," said Schumaker, "but seeing it can't be relevant, I don't reckon I'll be bothered. My client holds a document giving him ownership and no book can change that."

"Are you resting on that?" asked Judge Conner.

"I'm resting on my client's integrity," said Schumaker.

"Most ethical," said Judge Conner. He tapped with his gavel. "Case held over. Court adjourned."

"Held over?" said Schumaker.

"Your learned friend, Mr. Schumaker, has most properly drawn the court's attention to an encyclopaedic reference which suggests you need to find witnesses qualified to testify as to the age of the paper used for the document in dispute. This reference, Mr. Schumaker, confirms that your learned friend was correct in concluding that the grant made in 1790 to your client has possibly been set down on paper manufactured after 1814. You will see, therefore, that I can pass no judgement until this particular question has been resolved. Case held over." Again the gavel tapped.

The courtroom rose on the departure of the judge.

"Pa," whispered Lisbet, "didn't I tell you to hire Mr. Rawlings, didn't I? That Herman Schumaker, he's just downright feeble. Why, Judge Conner was looking at him as if he couldn't understand why anyone would let him into a courtroom, let alone hire him."

"Goddamnit," muttered her father, "it has nothing to do with Schumaker." He edged out and walked down to speak to the lawyer, who was patting the bewildered Sancho on the shoulder. The schoolroom began to empty on a high-pitched buzz. Isabella and Luisa sat down again. Jason joined them. Isabella looked glowingly at him.

"I am speechless with delight," said Luisa.

"And I am very happy," said Isabella, looking vividly so. "Señor Rawlings, thank you."

"We've only won a few months' grace," said Jason.

"We have won the case," said Isabella, "the document is a forgery."

"It looks like that, perhaps," said Jason. "But Sancho López doesn't fit the role. There's something very odd about it. We were lucky in finding that information on watermarks, but it's still possible the watermark in question may have been used before. You showed me the paper your grandfather used, and we know it came from Spain; it too bore the crowned ibex. But some of his older documents bore the previous watermark—the ibex without the crown."

"It's of no consequence," said Isabella. Under her green bonnet bright triumph sparkled, her eyes richly expressive of it. "You were too clever for them. They will not come to court again."

"They might, if they can find an expert to testify in their favour." Jason wore no air of triumph or satisfaction himself. He was detached, reflective. "Well, if they do you must use your San Antonio lawyer, for almost certainly I shall be gone by then."

"Señor?" said Isabella, and looked as if he had dealt her triumph an unfair blow.

"We understand, señor," said Luisa, and gave her sister a nudge of rebuke.

"Yes, of course," said Isabella, but still looked as if she would not allow her appointed advocate to desert her.

An old woman left her seat at the back of the room. She moved with the aid of a stick. She wore a black scarf around her white head. At the door Sancho López came up with her and took her arm.

"I am confused," he said. "What happened?"

"Come home," said his mother, setting her mouth and staring fiercely in front of her as she limped into the sunlight.

Colonel Hendriks walked across the front of the room and bowed to the Cordova sisters with the cynical grace of a man who had been cheated, not defeated.

"Señorita, my congratulations on your choice of attorney," he said. His smile was fixed. "Mr. Rawlings, you've foxed us all. By God, first you empty my pockets of change, now you deprive me of my chance to buy land. That's right unkind of you, sir. The document is no forgery."

"Would you wager on it, Colonel?" said Jason.

The Colonel's handsome face coloured.

"I'll have it sent to Austin, Mr. Rawlings," he said, "by God I will."

"But you'll not wager?" said Jason.

The Colonel turned abruptly to Isabella.

"Señorita," he said, "I still want that piece of land. Let me buy it from you, then, instead of from López. I do recommend a peaceful solution."

"There is no Cordova land for sale, Colonel Hendriks," said Isabella kindly but firmly. "I am sorry. Señor Rawlings, it is quiet now. Will you please take us home?"

Lisbet was still sitting as she watched them leave. Isabella sailed regally down the aisle of the courtroom and Lisbet bit her lip at the warm beauty of the woman. Jason gave her a friendly nod. Lisbet responded with a bittersweet smile. Outside, the Cordova carriage appeared, as people stood around, eyeing them with a mixture of admiration and resentment. Luisa permitted herself a responsive little smile. Isabella's air was gracious.

A woman said to a man, "That lawyer, they brung him all the way from England, I heard tell."

"Reckon that's right," said the man. "There ain't none foxier than them English."

Jason, seeing the sisters comfortably settled, said, "You'll excuse me now, señoritas?"

"Isabella may, I will not," said Luisa.

"Nor I," said Isabella.

"We wish you to see us home and share *merienda* with us," said Luisa. *Merienda* was the midday meal eaten in the open air.

"Señor, it is a command," said Isabella.

"Yes, I agree," said Luisa, "this time it is a command. Señor?" She moved her skirts to allow Jason to board the carriage, and they drove off down the street, leaving the curious looking after them.

"Damned if I ain't mighty taken with that Isabella," said the man who had his own opinion about the foxiness of English lawyers, "damned if I ain't."

"Her?" said another man.

"She's got spunk. Ain't no one else in Westboro as ready to spit in Colonel Hendriks' eye as she is."

The dust rose behind the bowling carriage and hovered like flecks of gold in the bright, hot air.

"Someone may show his hand now," said Jason.

"The someone who forged the document?" said Isabella, dwelling on his sun-darkened countenance as he stared sombrely at his boots.

"I candidly don't know," said Jason. "Señorita, you must buy that piece of land yourself."

"Buy it? But it belongs to me."

"As your lawyer—"

"Which you are not, señor."

"Isabella, how can you be so ungracious?" said Luisa.

Isabella flushed. She had only meant her comment to be teasing. Señor Rawlings did not look offended himself, but she realised she must have sounded very ungracious. It gave her a sense of acute dismay.

"Señor Rawlings, I did not mean—really I did not—"

"I know," said Jason, and smiled. Isabella felt quite a strange amount of relief.

"Are we out of town?" she asked. She had her back to the receding street.

"I think you can say we are," said Jason.

"There is no one watching us?"

"We're out of sight," said Luisa, sitting beside Jason.

"Then I can now express myself," said Isabella, and threw up her hands and cried, "*Olé!*"

Luisa laughed and echoed her sister. "*Olé!*"

"Señoritas, calm yourselves," said Jason.

"Oh, boo," said Isabella. Everyone laughed then, except Apulca, who masked his satisfaction with gravity.

They ate their light meal at a table under an orange tree on the patio. A wrought-iron balcony built under the windows ran around all four walls, and climbing plants clung to the walls and reached to clasp the ironwork. In this atmosphere of bright colour Jason made his first encounter with Mexican omelettes. These came lightly and warmly to the Cordova table, and meltingly to the mouth. He demolished three with no trouble at all.

"Señor Rawlings," said Isabella, her rich colouring enhanced by her dress of summer white, "I said you were not a lawyer and Luisa said I was ungracious."

"We have already passed that moment," said Jason.

"I am returning to it because—"

"Isabella," said Luisa, "it was the way you said it, and so soon after Señor Rawlings had won such a splendid victory for us."

"Oh, shoo, little squirrel." Isabella, wineglass in her hand, shook her head at Luisa. "Señor, you have probably observed that my sister is given to interruptions. I am rarely allowed to pursue a conversation properly."

"Oh, I think you do exceedingly well, Isabella, really I do," said Luisa, inveterate tongue in cheek.

Isabella laughed. She was always able to enjoy Luisa's little sallies.

"Señor," she said, the sun on her face and in her eyes, her parasol lying unopened beside her chair, "I hope I shall now at least be allowed to say that I think you our friend, and that I would rather you always be our friend than our lawyer. That is what I meant in wanting to return to that moment. Señor, while you are here Cordova is always open to you."

She was expansive in her appeal, and he could not deny she was incomparably lovely. But he was not here to court any woman, not even Venus herself, and so he only said, "I shall be here until your father returns."

"You are very mysterious about my father," said Isabella. "Why do you not go to Austin if you are so anxious to see him?"

"Do you have his address?" asked Jason.

"No. He is casual about such things."

"Then if I go to Austin," said Jason, "I may not find him. Nor should I want to arrive on the day he leaves to return here."

"Señor," said Luisa, "does he owe you money? He is addicted to gambling, I fear."

"Money? No," said Jason. "How could he? I've never met him, though I hope to. Therefore, I'll wait for him."

"Is it so important not to miss him?" asked Isabella, wondering why his eyes were sometimes so apparently remote from what was immediately around him.

"Friends should not be too inquisitive," said Luisa, and gave Jason a little smile as if they shared a secret. Isabella saw it and stiffened. She did not know why it disturbed her so, except that Luisa must be brought about if her affections were heading in that direction. Señor Rawlings was not an unimpressive man and Luisa was not an unimpressionable girl. But the man for her was Fernando Alba, whose family lived three hundred miles to the west. Fernando had already declared an interest, and Luisa had the softest spot for him. It would be a mistake to have her develop feelings for Señor Rawlings. No Cordova could marry into a race notorious for its piratical acquisitiveness and its heretical Protestantism— What am I doing, worrying like this? thought Isabella.

"Señor," said Luisa, "Isabella has suggested we might invite you to ride with us sometime and show you a little of Cordova."

"Most kind," said Jason, but did not commit himself.

"Oh, it will be a pleasure," said Luisa, showing an enthusiasm that disturbed Isabella a little more. But they shared the wish to show him Cordova.

"Señor," she said, "you are welcome whenever it is convenient to you, and the pleasure will be especially mine. I should be modest, I know, but I cannot refrain from saying that Cordova is grand and beautiful, and that it should be seen. So you will come, won't you, whenever you have a day to spare?"

"Thank you," said Jason, again not committing himself. Not wishing for reasons of his own to become further involved, he went on irrelevantly. "Are you satisfied now, señorita, that Judge Conner was in no way inclined to deal unfairly with you? That you were not at risk under the laws of the Houston government?"

"Oh, I assure you," said Isabella with warm earnestness, but with a smile, "one is extremely grateful for exceptions."

"I was impressed myself," said Luisa.

Jason finished his wine and wiped his mouth with the snowy napkin at hand. "That was an excellent meal, señoritas, thank you. I must go on my way now."

Isabella felt disappointment. She had thought he would stay a while, linger with them. It was, after all, an occasion for celebration, and one he was entitled to share.

Luisa, who loved company and did not have enough of it, said, "Señor, you need not be in any hurry on our account."

"It's kind of you," said Jason, "but I must be on my way." He rose to his feet. "Señorita," he said to Isabella, "I should buy that land from Sancho López if I were you."

"But it's my own land," protested Isabella.

"It was just a thought of mine."

They said goodbye to him outside the house, José driving him back to Westboro in the buggy.

Luisa, watching him go, said, "He is very fine, I think."

Isabella felt disturbed again.

"Luisa, are you falling in love with him?"

Luisa looked astonished.

"Falling in love with him? I've only just met him. He's an interesting man, but love hasn't occurred to me. Why are you looking so concerned?"

"I'm only curious," said Isabella, vivid in the sunshine.

"Oh, I see," said Luisa, "if I were to fall in love with him, you would not consider him suitable. Do you think him not much more than a clerk, after all?"

"Luisa!" Isabella was visibly upset. "I hope I'd never be as miserable a creature as that!"

Apulca, standing by the door of the house, folded his arms,

closed his ears to the sound of heated words, turned his eyes up to the sky, and silently contemplated the tranquility of the endless blue.

"Ah," said Luisa, looking hard at her flushed sister, "so that is it."

"What is?" asked Isabella, suspicious of Luisa's sweet smile.

"You are falling in love with him yourself."

"Luisa!" Isabella had never heard anything so crazy. There was only one man who had ever made her blood tingle, and it was certainly not Jason Rawlings.

"You were jealous, that's what it was—"

"Oh, I shall slap you!" cried Isabella.

"—but you need not be."

"Nor am I! Luisa, you are quite mad."

Luisa laughed. She had a light heart and a younger sister's tendency to tease.

"Poor Isabella," she said.

"Oh, this is ridiculous," breathed Isabella. "I, in love? With a wandering adventurer?"

"Worse," said Luisa, "with a descendant of pirates."

"Luisa, that's the silliest thing I've ever heard," said Isabella, "and I hardly know him."

"Neither do I," said Luisa demurely, "but I'm not the one who's blushing."

"I am not blushing! I'm just furious with your nonsense." Isabella turned with a flouncing rush of skirts. "No more. I'll not listen to another word."

"What does it matter that he isn't Spanish and doesn't own an *estancia*? If you wish to be in love with him—"

"I don't wish! Luisa, stop this!"

Luisa laughed again. She had never seen her sister so flushed and flummoxed.

"Well, I'd not stand in your way, Isabella. I'm already affectionately disposed towards Fernando Alba. And although Señor Rawlings is a descendant of pirates, at least he's a Catholic."

"As if that makes— Luisa, he's a Catholic? How do you know?"

"I came by some conversation with him last night while you were looking for Manuel and the encyclopaedia, that's how I know. So you see?"

"No, I don't see," said Isabella, "and you're a teasing little monkey."

"Ah, well," said Luisa lightly.

Isabella, realising that persistence on this tack could only head her on to the rocks, steered herself on to a less tricky course. "Luisa, to be serious, do you think we thanked Señor Rawlings enough? On reflection, I can't remember actually overwhelming him with gratitude."

"Then you should write him a note to thank him again for it. Won't do to have him think you are guilty of a lack of appreciation. And it will also give you the opportunity to invite him to ride with us."

"We've already invited him," said Isabella, "and I'm not going to make the mistake of pressing him. But I will send him a note to say how very grateful we are."

The note was written and delivered to Jason later that day. José took it.

*Dear Señor Rawlings. I am in a little distress, thinking I did not thank you sufficiently for the way you contrived a victory for us today. So I wish to let you know I am immensely grateful, that I really cannot thank you enough. If I did not show just how happy I was with the result, please forgive me. Luisa and I hope we may see you again quite soon, and I wish to sign myself your grateful friend. Isabella Cordova.*

Jason frowned over it. It really would have been better if she had let matters stand.

Jason watched the street from the window of his room, drying his hands on the towel. He was not looking for anything; he was lying in wait. There was some time to go—about two weeks.

The moving towel became still.

It was there, as sharp as ever, the memory of the day when he had arrived home from India after an absence of a year. He had travelled immediately to the family house in Dorset. His father was in London, held by the lure of clubs and gaming tables, and it was his sister Constance who was burdened with the painful necessity of telling him his wife had left him. In Constance's opinion she had chosen to follow in the footsteps of other shortsighted women who had exchanged the responsibilities of marriage for a senseless variety of sins.

"There's no gain in it," said Constance, "there never can be for a woman: we're too vulnerable. To spend only a few hours in dalliance with a man can imprison a woman for years in a dark hole of tears and regrets. There's no man who has to pay the same price as a woman in adultery. I vow Edwina will find that out all too soon. You must forgive and pity her, poor woman."

He could pity her: he could not forgive her. Fair, shapely, and with eyes that swam greenly between lashes as long as the wings of a bee, she could, with no more than one smile, win from him permission to dance on the lawn at midnight—if that was her whim. She was inclined, in fact, to have such whims. She was as much of a madcap as Lady Caroline Lamb had been, and regretted that she had neither Lady Caroline's wealth nor her former entry into the best houses in the land. In the end, Lady Caroline's whims had barred her from every house.

Life was quiet for Edwina in the county of Dorset, much too far from London, and Bath in Somerset had passed its palmiest Regency days. Jason and Edwina had been married only a year when he was posted to India, to the North-West Frontier, where the Pathans were causing problems. He could have taken Edwina with him, but she had heard too much about the heat of India and the rigid protocol governing the social round of officers' wives. She begged him not to press her, but to go without her, to do his duty and return to her at the end of his tour. That was to be in twelve months, and then he had promised to relinquish his Army career, which he had taken up after leaving university. They could move to London then.

It was in London that they had met. There they had at once fallen in love and married, she with no thought beyond the fact that she wanted him more than she had wanted anything. She had never seen a longer-legged cavalry officer or a more malely exciting one. All the same, she could not bear the sticky, boring thought of India. She begged him, on the day he departed, not to place himself at risk or she would spend their year of separation quite sleepless.

He would have liked her with him, but felt he had his kindest moment in agreeing to let her stay at home. And India was as she said it would be; she would have expired from heat and boredom. Hers was a liking for the sophisticated, not the exotic. They would have seen little of each other, for the unruly Pathans kept the British units constantly engaged. If she was impatient to have him back, he for his part felt crucifyingly incomplete without her. She hung in his mind like a bright, clear coolness, fair and fresh and white. He endured the heat and the sweat by day, piercing cold at night, with the cavalry units on constant alert. By night the Pathans crept down from the hills to swarm over the plains at dawn, where the cavalry engaged them. The cavalry were there entirely for the sake of maintaining the government-sponsored power of the East India Company. But all resistance was broken before the end of the year, and when Jason reached Calcutta he was able to write Edwina saying he would be sailing in two weeks.

His lust for life and his faith in women took a crippling blow at the news of Edwina's desertion. His sister knew of no way of easing the blow. She gave him what facts she could; Edwina had left only a brief note.

*Dear Constance. I have gone. Tell Jason, I cannot. I am sorry, but I am in love, hopelessly. I do not excuse myself. Worthless, I sign myself only, Edwina.*

No one knew who the man was. Edwina had been spending much time in London, ostensibly with friends of her family; but Constance, making enquiries after her defection, soon ascertained she had not seen those friends for months. The London friends informed Constance that Edwina, confessing herself more wedded to the excitements of London than to an absent husband, quarrelled with them the moment they tried to remonstrate with her. No, they could not give details of her indiscretions, for it would not be true to say they were in possession of anything more than rumours and gossip. The rumours, however, were strong enough to make them suggest to Edwina that she scotch each one. Edwina said she did not live by feeding on rumours, nor should they —her life was her own and no one else's. There were some people who could happily sit and count their fingers, and others who had to chase rainbows; she did not lecture people herself, therefore she did not expect them to lecture her. She would only say that sometimes some people actually caught a rainbow.

No, they could give no information at all on the man who had seduced her from her responsibilities and persuaded her to run away with him. Nor could Constance, when making further enquiries, find such information in anyone else. In her indiscretion, Edwina had in one sense been discretion itself. She left behind, it seemed, nothing by which her lover could be identified.

So Jason went in search of her. And the man. He knew from the start that the ice and fire which took possession of him were going to stay with him until he had killed the man and stood face to face with Edwina. He knew the years might drain uselessly away, that he might forfeit half his life in pursuit of a bitter, compulsive satisfaction, but his obsession left him no alternative. Only when he had experienced the moment of confrontation and truth would the ice thaw and the fire die.

His first clue came after weeks of scouring London. The grand houses and fashionable salons had shown him only blank faces. He was quite aware that the people who lived in or patronised such places were not the kind to give information on erring wives to cuckolded husbands. It was a clerk at a hotel who finally put him on the track. Studying the framed miniature of Edwina produced by Jason, the clerk said yes, he was sure that was the likeness of a lady who had visited the hotel some months ago.

She had stayed at the hotel?

Not on that occasion. She was a charming lady, easily remembered because of her looks and gaiety. She had arrived with companions, men and women, and dined in the restaurant with them. Then a few weeks later she returned to stay for a night.

Was that set down?

The hotel register, so the clerk said, was confidential. But thank you, sir, you may inspect it since I see you are in determined concern over the matter. Let me help. The day in question, I recall, was a Sunday, a quiet day. Her name escapes me, but will come to me when I see it. Ah, there it is. Mrs. E. Sylvestre. That, I can promise you, sir, is the signature of the lady whose miniature you hold.

Was she by herself?

~ 81 ~

Indeed, sir. But she had a full complement of luggage. She left about noon the next day. A hackney carriage called for her. She was most gracious with everyone, most charming. No, unfortunately, sir, I cannot say where she went to from here, but I assure you that is her portrait. We are trained to remember our patrons so that when they return they are not welcomed as strangers. And, of course, some are remembered more easily than others. Thank you, sir.

Painstakingly, Jason made enquiries of all the public hackney carriage drivers he could find, but without success. Then two small thoughts moulded to become a hope. One, Sylvestre might be the name of a foreigner. Two, Edwina had had a full complement of luggage. That took him on a round of the passenger offices of shipping companies. He was eventually given information that took him from the Old World to the New. First to New York, where he asked his questions of hotel servants. He was patient, dedicated, and purposeful. He kept his distance from people. He wished no friendships, no distractions. It all showed in the unreceptive bleakness of his eyes and the hardening line of his features. His love for Edwina had burned itself out, but the other fire still flamed, fed by the fuel of his obsessive desire to come face to face with her. Nor was there the slightest weakening of his resolve to kill her lover. A man who robbed a soldier of his wife was far more deserving of six feet of earth.

The hunt was a slow one, tedious and tortuous. The trail was all too easily lost, time and again. A hundred questions a day, every day; these and perseverance brought him back on the scent each time. He spent three months in New York, almost four in Philadelphia, and over four in Washington. It seemed that the quarry were dallying in cities, enjoying what each had to offer those in love and at play. He picked up clues not only at hotels but at theatres. Edwina left striking impressions behind her, and he had a description of the man now.

He thought, after tracing them to a Washington hotel, that he had subsequently lost them for good. But because he simply could not chase hopefully around the vast continent of America, Washington kept him penned. His patience and persistence were rewarded by a Washington itinerant, a cab driver. The cabbie, having looked long and hard at the miniature, thought that for a dollar he could dig up a recollection or two. Scrutinising the little portrait a second time, after receipt of the greenback, he became positive. Sure, that was the lady he had picked up from the hospital maybe three months ago. He reckoned she was English. That so, English? That was her, then. They had a way of coming sweet to the ear, English ladies, and there were always some in Washington. Drove this one to a house where she took herself and the baby inside. Sure it was a baby, it was no rag doll—it hollered. Which house? Take you there for fifty cents.

From that house in Washington he went to Baltimore, where one or two bright Maryland belles eyed him boldly from under deceptively demure lashes. He was hardly aware of them. He was in Baltimore for months. Then he crossed to St. Louis, and after a while there travelled down the Mississippi to Memphis. He lost the trail a dozen times, found it again just as often. He reached New Orleans. Information gained from a hotel there after two weeks sent him all the way back to Memphis, where he discovered that the information had no value except to suggest that the quarry had become aware he was hunting them and had laid a false trail. He returned to New Orleans and there for five months he scoured and searched. He received a letter from his sister Constance towards the end of this period, having written to her during his previous visit. He had not expected a reply, for he had not known he would be coming back to that city and using the same economical lodgings. Constance wrote in the hope of reaching him with the news that his father had died and left an immense mortgage hanging around her neck, and that she would like him to come home so that she could hang it around his, where it rightly belonged.

He sent a brief reply: He did not know when he would be home. There should be monies coming in from the estate, and as long as she paid the interest with these that should keep the wolves out.

It was at the end of five months in New Orleans that he found Edwina, in a house on St. Charles Avenue. It connected with the house next door, and the house next door was a sumptuous but discreet establishment graced by beautiful octoroon girls, potential paramours of the rich gentry of New Orleans. Edwina was in a room on the first floor of the more modest house. It was early evening and she had been dead since morning, having taken poison at dawn. She lay in her bed, awaiting the arrival of the undertaker. Fortunately, she had a patron, a friend, a Monsieur Johnson, who owned the house and also the establishment next door. He was not without influence; and in kind, compassionate generosity had made arrangements to ensure she did not receive the anonymous burial of a suicide. He himself had departed on urgent business, and it was possible he would not return until things were, ah, tidy again. The smooth-faced, hard-eyed housekeeper, an imported citizeness of France, would have imparted none of this information, or even invited the visitor in, had he not put the fear of God into her.

First he insisted on seeing a lady whom he had been told resided there.

"Only Monsieur Johnson resides here—"

"This lady." Jason produced the miniature.

The housekeeper looked at the portrait, then up into the blue eyes like ice. He spoke; the housekeeper listened. The lady was his wife. That was understood? He had no wish to call in the law officers. That was understood too? He required only his wife.

The housekeeper, cold shivers disturbing the warmth of her body, let him in. She wept brokenly without shedding a tear, begged him to bear the news that the poor lady was dead, explained how good Monsieur Johnson had been, and then led the way up the carpeted staircase.

And so, standing beside the silken-draped bed in a room exquisitely furnished, Jason Rawlings was at last able to look into his wife's face. For three years he had longed for this. Her face was calm and without lines, almost lovely in its tranquility, although there was a faint blueness on her lips and the lightest of shadows beneath her closed eyes. She was still fair. Against the snowy white of the pillows her hair looked golden. She had lost a little flesh. But no one could have said that there lay a woman tainted by her excessive love of pleasure.

He did not feel hate. His love, once so total, came to life again as pity. For three years she had lived as he supposed she wanted to, amid the excitements of different cities. Yet by her own hand she had perished. They had had one year together, a year which had meant much to him—but perhaps not quite so much to her. Maybe she had enjoyed her few years around the candle flame, and perhaps even as she took the poison she might have told herself she would have done the same things again. The world and its tinselled magic had called. The house in Dorset could not have meant much more to her than rusticity.

He could not weep for her, but he could feel sad regret for her lack of faith in the future they might have had. There would have been good days as well as the dull ones. There could have been children. Even if she was a woman who could not have grown old gracefully, had she never realised that the most glittering ballroom could not cast its spell forever? She could have found some compensations with him in Dorset, in the heady scents of summer, the hoydenish atmosphere of spring, and the affection of friends. Instead she had chosen a way of life that had led her to end it while she was still young.

He put a hand to her hair. It still felt soft and rich.

The fire of his obsessive purpose died. Only the ice was left.

The door opened. He thought it could only be the housekeeper. He looked round. A young woman, quite beautiful, with huge amber-brown eyes and a wealth of dark glossy hair, regarded him with a curiously expressive mournfulness, like an unspoken lament. Her skin had the colour and perfection of the palest gold, and she wore a long green silk wrap that glimmered around her curving body. He had been long enough in New Orleans to feel certain she was an octoroon. So many of them were astonishingly beautiful, yet they had a future that lasted only as long as their beauty. Unless their patrons gave them a house and a pension.

"Who are you?" he asked.

"M'sieu? I am Antoinette." Her English, overlaid only by the softest accent of a French-speaking citizen of New Orleans, was almost flawless.

"Antoinette." It was an emotionless restatement of her name.

"Oh, there are ten thousand Antoinettes in New Orleans, m'sieu." Her faint smile was sad, her voice tinged with a charming little huskiness that came of her sadness. Hesitantly, she said, "I am told—m'sieu, is it true, you are the husband?"

"Yes."

"You are sorry for her, m'sieu? You have come to bury her, not to rend her?"

She spoke softly and such was her education that she was able to paraphrase Shakespeare. Knowing what he did of New Orleans, with its unbreakable associations with the old aristocratic feudalism of France, its racial divisiveness and its stern belief that birth

~ 85 ~

governed the individual's place in life, he was aware how impossible it was for the octoroon women, however beautiful, to find any real place at all. They belonged neither to the whites nor to the blacks.

"I came to find her, Antoinette."

"M'sieu, she knew you would, one day. I may enter, m'sieu?"

"Close the door."

She did so, quietly, and came to the bedside. The most highborn duchess could not have crossed the floor more gracefully, more flowingly. She was a creature of exquisite movement.

She looked down at Edwina.

"She laughed at life, m'sieu. It was destroying her, but she still laughed. Only when she spoke of you was she sad. She said, 'Antoinette, he will catch me one day and then I shall curl up and die.' M'sieu, here is a letter." Antoinette brought the missive from out of her wrap. "She gave it to me last night. She said, 'If he comes one day, give it to him. If he does not come, it's of no importance. But give it to no one else.' M'sieu?"

She offered him the letter, looking into his bitter eyes. He took it from her. She brought a chair forward and placed it beside the bed. When he sat, she left him. He read:

*My dearest, my sad one. I know you are sad. I know you are angry too, that you are looking for me. It is too late now. But I love you, will you believe me? It is not a perfect love because I am a very imperfect woman, but it is a better love than I have had for others, I know that too.*

*I met him in London, the first one. I could not stay in Dorset— nor could your father. Constance could, but then she likes cows and meadows and wet grass, and so she has joy in these things. Mr. X was so charming, so gay. I shall call him that because he was the unknown quantity to you and to me when you and I were in love. I have no strength, I cannot say no when I am tempted by the things I want. I must do what I want to do, and that is a great and expensive weakness, isn't it?*

*Mr. X was a man who did not like cows and meadows either. But although a woman without strength, I was not conquered in five minutes. That is my only saving grace, that I did not fall immediately into his arms. He persisted, detecting my weakness and my love for champagne. In Dorset there is ale which I am told is* unsurpassed, but it is champagne I adore. I failed you after the excitement of a London ball, at which attended the great, towering, and magnificently wicked Duke of Cumberland himself. Mr. X took me to the rooms of a friend in Albany. It is the discreetest place in London, Albany; there I was unfaithful to you.

I was unfaithful many times after that. In the end I could not return to you. Mr. X wished to take me to America with him and I had to go. There was a child, you see. I did not tell him I was enceinte at the time—because, curiously, although he has so much charm I did not feel paternity would excessively delight him. The child was born in Philadelphia, suffered a little illness in Washington, and caused Mr. X to become somewhat peevish. Wretchedly infatuated woman that I still was, his peevishness was my sorrow. We were both made to enjoy life, not to be burdened with it. There is a woman in Baltimore called Sarah Blazey. She is a foster mother to the child, Clare. Please believe me, selfish though I am, there is a little piece of my heart in Sarah Blazey's house.

While we were in St. Louis about a year ago, we met a Mr. Johnson from New Orleans. He expressed delight in me. He has a singular admiration for ladies from England. Though this comes, I regret to say, from his knowledge that there is a demand in New Orleans for those whose refinement is unquestionable but who have fallen on hard times. Mr. X, who had never been quite the same after suffering all the inconveniences caused by my having his child, was cooling considerably towards me. And, moreover, he was also running short of funds. He professed himself under an obligation to go immediately to New York to conduct a financial transaction, and to travel without baggage. We had intended going to New Orleans, and he considered I ought not to miss its own particular excitements on his account. Mr. Johnson assured me he would be enchanted to escort me there, and that my welfare would command the warmest attention. Thereupon the two gentlemen, Mr. X and Mr. Johnson, conferred at length, following which and in the most civilised fashion I was handed over by Mr. X to Mr. Johnson, with whom I travelled to Memphis by steamboat, leaving Mr. X to go his own unfettered way.

We stayed in a Memphis hotel for a while, where Mr. Johnson advised me that he had not been mistaken in his first impressions

*of me. He vowed indeed that I was a tender joy to him and would
continue to be. I am confessing all, am I not? It was when we
were returning to the hotel one day that a chambermaid who
had been on the lookout for us hastened to intercept us. You were
there, in the hotel and waiting. Fortunately for Mr. Johnson, who
can exercise as much charm as Mr. X, the chambermaid suspected
from your look that you were not amicably disposed towards us.
You had questioned her as well as others there. She told you, I believe, that she did not think we were the people you were enquiring after, for although I bore a similarity to the lady in question,
the gentleman was quite unlike your description of Mr. X. You
were obviously sure the lady was me, however, so you were waiting. The chambermaid said you looked like a man in search of the
devil. I might have said two devils and their mistress. Mr. Johnson
was a little alarmed at the prospect of an encounter with you, and
thus we turned about and left later that day for New Orleans, the
chambermaid arranging for our luggage to be smuggled out and
taken to the steamboat office for us.*

*On arrival in New Orleans, Mr. Johnson, by means of generous
donations, arranged at an hotel for you to be given the most mis-
leading information should you chance to call. But I think you
will still persevere, no matter how well Mr. Johnson may have had
you misled. Cavalry officers don't quit the field voluntarily, do
they?*

Jason remembered the incident and his savage disappointment
that although he had earthed his quarry they never surfaced. The
chambermaid had been protecting Edwina, of course, not Johnson, for it was Edwina's charm that would have fostered an allegiance, not the man's. He remembered too that there had come a
time in the hunt when answers to his questions had begun to puz-
zle him, when although a person's recollection of Edwina left no
doubts, the description of the man she was with did not tally with
that which had gone before. He understood now: she had
changed partners. She had had no option.

*Mr. Johnson, with affectionate generosity, installed me in his
house in New Orleans. His regard for me was constant, or almost
constant. Frequently he professed himself proud of me, and six
months ago invited a dear friend of his to come and gaze at me.
His friend, I vow, seemed enchanted. Mr. Johnson drew me aside*

*and explained that his friend had done him so many cherished favours that he could never adequately repay him by his own endeavours. The best he could do was to offer to share one of his more exquisite treasures with him. I said I hoped I was not the treasure he had in mind, to which he responded with the utmost frankness that as far as his friend was concerned I was the only treasure. If I lacked a true appreciation of the circumstances he would with profound regret have to relinquish me. To whom? I asked. He replied that on the streets of New Orleans I could take my pick of amorous dandies.*

*I am not a woman brave enough to stomach such a fall as that. Accordingly I brought Mr. Johnson's dear friend to my bed. From time to time other dear friends followed.*

*Now I am ill, my sad one. It is the New Orleans illness, one that in my weakness I have brought on myself and one that in my distaste and cowardice I cannot face. My only consolation is that some of Mr. Johnson's dear friends may perhaps not be feeling too well either. Nor even Mr. Johnson himself, perhaps.*

*It is a very melodramatic story, isn't it? Unfortunately, the leading lady's part fitted her all too well.*

*Do not search for Mr. X, do not go after him. Do not waste your years. Search instead for another wife, a stronger one, who will love you at least a little more than she loves herself. And be kind, if you can, to a girl called Antoinette.*

*Perhaps you will never come, perhaps you will never read any of this. But I wished to write it down and have done so. And I will write down also what will be my last words to you. I have known many men now. You are the best of them. I can only remember how sweet was my brief time with you. That is true, believe me. Goodbye. I am so sorry. Edwina.*

She had not excused herself or asked him to forgive her. He looked again at her. The evening was warm and the sunlight crept lazily through the shutters. There were shadows on her face. But the faint blueness had gone from her lips and they were pink. He touched her with his fingertips, gently pushing back her eyelids. The green eyes, though blank with death, were still as soft as the first summer light over the Dorset hills.

He sat reflective and quiet, his pity for her as real as his love had once been.

"M'sieu?" It was Antoinette. She carried a tray. On it was coffee, and also cognac. She saw his face, lean and hard, but his eyes were not so bleak now. They were sad. "You forgive her, m'sieu? You understand?"

"I understand butterflies," he said.

"Butterflies?"

"What else can some women be? Life for women is not the same as it is for men. Vulnerability is with them at birth, and remains with them all their lives. So some of them choose a brief existence in the sun, or what they think is the sun."

"M'sieu," said Antoinette, her huge eyes full of soft shadows, "your wife was an English lady, and lived with laughter even when I knew she was unhappy. But she was very proud. I was her friend, she told me so, and I am proud too. We laughed together, many times, and she would tell me to go. 'Go,' she would say, 'go, for you are young and strong. For myself I cannot go, I cannot lie in any bed now except a soft one. But you are strong. So go.' M'sieu, how can I go any more than she could, whether I am strong or not?"

She was telling him, of course, that she was a bonded creature. She poured the strong black coffee. He took it from her and drank it. She gave him the brandy, golden in its transparent balloon. It brought new fire, but it did not melt his ice.

"Thank you, Antoinette," he said, and she studied him, a little covertly, a little shyly. And she wondered why his wife had left him.

"You will bury her, m'sieu?" she said in soft earnestness. "The funeral is arranged, and if you are there she will not be alone. She did not like to be alone."

"Since you were her friend, Antoinette, we will go together."

"Oh, if I may come with you, m'sieu, I will be in debt to you," she said, her eyes luminous.

"When is the funeral?"

"Tomorrow morning. M'sieu?"

"Yes?" He responded abstractedly.

"She will be glad to have you with her."

She was a strangely gentle creature, he thought. She cast compassion over the room, over the dead and the living. "Shall we cover her?" he suggested.

"I will do it, m'sieu." She drew the sheets over the fair head, murmuring, "*Adieu, ma chérie.*" She glanced at Jason, hesitated, then said, "M'sieu, do you wish to stay the night? There is no one who will say no to you and *le maître* will not be back."

"Do you mean a man called Johnson?"

The large eyes expressed warning.

"Yes, m'sieu. But he will not be back. Not until she has been buried and he knows you have gone. He will know now, m'sieu, that you are here. He will know you are her husband. He will wait for you to go. M'sieu, you will not pull his house down? It would not be wise. I will take you to a room. You must leave her for a while, you must let her lie in peace."

He went with her to a room across the landing. The room was dim, the shutters closed. New Orleans citizens endured the sun out of doors, but never permitted it to pass a threshold or enter a window. If one wished sunlight when at home, there was, in most of the old Creole houses, an inner courtyard, paved and quiet and open.

"Do you wish food, m'sieu?" asked Antoinette.

"Thank you, no," said Jason, sombre.

"Or for me to stay to talk with you?" She hesitated again before adding, "I do not have to appear this evening."

He understood that. She meant she did not have to present herself for inspection in the establishment next door. She was, with her grace and beauty, an octoroon girl to be coveted. Many of the more affluent gentlemen of the city were glad to acquire such girls. Jason wondered, in a detached way, why this exquisitely lovely girl had not been acquired by a discerning Creole long ago.

"Do you live in this house?" he asked.

"That is so, m'sieu," she said, glimmering in the dimness. "I was the help and companion of your wife. She would have no one else. We were friends, you see. I am so sad about her, but I am very glad you have found her and will be with her tomorrow. Forgive her, please forgive her."

"Am I holy enough to dispense forgiveness? It's better, isn't it, to understand or to try to understand. Edwina was born to be a brief blaze of colour, perhaps, in the eyes of people who glimpsed her in passing. She knew herself. It's all in her letter, Antoinette. She did not ask to be forgiven. Nor to be understood. But I think she would have preferred understanding."

"Yes, m'sieu," said Antoinette softly. "You wish nothing at all?"

"Nothing, thank you."

"Then *bon soir*, m'sieu. I will wake you in the morning."

The door closed soundlessly.

9

Antoinette was electrifyingly beautiful in black. The pale gold lustre of her skin was almost translucent in its delicacy behind her black veil, and her eyes were liquid with moistness. She and he were the only mourners. Dawn had been cloudy, but the sun broke through as they sprinkled dust on the descending coffin. Silently Antoinette said her farewell to the only white woman who had been her friend. Silently Jason watched the first spadeful of earth thrown. Then together they left the cemetery.

In the city the clarity of the Gulf air was besieged by the miasmatic odours of sanitation so minimal it scarcely existed. Whatever New Orleans spent its money on, very little was set aside for the provision of drains and sewers. The Creoles ignored such an earthy factor. They considered that civilised perfection was exclusively to do with cuisine most exquisite and culture most sublime. Plumbing and sewerage were matters for other people perhaps, not for them. Every meal was a banquet, including breakfast, and culture meant such things as the Théâtre d'Orléans, individually designed livery for household slaves, the sensuous nurturing of beautiful octoroons, and the subtle and stubborn rejection of everything American or Anglo-Saxon.

In the Faubourg Orléans, beginning to acquire its look of morning bustle, Jason asked Antoinette whether she would like to stop and drink coffee.

She looked at him a little uncertainly through her veil, wondering if he realised white gentlemen did not take octoroon girls into the coffee shops of New Orleans.

"It would be better, m'sieu, to return to the house for that."

He saw the sense of it. He was willing to act as if she were white, but recognised she did not want to risk embarrassments arising out of the doubts of some sharp-eyed café owner. In the dignity of her mourning black and with her skin so light she could have passed for white in many countries and many cities. But New Orleans had an instinct for picking out a yaller gal, however pale her skin. They called the beautiful mulattoes that—yaller gals. Jason felt for this enchanting creature, who would dread the peering eyes, the polite questions. Her grooming, her grace, and her natural intelligence made her a person exquisite, but her mixed blood condemned her to a twilight world.

"We'll go back to the house, then," he said, "and have coffee there."

"*Merci*, m'sieu." In her relief she gave him a faint smile of gratitude. He looked around for a cab. She watched him. He was quite different from the small, dark Creoles, who were dandified almost to the point of decadence. He was very long-legged and his muscular body was slender. His bottle-green coat and buff trousers were impressively well tailored, even if there was perhaps a suggestion that it was years since they had known the nap of newness. His top hat, with its slightly curled brim, distinguished him, although if one looked closely the marks of repaired dents could be seen. She wondered, as she had when she first saw him, why it was that his wife had preferred other men.

A cabriolet pulled up. The cabbie peered at Antoinette. Bravely she lifted her chin and disregarded him. Jason handed her aboard and met the cabbie's eye.

"St. Charles Avenue, *tout de suite, mon ami*."

The cabbie did not argue. They travelled back in style to the house, Antoinette very conscious of her escort and his calm indifference to rules written and unwritten. He was not at all concerned about either, it seemed. No Creole gentleman would have ridden like this in public with her; Monsieur Rawlings did not seem to mind at all.

She sat upright and looked flawlessly aristocratic. New Orleans seemed to have too many people on the streets. But the city, with its impossibly narrow thoroughfares, always did seem crowded—simply because it provided pedestrians and vehicles so little room. White people sauntered, Creole ladies strolled beneath their ubiquitous parasols. To make haste was to turn them into very ordinary people. Blacks were either hurrying or dawdling, depending on the mood of their masters and the nature of their errands.

Antoinette said, "M'sieu, I should really be chaperoned. It is not the thing for me to be unaccompanied."

"You're not unaccompanied," said Jason, "you're with me. New Orleans must grow up—you must help it to. In any case, you're wearing gloves; no one is to know you aren't married to me. Are you worrying? You need not. If people are looking at you, it isn't because they're wondering if you're Creole or not, or even whether you are married to me. People always look at lovely young ladies."

Beneath her veil she coloured. She knew he was not paying her an insincere compliment.

"M'sieu, I cannot help New Orleans to grow up."

"I know you can't." Jason, for all that his mind was on Edwina and the man who had taken her, cheapened her, and passed her on to a procurer, did not find it too much effort to give his attention to this remarkably appealing girl. "The world is full of idiots, and perhaps there are more here than anywhere. Possibly, except for people like you, we're all idiots."

Antoinette made an impulsive but graceful gesture of disagreement, and two black girls, brightly swathed, their hair bound by yellow cotton tignons, glanced up at her. Their sighs were indicative, perhaps, of their assumption that though she was in mourning she was white and free.

"M'sieu," she said with a little smile, "you are least of all an idiot. One has only to be in your company a few minutes to be very sure of that. But I am less sure about myself. It is possible, of course, that if I were compared with the graceless idiots of New York, or the excusable idiots of Paris, I should not be considered quite the most hopeless."

"What are graceless idiots?" asked Jason.

"Is it permitted to say that they are those who are simply stupid, m'sieu?"

"It's permitted. And excusable ones?"

"Those whose foolishness is lovable," she suggested.

"That's permitted too, and also acceptable." He smiled.

They reached the house on St. Charles Avenue. The house-keeper let them in. Searching to indulge her disagreeable mood, she shook her head at Antoinette.

"Where is your chaperone, where? To go out, to enter streets, where anyone might have seen you—what were you about and what will people think?"

Antoinette flushed with dismay and embarrassment. The incredibly artificial nature of the grumbling complaint would have made Jason dump the ridiculous hag into a cold bath had it not been for the fact that this very artificiality meant so much to Antoinette and her kind. Without its façade, they would have felt as naked as cattle. In manners, courtesies, and etiquette they were taught that they reflected all the graces of virtuous young Creole ladies, and when they became the mistresses of rich patrons their behaviour was still required to be faultless and beyond reproach.

"I am sorry, madame," said Antoinette, "but it was such a sad occasion, and I was forgetful. You will forgive me? I will dress your hair for you tomorrow. See, m'sieu, what fine hair Madame has?" Lightly and delicately Antoinette's hands winged around the housekeeper's stiffly curled locks. "It is a joy to dress it for her. Madame, you will not tell le maître I had no chaperone? It was the funeral, it—"

"Ah, it is over. Good." Madame Coulbert crossed herself. She looked hopefully at Jason. "You are leaving now, m'sieu?"

"Not yet, madame." Jason eyed her like a man who would not stand in the way of her early demise. Her glance fell. "I should like to see your employer before I leave. I wish to talk to him about my wife. That is, my late wife."

"I am not sure," she said, and began to mumble.

"You may take it, madame, that I am very sure. But it will not be an unfriendly talk. Advise him so."

"Yes, m'sieu." Madame Coulbert was nervous, flustered. "Of course, m'sieu. If I can contact him."

"I feel certain you can. And I am in no hurry. I am able to wait."

"Naturally, you are welcome to a room, m'sieu. It was a tragedy —your poor wife—but not everyone lives to a great age in New Orleans."

"Also, it was my fault Antoinette went to the cemetery without

~ 95 ~

a chaperone." Jason spoke evenly, his clipped voice clear, his words precise. "Attach no blame to her."

"No. Of course not, m'sieu. Nothing will be said of it." The housekeeper was perceptibly uneasy. His wife had died in her master's house. She had poisoned herself. The authorities did not know that. But he, the husband, did. Madame Coulbert wished she had not gabbed it all out. But he had looked at her and she had felt a tightness around her neck. He had the eyes of a Seminole Indian with a blood debt to settle.

She effaced herself, and Jason and Antoinette went up the stairs to the first floor.

"M'sieu," whispered Antoinette, "she is not a good woman, that one. She is without warmth. But she is afraid of you. It is the way you look at her and speak to her."

"It doesn't make you afraid?" he said with a smile.

"But, m'sieu, you have not looked at me like that or spoken to me like that," she said. "You have only been very kind. If you wish to sit for a while now there is a *petit salon* which is quite comfortable. I will bring coffee to you."

She took him into a small sitting room, expensively and taste-fully furnished with imported pieces from France. The decor was white, gilt, and blue. Antoinette was in a mood of warm under-standing, wishing to provide him with privacy, comfort, and sym-pathy. She slipped away to prepare coffee.

Jason thought about Edwina. He had always felt that when he did find her every bitter word stored in his mind would be spoken. She had escaped them all by taking her own life. He had nothing for her now but regret and pity. Despite all that she had done, of her own free will, simply to appease her need for gaiety, she must have died in despair. Her letter was a brittle parody of events, full of mockery of herself and her lovers. The waste was tragic. She had been like a bright flower always in bloom. One reason, the primary reason, why he had managed never to completely lose her trail was that there was always someone, somewhere, who remem-bered her out of hundreds of others. She looked as if she had come fresh from a garden, one articulate hotel proprietor had said. And she had finished up in a decadent hothouse to wilt and to die.

Now there was only the man. Her Mr. X. Sylvestre. Who had not merely discarded her, but handed her over to corruption.

Well, he would find Sylvestre, if it took him another three years. It was in the cards that it would take him a lot less. Because corruption, which went by the name of Johnson, should prove an invaluable source of information.

Antoinette returned, bringing the coffee. She set the tray down on a glass-topped tulipwood table. Modestly she said, "M'sieu, I thought—that is, it is not as if there should be the usual proprieties, perhaps?"

He saw there were two cups on the tray and said, "No, it is not, and I thought we had already agreed to take coffee together."

"Oh, but I should not want to discard the accepted formalities without your approval," she said earnestly. "It is the careful observation of such things which makes us civilised, and many little faults can be forgiven in people if they are at least courteous and conforming. Is it not so, m'sieu?"

"Are you saying, Antoinette, that it would be more conforming of us to take coffee separately instead of together? There is no chaperone, is that it?"

"M'sieu," she said, "you are a gentleman and I—"

"Yes, you are a young unmarried lady and a most attractive one." Jason simulated a gravity to match her earnestness. "But I think neither of us is in danger. Therefore, we will enjoy coffee together. We can also converse, I imagine, without too much risk. I think you like talking."

Antoinette smiled, and her enormous amber-brown eyes looked meltingly soft.

"It is an opportunity to exercise my English," she said. "My English is not too faulty, m'sieu?"

"Your English is perfect. So sit down, please, and pour coffee for both of us."

"Yes, m'sieu," she said, and sat down with a movement that was sinuously effortless, a collective flow of smooth, coordinated limbs which established her in light, graceful occupation of a blue and gold Louis XV chair. Her petticoats whispered, sighed, and settled.

"Tell me about the man Johnson," he said as she poured the coffee. It came out black and stiff, like all Creole coffee.

"M'sieu," she said, betraying a little anxiety, "you must tread with care. He is not an unimportant man."

"I shall tread with great care, Antoinette."

"You are wondering how he treated your wife?" she said, handing him his coffee.

"I know how he treated her. But he wasn't the one who took her from me. Antoinette, is Johnson a man who would rather buy his way out of trouble than extract himself in a riskier way?"

Antoinette clasped her fine, pale hands in her lap.

"M'sieu," she said, "he would always prefer to use either his influence or his money. He goes hand in glove with the law. So the law looks the other way at times. But when his influence or his money cannot provide a solution, he knows it is dangerous for him to have too many throats cut. His establishment must not be tainted by scandal. No Creole would set foot in it if it were."

"We can assume, then, can we, that he favours bribery above murder?"

"Oh, m'sieu, be careful if you intend to make him pay for what he has done," said Antoinette with a new rush of anxiety. "I should not want anything to happen to you."

"Nor I to you. Antoinette, why is it you have no patron?"

It was a cause for curiosity, the fact that so beautiful and appealing an octoroon was not by now the pleasure and joy of a moneyed New Orleans aristocrat. She would surely delight the most discriminating of proud Creoles. The light-skinned mulatto girls, providing they had all the graces as well as beauty, could look forward to being bought by the self-indulgent rich, usually the Creoles, and installed in a house or an apartment of luxury. Carefully brought up to become ladies of loving joy, they made faithful mistresses. It was as high as they could climb, and how long they maintained their position depended on how long they retained their ability to please the eye, delight the ear, and pleasure the senses. Their capacity to please in all things could be infinite, for, like the geisha girls of Japan, they were schooled in the many ways of serving a man, and in them was instilled the belief that to give such service was to achieve their own kind of fulfilment. So willingly did these octoroons, in their wistful desire to be loved and protected, accept what New Orleans society ordained for them that many benefactors, even the proud Creoles, acquired for them an affection which ensured their enslaved mistresses would never want. They retired richly laden. Others—too many of them—grew fat after a number of years, for they were addicted, amid the luxury and idleness in which they lived, to just the things which would make them fat. No Creole would retain a mistress of whom he could not be proud, even though she never appeared in public with him. An overweight one was likely to be pensioned off in a way that was generous, but left her without any further purpose in life except to grow fatter. And there were some who were not pensioned off, but disposed of by being sold to someone who just wanted another servant.

Antoinette had extraordinary style and charm. Among a class of women noted for their remarkable beauty there could be few superior to her, thought Jason. So why had not some Creole set her up? She did not seem too eager to give the reason. She looked at her hands, the long slim fingers as sensitive as her feelings for the proprieties.

"Never mind," he said.

"M'sieu," she said with an effort, "I must wait for a patron who will wish to acquire me despite my imperfection."

There was a very sensitive issue here. Her skin was dusky with burning.

"I see no imperfection, nor remark any," he said.

"M'sieu," she whispered unhappily, "I am not a virgin."

He should not have asked his question. She was on fire with shame. An octoroon girl could own no worse imperfection. No matter how beautiful she presented herself to those who came to the establishment to inspect her and assess her, no matter how well-inducted, well-read, and well-versed she was, in the eyes of the polished gentlemen of New Orleans her loss of virginity made all her virtues count for nothing. Except perhaps to a man whose compassion and discernment counted for more than his sense of tradition. The Creoles, disdaining all that was not Creole, cultivated perfection in all things relevant to the civilised enjoyment of life. Food, style, manners, possessions, clothes, and women. They came to an establishment to meet quadroons, octoroons, and other "yallers," always on the understanding that perfection was guaranteed. No establishment which valued its reputation would produce for any client a girl who was not inviolate. There were exceptions, though never deceptions. Some clients outside of the Creoles were willing to meet a girl whose beauty and appeal might be irresistible enough to make her loss of virginity seem unimportant, particularly if she were well recommended by her proprietor. But no proprietor would dream of recommending her to a Creole, even if she surpassed Venus herself. However, there were other gentlemen, other rich men. She could meet such men, look beautiful for them, charm them with her voice and impress them with her deportment. No pressure was put on a client. The girl herself had to convince a prospective patron that she was well worth acquiring, despite her unfortunate imperfection.

"Well, it doesn't signify disaster to me," said Jason, lazily casual, "for I make no claim to innocence myself."

She raised her downcast eyes, her burning blood receding. There was a faint smile on his face. Whatever other men might think of her lack of physical immaculacy, he seemed not at all concerned.

"M'sieu," she said, returning his smile, "you are imperfect too? Oh, that is *drôle*."

"Do you have duties in this house?"

"There will be little for me to do now that your wife—now that she is gone."

"Then this afternoon we'll find a carriage of some kind and you can show me New Orleans. Will you do that?"

Antoinette took on a warm glow.

"You wish that, m'sieu, to ride out with me? It is not considered—"

"Never mind how it's considered by others. Myself, I should consider it very agreeable. And I don't, in any case, wish to sit around all day. If there's your reputation as an eligible young lady to worry about, then we can take either a closed carriage or a chaperone."

Her laugh was softly husky.

"To properly observe all the conventions, m'sieu, there should be a chaperone, whatever carriage we take."

"If you wish," said Jason, "if you feel she is necessary."

"On the other hand," said Antoinette, only the softest whisper of an accent caressing her English, "it would be very boring for her, and in a closed carriage her presence could perhaps be assumed. It is only in an open carriage that the visible absence—"

"Visible absence?"

"Yes, m'sieu. The visible absence of a chaperone would indicate that the lady is either married or that her escort is otherwise related to her."

"I sometimes find this sort of thing amusing," said Jason.

Antoinette was slightly shocked.

"M'sieu, it is not the sort of thing that has ever been found amusing in New Orleans."

"God's life, I know it. But it's not always indicative of an enlightened society."

"Society is more enlightened in England, m'sieu?"

"In England, puritanism, hypocrisy, and flexibility all flourish. You may indulge in one or the other, or even all three if you care to."

"I am astonished, m'sieu," she said, "but how can I argue it when I have never been outside New Orleans?" She was enjoying the conversation. "Have you not seen our city that you wish me to show it to you?"

"I've seen a little of it." In fact, in his tireless scouring of the place he had seen most of it. But not in any spirit of interested discovery. "You shall show me more of it."

For the first time he felt no sense of consuming urgency. Edwina was now no part of his search. There was only Sylvestre—and Johnson could tell him a great deal about Sylvestre. Johnson had to, when he returned. In the meantime there was Antoinette, who had been Edwina's friend in this finely furnished house, and was a breathtakingly beautiful girl without any future except as some man's purchased pleasure. The pity he felt for Edwina embraced Antoinette.

"M'sieu," she said softly, "I shall be most happy to go with you."

# 10

Because of Edwina, buried that morning, Antoinette did not change out of her black. She wore it in deep sincerity, and in sincerity it imparted its air of lament. Because she also wore the black veil they rode in an open carriage after all, for the veil masked the flawless skin and muted the luminous quality of her eyes. Any perceptive citizen beholding such skin and such lambent eyes would have wagered them incontestably characteristic of an octoroon. Her veil, however, and the way she held herself, made any curious onlookers wonder more about who she was than what she was. The carriage itself complemented her mourning elegance, for it was a shining black phaeton drawn by a pair and it belonged to Johnson. Madame Coulbert, being asked by Jason if a conveyance was available, did not feel strong enough to take up a negative attitude, for she was sure he was capable of quietly strangling her. She had the phaeton and a Negro driver placed at his disposal, and also gave permission for Antoinette to accompany him. Yes, she was certain he would take good care of the young lady if she was not to be chaperoned, but he was to understand she must remain heavily veiled.

"She must not be recognised, m'sieu."

"Why? For a very special reason, madame?"

"I can say no more, m'sieu," said the housekeeper. "Please accept my word."

"Very well."

To most observers on the streets that afternoon it seemed that the man in the stylish green coat, buff trousers, and brown top hat had an exceptionally striking wife. It was a pity that so attractive a woman was shrouded in mourning, but to her credit it did not detract from her aristocratic air.

New Orleans in 1839 looked like a city that had been thrown together rather than systematically built. Many streets, especially in the old quarter, were so narrow that the flat-fronted houses might have been said to open their doors on to their neighbours opposite. The galleries that relieved the monotonous flatness, wrought-iron balconies of Spanish style, were so companionably poised that to stand on one was to bring a gentleman within kissing distance of any lady who cared to step out on to the one immediately facing. There were no paved sidewalks; indeed there were no sidewalks of any kind. There were only the cobbles of the streets, in the gutters of which a mixture of foul water and rotting refuse could lie and stagnate for weeks. Typhoid was so common, so deadly, and so frequent that it was the regular decimator of New Orleans life.

Nevertheless, the continental air of the city and its people was flamboyant and colourful. In the sunshine, with the heat tempered by the Gulf breezes, the Negroes showed faces shining and by no means sulky. Born into slavery, most of them were unable to envisage a freedom which meant they would have to forage for themselves; those who could envisage it had a deep, burning desire to achieve it.

The black girls and women wore colours quite vivid, their cotton tignons the mark of their bondage. Hats and bonnets were for white ladies, as were the gay parasols with their fluttering ribbons.

Antoinette was a knowledgeable and elucidatory guide. "There," she said with a gesture of her gloved hand, "that building is so old, m'sieu, that there is probably nothing older in New Orleans except some of the cab horses." They had reached the ancient quarter and she wished him to see the house on Chartres Street which dated back to 1730. "In there once lived the *Filles à la cassette*, without whom New Orleans would have remained unrefined and regrettably uncivilised for many, many years."

"*Filles à la cassette?*"

"Oh, but yes," she said. "In English you would call them the Casket girls. It was this way—m'sieu, you will not let me bore you?"

"I'm not as easily bored as my wife was." He could say that without bitterness now.

"Oh, I assure you, m'sieu, as long as there was something to laugh at, even herself, she was never bored. Although sometimes there was a look on her face. But not to do with boredom, no. With her mistakes perhaps?" She was earnest to protect her own image of Edwina, the white woman who had been a precious friend to her. Her voice was soft but clear, even within the heavy veil.

"The Casket girls, Antoinette, what about them?" Jason was permitting himself an interval of normal life at last, for this extraordinary girl was enchanting.

"It was this way, m'sieu," she said as they sat in the stationary phaeton. The Louisiana sun lifted the earth's moisture and dried it, but could do nothing about the gutter refuse except hasten its decomposition. Nearby the Place d'Armes was full of people and vendors and street cries. "Very long ago, quite as long ago as when New Orleans was just a settlement, the only ladies here were not the most admirable. They were regrettably unrefined. You comprehend, m'sieu?"

"I am having no difficulty, Antoinette." He hid his smile. For the moment his mind and his body were lingering. A flower seller arrived and held up a spray of golden mimosa.

"Madame?" she said sympathetically to the black-draped Antoinette.

Jason bought the spray. The flower seller in her patois said he was an understanding gentleman and a generous one, which meant that he knew the mimosa would brighten the lady's sadness and that he would not ask for any change. Jason waved her away and she went bouncing off. He gave the spray to Antoinette. Beneath the veil she coloured and she took the mimosa with a smile that was emotional.

"*Merci*, m'sieu," she said, "you are kindness itself."

"Continue," he said. "Please continue your story, Antoinette."

"Yes. *Allons*, there were only these—shall we say, dubious ladies, m'sieu?"

"I am agreeable," said Jason.

"So Governor Bienville, a man of eminence and understanding, decided that nothing at all worthwhile would come of New Orleans unless the settlers were provided with good women who would make good wives. It is not possible to turn any community into a civilised one without the refinement that comes naturally with good women who make good wives. That is so, m'sieu? We are agreed on that?"

"We are agreed."

"The influence of good wives is extremely profound, is it not?" she said.

"We are agreed," he said, and wondered if she, with her life so prescribed, ever dwelt on the thought that she would probably never become a wife.

And Antoinette, about to continue, suddenly looked a little stricken because his wife, of course, had not been a good one.

"Oh, m'sieu, I—"

"Continue," he said.

"Yes, m'sieu," she said, and smiled because he was smiling. "Governor Bienville was also agreed."

"Then we're in exalted company, Antoinette, he being so eminent a person."

"Oh, indeed," said Antoinette gravely. "So when his term of office was finished and he was able to return home to France, he assured the settlers before he left that when he was back in France, he would do his best to find good women for them. He would arrange for these women to voyage to New Orleans, where the more worthy settlers could meet them and decide who might best marry whom, so that they could build their own *bonbonnières* together."

"I fancy *bonbonnières* are going to escape me unless you translate."

"A *bonbonnière*, m'sieu, is a nice *petit* furnished house. Voilà, m'sieu, it was almost no sooner promised than accomplished, if you will allow for the reasonable interval of time. Yes?"

"I think we can allow that."

Antoinette smiled because he was so agreeably in tune with the moment.

"So? So they arrived, the good young women with their most precious little belongings in their caskets, and that house, m'sieu, is where they lived in the care of the Ursuline nuns, they and others who continued to come. And with them came refinements and courtesies and customs. It was not easy, oh no. At first, the houses were only log cabins with roofs of bark, and in between each house were green ponds full of reptiles. M'sieu, that would not have made it easy even for the very best of good women, would it?"

"No. But they persevered and endured, and in the end, no doubt, they triumphed, as good women do."

"Oh, yes, indeed, m'sieu," she said with warm earnestness, but her eyes were hugely amused behind her veil. "And now New Orleans is a city of culture and many, many refinements."

Jason might have said the gutters left a lot to be desired, but then so did the streets and thoroughfares of other cities, in both the Old World and the New.

"It has its own atmosphere," he said.

"M'sieu, shall we now go on our way again?"

They resumed their leisurely exploration. Despite her sadness for Edwina, Antoinette had moments of melting happiness. Never before had she ridden in an open carriage with a white man, never before had any white man been the kind of companion to her that Monsieur Rawlings was. He turned only cold eyes on Madame Coulbert. Yet for her he had smiles and kindness. She felt sensations that were extraordinarily warm. She gave of her best as a guide. She drew his attention to the area largely settled by Jesuits, explaining to him that they did much to provide early New Orleans with such necessities as wax, figs, and sugar. She wished him to know that she had not received this information from the Jesuits themselves. She had simply read about them. She read about anything and everything, and had once consumed an English dictionary from cover to cover: any book, any printed word, represented joy to her.

Jason thought her touchingly appealing. She was as finely mannered as a lady-in-waiting, and any lady-in-waiting was invariably a more impeccable figure than a queen herself. Yet, as an octoroon, Antoinette had a future that was a mockery of what she deserved. Here was a child of fate whose accident of birth would prevent her pouring out her gifts to the world. He had taken her out because of a desire to see how she would behave and react, because for once he was not concerned wholly with himself and his obsessions. His need to destroy Sylvestre was still there, but in company with Antoinette it had been pushed into the background.

"I fancy you like your city," he said.

"Like it, m'sieu?" she said, and seemed oddly surprised.

"Don't you?" he persisted.

The answer did not come at once. When it did it arrived almost nervously, as if she had doubts as to whether she was in wisdom at committing herself.

"No, m'sieu."

"No?" Jason glanced at her. Behind the veil her eyes communicated nothing for once. "But you know it so well, like someone who loves it."

"I know it very well, m'sieu, but that does not mean—m'sieu, it does not matter, it is of no consequence."

The carriage was temporarily hemmed in. There seemed more vendors than customers. Most were selling food and drink. Oysters, pies, rice cakes. Soft drinks. No one drank the water. It was undeniably poisonous. Jason, waiting until they were moving again, said, "What is wrong with New Orleans?" He thought he knew what was wrong with it for her, but asked his question.

Antoinette drew a breath and said quietly, "It is the only city for some people, m'sieu, but for me it is always my cage."

So, then. She was not as conditioned as most of her kind. She had been brought up in an atmosphere of imitative gentility, to become a copy of a modest, well-behaved Creole girl. But there it stopped; life for any mulatto girl pointed in only one direction. Antoinette's colouring was so delicate that she could have passed for white the world over. Except in discerning New Orleans, where she could not hope to become more than the property of a wealthy patron. No white man would ever marry Antoinette. And she, because she had obviously been educated and tutored, would never contemplate marriage to a black—that would destroy completely any desperate hopes she might have of rising above her circumstances. She knew the limitations her mixed blood thrust upon her life, and because of her intelligence she probably thought about those limitations in a way other octoroons never would. New Orleans was her cage, she had said, emotionally stating what was an inescapable fact.

"You'd prefer to leave New Orleans, Antoinette, to live elsewhere?"

"M'sieu, I am in the care of *le maître*."

She meant the man Johnson, whose possession of her was also an inescapable fact. Undoubtedly at some time he would sell her. It was odd, very odd, that even though she was not a virgin, the man had not received an acceptable offer for her. Jason could not believe that even in New Orleans there was no one willing to take such a girl as this as his mistress.

"So, you are in his care," he said. "Until he finds a patron for you. Is that right?"

Antoinette had lost her look of happiness.

"He is not unkind in his consideration of my best interests," she said as the driver took the phaeton out of the square. "He will not sell me to someone who is not a gentleman."

"Will he not?" said Jason critically.

"Oh, m'sieu, he deals only with gentlemen, and among them are members of some of the very best families in New Orleans. Oh, I assure you, m'sieu." She wished him not to think her prospects anything but excellent. Nor herself could she contemplate with less than anguish the thought of ending up in the bed of some tobacco-chewing planter. "Perhaps there is a little disadvantage for me in that Monsieur Johnson has such an irreproachable clientele, because so many of them would not look seriously at any young lady who has imperfections. But he is sure I shall not forever lack a loving patron. He has given me the benefit of his protection—"

"Protection?"

"It is a word of acceptable meaning, m'sieu?" she said, and he thought her suddenly self-derisive.

"It might be to Johnson."

"Although I do not know my parents, I am assured my mother was a woman of sweetness and my father a Creole of peerless repute. It was because of my parentage that when I was seventeen Monsieur Johnson consented to make himself responsible for my future."

"As a favour to your unknown father?" said Jason, and asked himself what man who had fathered such a girl would not himself want to be responsible for her future.

"That is possible, m'sieu." Antoinette seemed to want to talk and confide and he did not stop her. As a child, obviously of a Creole and his mulatto mistress, she was raised in a convent. There she was educated in basic subjects like reading and writing. And there she was taught the tenets of the true religion, and each tenet had something to do with the necessity of accepting it was God's hand which guided and directed all things and all people. One must learn humility, one must be neither doubting nor questioning. She was not taught history or economics, philosophy or politics, but she was taught English. She did not think that by the time she was fifteen she had been found wanting in either attitude or aptitude, and was blessed more than once by the Mother Superior for her fund of humility. But she also was gently reprimanded for her covetous tendency to acquire reading matter not on the recommended list, by surreptitiously lifting books from the convent library and smuggling them into her cell, where she devoured the most Catholic or obscure literature with bliss.

Twice a year she was called before the Mother Superior to undergo a kind but shrewd catechism. She always felt on these occasions that there was someone else in the room, someone who sat behind the high carved screen that stood in a corner of the sanctum.

At fifteen she left the convent to work for an extremely correct and reputable French family. There was no family more correct. Correspondingly their coloured servants were just as correct. Punctiliousness flowed from *grand'mère* down to the lowest of the bonded minions. It was a household in which a fifteen-year-old octoroon girl fresh from a convent, could feel secure. Antoinette, because of her natural grace and pleasing ways, became the eldest daughter's maid. The behaviour of the daughter and the rest of the family was to her an example of all that was admirable in civilised human relationships and she was complimented on the niceties of her own behaviour. In such a perfect environment, whatever Eve or Adam presented an apple, one might surely take it and bite it, and lose not a wink of sleep.

Antoinette supposed that the extra kindness she received from the nineteen-year-old son were all part of the pattern, although she was a little uncomfortable about the little caresses he began to bestow. However, because the household generally could not be faulted, and because she had been taught that all people had their place and all people their ordained ways, she accepted the gestures of kind affection. People in high places bestowed, and people in lower stations received, the latter with gratitude and humility. She considered herself at grievous fault in not feeling too much gratitude, and so compensated by envincing such mute humility.

Her understanding of proper relationships became very confused, however, when the young man pulled her out of the crowds during the Mardi Gras celebrations and took her back to the house. All the family were out, even *grand'mère*, for that was how it was during the Mardi Gras. The young man insisted on celebrations of their own. Drinking wine in his room with him increased her confusion, and began to put her into grave doubt. But there was the rule of obedience to observe, and also the fact that she had never drunk wine like this before. It made her very light-headed, and it made him discard the correct and strict family rules concerning female servants.

The family, arriving home in the early hours, discovered her in bed with the erring son. She was just seventeen. During the afternoon of the next day an altercation took place. Altercations were so unusual they were hardly known. She was not present, but she knew it was to do with the fact that she had been seduced, about which she was in an agony of shame. She heard voices as she was passing the door of a room, going on an errand. She heard one voice which was not raised, as were the voices of the angry father and the hotly defensive son. It was a much colder voice. It had more impact: it cut across the altercation and rooted her to the spot.

"Antoinette was not to be trained for promiscuity but faithfulness, and just at the moment when she was ready to be placed into the right hands she has been robbed. Now there is little chance of passing her from those guiding hands into the possession of the kind of gentleman I would have wished."

A woman arrived two days later, a matronly mulatto, and Antoinette was taken to a house where she was received by a Monsieur Johnson, an American citizen of New Orleans. He surveyed her with kind interest, asked her kind questions, and gave her kind smiles. Then he told her she was not to worry at what had happened to her, that he would swear by the trumpets of Jericho to place her in the arms of a man not only of exemplary birth but of generous understanding. In short, a scion of New Orleans nobility. She did not fully comprehend at that time exactly what he meant. She was placed in the charge of the matronly mulatto, who tutored her in the arts pertaining to being all things to a gentleman except his wife. She began then to understand what her life was all about, what she was designed for and what some would have said was ordained for her.

That had been two years ago. Since then she had been introduced to many distinguished gentlemen in the salon of the house next door, some young and some mature. But none of them, it seemed, found her looks or her grace outstanding enough to quite make up for her lost virtue. There had been other gentlemen, not quite so distinguished, who came at specially arranged times so that Monsieur Johnson's more elite clientele did not have to rub elbows with them. Many of these gentlemen professed themselves extremely interested. Each offered for her and each offer was accepted for consideration. But a day or two later Monsieur Johnson would advise her that the particular gentleman in question was not quite suitable. She began to wonder who made these decisions. It could not be Monsieur Johnson, or he would not have considered the offers in the first place, and he would not have presented her to any gentleman of whom he did not have forehand knowledge.

Jason understood as well as any man why her prospects of finding a distinguished patron were limited. So rigid were the traditions relating to the acquisition of a mulatto mistress that no New Orleans gentleman of quality would put himself in the untenable position of confessing that the light of his clandestine life had known another man before him. Such prior carnal knowledge had about it a suggestion that she might not prove faithful, which would deal his pride and his charity a wounding blow. It was not to be contemplated.

"Antoinette, did you want to tell me all this?"

"M'sieu," she said, "you asked me if I liked New Orleans. What I have told you is all to do with the answer I gave you. But—" She hesitated.

"Say what you wish to, Antoinette."

"I only wish to say I hope you do not think less of me."

"I think you a young lady of sweet gifts, as I did when I first saw you. Antoinette, open your cage. Leave it and fly far away."

"That is poetic, m'sieu," she said, "but impossible, as you must know."

Madame Coulbert showed herself when they got back. She was pleased to advise Monsieur Rawlings that Monsieur Johnson would be back tomorrow and generously disposed to listen to him.

"Tomorrow? That will do," said Jason. "I shall still be here."

Reaction claimed him that night; he could not sleep. He relived the years of hunting and searching. He relived the moment when he had looked down into Edwina's peacefully dead face. The elusive image of the man Sylvestre chased around in the darkness. He lay awake for hours until his brain was exhausted and the medley of thoughts and images collapsed and drained away. A moment of clarity came just before he drifted into sleep. His immediate course charted itself. There were two landmarks: one led to Sylvestre; the other to a girl and a child.

# 11

He slept late. Breakfast was brought to him by a servant. An astonishing array of meats in richly glutinous sauce, formidably seasoned with a legion of different spices, appeared before his eyes. As an accompaniment came bread dipped in a smothering pond of well-beaten eggs and fried in fat. Jason had encountered this typical New Orleans breakfast before. Salubriously gastronomic as far as Creoles were concerned, it could be received by an Anglo-Saxon stomach only with outraged shudders. Jason liked to accord his own stomach simple respect. He considered good meat should never be cooked except in its own juices. Only indifferent meat needed the disguises offered by rich sauces. Vegetables should come to the table as fresh as possible and complaining of no uncomplimentary embellishments.

He sent the meal away quite courteously and asked for only fruit and coffee. Five months in New Orleans had taught him that survival for an Anglo-Saxon visitor could be helped by a selective choice of foods. Up till now in this house Antoinette had looked after his stomach, and instinctively or otherwise had served him simple dishes. He sought the housekeeper after he had eaten and dressed. She was in her cubbyhole room downstairs, and opened the door to his knock.

"Madame," he said, "when may I expect your employer?"

"Monsieur Johnson? In an hour, m'sieu, in an hour. I am assured of that."

"In an hour, then. Madame, where is Antoinette, who has been a great help to me?"

Madame Coulbert was not sure whether to answer frankly or obliquely. She did not trust what lay behind those stony blue eyes. She felt the wrong kind of answer would not prove at all profitable. It was the worst luck in the world that this hardheaded

*Anglais* had arrived precisely on the day when his wife had been stupid enough to kill herself. It was a coincidence of unnameable ill luck.

"Ah, Antoinette," she said. That could do no harm, that noncommittal response.

"Yes. Where is she?"

It was there, the look that told her he was not going to be denied. So she said, "Antoinette has moved to live with the other young ladies next door. Monsieur Johnson allowed her to live here because your poor wife—" She crossed herself—she thought that would do no harm either. "Your wife wished it, and in natural kindness Monsieur Johnson arranged it."

"In Monsieur Johnson I'm to meet a paragon, it seems."

"M'sieu, he is spoken of very highly," said the housekeeper, veiling her eyes. "You will understand, however, that it is better now for Antoinette to be with the other young ladies. She has little in common with the servants here and is, as I am sure you have noticed, quite superior to them all. Your interest in her has been kind, m'sieu, but you may rest assured that Monsieur Johnson has great hopes for her. She is so refined."

"She will be pleased to hear it."

He took himself off to the livery stables, where he had a few crisp words to say to the proprietor, who, in lazy generosity, had been feeding his horse Napoleon too much oats. Oats were cheap, and the tendency was to slip on the bag and leave it. The proprietor agreed he had been at fault, but the horse had made no complaint, and some exercise would soon cure his fat look. Jason attended to that himself, trotting the animal out of town and taking the river road northwards. Napoleon, a great cavalry horse, had left England with him, crossed the ocean, and had carried him on his long, wandering searching from New York down to New Orleans. It had been the kind of journey the beast was not used to, and at times he had exhibited both disdain and fractiousness. He let it be known now that he did not favour the sudden transition from comfort to hard work, albeit his sinews and tendons did—he shied and kicked. Jason cuffed him and let it be known in turn that there were to be no tantrums. Napoleon shed his liverishness. Jason put him to the gallop. Plantations stretched away. Fields of palmetto, clumps of oak and cypress, carpets of lilies and expanses of sweet-smelling acacias bordered the estates.

Honeysuckle offered its fragrance and red oleanders their brilliance. The mimosa sprinkled the immediate world with gold. But both horse and rider galloped by oblivious.

Jason ran the excesses out of his mount. The horse did not thank him for it, but sweated profusely and stomach-grumbled. However, they had been together for many years and there were no hard feelings by the time they returned to the city, where Jason called on a man he had come to know, a Mr. Farquhar. Jason conversed with him for a while, then took Napoleon back to the stables. Both felt better at that stage; Jason said so by pulling the beast's right ear, and an amiable snort told him all was forgiven. The proprietor was requested to get the animal rubbed down and to ensue it was in a fit condition to travel tomorrow. The proprietor vowed obedience, vigilance, and competence. Jason vowed there would be no payment forthcoming if the horse again resembled an overblown barrel.

Madame Coulbert noted Jason's return to the house, and effected one of her more obsequious appearances to inform him that Monsieur Johnson was waiting to receive him, and had been for almost an hour. Jason, his expression that of a man to whom Monsieur Johnson was about as important as one more flea, told her to delay a moment while he went upstairs. He returned, a sword belt buckled around his waist and under his coat. She saw the scabbard, old, oiled and black, and the hilt of the sabre it contained. A little greyness took hold of her.

"Now, madame, you may take me to him," he said.

She took him to her employer's ground-floor study. Johnson rose up from his desk, dismissed the housekeeper with a wave of his hand, and followed this with a friendly flourish that invited Jason to seat himself. Jason remained standing. He studied his man. The American did not look like a pimp. He was approaching middle age, and his sober-hued garments were of such excellent fit and style that they would not have displeased that doyen of fashion, Beau Brummell himself. He had keen eyes, sensitive nostrils, and a short firm upper lip that sat in poised calmness above a full lower lip. He exuded the air of a gentleman and looked like one, his pallor just delicate enough to have found favour in the salons of London. One would have to be in a crusty mood to find any outward fault in the man, and Jason was not in a crusty mood: he was inflexibly disposed, that was all.

This was the man who had given Edwina a push down the slope to self-destruction. But he was not the man who had set her on it. Jason had long since come to terms with emotional trivia, and found it fairly easy to control little irritations and useless tempers. He could even set aside fury as far as Johnson was concerned, for Johnson represented a steppingstone and a purse. There was no point in strangling him or slicing him to pieces. From him Jason required information, necessary funds, and an agreement.

"Sir, my felicitations," said the gentlemanly gentleman, opening on an agreeable note and in an unspoiled New England accent.

"Inadequate," said Jason, crisp and uncompromising, "you owe me far more than felicitations."

Johnson shook his head sadly.

"A tragedy, I give it to you frankly, a tragedy, sir. A dear woman. What can I say?" Johnson conveyed the openness of a man in honourable grief and regret. "I was informed she was divorced. Not the remotest idea ever crossed my mind that she was not a free woman. I was assured she was her own mistress. You have my word, sir, that there was no coercion." Here he paused to sigh. "The dear woman came willingly with me after I met her in St. Louis. She—"

"Damn my ears, are they deceiving me?" said Jason.

"Sir?" Johnson lifted a pained eyebrow. "I will have you know—"

"I suggest you save your breath." Jason, coat unbuttoned, placed a hand on the hilt of his sabre. A slight frown joined the pained eyebrow. "In St. Louis you took her off the hands of another man. And at an agreed price, no doubt, the other man being short of funds. You brought her here. You loaned her to other men from time to time—also at an agreed price, without any doubt. Two days ago she took her own life. She had the New Orleans complaint."

"My dear God." Johnson's delicate pallor became stark. Shock stared from his eyes, and hideous worry. "I never knew that."

"I hope the information is helpful to you," said Jason icily. "And to your friends."

"I'm grateful, sir, but aghast. My dear God," said Johnson again, "I must see my doctor."

"Not immediately," said Jason, "we haven't finished our conversation."

"Where could the dear woman—"

"Where? Are you a fool? She acquired it either from one of your friends or from the man who handed her over to you. And that is giving you yourself the benefit of the doubt, as well as assuming the circle was no bigger."

"My friends are gentlemen, sir."

"Gentlemen are less immune than ordinary people," said Jason, "they're more promiscuous. Are you suffering from the heat, Mr. Johnson?"

Johnson was wiping his lips and dabbing at his forehead with a square of mauve silk.

"I'm in distress, sir, distress," he said.

"For my wife's misfortune or your health?" asked Jason.

"Damn it, I'm not an unfeeling man."

"Nor I, and I'm entitled, I think, to call you out."

"No, sir, not recommended at all, at all," said Johnson.

"Well, it isn't what I have in mind at the moment, by God. What I want from you, among other things, is information on a man called Sylvestre, the man who looked after my wife's welfare immediately prior to you. I want to know all that you know about him and exactly where he went after you parted from him. I mean to have this information. Do you understand?"

"I assure you, sir, in view of the pain you feel, that I'm at your service." Johnson dabbed his lips again, then put his square of silk loosely away. "I can't hide my regrets. Never, had I known she was a gentleman's wife, would I have contrived a situation offensive to the honourable state of marriage. And no, sir, I can't let you think I would have—ah—loaned her to other men. She—"

"I am in possession, Mr. Johnson, not of thoughts but facts." Jason was coldly precise. "With your help my wife destroyed herself. You owe her to me, if I may put it like that, but it's a debt you can't pay. The alternative is an acceptable exchange. My wife will remain here in New Orleans. In her place I will take Antoinette."

Johnson, pale in his worry over his health, recovered a little. That proposition was of the kind he understood. And it meant that law officers would not be called in, that he would not have to consider arranging for the Englishman's throat to be cut. But damn the fellow's wife for having been stupid enough to get herself into a state of pox, and then a state of mind where she had to kill herself. She had been a lucrative sideline. Certain clients had paid handsomely for the rare privilege of bedding a fair English rose. And damn the fix everything had put him in. Rawlings looked the kind of man more inclined to make demands than engage in negotiations. But he would have to negotiate concerning Antoinette. There was no way out of that for either of them.

"I'm willing to discuss your proposition, sir."

"It's not a proposition," said Jason, "it's a statement."

"All the same, sir, all the same. Now I'll not deny you've suffered a blow, but Antoinette is an exceptional young lady, as you'll allow."

"I do allow it," said Jason. "But a man's wife is the fount of his honour. She may be weak, she may be intemperate, but she is always his wife, his major responsibility. For my wife, Mr. Johnson, you owe me far more than you can pay. However, I'll settle for Antoinette and four hundred dollars. And the information previously mentioned. I'll have no arguments. I have named what I will have and there it stands."

Johnson's fingers drummed the desk. His drawn brows conveyed hurt protest.

"Sir, I swear that for Antoinette some gentleman will eventually offer as much as—"

"No gentleman of the kind you have in mind will offer anything for her, exceptional though she is. Such offers in this city are only for immaculate girls. You know you are either going to sell her to someone who is not her idea of a gentleman—whatever yours is—or keep her for the occasional pleasure of libertines. And I doubt if either alternative is going to be allowed, for Antoinette is her father's daughter. If she were not you would have sold her to some second-rate but moneyed planter ages ago. Isn't that correct?"

Johnson felt the same way about the stony blue eyes as his housekeeper did. He laid silent curses on the fellow, for he looked quite capable of slicing off a man's head and hang the consequences. There was satisfaction to be had in momentarily playing with the idea of having him join his wife in the cemetery; it could be managed without difficulty. A fresh hole dug beside the woman and the man dropped in neatly and very dead, everything accomplished so quietly and tidily in the middle of the night that the cemetery would show no signs of visitation and the earth no sign of spadework. Who would ask questions?

That was the risk. Someone might. What friends did the fellow have?

"Mr. Rawlings—"

"Mr. Johnson." Jason sounded as if his patience was being pulled about. "You are turning me over, are you? Considering the advantages of disposing of me? Not recommended at all, sir, not at all, if I may quote you. Take my advice, think only in terms of what is good for you, and your business. There's a letter in the hands of a lawyer here, a letter deposited by me."

Johnson's moment of satisfying indulgence died its death. Like himself, some men took out insurance during times of risk.

"Sir, I accept without quibble your feelings concerning the death of your wife—"

"My feelings concerning everything are all directed towards you at the moment," said Jason. "You procured my wife. A great mistake and a serious offence."

"Procured?" Johnson looked shocked. "I protest, sir, I protest most vigorously. But I agree there's an element of distress that makes argument seem—ah—petty. I can't deny your right to ask for restitution, though I do plead, sir, that I myself was misled. You mentioned two hundred dollars, sir—"

"Four hundred."

"Four hundred. Ah, that was the figure, was it? And certain information." Johnson cleared his throat. "I concur, sir. But I must tell you I can't let you take Antoinette unless a certain gentleman gives his full consent. My own consent counts for nothing at all, without his. My housekeeper told you, I believe, to make sure the girl was not recognised when you drove out with her. This certain gentleman was on her mind, a gentleman concerned with Antoinette's welfare. He would not, sir, have approved of her being in company with a man of whom he knew nothing." Johnson drummed the table again. "Only with his consent can you take the girl."

"Then get it."

"Hear me, sir." Johnson adopted a new air, that of a gentleman willing to give kind advice. "You have sweet joys in mind, consolation for the tragic loss of your wife, I warrant. You have taste. I know these—ah—girls. You're taken, I figure, with Antoinette's disposition, her sweetness, her virtues and her virtuosity. But where would you go with her? Outside of New Orleans or Louisiana she will languish—any of them would. They are the hothouse flowers of our garden. In New Orleans they flourish, they bloom; you have never seen such exotic beauty. You'll take Antoinette to New York? She will look ten years older after the first winter there. You will take her to England, make her spend weeks aboard a ship on the Atlantic? When you dock in Bristol, sir, you will carry ashore an old woman. Believe me, Mr. Rawlings, they are creatures of colour and light, and some are fairer than Egypt. But there are weaknesses in all of them and they are understood to perfection only by the Creoles."

Jason stood his ground, not a flicker of yielding in his expression.

"There are always exceptions, Mr. Johnson. In any case, Antoinette is not to be my hothouse plant. I don't intend to take her out of one cage and put her in another. If despite her health and intelligence she does display a weakness, it will only be that which overtakes a bird freed from its wickerwork prison. If she's unable to adapt herself to freedom she can return to her cage."

"You speak of freedom, sir?"

"I speak of what I intend, Mr. Johnson, and that is to accept Antoinette in part exchange for my wife. That, however, does not mean she's to be bonded to me."

"You are an evangelist, sir," said Johnson pityingly.

"And you, my friend, unless you do as I wish, are set to be embraced by hell."

The keen eyes narrowed, the full bottom lip thrust out.

"Sir, I do not recommend a violent level of conversation."

"Nor I. Tell me about the man called Sylvestre, the man who handed my wife over to you."


The atmosphere of the salon was wholly pleasing. The conversation flowed but no voice was loud. The decor was tasteful, the velvets subdued, the gilt-framed mirrors escaping the criticism of being ornate. A huge cut-glass chandelier provided light, its delicate chiming crystals softly tinkling whenever they were fingered by caressing draughts of warm air. The flower arrangements were colourful but not overpowering. The chairs were padded in light blue. At the piano in one corner sat a young and lovely girl in white, touching the keys giftedly, her chaperone to one side and a handsome gentleman turning her music.

There were some twenty girls present and several professional chaperones. Gentlemen, meeting the girls, looking them over, conversing with them, were as courteous as if the young lovelies claimed blood as pure as that of Creole girls. Fluttering their fans, the octoroons graced the salon with both beauty and modesty. Their white gowns were exquisitely symbolic of their purity. Their hair ranged in colour from dark to pale auburn, and no locks showed the crinkly or frizzy properties of the Negro. Few had more than the smallest amount of Negro blood in them.

The gentlemen, dandies all whatever their age, were quite as exquisite, sartorially, as the girls. Brocaded frock coats, jewel-studded waistcoats, close-fitting trousers, silk shirts with ruffles or cravats artfully folded, epitomised the New Orleans gentleman of quality. They were there to survey, to reconnoitre, to approach, to be introduced, and to conduct their ploys. A closer survey was made when they engaged with demure beauties who especially took their eye, although conversation was itself very important in establishing whether a girl had wit or charm, or only gaucherie. One naturally wished to discover if a potential mistress had an aptitude for entertaining a gentleman outside the bed or posed the dangerous possibility of boring him.

The façade of gentility and respectability was extraordinary, the professional chaperones practising a protective severity that lacked nothing in credibility. For the sake of their prospects, the virginity of these pale-skinned mulatto girls was as important to preserve and postulate as that of the daughters of the most ancient families in New Orleans.

There were other octoroons present. Set apart from the rest, their domain of reception was a large, curtained alcove. The curtains were partly open. They too had their chaperones, though not their innocence, for their gowns were not white. In hope they waited to receive any gentlemen who might be disposed to consider their assets in advance of their liabilities. While they waited, they sat and talked or slowly paraded. They never, however, stepped outside the alcove. Antoinette was one of these two girls. She was back in circulation after a respite of a few days. She wore a full-skirted gown of deep emerald green, the crinoline effect giving the impression that she did not walk but floated. The fine lace of ankle-length pantaloons peeped below fluttering petticoats each time she turned. Her eyes were soft with reflected light, her smile one of trained sweetness, though some might have said that this evening the sweetness was wistful. She looked what she was, the most gracefully beautiful creature in the place. From the salon, one or two gentlemen eyed her with regret, a regret that in the strict interests of tradition they could not ask to meet her.

Johnson appeared in the curtained doorway to the salon. He held the velvet aside, and Jason stepped in. It was the cut of his green coat and the style of his breeches which made the Creole elite accept his entrance without the lift of any eyebrows, for though the garments were far from new they were so distinctly tailored as to make the man inside them an undeniable gentleman. Not all the citizens of New Orleans were sufficiently *au fait* with fashion as to be able to judge the extent of a man's social acceptability merely on the cut of his buttonholes, but the Creole dandies were so gifted. Jason's garments were London-tailored, their lack of newness, the privilege of a gentleman's eccentricity.

Antoinette saw him at once. Her face paled, then crimsoned. Momentarily her poise crumpled, and one gloved hand went up to her throat. Her eyes turned into enormous pools of shame and unhappiness. The seated mulatto chaperone rose and tapped her lightly on the arm with her fan. Antoinette lifted her chin, took a deep breath, and addressed a desperately light remark to her companion, an octoroon as slender-waisted as herself.

Jason, accompanied by Johnson, strolled through the salon while modest eyes regarded him above spread fans. Little sighs sent warm breath to caress the fans. He entered the alcove. There Johnson formally introduced him to Antoinette, and Antoinette dipped in a magnificently flowing curtsey. But as she rose her blood rushed again and her eyes in distress beseeched his understanding. Jason smiled and gave her his arm. She rested her gloved hand on it. The chaperone ventured up but *le maître* gestured and she sat down again. She was not needed. Her charge had permission to engage privately with the newcomer. That looked promising. The chaperone, fighting at forty the steady encroachment of well-fed flesh, was happy for Antoinette, and also for the development that enabled her to remain seated.

The piano trilled a succession of light notes as Jason led Antoinette through a door in the rear of the alcove and into the quiet of a private room. Johnson closed the door on them and in malice hoped that the cursed fellow would be rebuffed. Antoinette, suddenly alone with Jason in a room where many a gentleman had finalised details of an acquisition, became burningly agitated. There was sweetness in thinking him her friend, there was shame in being bought by him. He had obviously contracted with *le maître* to purchase her and because he was an unusual man he had been granted the privilege of discussing the matter with her alone. Her colour flamed.

"Please sit down," said Jason. "I wish to talk to you."

She seated herself on a couch, her crinoline spreading and rustling. Her mouth trembled.

"M'sieu," she said with an effort, "why are you here, why are you in this place?"

"To find out whether I understand you or not."

She lowered her unhappy eyes.

"M'sieu, you and I have talked together and from this you know me. Is it necessary also to understand me?"

She was in obvious distress. He guessed why.

"Antoinette, you are talking of one thing," he said. "I wish to talk of another."

"In this place, m'sieu," she said, "it all leads to the same thing."

"I see. Do you imagine, then, that I think so little of you that I'm here to buy you and set you up? That isn't my intention at all."

She lifted her head. Her colour was high, her gloved hands tight around her folded fan.

"M'sieu, you of all men have been kinder to me than any," she said.

"Why are you so distressed?" he asked.

Her mouth trembled.

"It was just—m'sieu, when I saw you enter the salon I thought you had come to enquire after one of the more acceptable young ladies."

"More acceptable?"

"You are aware of my meaning, I think." She was still a little unhappy. "But then you approached me, and I wished the floor to open."

"Do I take it, then," said Jason with a wry smile, "that you would have preferred me to keep to what you call the more acceptable?"

"Oh, no!" Her face burned again. *"Non, non!* That is not what I meant. I meant—oh, I am in confusion. How can I say it? Oh, it was just that I did not like to see you in this place, or you to see me. Although it seems so elegant and refined, m'sieu, it is only a marketplace, isn't it, where gentlemen come to look at the wares. Showing you New Orleans, that was happiness; one I shall always remember. But having you see me here—oh, I am ashamed."

"You need not be." Jason spoke firmly. "It is not you who designed this way of life for yourself. Do you think I don't know that you have a mind of your own, that you're sensitive and very young?"

"M'sieu, I am nineteen," she said, "and that is very old for a place like this."

"Would you like to be free of it?" he asked.

"Free?" That made her look wonderingly at him.

"Would you?"

"I would give my very life to be free," she said breathlessly.

"You won't need to pay as high a price as that. You'll only need to be adaptable. It would mean leaving New Orleans."

"M'sieu, oh, I could not be free unless I did, could I?"

"I doubt it," said Jason.

"But how am I to be free?" Incredulity was beginning to replace wonderment. "You will get Monsieur Johnson to release me and send me North to the abolitionists?"

"I don't fancy that would suit you," said Jason, "and I've no liking for the idea myself, though in the last resort it would be better than a cage. Listen carefully, for you must make up your mind quickly. Antoinette, my wife had a child by the man who took her from me."

"Oh." She bowed her head. "M'sieu, that was something she never told me."

"It was something she was at pains to tell me. I wondered why. Having thought about it, I think I know. The child, a girl called Clare, is with a woman in Baltimore, who has obviously been given money to foster her. I think Edwina, in mentioning the child and where she is, hoped I would help to redeem her mistakes, for she even gave me the woman's name. But before I can collect that child, I must settle an account with the man. I've arranged with your nominal owner, Johnson, to take you away from here, if you are willing. I'd like you to go to Baltimore, escorted by a trustworthy acquaintance of mine. I'll give you a letter for the woman who has the child, and some money. In Baltimore, with the help of your escort, a Mr. Farquhar, you are to find convenient lodgings for yourself and the child. You are to get to know the child, to look after her, and sometime in the future I'll be in Baltimore myself. Then I'll collect you and the child and take you both to England. There you may choose for yourself the life you wish to lead. You may, if you so desire, be governess to the child, and live in our family house in Dorset. You—"

"M'sieu, what are you saying?" Antoinette, all huge incredulous eyes, could not grasp what to her was an immensity of joy. "You are going too fast—what you have said cannot be true—m'sieu, I am so giddy I am quite without my senses. You have bought me from Monsieur Johnson?"

"I have not." Jason smiled and shook his head. "We are not allowed in my country to buy people, although we've been in the business of supplying human wares to Americans. I've spoken to Johnson, and subject to the agreement of some certain gentleman —which agreement I will have, I swear—you will be released and out of bondage. Johnson feels you can't exist outside of New Orleans. My understanding of you is that you can and will— indeed, by God's life, you must. So you shall have the chance to prove yourself. You may not think it the most exhilarating way to prove yourself at first, going to Baltimore to look after a child neither of us knows, and you may certainly not wish to go to England—"

"As if I would not!" Antoinette, radiant, let her words fly. "I would go anywhere with you or for you. Willingly and happily I will go to Baltimore to take care of your wife's child. M'sieu, you have my gratitude for having such trust in me. I am so overwhelmed, you cannot know what you are doing for me. It is true, you will do it?"

"Between us, Antoinette, it represents the best thing we can do for my foolish, unhappy wife." Jason looked into eyes swimming with brilliance. "You'll be doing most of it. I shall only supply a letter and part of some money I am about to come into. I am asking you to take on a great responsibility, throwing you out into a world you know nothing of, so I don't fancy I'm showing you unqualified kindness. But I have faith in you, Antoinette. If you agree to all this I think I'll find you managing very well in Baltimore. You are to deposit the address of your lodgings there with the manager of the British shipping offices, so that I shall know how to locate you. Do you understand all this? I should tell you that if you do—and if you are quite sure about everything—you are to start for Baltimore tomorrow."

Antoinette, dizzy with rapture and emotional with gratitude, could not speak for a moment. She wished he might know that of what he spoke so calmly represented inexpressible joy to her. She swallowed.

"M'sieu," she said, "I understand all of it. I will go to Baltimore with the gentleman you mentioned. I will collect the child and give her all my care and love. I will love her very much. In Baltimore we will wait for you, and then go to England with you. M'sieu, there is so much more I could say, but you must know it is sometimes not possible to find even a single word."

Soberly Jason said, "Before you decide that England means paradise compared with New Orleans, let me tell you we're a very insular and prejudiced people. Each nation swears by its own greatness. We do not swear by ours, we take it for granted as God-given. You are just as likely to be bitterly hurt in England as here. I wish to save you that kind of unhappiness. You are remarkably endowed with gifts, and if you also have aptitude you may be the equal of any young lady in England, as long as no one thinks you anything but white. We shall deal in common sense, then. You will be white. That will protect you against hurt, and create opportunities for you that wouldn't otherwise occur. Pride, Antoinette, must accordingly yield. Do you understand that too?"

"M'sieu, I shall not be hindered by pride. But opportunities?"

"You can be much more than a governess," said Jason. "There will be men who will no sooner lay eyes on you than they'll want to marry you. You will probably be able to take your pick of the most elegant gentlemen."

"I have no taste for elegant gentlemen," said Antoinette.

"That won't discourage them," said Jason. "They'll consider you the most beautiful young lady in Dorset."

Warm colour swept her. The world was full of men, England might be crowded with them, but she knew there would be none who would ever mean more to her than Monsieur Rawlings.

"M'sieu," she said in a formal little way, "although you have not bought me from *le maître*, you have in some way persuaded him to set me free. Being free, may I accordingly decide for myself what I wish?"

"You may."

"Then, I wish no gentleman, only to care for your wife's child. I do not understand why she left you, though I do know now why she realised in the end that she had made a mistake. M'sieu?" She smiled then.

"Yes?"

"You will protect me from all ardent gentlemen?"

"I can make you my ward," said Jason, caring for the enchanting girl.

"Ward?"

"It means I should be your legal guardian and have the right to protect you."

"Is that to assume I should become your daughter?" she asked.

"It would be as near to that as it could be."

"Oh, m'sieu," she said with a husky laugh, "you are hardly old enough to be my father, and there are many young ladies of my age who would never wish to be merely your daughter. But I will be whatever you think best."

"You need only be yourself," said Jason. "Later tonight, Johnson has arranged for me to meet the man who must approve your release. But I shall have you out of here whatever the outcome, be sure of that."

"The saints, m'sieu, would not take my hopes from me now," she said with her soft earnestness.

"Well, trust the saints, and me too. You shall leave tomorrow for Baltimore. I must go to Texas."

Her eyes clouded and darkened.

"Your wife wished you not to go after the man, m'sieu. He will perhaps know you before you know him. While you are still looking into other faces, he will strike."

"Trust me. I shall see you in Baltimore."

# 12

The touch of mystery and drama was to Jason almost farcical. The man had insisted that only one lamp be lit, and that it be so positioned as to leave him in black shadow and Jason with his face dimly illuminated. The time was midnight. Also dramatic.

"Who are you, m'sieu?" The voice was cool but cultured, the accent Creole.

"Are we to exchange names as well as questions?" asked Jason, who had agreed to enter the presence of the Creole but was in no mood to suffer an inquisition.

"I want nothing from you," said the cold voice of the shadow. "You want something from me. I owe you neither my name nor my indulgence. You owe me reassurance."

"Concerning Antoinette?"

"Concerning your suitability to become her owner."

"I don't intend to become her owner, but her guardian," said Jason.

"Most worthy, m'sieu, most charitable." A faint note of disdain arrived.

"I have no designs on her. I am a man who would always rather have a wife in my house than a mistress over a shop."

"And I, m'sieu, am a man who, for the sake of a life that is precious to me, can use a very long arm."

"Very interesting," said Jason, aware of a black cape, a black hat, and a nameless face. "Would you find it just as interesting, m'sieu, to know that I have an arm that has reached from England to America?"

"It is for the good of the girl that I am here," said the Creole, "and I must be sure that you, too, are for her good. Unless you can satisfy me, she will not leave New Orleans. I will not risk her enduring degradation and misery."

"You have done nothing," said Jason frigidly, "that hasn't contributed in every way to her inevitable degradation here. It may not be degradation for many of her kind, but for Antoinette the bondage of her body to a gentleman of New Orleans is an unbearable humiliation."

The man in the shadows nodded.

"Pray continue, m'sieu."

"You are proud, I daresay, of New Orleans, its history and traditions. Consider, therefore, why it should not be able to offer a young woman of grace and beauty more than a cage. You know Antoinette, obviously. You know her well, though she has never known you. Who is less deserving of such a cage than she? I am no sophisticate, nor am I a gentleman of New Orleans, but after no more than five minutes in her company I would swear before God and all the angels that there is a girl of such gifts as to shame all who would not lift a finger to save her. If you are genuinely concerned for her, let her go, let her escape a future she cannot bear. It is not necessary for you to know me or my family. It is only necessary for you to have my word that I will protect her, not destroy her."

"The English, m'sieu," said the dark Creole, "are noted more for their arrogance than their charity. What is in *your* traditions and *your* history to make me believe that you will not first regard Antoinette as a *mulatresse* and therefore inferior? I will accept no criticisms of New Orleans from the English. Yes, there is intolerance in many of our edicts concerning slaves—but if we were to free them tomorrow and send them all to England, the milk and honey they would receive would not be enough to keep one of them alive for longer than a week."

"Your point is appreciated," said Jason, "but I am not arranging to take all your slaves, only Antoinette. I will see that she survives. I will take her whether you approve or not, and the only concession I'll make is to offer to render a report each year on her progress. And if at any time she asks to return she may do so."

"M'sieu, I could have her removed tonight, have her taken to where you would never find her."

"No doubt," said Jason. "But when it comes, as it must, to a resumption of her way of life here, what will you be able to offer her? What can you offer her? Only the hope that she may end up with someone who will be understanding enough to make her degradation near tolerable. Do you not realise what enslaved prostitution will do to a woman both sensitive and intelligent? Consider, if you remove her tonight, what you will have done for her good. Before I relinquished my commission I served with the Queen's 7th Lancers. That is all I will tell you of myself. But you have my word I mean her no harm, no humiliation."

The slightest of sighs escaped the Creole.

"I have looked to her welfare, m'sieu, as much as a caring man might. I have looked at her. I have listened to her, though she has never been aware of it. I have refused to let one man after another acquire her, for I too wished to ensure that first and foremost she received understanding. She is a creature of light, as her mother was. Such are the limitations we have imposed on ourselves with our traditions and edicts that we have imprisoned our compassion in chains of our own making. And so it is not possible in certain cases for a father to take his own daughter into his house. Monsieur Johnson told me your name is Rawlings. If that is your name that is all I truly know of you, except that you say you have been an officer. However, I have listened to you, and you may take Antoinette. Render me the yearly report you have promised. I accept your word in all things and put my trust in your promise. Address the report to M. Giraud in the care of Monsieur Johnson. That is not my name but it will do. M'sieu, if I am in your debt, if you are able to make Antoinette embrace life joyfully, then be assured I shall not be ungrateful."

"She will be in my care. You may rest on it."


Mr. Dillman Farquhar was an abolitionist. He did not advertise his vocation, however, not in New Orleans. One might enter a den of sleeping lions but one did not wake them up. He posed very creditably as a tracker of escaped slaves. Announcements concerning such slaves, together with details of rewards for their recapture, were thick and black in newspapers. Mr. Farquhar called on angry owners, asking for further details of the "nigras" in question, declaring that once he had them no man could land quicker on the tails of the running blacks. Owners, not unaware of the wiliness of infiltrating abolitionists, reached for their muskets the moment an uninvited visitor proved suspect; but Mr. Farquhar was a genially convincing man. Given leave to speak to an owner's slaves about an escapee, he used the opportunity to take stock of conditions and to give the Negroes advice on how to best reach the North if they decided to run one day.

He was not a tall man, but he was very broad, and as solid as an oak. He had a circular bald patch which gave him a monkish look when his hat was off, though it seldom was. His eyes were bright, his expression jovial, and his teeth strong-looking if tobacco-stained. Born in an English rural community, his father an agricultural labourer, he had at the age of ten accompanied his parents to a new life in America, the land of enterprise and evangelism. His conversation was extrovert and cheerful, his accent and phraseology still spiced with the quality of rural England, and he looked always on the bright side of life. He considered it a day of days to meet Mademoiselle Antoinette Giraud. He was sure he had never beheld so melting a young lady or one with such superb eyes. He would swear to it, he informed her, that she was undoubtedly descended from the royalest house in Europe.

"I am flattered, m'sieu," said Antoinette, watching Johnson's Negroes loading her luggage on to the carriage, "but I would hardly say it was true."

"No, I daresay you wouldn't," said Mr. Farquhar, "which don't make it less likely—only more so."

"More so?" Antoinette smiled, and no one knew the fever she was in, the height of the clouds she rode.

"Ma'moiselle, I figure true graciousness and modesty only come with true royals, and though I never met any princess, not even a Pawnee one, it's my opinion you own twice as much as most."

"M'sieu," said Antoinette, "we cannot begin our journey with you thinking me far from what I am. That will never do."

"There, don't you worry your head none," said Mr. Farquhar, "it'll do for me. So maybe you're not the Queen of Siam. You're still going to be protected as if you are. Ma'moiselle, it's a privilege."

"Thank you," said Antoinette, and lowered the veil she had put up for him. She had asked Jason if she might wear her black again, so that she could depart from New Orleans in a way that would pay her last respects to Edwina, his wife and her friend. True, she was leaving New Orleans gladly, but he would not mind her wearing black, would he? Jason did not argue. He knew her sentiments to be genuine. There was nobody she wished to say goodbye to other than Edwina. Her face was turned to the North, to Baltimore, her eyes already washed by the grey Atlantic, the ocean that carried ships to Europe. New Orleans had given birth to her, but had withheld love. Her future had haunted her as the past haunted others. She had not a single regret at leaving the city. Her heart was thumping, pounding, fluttering, soaring, and she would not have been surprised if it had flown off in advance of her body. If anything at all kept it earthbound, it was the realisation that while she was in Baltimore, Monsieur Rawlings would be in Texas, looking for the man who had robbed him of his wife. That made her unhappy, for she knew it could only end with one or the other losing his life. It was not that the other man deserved to keep his, but quite unbearable to think that Monsieur Rawlings might lose his. For he was the man who had set her free.

Except that she was in a more sensitive bondage now.

The Negroes put up the last of the luggage. Mr. Farquhar gave her his hand and she stepped aboard. Suddenly she felt in pain. She tried to speak calmly as she said, "Monsieur Rawlings is not coming to say goodbye to us?"

"We shan't leave until he does," said Mr. Farquhar stoutly. "It's my opinion, Your Highness, that he's enjoying a last few minutes putting the fear of Abraham into the heart of the preyer on human souls, Beelzebub Johnson."

Antoinette, not quite convinced, said, "I think he has many things to attend to, besides leaving Monsieur Johnson chastened. You do not feel he has forgotten us, forgotten that we are going?"

"Never." Mr. Farquhar grinned broadly. "You just sit tight, Princess."

"Why do you call me these names, m'sieu?"

"Because I reckon they fit you. Don't worry, we'll manage." They were to travel by steamboat on the first stage of their journey. He knew the nose and instinct Southerners had for the merest hint of coloured blood: there were no free coloureds in their book. And there was the fact of Antoinette having no female companion or chaperone. Well, he was going to have her travel as his niece, and keep her out of sight as much as he could in the cabin he had booked for her yesterday, after talking with Rawlings.

Antoinette sat as patiently as she could, but her mouth was

trembling under her veil. Then the long-legged figure appeared, coming out of the house, a servant carrying his large pack. Jason nodded to him and the man set off, making for the livery stables.

"My apologies, Mr. Farquhar," said Jason, "I think I've been keeping you."

"Nothing to fret about," said the genial one, "plenty of time to catch the boat."

"You'll take good care of her?"

"Never doubt it. My own departure from this sink of iniquity is kind of overdue. They're beginning to sniff me out, like I told you. I don't fancy a New Orleans rope, it's harmful to the neck. Baltimore will suit me for a while. Your sweet gal will be as safe with me as with you, my hand on't. I'll be like a lion, my friend. I aim to bite the head off any man who gets within spittin' distance of her. That makes you smile?"

"No."

"I reckoned I saw a flicker," said Mr. Farquhar affably.

"Only indicative of my faith in you as a lion," said Jason.

"Well, between us we shall save her soul for the Lord," said Mr. Farquhar. "You'll pardon me if I kick my heels a mite. She wants to say goodbye to you."

He strolled off a few paces.

Jason climbed into the carriage. He wore his travelling clothes, a wide-brimmed round black hat, well-weathered soft leather shirt and corded breeches. To Antoinette he looked as one God must have designed of strength and valour, but then her eyes were those of a young woman intoxicated by the heady wine of a new life. She was in quite the most emotional state she had ever known. Johnson appeared in the doorway of the house, Madame Coulbert with him, her house keys ringed to her belt. He looked at Antoinette and bowed to her in exaggerated irony. He had not come off too badly. The Creole had reimbursed him for time given, trouble encountered, inconveniences suffered, and loss made. He turned back into the house. Madame Coulbert followed him and closed the door.

"They have shut you out, Antoinette," smiled Jason.

"Yes," said Antoinette unsteadily, "but how much better that is than being shut in. M'sieu, I owe you so much but I am so worried."

"Are you already in regret?" asked Jason.

"Oh, no," she swiftly assured him. "I am on wings of joy, but I am also unhappy. I have heard Texas is a wild country, that men count life very cheaply. M'sieu, you will take care?"

"I shall not be careless, that at least you may rely on."

She thought he looked formidable enough to put fear into his man when he found him, but what if he turned his back at the wrong moment?

"You will not be too long coming to Baltimore?" she said.

"Several weeks should not be too long. He's elusive, my man, but I think I know where I may find him, and find him I must."

"I shall pray for you, m'sieu."

He looked around. The air was warm and balmy. New Orleans by morning was at its softest, its miasmatic odours not yet risen.

"Antoinette, remember what I said an hour ago. Find lodgings before you look for Sarah Blazey. When you do find her you may also find a little trouble. If she's a good soul and has become fond of the child, the trouble will be of an emotional kind. If she refuses to release Clare, don't quarrel with her but keep an eye on her and Clare in whatever way you can. You have the letter I gave you and the money?"

"Yes. M'sieu, you have given me over three hundred dollars."

"You will need it," said Jason, "and will know how to use it. For myself, I've enough, I think, to see me to Texas and back."

"But I have even more than what you have given me, m'sieu, I have a fortune," she said. "There was a packet delivered to me a little while ago with a thousand dollars in it."

"Heavens, girl." Jason smiled. "Do you know who sent it?"

"I think, m'sieu, it was sent by the gentleman who made all the decisions for Monsieur Johnson. There was no message. Do you know?"

"I'm fairly sure your guess is right," said Jason. "Antoinette, you are also rich."

Antoinette's smile was misty through her veil.

"M'sieu, I *am* rich," she said softly. "I have known your wife, and now I know you. I am the most blessed of women. Except— oh, you will take care, will you not?"

"Rely on me to see you in Baltimore eventually. So for now it is only *au revoir*."

"Yes, m'sieu." Her head was low.

"What is wrong?"

"Oh, I am so grateful—"

"But so am I." He stepped down from the carriage. "Clare is my wife's child, and I'm asking you to perform miracles on her behalf. Give me your hand." She put it out. He took it, pressed it, and lightly kissed the gloved fingers. Her eyes swam. "*Au revoir*, Antoinette."

"M'sieu—take very good care."

He waved as the carriage set off, carrying her and the redoubtable Mr. Dillman Farquhar on their way to catch the Mississippi steamboat. Mr. Farquhar raised his hat. Antoinette's hand fluttered, and her eyes shed hot tears.

From Louisiana, Jason resumed his chase, crossing the Red River at Shreve's Landing, with the Texas border due west on the trail. He was back on the same kind of chase then, but with information that made it less difficult, less frustrating. Johnson had very clearly described his man and his destination. The trail, therefore, was not so easy to lose now, and the questions he asked were for confirmation, not information. He knew by instinct these days whose ears were receptive to questions, whose hands were worth silvering for the frankest replies. There was always such a person at the stagecoach stops. Napoleon carried him steadily on; confirmation pointed him ahead. Johnson, it seemed, had not lied. His man was heading for the destination which, said Johnson, had dropped casually from his lips over a game of cards.

He did not dawdle, yet all the same he took his time. He did not want to wear Napoleon down to his withers, nor did his old cavalry mount intend to let him.

Mrs. Purdy knocked on Jason's door and handed him a letter. He slit it open.

*Colonel Hendriks and Elisabeth present their compliments and*

*request the pleasure of your company to supper tomorrow evening
at seven, and without fail, for having been disappointed in court
today, they insist on not being disappointed at table tomorrow.*

*PS. I declare, sir, you are a wretch. Do not make matters worse
by refusing to come. Lisbet.*

"There's a darkie waiting for a reply, Mr. Rawlings," said Mrs.
Purdy, looking as roundly cuddlesome as ever.

"Tell him, would you, to tell Miss Lisbet yes," said Jason.

Laura Purdy sat sewing by the light of the lamp. The bar was
doing good business this evening and Sam was managing fine. She
would have been willing to help. It was not unusual for husband
and wife to serve, and a woman's presence kept the customers be-
having fairly respectably. But Sam would not have her in the saloon. He reckoned there were always one or two drifters ready to
regard the presence of any woman as a challenge.

Someone tapped. She looked up and Colonel Hendriks put his
head in. Mrs. Purdy blushed.

"You'll forgive me, ma'am," he said. "I just dropped by, but the
card game is poor. So I thought to pay you my respects before I
left."

He entered the room, closing the door behind him. She put her
sewing down and got to her feet. He smiled.

"Colonel Hendriks, sir, the door—"

"I dislike paying my respects with a door open," he said, and
his white teeth showed as his smile broadened. "And I can't talk
to Sam in front of outsiders. So I'll talk to you."

"Talk to Sam?" Her colour was up, her pulse fluttering.

"I've made up my mind to build the hotel," he said. "Westboro
needs one. I don't figure to make Hendriks a hotel for all the cotton buyers who come sniffing."

Mrs. Purdy glowed with hope.

"Colonel Hendriks, you ain't—you don't mean you'll build
without someone in mind?"

"I need to have in mind people I'm confident would run it as it
should be run," he said, eyeing her roundness, as if it had something to do with competence.

"You'll give Sam the chance, won't you? He's good at running
things, and even keeping books. We both would surely like the
chance; it's what we want."

"I haven't precisely set my mind on names yet, Miz Purdy, but I can't say I'm not willing for you and Sam to apply. I declare, Laura, an application couldn't come from a prettier woman."

She blushed again. He was handsome, persuasive, and the weakness of a woman beguiled made her tremble. His power and influence could do so much for her and Sam, especially if he gave them a stake in the hotel. Sam realised it as much as she did, but whereas she knew there were certain ways and means, he did not. Or if he did, he would not have entertained them. Nor would she have, a while ago. They had had a hard time, striking southwest into Texas several years ago, and not until Colonel Hendriks had helped to set them up with their saloon and rooms did they begin to feel life had taken a better turn. It had cost her something for Sam to be given that chance. She had paid in two instalments. The first on Colonel Hendriks' promise, the second when she and Sam were in occupation. It still made her hot, however, whenever she thought of it. But she had done it for Sam, who worked so hard, who had failed so often despite his efforts. The Colonel had been handsomely ardent and it had not been as unbearable as she feared, not physically. Physically she had been swept into a heated flood; it was her conscience that suffered.

"Colonel Hendriks—"

"Hush your pretty mouth," murmured the Colonel, and put his hand under her chin and turned her face up. He bent his head and kissed her warmly. "There, my respects, Laura, and a promise to keep Sam in mind. And you."

She turned away and said, "I can't look at myself sometimes, I surely can't."

"I have no trouble looking at you," he said.

"You'll give us first chance with the hotel?" she said.

"I guess you're irresistible," he said, and embraced her curvaceous body. She flushed crimson.

"If Sam comes in I will surely die," she breathed.

"Sam never leaves his bar, you know that. And I know that."

"I can't do wrong by Sam, I can't, not again."

He smiled. She was warm and soft against him.

"Come out to Hendriks tomorrow afternoon. Tell Sam I want a recipe from you. We've a guest for supper in the evening."

Scarlet, she said, "Colonel Hendriks, must I?"

"I leave it entirely in your own sweet hands, Laura, but I swear

I don't know why I don't help you do wrong here and now. I've never seen you blushing prettier."

He laughed and left her hot, confused, and fatally weak.

Jason lay awake. It was in his bones, the certainty that now he only had to wait for his man. The certainty burned the ice. There was one note of irony—the assistance he had given to the daughters of Esteban Sylvestre y Cordova.

Sleepless, he heard the footsteps on the stairs, the slight creak of the landing boards. A spur clicked. He sensed the arrival at his door and was out of bed silently and speedily. The door began to open. The men slithered in, two of them. The moonlight cut across the room, over the empty bed. They turned and the point of a sabre tickled the chest of the foremost man.

"Ah, señor," he murmured, and the second man closed the door. Their high sombreros and leather-chapped trousers proclaimed them vaqueros. They smelled of grass and range and cattle.

"Speak up, my friends," said Jason.

"Will you come with us, señor?" asked the second man, and the long knife of the vaquero glittered in his hand.

"I am compelled?"

"Señor, what good will this do you?" The first man touched the shining sword, the point of which bit into yielding buckskin. "We have orders to take you with us. You are welcome to make a hole in me, but you will lose an ear. Pedro can take off the tail of a running fox. A standing ear, señor, is no problem. Come with us. There is only a conversation at the end of it."

"With whom? You are Cordova vaqueros?"

"Come with us and see for yourself."

"I'll come my friends, but you go first," said Jason. He slipped into his clothes, and the Mexicans went ahead, down the stairs to the rear exit. They had their horses and one for him. His was skittish. He thumped the brute. They rode out of Westboro and into what was left of San Carlos, where they turned right along a dusty track until they reached an old adobe house. There they tethered their horses and went inside. Candles burned. In a room where there was an oil lamp as well sat an old woman. But her back was straight and the fine bones that were the foundation of a beauty in a woman remained. The beauty had retreated with the ageing of the flesh and the lines had become deeply established. Yet there was still quality and character, and her eyes were fiercely alive.

"Señor," she said in a biting voice, "you are out of bed."

"Señora, so are you."

"*Quia!* What nonsense. I have slept my time. I am not called to bed by the clock. Señor, you will sit with me for a few minutes."

The vaqueros pushed a chair forward. Jason sat down. The old woman surveyed him with the eyes of a robbed eagle. She gestured at the men. They disappeared. She leaned forward, clasping a stick, its point on the tiled floor.

"Señor, you are not an honourable man. This morning you called my son Sancho a liar."

"Señora, I did not."

"You are a lawyer. Lawyers are devious in their use of words. While a thousand people will say they have named a man a liar, they will say not so, not so. They will say they only suggested the man has a bad memory. My son Sancho does not have a good memory, but neither does he have a dishonest tongue. Simple men, señor, speak simply. A lie evades them, for a lie is a complex thing."

Jason, intrigued, said, "I made a point, señora, not an accusation."

"The point you made, señor, burdened my son with the cloak of deceit. What should my friends do with such a lawyer if not feed his tongue to the vultures?"

"Señora," said Jason, "tell me about the document."

"It is a good piece of paper, not false," she said.

"I believe you, señora, but now you will have to show in some way that the paper is as old as the date it bears."

"*Inglés,* why do you wish to cheat Sancho of money that will make life pleasanter for him as he grows old?"

"I've no wish to cheat anyone. I have only acted for Señorita Isabella Cordova, who will not accept that the document is genuine."

"Señorita Isabella Cordova—pah!" The old lady rapped his boot with her stick. "That one! She could have bought the land from Sancho at a fair price. We asked only for enough to keep him in a little comfort. She would not listen, she would not even look at the document. Señor, are you a dishonourable man? Your face does not say so, but I am not sure I like your eyes."

"They're the only ones I have." Jason smiled. His increasing involvement with the dispute was unwelcome, despite its ironic factor, for it was something to engage his time and interest while he waited. "Señora, I have never been called dishonourable. I win at cards sometimes, but then I play well. In acting for Señorita Cordova, I thought myself fighting Colonel Hendriks. What am I discovering now, that I am fighting you?"

A large brown spider scurried across the floor.

"Señor," she said, "why do you act for Spanish Texans and not for your cousins, the Americanos? The *Inglés* have no love for the Spanish."

"That doesn't mean we should all love Colonel Hendriks."

She chuckled at that. It bubbled in her throat.

"*Inglés,* that is a good answer. She does not deserve your brains, Señorita Cordova. She is a woman so proud she will end up living on top of a mountain, far above all other people."

"She is not quite like that, señora."

"Ah, you have looked into those eyes of hers, have you?" Again Señora López chuckled. "Much good will it do you. She will never wed into the *Inglés.*"

"She has not been asked to."

"Why are you here, señor, in Cordova country?"

"I am waiting for a man."

"Hm." She peered at him. "Señor, I say to you, did we wish to sell this piece of land to Americanos? No. That is not the way to keep Texas in our hands, by selling it piece by piece to Americanos. But when anger quarrels with reason, the nose is cut off to spite the face."

"You agreed to give Colonel Hendriks an option to buy because you were angry with Señorita Cordova?"

She made an impatient gesture.

"Many times we offered to sell the document to her for two thousand dollars. Señor, the land in question is worth much more than that, much more. She refused. In the end, hearing that the Americano wished to get his hands on part of Cordova, we offered him that which this document gives Sancho title to. He asked for what he called an option, and Sancho signed a paper."

"He asked for an option, señora, because he too was unsure,

made so by Señorita Cordova's conviction that it was not a valid grant. That's why he wanted a ruling from a court of law. Had he secured it, he would have taken up his option. He is not going to purchase land from you until he is certain the title is genuine."

"Ah, that Yankee gringo." The stick tapped the tiles as the spider's mate made its dash to catch up with wife and fate. "And you, señor, you have made Sancho look a liar and in such a way that it would be better for Pedro and García to feed you to the coyotes."

"That is an unhappy advance on just my tongue," said Jason, "but unless that document is genuine you could feed me to the lions, which would eat my bones and all, without it making the slightest difference to your case. It would be better, in my opinion, to think of other solutions. Confide in me, señora."

The fierce eyes were brooding, holding his in the flickering light. The heat and the flames of the lamp and candles drew in the night insects. Huge moths danced in the venturesome way of compulsive suicides, scorched wing tips beating. But the flies, at least, were dormant.

"Señor, many years ago that land was willed to my son by Don Carlos."

"The question, señora, is why he should do such a thing."

The lined lids veiled her eyes.

"It was payment, señor."

"For what?"

"For favours." Her face drew in the shadows of the past.

"What inference am I to draw, señora?"

"You are a man." Her voice was biting again. "You will draw the inference of a man. You will disregard the wild blood of the young, the confusions of incomprehensible emotions, and the mysteries of God. What place do they have in favours given and a gift bestowed?"

Jason was silent. His faith in the reason and loyalty of women was an embittered, cynical one. Yet there was Antoinette. And Señora López, fighting fiercely for her son, so fiercely that secrets were on her lips.

He said after a while, "It was not just for favours, señora."

"Ah, your mind is as cold as your eyes, señor. Here is an old woman talking of hot blood and wild youth, and here is a man who puts one and one together and makes three. He is not content to leave it a mystery, to say it concerns only those who lay together under the sun. No, he must draw his inferences and come to his cold conclusions."

"Which is what you knew I could not avoid," said Jason. "That is why Don Carlos gifted the land to you."

"To my son."

"You are a widow, señora?"

"The man who married me was a good man, señor, but died a long time ago."

A moth, vanquished by a flame, fell.

"Señora, there's more to tell, I think," said Jason. "The document?"

She brooded.

"I will tell you, *Inglés*. I think you are not, after all, a dishonourable man. The original document was lost in a fire. But Don Carlos still had many years to live then. His only desire was that none should know of his bequest until after he was dead. I honoured that, señor. Never in all those years did I speak of the fact that he had paid my son for favours given by me."

"That was not the way of it, señora, nor is it the way you should put it."

"I put it as you would, as others would," she said fiercely.

"No, señora, not as I would. A child was born of love, not of favours. To scourge yourself is to be in as much pride as Isabella Cordova."

Señora López smiled.

"What was I saying?" she asked.

"That you lost the original document in a fire."

"Yes. Yes. But Don Carlos had a copy—"

"A copy?"

"Do I mumble, señor? No. I do not. He wrote out a new document from the copy. It was the same in every detail, including the date and the signatures of the witnesses, two faithful servants of his. There, señor, what does your mind make of that?"

"It puts me between the devil and the deep," said Jason. "It was the very devil indeed to copy so precisely. One variation was permissible. The date. As it is, that date stands on paper possibly not manufactured until years later."

"Ha, who was to know, *Inglés*, that you would come peering and prying, that the paper itself mattered?"

"It could cost your son his gift. We must find a way out. Señorita Cordova must be satisfied and so must you."

She quizzed him with very bright eyes.

"Señor, now whose hand are you taking?"

"Yours," said Jason, "I am in love with you."

"Ah," she said, "are my eyes, then, more beautiful than hers?"

"Also," said Jason, "I wish to save my tongue."

"*Quia*," she said again, but she smiled. "Señor, if there is a solution that leaves the Americano empty-handed, I shall not complain."

"Well, the Americans left the British empty-handed after all our years of establishing the colonies, so I'll not weep tears myself. Does the option name a price?"

"Price? No." She shook her shawl-covered head. "He suggested four thousand dollars, knowing it was offered to Señorita Cordova for half that. But he did not write it down."

"Then perhaps we can outfox him, señora. You will write him, stating that although he may now be thinking otherwise, the bequest is genuine. You will ask him if he intends to take up his option, and if so the price is twenty-five thousand dollars."

"That, señor, is a fortune," she said calmly. "For that amount he would want all of Cordova and the Rio Grande as well."

"Now, señora," said Jason, "since he's no longer sure Sancho can get his claim confirmed, irrespective of what you say, he'll relinquish the option and try again to deal directly with Señorita Cordova. I repeat, you must put your request and your terms in writing."

"You will do it for me. Sancho will sign it. My writing, señor, is limited. So is Sancho's. And then you will approach Señorita Cordova?"

"I will steel myself for that," he said, and she chuckled again. "We must bend her pride, señora. We must make her see the sense of ensuring the land is hers."

"That will be better than letting the Americanos have it. With each turn of the sun their flood rises and spreads. The people of Texas will soon be submerged. Perhaps, if he has money, Sancho will at least be able to keep his head above the waters."

"We will ask Señorita Cordova to pay four thousand dollars."

Her eyes were full of the reflections of the flickering light.

"Señor, that is much more than we asked of her before."

"It is what Colonel Hendriks offered and is not less than your family deserves."

"Señor, with your Isabella I do not advise a humble voice, but a strong one. Then it will be settled."

"*Buenos noches, señora.*"

"You will not lose your tongue, señor."


"Isabella! Isabella! Who is here, do you think?"

"I am, little wagtail." Isabella, standing before her dressing table, turned as her sister flew into the room. Her mahogany-framed mirror flashed her bright reflection.

"No, not you. You are always here. Come downstairs."

"Who has called that you're so flushed?" smiled Isabella. Casually, she suggested, "Señor Rawlings?"

"Oh? Why should you think Señor Rawlings?"

Yes, thought Isabella, why? Except that she had sent him her desperate little note, asking his pardon, and he had neither replied nor called.

"Well, I should like to know he's forgiven me," she confessed.

"Of course he will, he is a gentleman," said Luisa. "But come down and meet Fernando and someone else."

"Oh, Fernando is why you're flushed? But who is someone else?"

"Very well, I'll put you in a flutter, then," laughed Luisa. "It's Fernando's uncle. Philip. There, now who is flushed?"

"I am not," said Isabella, though her blood leapt a little.

"But you are." Luisa laughed again. "Ah, who dreamt of horses when she was young?"

"Luisa, I'm hardly old yet." Isabella turned back to the mirror and lightly touched her bunched curls. "Let us go down, then."

The two men, still showing the dust of travel, were slapping it from the sleeves of their coats when the sisters entered. Fernando Alba, a young man of twenty-one, heir to the estate held by his family west of Cordova, was dark and slight, moustache bravely sprouting. His uncle, Philip de Ravero, forty years old, was taller, stronger of build and lighter in colour. His brown hair was streaked with tints of gold and he had a bold, bright expressiveness that proclaimed him an extrovert of permanent cheer. Cordova had seen much of him in former years. Isabella, when sixteen and then seventeen, thought him a reborn Cortez. His was the air of brave, laughing adventure, he sat a horse in splendid command of both animal and earth, and he roamed the South Americas like a cavalier. She fell madly and passionately in love with him, so that whenever he was at Cordova she lived in either high heaven or deep despair, depending on the kind of attention he gave her. He had no wife. He said he had never had the time to court any lady, that the world had never stood still long enough for him. While Isabella was still seventeen, Philip left Texas to go East, swearing that unless he saw Spain and Europe then, they would retreat beyond accessibility. His going left her heartbroken.

Philip looked up from his dust-slapping as the two young ladies entered. His brown eyes gleamed, his teeth shone.

"Luisa, who is this, in faith?" he exclaimed. "I begged you to fetch your sister and you bring— Is Texas a monarchy and not a republic? Is this the most royal Princess of Texas?"

"Oh, she's excessively royal," said Luisa, "but some of the time she's almost like the rest of us, and can be called Isabella."

"Isabella," smiled Fernando, "salutations." He kissed her hand.

"Fernando, how good to see you," said Isabella, "and who is your friend?"

"A wandering clown of sorts," said Fernando, which made Luisa laugh and eye him happily.

"Oh, the devil," said Philip, "I'm put down by the impertinence of a nephew and the wit of a lady most high." He burst into laughter. Robustly infectious, it carried around the room, enchanting smiles. "Isabella, am I to believe you are you?" He advanced, took her hand, and looked into her eyes. "So tall, so magnificent." He took her other hand and lifted each to his lips. "What is Texas against Castile? Leave Cordova, go to Spain. Spain will unseat María Cristina and crown you in place of her pale daughter."

Isabella, mesmerised, was drawn into warm, bright seas. They washed caressingly over her. How alive Philip was. He had reached maturity, but looked as if he would never grow old. None of his zest had gone, none of his vitality. He exuded a rich, exhilarating knowledge of life and its wonders.

"I can manage Cordova," she said, surfacing, "but Spain would be a little too much for me."

"But, *cara mía, cara mía!*—modesty has no place in the shadow of perfection." Philip flung modesty out of the way with an extravagant gesture. "By all the sweet angels, Isabella, you look equal to commanding an empire."

That compliment was a bit florid, she thought. It had brought what was almost a giggle from Luisa.

"Philip, I assure you—and Luisa will assure you too—that as an empress I should quickly be found wanting."

His bright, bold eyes teased her. She felt herself flushing.

"In not being here to see you grow up," he said, "I've missed magic."

"I was grown up before you left," she smiled.

"Isabella, you were young and sweet then, yes—but you hadn't acquired magnificence. By every blade of the Texas grass, you're a woman to behold."

"Fernando," murmured Luisa, "do you think we're in the way?"

"Some reunions aren't merely a feast of words and flowers, they're a banquet," said Fernando, "so yes, I think we may very well be in the way."

"You see?" said Philip to Isabella, putting a soulful hand to his cheerful heart. "Everyone has grown up." He laughed again, with gusto. "Beauty has blossomed out of sweet youth, and for all my years I can only stand and stare." His eyes sought Isabella's wide mouth and lingered on her lips. It embarrassed her. And as he took her hands again, lightly squeezing them, the warm seas receded and she knew herself to be no longer a breathless, infatuated girl. Six years ago a squeeze from his hands would have put her in bliss. Now, in front of Luisa and Fernando, it only made her uncomfortable. "But what are words, in any event?" laughed Philip, applying another squeeze.

Why she thought it an unsophisticated familiarity she did not know. Gently she disengaged her hands. She was not sixteen or seventeen. She was twenty-two. She had grown up and it was the oddest shock to feel that Philip had not grown up at all. He was engagingly, handsomely boyish, and at his age he had no right to be. It might appeal to some women, make them feel young themselves, but it did not appeal to her.

I was in love, she thought, with a high-spirited boy of thirty-four—who is still a boy at forty. Or am I in fault? Have I, in just five or six years, become very old?

It did not matter. While Philip was here he would make Cordova a place of laughter.

"Philip, you and Fernando, you're here to visit, to stay a while?" she said. "Are you to tell us of your adventures abroad? You've been—where have you been?"

"My sweet one," said Philip, "we'll be grateful for a bed tonight, but must be on our way first thing in the morning to see our cousins in San Antonio. As for me, I've been to Europe and back and taken my time."

"So has Father," said Luisa.

"And why not?" smiled Philip. "What is the point of not taking time, of galloping from one place to another in a frenzy? One must linger, observe, participate, and digest. Spain, I fear, was a mixed canvas, for while it has fine arts it also had intemperate politics and drained vigour. Europe was so diverse that it was better to enjoy its colours than attempt to understand its patterns. And the cities, ah, yes, dear girls, in Spain there was Madrid, and in France there was Paris."

"Yes," said Isabella, "I've heard that is where Madrid and Paris are."

Philip, carrying on regardless of that little dart, said, "Paris, my sweets. So French. There I met France itself and might have been rendered an insignificance had I not decided to set my own mark on the place. Let me tell you . . ."

Isabella thought: Oh, Santa María, I am going to be bored. What is the matter with me?

Philip went on, so swampingly rhetorical that nothing might have stopped him had she not seized on the tiniest check in his tidal flow to tell him that as he and Fernando were to stay overnight they must see what had happened on the first floor. Then they would all take wine together out on the patio.

On the first floor a small room had been converted into a bathroom, and it was no longer necessary to carry a bath and fill it in a guest's bedroom. Philip and Fernando must see it. They saw it. Philip, rousingly impressed, almost composed a song about it. Fernando and Luisa stole downstairs again, and it took Isabella another five minutes to prise Philip loose from his enthusiastic inspection of the miracle of Cordova plumbing. Descending the stairs with him, she felt his arm cheerfully encircling her waist. It may have been gallantry; it may not. In any case, while seeking to discourage him Isabella failed to keep her skirts hitched and one heel caught in a petticoat, causing her to fall. Philip caught her, swung her over the last few stairs in a flying whirl, and deposited her safely on the floor of the hall amid his burst of laughter. But in her whirl her skirt and petticoats billowed, revealing the delicacy of her lacy white pantaloons.

A servant, preceding a caller, stopped in goggling reaction to this extraordinary display of lingerie by the señorita, then blanked out his astonishment. The caller raised his eyes tactfully to the high ceiling. Isabella crimsoned. The very fact that his eyes were elsewhere told her what he had seen.

The servant said, "Señorita—"

"Yes, you may go, Manuel," she said.

Manuel bowed and disappeared. The bow, possibly, was for the delight she had given him. Certainly his face split into a huge smile as he entered the servants' quarters.

"Good morning, señorita," said Jason, finishing his inspection of the ceiling.

"Señor?" said Isabella, her face still hot.

"I rode out in the hope you might spare me a few moments."

"Yes?" She lacked all sense and comprehension for the moment, she was so discomfited. Oh, that boisterous Philip. Even now his smile was like a loud laugh. She made an effort and introduced the two men. Knowing Philip had a Spanish Texan's distrust of ambitious Americans, she took care to point out that Jason was English.

"Ah," said Philip and his smile was one of fixed politeness for a change. The English were no easier to love than the Americans. "Ah, English. One falls over them everywhere."

"Señor, do you blunder about, then?" said Jason.

"*Touché*," said Philip generously, and his smile took on its normal cheer.

Jason turned to Isabella.

"Señorita, if it's not convenient now, I'll call again later," he said.

Isabella came to. So, he had come, after all. He had forgiven her. It warmed her, dispelled the little sense of unhappiness that had stayed with her since yesterday.

"Philip," she said, "please join Luisa and Fernando, and please ring for refreshments, whatever you wish. I must speak with Señor

Rawlings; he has been acting for us in a land dispute. Señor Rawlings, there is the study. Shall we use that?"

The study was almost devoid of light, the shutters fully closed. Isabella opened them a little, and shafts of brightness entered to light up an inlaid oak escritoire. She turned to Jason. Fairly recovered now, her smile held the warmth of her nature.

"Señor Rawlings, I am so glad you have called. Please, I simply do not know why I behaved as I did yesterday. I was quite inadequate. You have forgiven me?"

"Señorita," said Jason, "I'd already forgotten it, if it ever happened. Certainly, I can't recall any inadequacies."

Isabella thought how much quieter a presence his was than Philip's, how much more compelling.

"Señor," she smiled, "you must do better than that. You must make me suffer a little, and then forgive me very positively."

"How am I to make you suffer?"

"By being very stiff and unbending, and refusing to let us show you Cordova." Her eyes warmly begged, her long lashes swept to veil them, then lifted to show him soft contrition. "I shall suffer, you see, by being very upset. Then you are to forgive me positively by finally accepting our invitation. Will you come tomorrow, please? It will take all day, and even then you will hardly see all of it. Our friends will be gone in the morning, so you must put up with just my company and Luisa's. You will come, won't you, please? I shall not be ungracious again, I promise."

Her vivid Spanish beauty was soft, her dark eyes lustrous. Jason saw himself becoming unadvisedly involved. He had already broken with his habit of shying away from any kind of involvement. This one had been ironic from the start—he did not want it to become impossible. Isabella Cordova was not just another small ship passing in the night. However, it was on her own head.

"Señorita, thank you. I'm flattered."

"Oh, no," she said quickly, "it was not meant to flatter you but to make you understand you are our friend. And it is agreeable of you to have forgiven me so generously. Señor—" She blushed. "Señor, you must have thought me very childish a few minutes ago—it was not what—oh, please tell me you didn't see."

"I did see," said Jason, "and wouldn't have missed it for anything."

"Oh," said Isabella, and crimsoned again. Jason coughed. She did not know where to look, but she essayed a quick glance. He seemed quite solemn.

"Yes, quite picturesque, señorita. Now, that document—"

"You are to dismiss it from your mind," she said.

"The document?"

"The picturesque," said Isabella.

"Very well. I need a few minutes with you, please. I've seen Señora López, Sancho's mother. Señorita, somewhere among your grandfather's papers I think you may find a copy of the bequest he made to Sancho."

Isabella was aware of a little shock of sharp disappointment. So that was why he had called, to talk about the document. She put her chin up, making her slim neck look lovely.

"You are mistaken, señor."

"Where are your grandfather's papers?"

"There." She gestured towards the escritoire. "But it's no use to look for something which does not exist."

"Nevertheless, I have your permission?"

Oh, how dare he stand up against her like this!

"No," she said.

Patiently he replied, "Señorita, there are times when it's wiser to test the improbable than to trust to assumption. Shall we go through the papers together?"

Angry that he should believe there was any need to do so, she said inflexibly, "We have guests. I cannot neglect them for the sake of the improbable."

At the look he gave her she felt a sense of dismay.

"Is it so much to ask," he said, "a few more minutes away from your guests to ensure justice is done to a woman and her son?"

That upset her out of all reason.

"Oh," she cried, "I did not think you the kind of man to transfer your allegiance as quickly as this!"

"Is that what you think? Very well, then. Good day, señorita."

"Stop!" she cried as he reached the door.

"Señorita?"

"Oh, I am sorry," she said emotionally, "but you are not to go off in a temper. How can we be friends if you do that?"

"I'm in no temper." He eyed her critically. "I'm afraid, señorita, you have yet to grow up."

That of all things! Isabella's eyes glittered with tears of fiery outrage.

"No one has ever—señor, leave my house!"

"I mean to," said Jason dispassionately. "There's no point in staying, and that's the truth of it."

He opened the door. An unbridgeable chasm of riven friendship yawned in her mind's eye. She ran at the door and slammed it shut again, barring his way. She turned on him, her face flushed, her breast heaving.

"You would dare to go without apologising?" she cried.

"If it's going to shake the heavens, no," he said. "Señorita, I apologise. I'm not sure what for, but you seem a little agitated—"

"Oh, you are not a gentleman, no, you are not!" Isabella, appalled as she was by her descent into such childish repartee, could not help herself.

"Well, you're a very fine lady, God's heaven you are, and amusing with it," said Jason. He realised it made no odds if he had come to the end of his brief span with her and reached for the door handle. Isabella put her back against the panels.

"No!" she gasped.

"What is the point of all this?" frowned Jason.

"I wish you would not make me feel so up and down!"

"Console yourself, señorita. To be neither up nor down can be very dull."

That was what she believed herself. She stared at him, her brown eyes hot, glimmering, and agitated. She did not want him to go, and that realisation was confusing her. She, who had sometimes still thought about Philip, and wondered if he would ever return to Cordova, had forgotten him only a short while after his arrival.

"Señor Rawlings, please."

"I fancy—"

"Wait." Flushed and emotional, she said, "You did not mean that remark, did you—that remark implying I was young and silly?"

"I only meant you'll realise one day that pride can be extravagant."

"But, Jason—" She coloured at her impulsive use of his name.

"Well?" Jason was taking refuge in his survey of the graceful escritoire. It kept his eyes off the handsomer shape.

"Señor, I confess to a little pride, but generally my moods are almost always extremely agreeable."

"Indeed, señorita, they are. Almost." He gave her a smile. It had nothing of the bravura of Philip's smiles, but it completely dispelled any lingering tension.

Suddenly Isabella began to laugh.

"Señor, you are an impossible lawyer," she said.

"We had decided, I thought, that I'm not a lawyer."

"Yes? So you are an acceptable man instead. Almost." She laughed again, full of relief that the quarrel was over. "You will concede that—a little sauce for the gander?"

"I think you earned it."

"Señor," she said cordially, "shall we go through my grandfather's papers together?"

There were many papers in the drawers and compartments of the escritoire, most of which looked as if they had not been touched for years. Even in the close-fitting drawers they had gathered dust. Isabella, having yielded without reservation, was as thorough as Jason in her examination of all they brought out. Nor did she mention her guests again, though half an hour went by. Then, opening up a plain, sealed packet that had lain inside a ribbon-tied sheaf of documents, she extracted and unfolded a sheet of paper. She drew a shocked breath. Jason looked up from a pile of other papers. Isabella thrust her discovery behind her, stared him out for the moment, then said despairingly, "Oh, day of ups and downs. Oh, day of wounded pride and an infallible lawyer."

"Show me," said Jason, extending his hand.

"It's nothing." Isabella tried hard. "Well, it's nothing much. Well, it's incomprehensible and I mean it so."

"Show me."

"I must tell you, señor, that I dislike your eyes. They are running down my back." Now she tried her sweetest, warmest, and sincerest smile. "You will not be angry with me, will you?"

"Why should I be?" Jason reasoned that the most compulsive object of the exercise was in its consumption of time. He had a week and more of it still to spare. "Whatever the outcome of this, it'll be of no benefit to me."

"The friendship of Cordova, that is of no benefit?" she said in a hurt voice.

He merely looked at her. Santa María, those eyes of his, piercingly blue. She sighed. Captivatingly she put on a woebegone expression and handed him the paper. It was a copy of the original bequest to Sancho López. Jason, studying it, thought of old proud Señora López and her long-kept secret.

"We should have thought of looking two days ago," he said.

"You are not angry with me?" She was sure he would be. The existence of that copy pointed most unhappily to her obstinacy. A little pride was one thing, any man would permit that; obstinacy was another. Her grandmother had always said that pride could burnish a woman's spirit, obstinacy render her solitary.

"Angry with you?" Jason looked up from the paper. "Except for a little trick or two, I stand on the sidelines in all this. All the same," he said, "we should still have looked."

"You are not on the sidelines, you are our friend," protested Isabella. "But who could have imagined my grandfather would have signed away land, land that he loved, to Sancho López?"

"He signed it away in love," said Jason. Isabella stared. "Your grandfather loved Señora López. I fancy that when she was young she was very beautiful. Her eyes tell you that, don't you think? But your grandfather, I imagine, was the heir then to Cordova—and marriage to a Mexican girl of little standing was impossible."

Astonished, Isabella gasped, "In love with Señora López?"

"Señorita, she wasn't always as she is now."

"No. But, Jason—señor—my grandfather—if you had known him—"

"I've seen his portrait. Tufted old white eagle, and fierce. That's it, isn't it? But he wasn't always like that, you know. He too had young blood once. Let me explain—but I think you must keep it all to yourself, as Señora López has since the time it happened." He told her of his conversation with the old lady, of the reason why the gift was made to Sancho, how the original document was destroyed and a new one made. Isabella listened without interruption. With her eyes on his face, she thought how absorbing he was, and how Philip, who must be years older, was not yet out of boyishness. "So, there you are," said Jason at the end. "All has been said for Señora López and her son. What do you think now?"

"Oh, you are a pleasure to listen to, even though every word has gone against me," she said impulsively.

"Señorita? That's hardly important, is it?"

"It has its little place in the scheme of things, and therefore I would not myself cast it aside," she said.

"Señorita—"

"Yes, I know. My grandfather. I can only say that for him to make a gift of such a priceless piece of land—when he loved all of Cordova—is difficult for me to take in."

"Perhaps he thought her love was just as priceless. She's a fine old lady."

"But why did he not make her a gift of money?"

Jason appeared to regard her as if she owned a lack of imagination that would have been remarkable even in a five-year-old. Isabella bit her lip.

"Perhaps, señorita," he explained carefully, "she did not ask for or want money. Perhaps she did not ask for anything. Perhaps he himself insisted on making this gift to her son. It's what a man of honour might have done."

"Señor, I beg you," she said with a rueful smile. "Please do not give me another look, but it is money she is asking for now."

"Not for herself, Isabella." Her name came naturally enough to please her. For once she liked the sound of it very much. "It's for her son. She knows land is of no use to Sancho. He doesn't have it in him to make it work for him. Señora López herself is poor, but she's a woman with memories, and they mean a lot more to her than land or dollars. She's come to a practical turn of mind in regard to Sancho, however, and sees no reason why he shouldn't have a few dollars for himself."

"If only my grandfather had told the family, or at least told me," said Isabella. "Señor, he confided in me so much, and was always more to me than my father was ever. I loved him dearly."

"Then you'll understand that what he shared with Señora López was for themselves alone. I doubt if even Sancho knows who his real father was. You must keep the secret, as Señora López kept it."

"Yet she told you, a stranger. Why you? I wonder."

"Perhaps because she knew I loved her," said Jason with a little smile.

"Señor?" Isabella looked like a woman suspended in dumb-founded limbo.

"Well, it was just a little something between us. We took to each other after an uncertain opening, I think. So I told her I

~ 153 ~

loved her and she gave me a poke with her stick—figuratively, that is."

Isabella's curls themselves seemed to dance with laughter.

"Was it painful figuratively, señor?"

"Bearable," said Jason. "Señorita, you must now buy what belongs to Sancho if you wish to retain that piece of land. You must be graciously repentant of your obstinacy."

She did not like that word, nor his readiness to apply it to her. It made her wince a little. Her pride rushed back, but she caught his eye and managed to think before speaking.

"You are right, yes," she said, "and I will be very repentant. But there is Colonel Hendriks—he still has an option."

"We hope to make him relinquish that." He explained how, which made her realise he had done much thinking for everybody. "And then you, señorita, will offer four thousand dollars and Sancho will hand the document to you."

"But they asked for only two thousand before."

"Four thousand is now very fair, I think. Don't you?"

"I fear, from the way you have engaged with me so far, that it would be no use thinking otherwise," said Isabella. "I will promise four thousand dollars, then. That amount will gild my graciousness, will it not?"

"Sancho will think so."

"It will be your victory," conceded Isabella. "Why have you done all this for Señora López and me?"

"I had nothing else on hand," said Jason, "and there's still our frustrated American friend to deal with."

That was not the answer she wanted. She said, "I am in your debt now. But why are you really here? It cannot be that you just wish to meet my father. Is it because you are looking for land? If so, I will take you all over Cordova and show you where you may grow cotton, or raise cattle, and I too could make a gift of— That is not said to offend you, to imply there is a fee to be paid, it is only said because you are a very good friend."

"You'd part with a slice of Cordova?" he asked.

"For you I might," she said, and colour came to tint her.

"I'm obliged," said Jason, with what she thought was the strangest smile, "but thank you, no. I belong to Dorset in England. And now I must take up no more of your time, you have your guests."

She had not realised that almost an hour had flown. They had argued, almost quarrelled, and then they had talked. And she had been absorbed.

"But you will stay a little longer, take some refreshment?" she said.

"It would be an intrusion," said Jason. "*Adiós*, señorita."

"*Adiós*, señor," she said, a little stiffly, and when he had gone wondered if he would be casual enough to forget to come tomorrow.

Later that day she sat with Luisa and their guests in the shade of the patio. They drank coffee. Philip, already comfortably established in the way of a guest who knows himself to be popular, had the brandy decanter at his elbow. Isabella watched him, wondering where love's sweet dream had gone. She was unaccountably restless, though not bored. Fernando was an engaging young man who made up for the egoistic perambulations of Philip, and Luisa had her own endearing little fund of words. All the same, Isabella was restless. She would have liked to ride, to have galloped with her vaqueros and let the warm wind rush at her face. But Philip and Fernando had already ridden for more than two days, and had further riding in front of them tomorrow.

So she had to sit and become more restless.

"The Englishman," said Philip suddenly, "who is he?"

"A friend," said Luisa without apology.

"A close friend?" said Fernando, smiling at her.

"A good friend," said Luisa.

"He's been acting for us, Philip. I told you," said Isabella. "It's almost settled now. But yes, he is a good friend." Except that he had casually dismissed what many other men would have stood on their heads for, a piece of fine Cordova land. That rankled. "We're showing him something of Cordova tomorrow."

"Then be careful not to let his horse run off with him," said Philip, "or he'll lose himself."

"I think not," said Isabella. "He isn't the kind of man to let a horse take control of him."

Philip smiled as if the angels had enlightened him.

"He's impressed you, Isabella," he said.

"He's just a man," replied Isabella casually, and Luisa looked at her and smiled.

"How long has he been in Texas?" asked Philip, studying his brandy with the benevolence of a connoisseur.

"Oh, he's just been wandering, I think," said Luisa.

"They do wander, the English," said Philip. "Mostly into other people's provinces. The difficulty then is to make them wander out again."

"It isn't only the English who do that," said Isabella. "They're no worse than the rest of us."

"Goodness, Isabella," said Luisa, for that was the first time her sister had said a kind word about those pirates from Britain.

"Well, we should be fair," said Isabella.

"Oh, fair by all means," said Philip, "but ridiculous, no. What of their thieving ways, sweet Isabella?"

"I'm assured the worst of their freebooters is dead."

"I'm willing to leave it at that," said Fernando equably.

"And I," said Luisa.

"Has he come to look for land?" asked Philip.

"No," said Isabella, disliking the slight bickering note of the conversation.

"He says he's come to meet my father," said Luisa.

"From England? All the way from England to meet your father?" Philip's laughter spread itself generously. "What is he after, then, a keen game of cards?"

Isabella smiled, but not at Philip's remark. She was thinking about Jason declaring his love for old Señora López. A soft little laugh escaped her and her eyes became reflective and dreamy.

She heard Fernando say, "Perhaps he's looking for a wife. If so, he's come to the right place—except that I'll watch very carefully where his eye lands."

Luisa pinked.

"Well, if ever a crisis is compounded," said Philip, "call on me, for I've my own little ways of tickling the English."

Isabella heard but did not comment.

Luisa said, "Don't be silly."

"Ah, but one never knows with the English," said Philip.

"When you were in Europe did you go to England?" asked Luisa.

"Did I? Yes, I did," said Philip, "and now I think I know it well."

"Do you?" murmured Isabella.

"It has one particular fault," said Philip.

"What fault is that?" asked Luisa.

"England, alas," said Philip, "is full of the English."

His laughter grated on Isabella.

# 14

Colonel Hendriks had not dressed with a Richmond grandeur; that might have ostentatiously outshone the guest. So he was soberly attired in a coat of dark grey faced with black brocade, trousers a shade lighter, and a white silk shirt modest in its ruffles. Lisbet presented herself in lilac. Jason arrived in his well-worn coat and trousers, all he had in addition to his practical travelling clothes. But Lisbet still thought he looked as if he might offer something more than the raw muscular bravado that was such a quality among the adventurous Americans of Texas. The husky aura of the Texan male—compounded of courage, hair, strength, and drive—and the awesome indestructibility of the enduring women, fascinated her, as did their gift for making one word do the work of twelve. Lisbet, as the Colonel's daughter, had frequently encountered this gift when trying to make homesteaders and other folk feel there was communication between the Hendrikses and them.

"Your home is real sweet, Miz Buckle. Have you been here long?"

"Nope."

"All the same, you surely have made things look pretty. Are all your family with you?"

"Can't tell."

"Oh? Why not?"

"Ain't counted 'em lately."

"It really is nice seeing new people settling in Westboro. We fondly hope you and your family will help us build a fine, prosperous county."

"Ain't stayin'."

"Oh, that makes me so sorry. Are you finding things unsatisfactory?"

"We ain't, hogs is."

"What's wrong?"

"Ain't had one sucker in eight months."

Could one hold a conversation with Jason Rawlings? Seeing he was from the old country, he could surely talk. He had talked enough in the courtroom, a pest on him.

"I'm delighted you could come, sir," said the Colonel.

"Kind of you," said Jason, "but I must allow you some reservations."

"Indeed you must," said Lisbet, "going against us as you did, seeing we're cousins and all."

"The British and Americans are cousins?" said Jason.

"It can't be denied, sir," said Lisbet, "nor would it be by Virginians, who owe so much to Sir Walter Raleigh." She had not been the greatest scholar at the Charleston academy, but history had interested her hugely. "Fie, sir, how could you twist poor Sancho's ears as you did, and put Pa in a mighty fret?"

"I'll speak for myself," said the Colonel. "I'm not beaten, only delayed."

"You'll bring up reinforcements?" said Jason.

"You mean qualified witnesses?"

"You'll not get Sancho's grant legalised otherwise."

"Rely on it, Mr. Rawlings," said the Colonel. "I'll re-engage one way or another. Shall we sit outside for a while and enjoy a drink before we dine?"

They went through the rambling house to the long timbered back porch which overlooked the great landscape of cotton. Cloud galaxies hung in fat white clusters high in the west. Below the billows of white, the blue of the evening sky was retreating before the advent of flushed gold. The pasture ground, fenced by split rails, was empty of animals except for those few horses not yet willing to be stabled, who stood in rolling-eyed suspicion of hovering black stable hands. At the slightest movement, the animals frisked away.

Joe the butler came out to see about drinks. Lisbet favoured fresh homemade lemonade with a dash of orange liqueur. The Colonel pressed Jason to try a planter's brew, Bourbon mint julep. Jason did, and when it came and he had taken a mouthful, he found himself thinking that if any whisky was worthy of its name it was a pity not to let it stand up for itself.

Lisbet was southern rose-pink. In Virginia it had been a social sin of almost heinous proportions to let the sun kiss one's skin. Yet in Texas the greater freedoms she enjoyed were inducing her to lift her face to the sun, and some gold had crept into her rose-pink. She was a slumbrous, feline creature, thought Jason, and though lacking the enchantment of Antoinette and the lustrous beauty of Isabella, might be considered an engaging tigress by some. Lazily her lashes stirred, drooped, lifted, and the glowing light of evening touched her eyes. Her lips curved under his regard and her teeth glinted.

"I presume," said the Colonel in his fruity drawl, "that as advocate for Cordova you'll not wish to discuss the dispute out of court?"

Jason could have pointed out that the case was not now what the Colonel thought it was. But he only said, "If there are any new developments which you fancy would advance Señorita Cordova's interests, I'd not stop you from mentioning them."

"Mr. Rawlings, have you no shame?" asked Lisbet.

"I lack a lawyer's more rigid scruples," said Jason quite truthfully.

"Oh, you were at poor Sancho López with no scruples at all yesterday," she said, "and set me biting the fingers off my gloves. Paper watermarks, oh fiddledeedee, sir."

"But relevant, all the same," said Jason. He observed two men on horseback in the distance, riding into the sunset. The Colonel followed his gaze.

"My eyes and ears, Mr. Rawlings," he said. "I've recently taken them on. I need boundary riders on a place this size to look and listen for predators."

"Predators?"

"Redskins, sir."

"They come to eat your cotton?" asked Jason politely.

"They'll come for anything," said the Colonel.

Joe came out again and handed the Colonel a letter. He opened it and read it. It seemed fairly brief, but it made the blood rush to his face.

"Pa?" said Lisbet, coming out of her dreamy speculations concerning their guest. Jason at once sensed she was her father's daughter, that what touched the Colonel touched her, that when he used his teeth she would stand with him and use her claws. Her father got up, his mouth set, his eyes choleric.

"I've got to ride out," he said. "You'll excuse me, Mr. Rawlings, but there's something I've got to settle right now."

"Pa," protested Lisbet, "I'm to dine alone with Mr. Rawlings?" But it was less a protest than an inquisitory feeler as to the reason for this turn of events.

"I regret it, apologise for it, but I can't help it." Again the Colonel said, "You'll excuse me, Mr. Rawlings." Then he strode away. Jason looked thoughtfully after him. He knew what was in the letter.

Lisbet's burning curiosity slipped its anchor and sailed away as Joe came to announce that supper was ready to be served. She waltzed into the dining room in a mood of intrigued anticipation, for she had a captive audience. She enjoyed her meal and made an exceptionally good job of ignoring Esmeralda, who, from a stubbornly entrenched position by the huge sideboard, played the role of chaperone with muttering resolution.

Lisbet was able to talk indeed, finding Jason a cool, reflective participant in conversation that never once touched on the boring bounty of the land, or the tiresome problems brought about by slaves who only bent their backs when the overseer was about. With Jason she discussed the consequences of the social straitjacket imposed on women by the strict conventions of Virginia.

"I do declare it's a backward state," she said, "for it surely does suffocate ladies. In desperation, Mr. Rawlings, some break free and act like beings so intoxicated that in no time they're down with born white trash."

"I congratulate you, Miss Hendriks, on escaping that."

"You are cool in your judgements, sir, very cool." The tip of her pink tongue caressed her bottom lip. "Tell me, what social rules are imposed on the ladies of London?"

"Which class of ladies?"

"I mean ladies of respectability, Mr. Rawlings."

"It's expected of them that they protect their respectability by committing their indiscretions in circumstances of unbreachable privacy. It parallels the French mode—except that in France it's called a laudable way of ordering social behaviour, and in England it's called hypocrisy. Either way, it enables the participants to enjoy the best of both worlds—if one accepts that it is the best."

"Mr. Rawlings, I surely think London is the place for a lady," she said with pleasure, "though I confess that were I lovingly attached to a gentleman—"

A mutter of outrage emanated so fiercely from Esmeralda that Lisbet hastily rectified her grievous error.

"—to my husband, sir, then I'd be undeviatingly faithful."

Jason's eyes grew bleakly stony as Lisbet went purringly on in a way that proclaimed she had all the makings of another Edwina. Esmeralda's face became rigid with shame and anger. Lisbet changed course and asked Jason what he thought about the great George Washington.

"A wooden revolutionary," said Jason, not given to being generously forgiving towards those who had damned and defamed the Redcoats in all ways. For it was the Redcoats, in his estimation, who had made Canada and America safe at last.

"Washington is dismissed like that?" Lisbet was taunting. "I declare you out of order, sir."

"No great flair as a soldier, even less as a general. Quite without imagination."

Lisbet's smooth, moist mouth parted in a sleepy smile of challenge.

"You're speaking, Mr. Rawlings, I think, as one who still feels sorely bruised by the licking Washington's troops gave to such as Burgoyne and Cornwallis."

"I am bruised, Miss Hendriks," said Jason with dangerous calm, "by biased interpretations of history."

"Mr. Rawlings, you all were licked."

Jason sighed. Esmeralda was burning to box Lisbet's ears.

"Are you entertaining me to supper, or endeavouring to provoke me?" asked Jason.

Lisbet's eyes opened wide.

"Mr. Rawlings, I declare I'm only opening a discussion. I'm fascinated by our great Americans, by Washington and Adams and Captain Lawrence and such, and wish to know what you think of them."

"You choose figures made greater by adulation than by achievement. Washington, for all the immense advantages of fighting on his home ground, would have failed without the help of the French. Your general was only fighting one war; the British were fighting two. Captain Lawrence, a fair figure of courage, I grant you, attacked Captain Broke with a heavier ship and a greater crew and lost the battle in minutes."

"He died a hero, sir—"

"Who made an incompetent assessment of the situation."

"—and if I may say so, General Washington's fight against British tyranny was a miracle of endeavour, sir."

She was in confident possession of the advantage, she thought, for the fact remained that the British had been beaten.

"Madam," said Jason, "you are a simpleton. There was no more benevolent tyranny. The revolution was mounted by riffraff and fastened on to by people like John Hancock, a pretty figure of innocence and victimisation in his smuggling activities, I must say."

That snapped her self-satisfied repose.

"I denounce your pettiness, sir!" she said, and sat up furiously. "Why, never did I hear any man so out of sense or good judgement. With taxation without representation, sir, you imposed monstrous and unjust burdens on the American people."

"Do you give representation to your Indians?"

"Indians? Pooh!"

"Madam, when you insist on opening a discussion you should first acquaint yourself with the facts of the subject, instead of indulging in the fantasies that come from wishful thinking."

Lisbet waved her napkin at him like a battle flag. Esmeralda moved and snatched it from her, and slammed it down on the table. Lisbet, heated, took no notice.

"I don't indulge in any fantasies, sir, but the truth!"

"Indeed?" he said, and she had never looked into colder eyes. "Well, you have succeeded, madam, in making the truth sound like rubbish. I would not describe the fantasy of monstrous burdens as anything but rubbish at its most infantile."

Lisbet could have scratched his eyes out.

"Sir," she cried, "where are your manners?"

"Gone, I fancy," he said, "in search of your intelligence—and for all the success they'll have, will probably never return to me."

She swooped to her feet, her lilac gown rustling around her agitated body.

"Mr. Rawlings, you may go, sir!"

Jason eyed her in disgust. Esmeralda broke in.

"Now, Miss Lisbet—"

"Be quiet! Sir," she declaimed to Jason, "I have asked you to leave, do you hear me?"

"I'm satisfied," said Jason, on his feet. "I should say, however, that the discussions which you turn into arguments, madam, are always likely to enter the hurly-burly. And if you can't stomach the hurly-burly, young lady, you should confine yourself to embroidery."

Lisbet bit off a scream.

"I vow you the most offensive creature I have ever met!"

"Miss Lisbet, Miss Lisbet!" Esmeralda was shocked and ashamed.

"Good night, Miss Hendriks," said Jason. "Good night, Esmeralda." He spared the agitated mammy a smile, and then took himself off so unconcernedly that Lisbet completely forgot every ladylike quality she was supposed to have. She shouted after him:

"When you meet the devil, Mr. Rawlings, he surely will know you for one of his own!"

She stormed about the dining room, kicking at her gown and underskirts and talking wildly to herself. Esmeralda followed her angrily around, scolding.

"I've never heard the like. I done told you that ain't no way for a lady to carry on—talkin' that way with a gennleman. I fair took sick an' died listening to you aimin' to get him meaner'n the devil hisself. I've never—"

"Meralda, you shut up, you hear me? I'm not going to have a man speak to me like that!"

"Miss Lisbet," said Esmeralda crossly, "you all done prompted him to, an' I come near to boxin' your ears myself."

"I don't care! No gentleman should so far forget his manners as to insult his hostess as he did—oh, I could scratch his nose off his face!"

"Miss Lisbet, I knows you," said Esmeralda, shaking a furious finger at her charge. "I knows you good, an' I reckon when it comes to manners there's times when you disremember you ever had any."

Lisbet turned smouldering eyes on her mammy.

"Meralda, I declare I don't know whether I could love that man like a crazy woman or hate him worse than a polecat."

"Señor Hendriks," said Señora López, her lamp casting its moving light and shadows, "that is the figure."

"Not the one we agreed, you old harridan," said Colonel Hendriks, shoving the letter in front of her nose. "This figure bears no relation to the original, and I'll not have it, you hear?"

"The price, señor, is the one set down in that letter."

"The hell it is."

"The land," she said, "has increased in value."

"Sixfold? Sixfold?" He glared at her. "And backed by a document shown to be dubious? I won't be played for a monkey, by God. What sets your new price, eh?"

"Many more Americanos are entering Texas, señor."

"So, yuh'd play them off against me, would you? With that worthless document?"

"It is not worthless, señor." The light set shadows flickering around her eyes.

"There's a witness to say you hold genuine title?"

"There is no witness, señor, and the document is not dubious in my mind."

"It is in the eyes of the law," said the Colonel lividly.

She met his angry look with the dispassion of the aged.

"The eyes of the law, señor, are not my eyes," she said.

"I don't give a damn for your eyes, old Mex. I'm not prepared to purchase from you and then find myself in dispute with Cordova. You get hold of Herman Schumaker and get him to fight the case for you in Houston. If you win I'll raise my offer to five thousand."

"The price, señor, is twenty-five thousand—and on the document as it stands."

"The hell it is, I tell you!" shouted the Colonel. "Don't you know a deed of transfer couldn't be drawn up without the necessary adjustments being made to the Cordova deeds? Get that into your head, woman. Is Isabella Cordova going to come dancing to our tune? I tell you, I'll only purchase when the law finds in your favour."

She sat quite still, her back straight, her eyes unblinking.

"Then Sancho will sell to someone else, señor," she said, "who-ever will buy."

"At that price and on that document, no one will buy, you hear me?"

"I do not ask you to give up your option, señor."

"I'm damn sure you don't," he growled, "but I wasn't born in a chicken shed. You crafty old hag, do you think you can bluff me into agreeing to a new price if I want to retain my option? Any option on that worthless piece of paper doesn't rate a nickel."

"I do not ask you to give it up," she said again, "but the price—"

"Twenty-five thousand dollars?" He brandished the letter in her face, shaking it under her nose once more. "I don't aim to fall for that. I've been generous with you—I could have told you the mo-ment Judge Conner declared the case held over that you owned a parcel of nothing. I could have torn up my option then for all the good it was. But I didn't, I was willing to give you time to get new evidence. You know I want that land and you're aiming to squeeze me; but I'm not buying pie in the sky. By God, there's my option." He took a paper from his pocket, smacked it against the letter, and shredded them both. "And tell Sancho I'll see the pair of you hanged before I'll let either of you play cat and mouse with me again." He flung the shreds into her lap.

"*Adiós*, señor," she said.

"No one will buy," he said, "because no one in Westboro County is going to step on my toes."

"*Adiós*, señor," she said again, for no other words were neces-sary.

# 15

"Oh, madame, it is charming, charming," said Antoinette.

Sarah Blazey allowed herself a stiff smile. Her little parlour, with its lace-curtained windows overlooking the cobbled street, was a picture of neat order and cleanliness. Nothing that could be polished was less than shining, nothing that was white looked less than pristine. And even the small child shone. She was two and a half and quite the neatest little bundle of goodness and clean white clothes. Clothes, in fact, almost smothered her. She wore everything a child should, including a bonnet. She was pretty and she was shy, and she was very good in the way she stood perfectly still, without a single fidget, not even of her fingers.

Sarah Blazey, a woman of thirty-five, took motherhood and housewifery seriously and conscientiously. In the presence of an appreciative visitor a little gratification was permissible.

"I reckon to keep my home as it should be kept," she said, "so's if folks had to eat their food off the floor no one would complain at eating off mine."

"It is so pretty," said Antoinette, gently and intuitively striking at the heart of gratification in the stiffly disciplined breast. "So refined."

"Children should grow up amid piety and cleanliness," said Mrs. Blazey.

"Oh, so true, madame. Here is a little one so clean and pious she is already an angel." And Antoinette smiled at the child, who looked up into the hugely bright eyes, earnest to impart love and laughter, and the child, who had lacked for nothing in all other things, stared in wonder.

"We have given her everything we have given our own," said Mrs. Blazey. She too wore a bonnet. She always did for visitors. She felt most suitably complete to receive them then. "She is as healthy as they are, and as good."

Antoinette thought of good soldiers, good soldiers on parade, moving not a muscle while an officer inspected them, a kind but stern officer who expected immediate obedience to his commands. How lovely she was, and with eyes surely as green as her mother's. But unless the child was told to, she would not even smile.

"Madame, she is very good indeed," said Antoinette. She supposed she herself might smile, and did. It was a smile full of respect and admiration. Mrs. Blazey received it with a stiff little nod of her head, modestly acknowledging it as her due.

"You may leave us now, child," she said, and the little one bobbed her bonnet to Antoinette, and left the room like a dainty, overdressed, and well-controlled marionette.

"You have been a good mother to her, madame," said Antoinette, "and her father will be grateful."

"Her father?" Mrs. Blazey's pleasant but humourless face was plainly sceptical.

"Her mother's husband," said Antoinette. It was her second visit to the little brick house on the cobbled Baltimore street. Yesterday, after days of searching in company with the invaluable Dillman Farquhar, she had located this domain of Mr. and Mrs. Blazey. She knocked, Mrs. Blazey answered, and Antoinette explained she was calling on the instructions of Monsieur Rawlings, the husband of Clare's mother. She handed over the letter Jason had written. Sarah Blazey read it and listened to further words from Antoinette. She declined, however, to produce the child until she had discussed the matter with her husband, a good and pious man, who worked for one of the tobacco exporters at the docks. She and Mr. Blazey had agreed to take the child and bring her up, for which they were to expect one hundred dollars a year, payable in advance. They had received the first payment and the second, but the third payment was well overdue. Antoinette at once offered to make the outstanding payment, but Mrs. Blazey said she would first discuss that with her husband too.

Now, today, Antoinette had been received and the child produced. It appeared that Mr. Blazey, having seen the letter, accepted that its content indicated a knowledge by Mr. Rawlings of the truth, and that his concern for the future of the child was genuine. Discussion on this could therefore take place, as long as it was understood no decision could be made that was not approved by the foster parents.

It was obvious to Antoinette that Sarah Blazey was not disposed to hand Clare over on the strength of Monsieur Rawlings' letter alone. It had been apparent yesterday, and although she had produced the child today, her reticence still remained. Having piously accepted the responsibility of bringing Clare up, she most likely deemed it her Christian duty to ensure that Antoinette's mission was not in the nature of monkey business. Antoinette understood that, and had the good sense to dress herself in black again. This mark of respect for the child's dead mother—a poor, misguided woman, said Mrs. Blazey, but a woman for all that— did not go unnoticed. Her gloves Antoinette kept on. She knew that Maryland people would not fail to guess why her fingernails did not have similar tints to theirs. She also knew she had a need to be careful, tactful, and patient if she were to win the Blazeys over.

"Is the mother's husband the father?" asked Mrs. Blazey.

"It is his wish to be," said Antoinette. "The natural father has disappeared."

"From the eyes of the people, perhaps," said Mrs. Blazey, "but not from the eyes of the Lord. The Lord will call on such a man, wherever he is, and lay His just wrath upon him for the sinner he is."

Antoinette thought of her years in the convent and the multitude of sins she had been earnestly instructed to avoid, and how she had sometimes wondered if even the Virgin Mary could remain immaculate, so great and numerous were the temptations of the universe.

"Madame," she said, "I am sure that Monsieur Rawlings will, in his care for the child, do much to redeem the sins of the father."

Sarah Blazey considered that sentiment while shrewdly regarding the speaker, a young woman of striking grace.

"You're French?" she said.

"Creole, madame."

Sarah Blazey did not think too much of the Creoles, but was charitable enough to allow for exceptions.

"Your parents?"

"Alas," said Antoinette sadly.

"I'm sorry." Mrs. Blazey's expression softened a fraction. "But if I recollect rightly, dying in New Orleans comes easier than living."

Antoinette, who had quickly discovered that the sanitation systems in Baltimore were little better than those of her native city, accepted the implied disparagement.

"Alas, madame."

"According to Mr. Rawlings, you're to have charge of the child."

"I am to be governess and nurse, madame. I am in modest circumstances, and Monsieur Rawlings in his goodness has offered me the post. It is not possible to improve the care you have given her, but I shall not betray this care, I assure you. I shall do all I can to see that she stays as sweet and good as she is now. Madame, she is such a credit to you, as Monsieur Rawlings will see for himself when he arrives."

"When will that be?" asked Mrs. Blazey.

"Truthfully, I cannot give an exact time. But when he does arrive and speaks with you, I am sure you will not be disappointed in him."

"The child was born to his wife, but he's not the father. Hm," said Mrs. Blazey. "But he wishes to have her. Is this why I won't be disappointed in him?"

Antoinette could have given a thousand words why, but only said, "His is a Christian act, isn't it?"

Mrs. Blazey pursed her lips, then said with stilted formality, "Will you take tea, Miss Giraud?"

Giraud was the name Antoinette had given at the convent and which she was using again. She had never taken tea. Tea, to the Creoles of New Orleans, was a poison only fit for the stomachs of the British. She braced herself for the trial.

"Thank you, madame, yes."

Mrs. Blazey looked almost pleased. She was proud of her brew. Tea had been out of favour in America for many years after the incident in Boston; and those who liked it had great difficulty in procuring it, and even drew disfavour from brewing it. It was reckoned that tea drinkers had British sympathies. Liberty had its paradoxes. For the liberty to drink tea and the liberty to frown on the tea drinkers were unable to coexist comfortably. However, a small reconciliation had come about.

They took tea. Rapport of a formal kind had been established. As for the beverage, Antoinette was astonished that people could punish themselves so unnecessarily, and took each mouthful with her eyes shut. Mrs. Blazey, presiding over a large brown pot, confessed that she alone liked tea. Mr. Blazey would not touch it, nor the children.

"It is most refreshing," said Antoinette bravely. "Madame, it is a sensitive subject, money, but there is this amount which is owed you. Has your husband said we may discuss it?"

"Mr. Blazey has said we don't rightly aspire to close the wrong doors. It may be discussed."

"I am happy, madame. I have Monsieur Rawlings' permission to make acceptable arrangements, and even if the child is given into my care in a short while, I think it only fair to make payment for the full year. That is agreeable?"

"I don't reckon we can take what we won't earn, Miss Giraud."

"Well," said Antoinette with firm nicety, "in my consideration you have earned it."

Mrs. Blazey hemmed a little and demurred a little, but in the end agreed to accept fifty dollars due for the six months gone. Since the child was in the melting pot at the moment, she said, discussion of any other monies should be left. So Antoinette gave her the fifty dollars and they parted on terms of mutual respect.

Antoinette called again the following day, when she met Clare for the second time. This time, for a few minutes longer. The child's behaviour was so intensely good and obedient that Antoinette suspected piety reigned so absolute in the house that it had banished every kind of appealing little mischief dear to the hearts of all children. It could not be said, however, that Clare looked as if she lacked care or attention. Only, thought Antoinette, a little happy natural love and warmth. Yes, warmth. The house itself seemed stiff with starch. However, some progress with the foster parents had surely been made, for Mrs. Blazey said she had further consulted with Mr. Blazey and Mr. Blazey had said that if he could be sure Clare was to be given a good home in England then he saw no objection to this. He would like to meet the prospective governess who was acting for Mr. Rawlings.

They met on Sunday, when the Blazeys had returned from church and after Antoinette had attended Mass. Mr. Blazey was a round-eyed, portly gentleman, fussy in his habits and frisky in his manner. He liked the children to sit still but he himself was forever flapping his coattails or pushing his thumbs into his waistcoat and rising and falling on the balls of his feet. But he was not unkind, and his piety was less industrious than his wife's. He admonished their children sternly enough at her behest, but sometimes at the end of a lecture he would smuggle a sweet to each of them.

He was frankly taken aback when he met Antoinette, and almost stood rigidly still on the balls of his feet. She was not his idea of a governess at all. She was his idea of all that was sweet and beautiful in a young lady. Her first smile captivated him. He could not summon up the faintest negative. He talked with her for a long time, then went out of the room and returned with

Clare in his arms. Mrs. Blazey looked on as he transferred the child, placing her in Antoinette's arms.

"You need to get to know each other and to like each other," he said.

"M'sieu, oh, that is kind," said Antoinette emotionally. He and Mrs. Blazey left the room. Antoinette gave the child a misty smile. Clare gazed at her silently.

"Oh, sweet one," said Antoinette, and kissed her.

Clare blushed. "I am good," she said.

"Good? Oh, *ma petite ange!*" Antoinette laughed and hugged the warm body.

Clare blinked, she smiled, and she cuddled closer.

# 16

Ponderously the steers ran before the mounted vaqueros. The dust rose in clouds. The cows bawled. No bony Texas longhorns, these, but the heavy, meaty cattle of Mexican strain, as wild in their way as the mustangs of the vaqueros. Jason smelt them through the blue scarf that covered his nose and mouth. The odour of the lumbering beasts was strong. The heat and the dust assailed him. He watched as the vaqueros, dark heads dust-covered, dark faces glistening, kept the rounded-up strays, the mavericks, heading westwards to rejoin the main herds on the plains of Cordova. Sombreros whirled in flailing hands, whips in some, and the grassy rolling range trembled to the thunder of galloping horses and running cattle. The sun laid a shimmering furnace over the waving grasses, and Jason thought again of another kind of grass, richly green and cool, and air laden with soft moisture.

Isabella and Luisa rode up to him. Spanish though they were by blood, they were Texans, born to the sun and the wind, and to the grasses that stood as high as the tail of a running pony. Isabella, in her black habit and round, brimmed hat, had the heat of the day on her face and the exhilaration of the teeming outdoors in her eyes. Luisa, in brown habit, had all the animation of her youth and health.

Isabella, slipping her scarf from her mouth, looked at Jason with laughing enquiry. She was not restless now, she was filled with *joie de vivre* and patently eager to know whether he was sharing some part of it. They had spent the morning riding the valleys, watching the vaqueros round up the strays, and now they were on the range. Jason was sitting Napoleon in his relaxed way, and she thought to herself: Here is a man for Texas, here is a man who might have been born of the country.

"What do you think now, señor?" She was beginning to call him Jason at times. At other times she reverted to the formal address, because when all was said and done she was Spanish, with the traditional sense of reserve and propriety.

"The grass is yellow," said Jason.

"That is all you think, the grass is yellow?" laughed Isabella, gloriously alive.

"It's the gold of Texas," said Luisa, watching her sister, whose eyes turned so often on the man who had come wandering in on Cordova.

"In Dorset, we'd make hay of it," said Jason.

"Are you complaining?" asked Isabella.

"No. Does it ever rain here?"

"Often, and when it does you have never seen such rain."

"How often is often?" he asked.

"Often is sometimes," said Luisa.

"Oh, twice a year at least," said Isabella.

"Señor, do you wish me to order you a thunderstorm?" said Luisa.

"Luisa," said Isabella, giving her mustang a little kick to quell its fidgets. "A thunderstorm might suit him well. He's a man for climatic extremes. A thunderstorm would be quite in keeping with the other elemental visitations he's experienced in Texas."

"It would beat his head off," laughed Luisa.

Jason smiled. But he does not give much away, thought Isabella, he has secrets and keeps them all to himself. Is one of his secrets a woman?

That thought made a question leap to her lips, and she could not stay it.

"Jason, you have never said, do you have a wife?"

He was quite expressionless as he said, "I have no wife, se-ñorita."

Luisa, watching her sister again, saw her turn her head to look into the distance and so hide what that answer did to her.

The travelling clouds of dust, almost obscuring the disappearing steers and vaqueros, grew hazy golden rims. The noise lessened and the pungency of sweating animals on the move drifted west-wards with the dust clouds. To the right of the immediate range rose the hill known as Cerro Jorobado. Humpback Ridge. Cedars massed at its feet.

"Señor?" said Luisa, for Jason seemed far away. He was not so far, however. He was simply wondering what he was doing here, when it would have been much more sensible to be sitting and waiting in Westboro, involving himself with no one.

"I'm very impressed," he said.

Glowing with pleasure, Isabella said, "With everything?"

"Most of all with the way your vaqueros ride."

Isabella liked that, loved it. She was proud of the Cordova vaqueros, of their skill and their loyalty. And Jason spoke as a horseman himself, a cavalryman. It was a generous compliment.

"Our vaqueros? They are born in the saddle," she said, "and can count a running herd better when their feet are in the stirrups than when they are on the ground. You saw them at work round-ing up the strays. The herd instinct isn't total; some steers are al-ways breaking away. It's necessary to collect them as quickly as possible or they would soon be lost to us. The Americans have acquired an appetite for Cordova beef, but no inclination to pay for it."

"I doubt you mean all of them," said Jason.

"You think me prejudiced?" she said.

"I think, generally, they own to as much honesty as other peo-ples. And they have great vigour. It's lazy people who are light-fingered, Isabella."

"Oh, out there are light-fingered Americans," said Isabella, making a little face at him. But she did not want to argue with him, for she was sure he would not let her come out of it at all well. And she did not want to experience again the emotional dis-turbance she had felt when quarrelling with him in the study. "Are you hungry?" she smiled.

"I am," he said.

"*Bueno*. Please come." She wheeled her horse, waited for Jason to come alongside, and then began to canter with him, Luisa following. Isabella's mustang thought little of this form of progress in these wide-open spaces and flung its head about. Isabella thumped it with her boot, but she said, "Shall we ride, Jason?"

"How far?" he asked.

"Half a kilometre. Luisa, shall we ride?"

"*Olé!*" cried Luisa.

They rode, they galloped—and even though Luisa and Isabella sidesaddled, they were as adept as the vaqueros themselves. The warm wind blew at them and the grasses opened up for them. In exhilaration Isabella touched her mustang with her spurs. Her mount flew. Napoleon blew snorts and went in chase. Jason gave him his head. The old, long-legged cavalry horse thundered in the wake of the mustang, devouring the ground, and from behind Luisa cried, "*Olé, olé!*"

Isabella had offered their guest a toothy mustang but Jason preferred the horse he knew so well to one which might be disposed to give him a hammering. Mustangs, always temperamental, disliked the feel of any riders with whom they were not familiar.

Napoleon came through like a four-legged cannon, and Isabella laughed in breathless delight as she saw Jason ahead of her. Oh, he could ride. Texas must have him—Cordova must have him.

They reached the supply waggon. There José and Apulca stood watching the Mexican cook. Baking on a shelf in a small, mobile oven were thin flat cakes of maize flour, the Mexican bread called tortilla. A large iron pan was being heated on bricks surrounding a timber fire. On the arrival of the patroness, the cook put steaks into the pan.

The sisters dismounted. Jason slipped from Napoleon and found Isabella at his elbow. Her face was flushed, delight in her eyes.

"Oh, there is Spanish in you, see how dark you are," she said. "You were born of conquistadores, not of pirates. You are a horseman, not a sailor. Luisa, did you see him go?"

Luisa, getting her breath, said, "Well, he's a cavalryman—and his blood was up and I did not expect him to dawdle."

"Little squirrel, that is very grudging," said Isabella.

"No, I am at his feet with admiration," laughed Luisa. "Remember, it was I who found your new Cortez."

Isabella blushed like a sweetly stung girl. That was what she had called Philip when she had suffered her infatuation for him—a reborn Cortez. Luisa knew that, and now had a world of teasing in her smile.

"It's Napoleon's feet you must languish at, Luisa," said Jason. "He is the virtuoso, not I. I only sit him. All else is claimed by him in the matter of performance."

"There, a modest Cortez," said Luisa. "What do you think of that, Isabella!"

"Oh, shoo!" said Isabella, looking burningly beautiful. She fanned herself with her hat, and her uncovered hair gleamed in the sun.

Jason said, "It's hot." He needed to be prosaic. Isabella's beauty was becoming a little too obtrusive. He looked at the sizzling steaks.

"They will be served with chili," said Isabella. "It is the Mexican way. Meat and chili are inseparable. And I think you like tortilla, yes?"

That was fairly prosaic too. But Jason did not reply. José and Apulca had their eyes on the Cerro Jorobado, and he had followed their gaze. The sun-baked heights were so sharply defined in the clear light as to seem deceptively close. It was the size of the horsed figures on a lower ridge that corrected the perspective —though they were brightly outlined too. And they were very still. Thirty or more. Indians: the plumage of their feathered headdresses was tipped with white.

"Comanches," said José uneasily. The Comanches fought everyone—Mexicans, Spanish, Americans, Navaho and other Indians.

The cook looked up from the steaks. Isabella, hat back on, peered from under the brim.

"They are paying us a visit," she said, and took her hat off and waved it. Her gesture was not acknowledged. The horsed Comanches stayed silent and still. It seemed as if their silence spread. The sounds of the vaqueros and the drove of steers were swallowed by distance.

"Is there a musket?" asked Jason. "If so, fire it."

"Comanches will not attack Cordova," said Isabella, but Luisa was visibly uncertain. "They are only looking."

"You're more confident than I am," said Jason, "and a fired musket might bring back your vaqueros."

"Isabella, I dislike the way they are looking," said Luisa.

Isabella glanced at Apulca. The Navaho drew his finger across his throat. The Comanches were like carved equestrian statues up there on the ridge. The day seemed suddenly windless. Nothing stirred, not even the yellow grasses.

"A war party?" said Jason.

"But they have never made war on Cordova," said Isabella.

"Señorita, bring back your vaqueros," he said. "Those Comanches look as if they're only waiting until your men are out of sight and hearing. They can see the drive from up there, I fancy."

Apulca primed the musket he always carried and fired it out of hand. The ball seared the bright air and the report boomed and echoed. The Comanches did not move. Apulca reloaded the gun.

"Señoritas, ride back to the house," said José.

"Well, we will all go," said Isabella.

"Señorita, with great respect," said José, "no. If we all ride they will catch us. You must go, with Señorita Luisa. We must stay to give you time."

Isabella paled, Luisa shivered.

"No," said Isabella faintly, "it will mean you may all—"

"You must go," said Jason. "José is right."

"No," gasped Isabella, and there was anguish now in her voice. José reached into the waggon and brought out muskets. "No," said Isabella again.

The Comanches began to move, picking their way down over the rocky slopes, moving one behind the other in single file. They were deliberate, purposeful. Apulca looked at Jason, then gestured at Isabella. Jason nodded and Isabella cried out as he lifted her from her feet, carried her swiftly to her horse, and set her on it. Luisa ran to her own mount. She knew what was to happen. Jason and their servants would do what they could to give her and Isabella time to get safely away. It was an hour's ride back to the house.

"Jason, no—I will not, I will not!" cried Isabella, frantic with fright for him and her servants. She had not believed there was any real threat until Apulca had drawn his finger across his throat.

"Go," said Jason tersely, unhitching the mustang and throwing the reins into her hands. He smote the horse and it went. Luisa followed. They must make as much distance as possible in the beginning, must reach the house in time to send help. In time? An hour? Jason and the others would be dead well before then. But Luisa rode urgently, Isabella frantically.

Apulca, slinging his musket, untied his horse from the waggon. His leaping ascent into the saddle was effortless. The Comanches were riding down the lower slopes, a weaving band of braves, heading for the massed cedars below. Apulca pointed to the west, touched his musket, and dug in his heels. The dry grass flew aside as he went in pursuit of the cattle drive. That left Jason, José, and the cook. The cook, Gonzales, was a fat man—but as difficult as a mountain to knock down.

"Señor," said José, "the vaqueros ride with their ears full of noise. So Apulca has gone to carry his musket thunder closer. Then perhaps they may hear him in time."

"Yes, I understood that, José."

They tied the horses behind the waggon. Jason loosened the sabre in the scabbard hanging from Napoleon's saddle. The cook gave out the muskets José had unloaded from the waggon. It was a major principle of survival; the carrying of firearms in Texas. They took cover under the waggon. The Comanches disappeared into the cedars. Jason, his musket barrel resting between wheel spokes, waited for them to reappear.

"José," he said, "how does one fight Indians?"

"Against the Comanches," said José, "it is best to blow one or two heads off as quickly as possible. The quicker the better, for speedy discouragement is the most chastening. If this is a Comanche war party, they have a purpose. We are not that purpose, for they could not have known we would be here. It is more likely to be the house, for they make war on everyone, señor, and it is possible they have decided war on Cordova is overdue. We are in their way, which is unfortunate, since they will want to remove us."

The sound of a fired musket came as an interruption from the distance.

"Apulca," said Jason.

"Apulca," agreed José. "Perhaps, señor, if we can blow three or four heads off instead of only one or two, it will be enough to make them think again. It is not customary for a Comanche war party to give up too many lives dealing with a secondary objective. Therefore good shooting may make them ride around us."

Jason received this piece of hopeful thinking without comment. He was angry. It was all too easy to foresee that in a few minutes his long years of relentless searching would have been for nothing. He would be chopped to pieces by tomahawks, or shot full of arrows. The senselessness of having put himself in this position increased his anger. He was not unused to facing a primitive violent enemy. The Pathans were every bit as fierce as red Indians, and had the same tendency to kill a man not once but a dozen times. But against the Pathans there had been a score of comrades on either side of one. Here, in the beaten path of a Texas range, one waggon and three men were not going to hold back thirty and more Comanches for longer than a few minutes. His hunger for the confrontation with the man Sylvestre had never diminished; to be robbed when it looked to be so close was unbearable. And to be robbed, indirectly, by Isabella was a savagely ironic blow. His fury was such that he wondered what kept him there waiting for the Comanches. Frustration clawed at the heart of his obsession. What was he doing, covering the retreat of daughters of Esteban Sylvestre y Cordova? Of all ironies, that was the most damnable. Fifteen clear minutes those young women needed to be sure of running free of the Comanches, and he was to try to help win that time for them. He was mad.

"Señor, do you see them?" It was a whisper from José.

"No. Nor can I hear them." The cedars were quiet, giving off not a sound, and the sun itself was a fiery silence.

"They are the very devils. They should have been almost at us by now."

"This is the devil of all devils," said Jason, which to José only meant that he was bitter because the day, which had seemed so full of simple life, had proved deceitful.

"Gonzales," whispered José, "do you see them?"

"No," muttered the cook, and wondered why the angels had cast him to play the role of hero.

José squinted. He did not want to die either, and was as inwardly frank about it as Gonzales. But there were the señoritas, the patroness and her sister. No man, however weak his flesh, could do that which would lessen their chance of escaping; one could only pray that death would be quick and merciful.

"Where the devil are they?" Jason wiped sweat from his face. By now the Comanches should be on them, like warriors disgorged from hell. But there was neither sight nor sound of them. How did they manage, those mounted Indians, to move through that cedar brake without so much as stirring a leaf or snapping a twig?

In the farther distance a musket fired again, its report faint. The array of cedars stretched away, a running shimmer of deep colour against the glinting rock of the Cerro Jorobado. The silence descended once more, and time itself hung suspended. It clamped a lock on their tongues. Their eyes strained into the fierce light. The harshness of the glare, along with the sweat in their eyes, caused their sight to blur and the cedars to dance. Gonzales wiped his eyelids with his fingers and essayed a hoarse whisper.

"José—"

"Silence!" hissed José.

Jason felt the first cold ripples of fear run down his back. Damn his stupidity, damn his involvement with Cordova. Damn the heat. Beneath the waggon they were out of the sun, but it was like being trapped in an oven. They peered along their musket barrels and continually flicked away the sweat.

"Señor, something is wrong," whispered José.

"God's life, do you think I'm unaware of that?"

José pointed to the right, where the cedar brake ended. Then to the left, where the trees stretched on, westwards.

"Señor, where are they?"

"Damnation, I take it they're still inside those trees, in front of us, watching us."

José cocked an ear as very faintly there came the sound of a shot. And then another. Well to the west.

"Señor?" said José.

"Oh, ye gods," said Jason. "They've gone after the vaqueros and the cattle."

"Truth lies inside a Comanche, not on his face," said José. "And it is a mistake to assume, as we did, that what they look as if they are going to do is what they really intend to do. They do not mean to burn Cordova, señor, as we thought, but to help themselves to our cattle. They will attack the vaqueros, take what steers they want, and vanish."

"I thought they only lived on buffalo."

"Another mistake, señor."

"Santa María," said Gonzales, "are you disappointed they prefer cattle to us, José?"

"I am wondering," said José, his perspiration running like tears, "if our vaqueros will decide whether to exchange the cattle for the light of tomorrow's sun."

"I am a coward," said Gonzales with a fat man's frankness, "and would give up a thousand head of cattle in order to wake up tomorrow."

"It is easy to give up a thousand head of cattle which do not belong to you," said José severely.

"There were about ten vaqueros," said Jason.

"Ten, señor, yes," said José.

"They need us."

"Ah, that is a brave remark, señor," said José, looking red and baked, "but not a sensible one. We thought we were about to die. We accepted that, because of the señoritas. That is what men must do for women, ordinary men or brave ones. But there is nothing we can do for the vaqueros, except to wish wisdom on them. They must give up the steers and run, señor. And if we are wise we will run too, while we have the chance."

Jason crawled out and stood up. The other two joined him. They listened but heard nothing. They saw only the hill, the cedars, and the rolling lie of the grassy range.

"A pest on it," said Jason, "we can't stand here doing nothing." He had forgotten his anger the moment it was obvious that the Comanches had turned west through the cedars and were out of sight when they emerged. He thought about the outnumbered vaqueros. He, José, and Gonzales had spent valuable time in useless occupation of a patch of ground under the waggon. As a soldier, that annoyed him.

"We must return to the house," said José. "That is the best we can do."

"Wait," said Jason, listening.

"Señor," said Gonzales, "José is right, we—"

"Wait," said Jason again, sure of faint sounds now.

"Yes, they are coming," said José. "I hear them too."

"Who are coming?" asked Jason.

"Either the Comanches or the vaqueros. Who else, señor?"

Gonzales' obesity quivered, as he too picked up the sounds of galloping horses. The sounds, muffled by grass and distance, rolled towards them from the southwest, not the west. That could have meant the Comanches, having broken out of the trees at a point not visible from the waggon, had crossed the line of the cattle drive and then turned, still out of sight, to come at the waggon again. Yet such a roundabout way, decided Jason, made no sense. Gonzales crossed himself. They listened and waited, muskets primed and every nerve alert to the possible necessity of diving for cover.

A single horseman appeared, riding fast. It was Apulca.

"There's one who's decided in favour of a tomorrow," said Jason.

"He is not alone, señor," said José.

A second rider appeared, followed by two more. Then several more. The Cordova vaqueros had made the wiser choice. Señorita Isabella would lose her mavericks, but not her vaqueros. She would not quarrel with that.

Apulca dismounted, almost before his mustang pulled up.

"Better we go," he said, and it was the first time Jason had heard him speak.

The vaqueros arrived, one after the other. Apulca's shots had finally alerted them, and it was while they were scouting hurriedly around that the Navaho had come up with them. They did not take all day to make decisions, but opted to ride immediately for the house. The moment they caught their first glimpse of the Comanches, coming in a direct line from the Cerro Jorobado, they knew it was themselves and the steers the Indians were after. The Comanches were savagely contemptuous of any Mexican who worked for Spanish or American paleface masters. The vaqueros streamed south. There was no pursuit. It seemed it was the cattle indeed the Indians wanted. But since only a blockhead would take the fierce Comanche branch of the Shoshone Indians for granted, the vaqueros did not stop to shake hands with each other. They turned east to head for the waggon at full speed. The Comanches would not attack the main herds farther west, for there were forty other vaqueros guarding them. They might, however, after securing the strays, decide to attack the house. In which case the patroness would need all the help she could get.

They explained all this with typical Mexican fervour, and

finished by advising Jason how they regretted the loss of the cattle. No doubt he would assure Señorita Isabella it was a loss they could not have prevented. Jason looked slightly rueful. There was only one person who had made a correct judgement. Isabella. She had said the Comanches would not attack the waggon party.

"What are a few cows, *amigos?*" he said to the vaqueros. "Nothing to what your patroness might have to say about other matters."

They rode for the house, Gonzales driving the rolling, creaking chuck waggon. Apulca stayed far in the rear, keeping an eye open for any sign of the Comanches. But the afternoon held its peace.

Isabella, white-faced and desperate, rounded up every ablebodied male servant she could find as soon as she and her sister reached the house. She made every movement a frantic running one, her skirts hitched, her voice calling wildly, her control near to the breaking point. Pictures of horror kept flashing into her mind, pictures of Jason and her servants being hacked to death.

Luisa gave what help she could, handing out muskets feverishly, and each with a prayer. Finally, with the body of servants mounted, Isabella ran from the house to her own horse. Luisa went after her, pulling at her sister, as she sought to climb into the saddle.

"Isabella, no! You can't!"

"Let me be! Luisa, please!" She thrust Luisa off. She was in the saddle and away then, her servants with her. She had never been so frightened. Not for herself, but for the four who had stayed. The torturing beat of her heart sent the fear physically hammering through her body, and anguish almost took the sight from her eyes. It was impossible, they would never get there in time. The Comanches would already have taken their trophies. All four scalps.

Oh, dear God, no! Santa María, Santa María!

They galloped wildly into the heat, muskets thumping against swaying backs, leather lashing the mustangs. Isabella rode as if by frenzy alone she could hold back the clock. Never had she known anything but love for the great, wild expanses of Cordova. She hated the liability of limitless space now. An hour, an hour, from the house to the waggon, that was what that liability meant at this moment.

It seemed to her to take an eternity of terrifying time to travel even a quarter of the way, and just when they had passed this mark the leading man pulled up so abruptly that his horse reared in furious resentment. Isabella came up with him, her eyes enormous with anguish, her expectations the very worst. He pointed. There, topping a shallow rise and riding down over the wide, beaten track towards them, were the vaqueros. Isabella put a gloved hand to her throat and her eyes went in wild search of other figures. There, there was José, and there in a distant dust cloud she made out the running, lurching waggon. And there, amid the vaqueros, was the black cavalry horse with Jason astride. Isabella swayed in her saddle, so giddying was her rush of blood.

The two parties met. Backslapping ensued, and the afternoon rang with the sounds of celebration and triumph. An escape from a band of Comanches was always a triumph, never mind that it would be related to the art of running away. Jason rode up to Isabella. Every emotion rent her senses, and an intensity of relief engulfed her. Her breathing was erratic, painful, and she could not raise a single word.

"Isabella?" he said. Isabella, visibly emotional, said nothing. "You lost only your cattle," he said. Isabella was silent. "That was all they wanted, it seemed, the cattle. Are you all right?" Isabella trembled violently. "Apulca is back there scouting, but I fancy they won't be visiting."

Her wide mouth was compressed, her teeth clenched. She turned her horse and without a word began to ride back home. Everyone followed, but silently. The vaqueros looked gloomy. The patroness was angry, after all. But, Mother of God, how could her cattle have been saved?

"Ah, señor," murmured José after a while, "it is a hard thing to be a woman, to have a heart and compassion in a country like this. It is easier to have no heart. But the señorita has a warm one and much compassion."

"Yes, no doubt," said Jason a little abruptly.

"And to have such a heart and no man to guard it for her against the cruelties of life, that is also hard, señor."

"There's Philip de Ravero," said Jason.

"Ah, yes," said José, looking at the lone figure of his patroness leading them all home, "a cheerful man, señor, a warbler of songs in a land of lions. A man, señor, who gaily comes and goes, and is perhaps no sooner in one place than he wishes to be in another. Of course, that is not to say the señorita thinks less than highly of him."

"It's little to do with me," said Jason.

"That is so, señor, that is so," said José, and smiled.

Luisa, watching in a fever from the house, saw them coming and ran out to meet her sister. Thankfully, tiredly, Isabella slid from her horse.

"Isabella—oh, how thankful I am—everyone is safe, then—see, they're all here."

"Yes," said Isabella, and took a deep grateful breath. Luisa saw her eyes were strangely wide.

"Isabella—"

"I must just go up to my room," said Isabella, and walked quickly into the house while the paved frontage filled with returning men. Luisa looked around for Jason. He was on his feet, rubbing Napoleon's nose. He gave Luisa a brief smile as she came up.

"Nothing happened," he said. "They took the cattle, that's all." He explained events and Luisa listened.

"Isabella was right, then, in thinking we should not be attacked," she said.

"But they would have attacked your vaqueros."

"Perhaps." She was very happy in her relief. "Apulca thought so, yes? But he did seem to believe we were in danger, though the Comanches have never made war on Cordova or its people before. We have a dispensation, I think, because we have never forbidden them our land. And it was an insurance, wasn't it, to let them have the cattle? But what is the matter with Isabella? She was so quiet, instead of being so pleased. Of course, she was desperately worried—"

"So was I," said Jason.

"But you stayed," said Luisa, "you stayed to give us time. We shall not forget—no, never."

"José and Gonzales also stayed."

"Oh, we are grateful to them too. Señor, you have been more than a friend, you—"

"I was there, Luisa, that was all. I must go now."

"Go?" Luisa looked at him in shock and surprise. "But how can you go yet? Isabella will—"

"I think your sister needs a few quiet minutes by herself, and I should get back to Westboro."

"Wait," said Luisa, and went into the house to see her sister. Isabella was at that moment coming down the stairs. Luisa thought she looked as if she had just shed tears, which was only understandable considering what had taken place. But she did not seem so strained, and smiled when Luisa met her.

"Isabella, Jason is going," announced Luisa.

"Going?" Isabella was startled.

"He seems to think he's outstayed his welcome."

"He said that?"

"No. But—"

Isabella left Luisa's voice hanging. Outside, the servants and vaqueros had dispersed, except for José and Apulca, the Navaho having just returned with nothing to report. They were with Jason, who was remounting Napoleon. Isabella flew up to him, giving the two servants an expressively dismissive wave of her hand. They discreetly took themselves off.

"Señor Rawlings," she said, "what are you doing?"

"I'm preparing," said Jason, "to depart."

"I do not advise it," said Isabella with dangerous sweetness.

"Well, it's good to see you're feeling better, Isabella—"

"I am not feeling better," said Isabella. "I am still in a state of nervous emotion—oh, I was so wildly relieved that I could say nothing, nothing at all—I thought the worst might have happened to you—that is, to all of you. But at least I have now recovered my speech, so am able to tell you that if you go I shall send my vaqueros to bring you back."

"I may rely on that?" said Jason, wishing that she did not appear so appealing to him.

"Oh, indeed you may," she said warmly. "Nobody has eaten yet. Everyone is famished, and there are no Comanches shooting arrows of fire at us. Didn't I say they would not attack us?"

"You did, but nobody seemed sure."

With the sun caressing her, Isabella smiled and said, "Yes, I agree, nobody was sure. I have quite forgiven you, and you are to stay and dine with us."

"For what am I forgiven?"

"For throwing me on to my horse." Isabella laughed then, all her emotions now quite containable. "Jason, you will dine with

~ 185 ~

us, won't you? Please? Luisa would like it too. It has been such a variable and eventful day, and it is time now to relax, isn't it?"

Jason knew it would be wiser to go, if only because of the father. It was anything but satisfying to his common sense to hear himself saying, "How can I refuse? Thank you."

Isabella, glowingly alive, plunged into warm impulsiveness.

"Jason, will you be gracious and please us very much? Will you be our guest, please? Will you stay here at Cordova until you wish to go wandering again?"

Here was fate's final twist of irony. He was being invited to sit and wait in the man's house. That mixed such spice with the ingredients of bitter resolution that it was irresistible.

"That may not work out too cordially," he said.

"Oh, it will be agreeable to all of us," said Isabella, a picture of rich Castilian beguilement, so wistful was she to have her way in this.

"I doubt it," said Jason, "but if you wish to risk it—"

"Yes, we will risk it," smiled Isabella.

"Thank you. Is there a bath in your house, Isabella?"

"But of course. There is actually a bathroom."

"Then if I could resist I can't now," he said.

Isabella laughed and set her laughter against the tears she had shed.

Jason sat at the harpsichord, Luisa stood by. Jason played and she sang. Isabella watched from the comfort of the couch, enjoying the music. Luisa, the teasing minx, put a hand on Jason's shoulder each time she leaned to turn the music page.

Jason sang an English song called "D'ye Ken John Peel?" He had quite a rich baritone. The song, he said, was fairly new, but it was very zestful and raced along infectiously. Isabella joined her sister when it was over, and turned the pages of the music book until she found a Spanish duet.

"You'd like that?" said Jason. "Let's make a dash at it, then." What a gay mockery of hospitality. He was the guest of two sisters whose father he was coldly resolved to kill. Perhaps a gentleman of true Spanish sensitivity would have long since advised them, in similar circumstances. Not caring half as much for this kind of chivalrous refinement as for ensuring that Sylvestre was not warned off, he kept his mouth shut and began sizing up the situation.

Luisa and Isabella could not save their father. Indeed, since they were proud of their Spanish blood, and of honour that could not be lightly cast aside, they might even understand that he had to face up to death. There was nothing else to do, then, but to play the part of a friendly guest and wait. "Are you ready now?" he asked, studying the music. "Let me hear you soar, my prima donnas. No tiny twitterings, but full voices. I'll thump loudly—"

"Jason," said Isabella, "we are not going to bawl our heads off because you have had two glasses of cognac. This is a sweet song."

"Yes, indeed," said Luisa, "very sweet. 'Two Birds in a Tree.' A little twittering is called for, in fact." She put her hand on his shoulder and pointed to a bar or two. Isabella, on his other side, leaned to peer at the bars, bringing her scented warmth close to him. Her white silk gown was low, her creamy skin glowing with health. Her curving bosom peeped, the valley softly dipping into the silk. Luisa looked and smiled. Isabella straightened up.

"Luisa," she said, "is right. In places she must twitter."

"No, no, that is your part," said Luisa.

"Certainly not," said Isabella, "the younger must always take that part."

"My dear young ladies," said Jason, "sing, please." He struck a chord. "And if you prefer you can leave the twittering to me."

But Manuel, after knocking loudly on the door, put his head in to say that Sancho López wished to see Señorita Isabella if she would be kind enough to receive him.

"Please excuse me," said Isabella, and went out. She returned ten minutes later. She looked as if the evening was making up for a worrying day. "There," she said happily, "the argument is all over. Sancho López came with his mother's tongue in his mouth, and I was as gracious, Jason, as you could wish. I have promised to buy back the land my grandfather bequeathed."

"You could have bought it months ago, and at a lower price," said Luisa.

"Ah," said Isabella sweetly, "but months ago I did not have Jason here to advise me."

"It's as well," said Luisa, "that he has been able to arrange everything so neatly for you."

"Luisa, there is no need to stir a finished stew," said Isabella. "I know how much he has helped us. But I said at the start, did I not, that he was the one to stand up for us. My perceptiveness in seeing that is satisfying."

"Oh, you and Jason are both extremely clever," said Luisa, "except that you are the more modest, Isabella."

Isabella laughed and clapped her hands. "Well, I think we have had a splendid day, after all," she said. "We have shown Señor Rawlings a little of Cordova, we have given our friends the Comanches a hundred head of cattle, and we have settled an annoying little land dispute. I asked Sancho López to come in and drink wine with us, but he was too shy. So I had Manuel find him a bottle to take back home with him. Now, what shall we three do to celebrate?"

"Sing," said Jason, and struck the chord once more.

So they sang.

Later Isabella went contentedly to bed while Luisa went upstairs in a happily sleepy state. Jason sank into sleep in the comfort of a guest room.

Before she closed her eyes, Isabella wondered why her sense of relief that day had been so intense that she had wanted to weep.

# 17

Lisbet Hendriks rode furiously, skirt and petticoats billowing. Esmeralda glimpsed her from a window as she came galloping up to the house from the tree-lined drive. She was at the girl as soon as Lisbet came up the steps.

"Miss Lisbet, you is downright deplorable! I'm gonna git your pa to lock you up. I's—"

"Meralda, you just quit bawling at me, you hear? Where is Pa?"

"He just come back from the cotton sheds, an' if he don't give you a bigger bawlin' when I tell him what you look like on that hoss agin, you gonna have to thank the good Lawd. I swear them fiel' niggers—"

"Fiddlesticks, you hear? Fiddlesticks," said Lisbet, and swept through the house. Her father was on the verandah. "Pa!"

Colonel Hendriks turned as she rushed up to him.

"I'm here," he said, taking the cigar from his mouth.

"Pa, listen to this. They're talking in town about a deal being arranged between Sancho López and Isabella Cordova."

"What deal?" The Colonel's face tightened.

"That parcel of land," said Lisbet angrily. "Sancho is going to let it go back to the Cordovas. Pa, they've tricked you. You gave up that option and left Sancho free to sell the land to them."

The Colonel swore. His face darkened.

"Where'd you hear this?"

"In the store. Mr. Harrison told me. He got it from customers. Pa, you surely do look fierce."

"That old Mexican biddy, María López, told me six months ago she'd never sell to that high and mighty Cordova bunch."

"It's Sancho who—"

"Sancho does what she tells him to. I've been tricked by no one but her. She's a damned old woman. She's changed her mind. She's tricked me—if it's true."

"I declare, Pa," said Lisbet, "you need to look further than Sancho's mother. You need to look until you catch sight of Mr. Smart Aleck himself—fancy-talking Jason Rawlings. From the moment he opened his mouth in that courtroom, he's been standing on your foot."

Esmeralda came out and stood muttering. Colonel Hendriks dropped his cigar on the boarded verandah and ground it under his boot.

"Meralda," he said, "go tell someone to saddle up my horse."

Esmeralda, seeing his flushed and mottled face, went without a word.

"Pa," said Lisbet, "are you all riding to town to talk to Mr. Rawlings? I'll ride with you. Except we'll have to go to Cordova—"

"I'm going to see Sancho López and his mother. Until I know different I don't have any quarrel with Rawlings, and I don't aim to take sides in your disagreement with him. I rate that gentleman a mighty cool customer, and can see the time coming when I might like to use that head of his."

"Now you just listen, Pa—"

"Hold your tongue." The Colonel's mood was dangerous and Lisbet knew it. But she was in a temper of her own.

"Don't you want to know that Mr. Rawlings is living at Cordova, playing at being adviser and comfort to her high-and-mightiness?"

The Colonel's face darkened to an uglier red.

"By God," he said, "is that the truth?"

"It surely is as I heard it," said Lisbet, "and it makes things fit together, doesn't it?"

"If that parcel of land is being bought by Isabella Cordova, then that means Sancho's grant is genuine, and that Rawlings got me bluffed out of the game. Well, I don't aim to quit for good. I want that land, and I mean to have it."

"Pa—"

"You stay here."

He collected his overseer, Ed Braddock, and rode into Westboro with him, where they picked up two other Americans. They went on to San Carlos. Folks watched them on their way, and the general opinion was that Colonel Hendriks was having a bad day.

"Looks like he's busting to spit from here to the Gulf," said one man.

"Ain't been done yet," said another. "Might just be done today."

The door of the adobe house of Señora López was ajar. The Colonel kicked it fully open.

"You go find Sancho," he said to Braddock, who took the other two men with him on the search. Sancho López would be sitting somewhere in the sun, soaking up wine.

Isabella, Luisa, and Jason watched as the wild mustang essayed moves of the most murderous kind in efforts to dislodge the vaquero on its back. Jason's interest was that of a cavalryman, which meant first of all that he did not see the mustangs in quite the same way as the vaqueros did. He had tamed horses new to the regiment in palmier and headier days. He had never used the head-checking methods of the vaqueros, who were as wild in their ways as the unbroken animals. But then he had never had to tame horses as hostile as mustangs, descendants of the breed brought to the South Americas by the Spanish conquistadores. They had all the traits of sensitively explosive fireworks.

The vaquero rose to the sky, his sombrero whirling arcs in his hand. The mustang landed on all fours, back arched, and almost immediately stood straight up on its hind legs. It threatened for a moment to keel backwards with its rider, but leapt instead for the poled fence of the corral. Dust flew as it swung to brush the vaquero against the rails. The vaquero dug in the bit, tightened fiercely, and the mustang reared, forelegs aiming blows at the fence.

Isabella's face was alight under the brim of her hat. There was so much dust that Jason felt a layer of it on his skin. But it seemed to have missed leaving its mark on Isabella. The skin of some women did seem miraculously resistant to inclemencies. Isabella's fine sheen was as unblemished now as it had been an hour ago when they had arrived at the corral to watch a number of unbroken mustangs suffer their first saddles and first riders. The vaqueros knew their business. As horsemen, they had no superiors. Jason acknowledged it. He also acknowledged that the vaqueros did not ask the mustangs to like them, only to accept them. That acceptance brought obedience. It was very necessary. The Cordovas did not sell any horse more disposed to bite off a man's head than accept his saddle. Breaking in cavalry horses was conducted on more patient lines. It was necessary to induce not only obedience but a rapport.

"You will bet on this one?" said Isabella.

"On the mustang?" said Jason.

"On the vaquero."

"Whether he stays on?" The noise of the battle between athletic man and snorting animal verged on pandemonium at times. A rail split, and a bucket, thought to be safe in a corner, went flying.

"You may bet either way," said Isabella.

"Who will cover my wager?" asked Jason.

"I will," she said. "There, what could be fairer?"

"What has come over you, inviting wagers?" asked Luisa.

"Chirp, chirp, little prairie bird," said Isabella. "Nothing has come over me. I don't think Mother would have objected to a little bet with a friend, and Father certainly would not."

"As fond as I am of my father," said Luisa, "I'd not hold up any of his ways as a reason for one of my own."

Isabella laughed. She felt the brilliance of the day was matched only by the magic of being alive. Life was with the future; she had looked back into the past after her grandfather died. He had never really become an old man, though his hair and beard were white. She missed him. He could make the house ring. It was a little something to be aware that there was a man around again; it was rather pleasant. Only her father's return from Austin was needed and Cordova would be alive once more. He wanted money, her father. He had come back from several years of travel to beg some from her, but she would not give it to him—not that kind of money. It would follow all the other money he had inherited, dissipated in the excitements of the cities. To her father, money was meant to be spent. The world, he said, was occupied by two kinds of people. The spenders and the receivers. All people could not be spenders, any more than all could be receivers. The spenders bestowed the means of existence on the receivers, and the receivers gave service to the spenders.

Not long after returning to Cordova, Isabella's father had started to get tired and restless. He had spent all he had received from her grandfather. She gave him a little, and he immediately took himself off for a few weeks to see what the new town of Austin might offer him. He would come back when his pockets were empty again. She would willingly have him back, but would not provide him with another small fortune. That would only put new wings on his feet.

The mustang reared again. For a split second horse and rider were a posed silhouette, black against the sun. Then the broncho launched itself forward, only to double up in midair. The vaquero, unseated, yelled and fell. The mustang celebrated with a powerful kick, a playful buck, and a trot to the rails. There it stopped, and rolled its eyes at Jason. The vaquero got to his feet, slapped on his sombrero, showed his teeth at the horse in a brittle grin, and shook his fist. The mustang retaliated with a viciously swerving run that knocked the vaquero off his feet and put him on his back again.

"Up, up," called Isabella, "*pronto, pronto!*"

The vaquero, his friends roaring, sat up and said, "Señorita, am I not better off as I am?"

"Jason," said Isabella, "can you show my vaqueros how it should be done?"

"Not without breaking my neck," said Jason.

"It is dangerous for anyone but the vaqueros," said Luisa.

"Yes, I know," said Isabella, "except that Jason has been a cavalryman."

"I am sure that is not the same," said Luisa.

"You are quite right," said Jason.

"I agree," said Isabella, but she would have liked to see him take on the mustang. She liked the way he sat a horse, and he had legs long enough to sit the best. The vaqueros, sitting on the top rail of the corral, were smiling. The mustang was eyeing them hungrily.

"Let me see what Napoleon can make of him," said Jason. He crossed a stretch of ground and untethered and mounted his long-serving steed. A vaquero opened the gate for Jason, and he rode Napoleon into the corral. The mustang sniffed and snorted. It put back its ears. Napoleon stood quite still. The mustang blew another warning snort, tossed its head, and retreated to the farthest point of the corral. Jason touched with his heels and Napoleon ambled to join the mustang. The mustang rolled back its upper lip. Napoleon sidled close, clearly interested in the coming manoeuvre. The mustang turned its quarters and aimed a kick. Napoleon, two hands higher, took umbrage, swung himself and pressed the mustang sideways against the rails. The wild horse glared and showed its teeth in a hideous grin. Napoleon churned ground and began to run. The mustang ran with him as if tied, Napoleon tightly constraining it. The mustang brushed the rails. They creaked. Jason did nothing except to keep the reins loose. The mustang turned, looking to bite Napoleon. Napoleon smacked into it from head to tail. Squeezed, the mustang halted, standing with eyes baleful. It kicked, then began to run again. Napoleon matched it, crowded it, and when it sought to swerve thudded it against the rails a second time. It reared back. Jason cuffed it. It sprang forward and Napoleon went with it, the two horses racing around the corral, Napoleon bullying the broncho weightily and persistently.

Jason took Napoleon towards the gate. It was opened. He rode through and the mustang was left bruised and sulky.

"That was extraordinary," said Isabella.

"It saves one's neck," said Jason, "and in a week would make the mustang easier to ride."

"A week? A week?" Isabella laughed. "That amount of time would be a luxury we cannot afford."

"I know. Taming a horse isn't quite the same as training it. I was giving Napoleon a diversion."

Isabella, sensitive because of her new emotions, said, "I am sorry, señor, if your horse finds Cordova boring."

They were interrupted by the arrival of a Mexican. He rode up to Isabella and spoke rapidly to her.

"You've found him?" Colonel Hendriks stared impatiently at Braddock, who nodded. "You took your time."

"Hidin' out on us, Colonel. I figure he got word we was lookin' for him. But we got him."

"Bring him in."

They pushed Sancho into the room. His mother, sitting by the unlit fire, glanced at him. Her fierce bright eyes warned him. Sancho was sweating.

"Señor?" he said to the Colonel, who looked liverish.

"I've been talking to your mother."

"My son speaks little English," said Señora López.

"He speaks enough," said the Colonel, "and I'll talk plainly. Sancho, you hear me?"

"Sí, señor."

"I've been asking your mother questions. I've received no answers. So I'll ask you. Get me?"

"Sí, señor." Sancho smiled uneasily.

"You made yourself scarce, did you, when you heard I was here?"

"Señor?" Sancho wiped away perspiration. His mother sighed for him, for his addiction to wine and his indolence. But he had no unholy vices—he was affectionate, and for all his simpleness she knew he would decide for himself which questions he would understand and answer and which he would not.

"You were hiding out," said the Colonel, "and cost my men time, a lot of time."

"Not hiding, señor, no."

"Well, ain't you a no-good greaser," said Braddock. "Sittin' on his fat pat he was, Colonel, behind the counter in the wineshop."

"Listen to me, Sancho," said the Colonel. "What made Señorita Cordova decide you held a genuine land grant, after all? Eh?"

"Señor?" Sancho's incomprehension was a worried blankness.

"And how much did she offer for it?"

"Señor?"

Colonel Hendriks made a gesture. Braddock shoved his fist forward. It hit Sancho in the back and sent him sprawling. Señora López tightened her grip on her stick and her eyes burned. Sancho got up without fuss and faced Colonel Hendriks in a way that was strangely dignified.

"Señor," he said in Spanish, "is that how to ask questions of a man?"

"What?" said the Colonel. "What's that you say?"

"My son wishes to know if that is how you ask questions of a man," said Señora López. "Señor Hendriks, Sancho has understood little of your questions. I have understood them all, also those you asked of me. I have answered none of them. I have only told you that what has happened between my family and the Cordovas is not the business of other people. My son will tell you the same."

"Your son will tell me what I want to know," said the Colonel. "If not here, then somewhere else. I can find a Spanish tongue to talk to him. Braddock, take him outside. We'll ride him back to Hendriks with us."

"Pardon me."

They turned. Jason had intruded himself into the room.

"Hold it," said Braddock.

"Señora." Jason gave Señora López a nod and a smile. Her eyes brightened.

"You are welcome, señor," she said.

"You have visitors," he said.

"That is so, señor," she said.

"Am I in the way?" he asked.

"You are not in my way," she said.

"Mr. Rawlings," said the Colonel, "I don't rightly feel I can tolerate your intrusion. I'd be obliged if you'd wait outside. I have a score to settle with you and I request you wait until I'm ready to engage with you."

"Colonel? Ah, it's you," said Jason. "I didn't notice you in so large a crowd. Good morning, sir. And is that my client I see also, Señor Sancho López? Indeed it is. Good morning, Señor López."

Perceptibly, a smile wrinkled its way through the lines in the face of Sancho's mother.

"Your client?" The Colonel's veined eyes were shot with temper.

"My commissions mount, Colonel," said Jason pleasantly. "I'm acting for Cordova, for Señora López and for her son. But I don't wish Mr. Schumaker to think I intend taking all the bread from his mouth. My stay is only temporary. What was it you were saying, Colonel?"

The Colonel, menacingly deliberate, said, "Mr. Rawlings, I'm beginning to feel you're not temporary at all. I figure, sir, that you intend to run the affairs of Westboro. I don't advise it. Westboro is the province of Texans, not foreigners."

"I'm representing Texans, Colonel."

"Ain't he a flat-mouth?" said Braddock to the other Americans.

"Wait outside, Mr. Rawlings," said the Colonel.

"We're pressed for space in here, I agree," said Jason. "I'll take my client with me." He tapped Sancho's arm. In Spanish he said, "Please accompany me, Señor López." Sancho glanced at his mother. She smiled and nodded.

"Leave him here," said the Colonel.

"You'll appreciate, Colonel," said Jason, "that I can't allow you to take him to Hendriks, which is what I think I heard you suggest. If he's to remain here, I'll remain with him."

"Braddock," said the Colonel, "I want no more pussyfooting around with this gentleman. See him out, see him on his way back to Washington, or wherever."

Braddock, always in favour of an honest, straightforward piece of talk, took Jason by the arm.

"I'm warranted to move you, mister," he said, "but that don't mean I want to shove you. You just act peaceful, and there'll be no shovin'."

"Just a moment," said Jason. He called for José. The door opened and José stood there. Crowding behind him were ten Cordova vaqueros. Through the open door came the smell of cows, mustangs, and Texas grasses.

"Señor?" enquired José politely.

"There are no problems, José. I only wished to know if you were there."

José drew back and closed the door.

"Them damn greasers," said Braddock heavily, "you figure on usin' them to break the law, mister?"

"Which law is that?" asked Jason. "The one giving citizens the right not to be hustled?"

"Any Mex tried to hustle me," said Braddock, "an' I'll shoot a law-abidin' hole in him bigger'n your head. You get them greasers outa here."

"How do you feel, señora?" asked Jason. "It's your house."

Señora López considered the question.

"Señor Rawlings," she said, "I am not used to so many people all at once. Perhaps you can arrange for everyone to leave."

"By God," said Colonel Hendriks, "you're pushing me, Mr. Rawlings, and I don't like it."

"It's embarrassing, perhaps," said Jason, "but my clients know they should not discuss their business without first consulting me. Have you had difficulty in communicating with them?"

"You listen to me, sir," said the Colonel. "I'll not be stopped by you, or anyone. I'm here to help open up Texas, to help others open it up. There's no one should sit on land when there are people willing to work it, willing to make Texas a great and powerful country. You take my recommendations back to the Cordovas. You tell them their land isn't for looking at. In a year there'll be a hundred thousand Texans who know different. Land is for people, sir—and the people mean to have it."

"I wouldn't quarrel with that, Colonel, as long as we're agreed on who we mean by Texans and people."

"Here, Mr. Rawlings, I'm the people," said the Colonel, and strode out. Braddock opened the door for him in time to enable him to make his exit without checking. It put Jason in mind of the exit of a general from a conference. Braddock and the two Americans followed, pushing their way through the vaqueros. José came into the room.

"You have put fleas into their ears, señor?" he said.

"We talked," said Jason.

"You are a disturbing gringo," said Señora López. "All this noise, all these men, all this trouble. Señor, it was quiet here in San Carlos until you stood up in court against my son. I have taken your advice, and what has it meant to me? The certainty that the Americans will pull my house down."

"Will they?"

"Of course." Señora López shook her stick at him. "I should have let my friends feed you to the lions that night. Why was I so foolish as to listen to you? And now see what you have done. Why did you come?"

"One of your friends brought word that the Colonel was paying a call on you."

She smiled.

"You came because of that?"

"Señorita Isabella herself agreed I should. I thought it as well to bring some of her men with me."

"Sancho, go and sit in the sun," she said. Sancho smiled, shrugged, and went to find peace. "Will you sit with me a moment, señor?"

"Willingly," said Jason, and found a chair. José went out to rejoin the waiting vaqueros.

"You do not know Texas," said Señora López. "Life here is a struggle, a battle. There are so many Americanos. There is space, señor, and the smell of riches—but they are elusive riches. Who can say if it is corn or wheat or cotton or cattle which will ensure those riches? Who can say it is this piece of land or that which will prove the better? Guns go off, señor, because the struggle is godless, and the life of another is not important in such circumstances. To kill a man because he stands in your way, that is not a great offence in Texas—only one of the more frequent customs. I have stood in the way of Colonel Hendriks. So has Sancho. It is likely, señor, that we shall pay for that."

"Did you think so when we discussed the matter the other night?" asked Jason.

"I did not think of it until I saw the look on the face of Colonel Hendriks a few minutes ago."

"That look was not for you or Sancho, señora, but for the Cordovas. And perhaps me."

She thought.

"So?" she said.

"You are not in his way now, señora. Nor Sancho."

"Ah, you see, that is what you have done, then. You have put yourself and Cordova at risk."

"Señorita Isabella was in the Colonel's way long before I arrived," said Jason.

She smiled.

"Ah, the señorita, the Cordova," she said. "Those eyes of hers have looked at you and seen in you a man to stand up for her. You are mesmerised, señor?"

"Not totally, señora."

"She wishes, that one, to be her grandfather's image, to be as he was, an eagle. But she is a woman, and no true woman can be a man—though she can grow claws."

"Isabella Cordova has claws?" said Jason.

The alert eyes in the aged face were bright.

"Her only claws, señor, are in her pride. And pride in a woman can cost her dear, unless a man can see beyond it. Señor, will you take wine with me?"

"With pleasure."

"There are bottles in my little cellar, señor, if you will be so kind. Give some to the vaqueros, but do not let them in on me or they will turn my house into a roaring *cantina*."

# 18

"What has happened? Where is Señor Rawlings?" Isabella was at the door of the house as José dismounted. Eight vaqueros remained in the saddle.

"Nothing has happened, señorita," said José. "When we arrived, Colonel Hendriks and his men departed. Señor Rawlings sent us back while he stayed to empty a bottle of wine with Señora López. He will return, he said, as soon as she falls asleep. We left two men to keep him company, to ride back with him."

Isabella looked sceptical.

"So," she said, "Colonel Hendriks rides to make war on Señora López and her son. But no sooner does Señor Rawlings appear than he departs with all his men."

"There were only three men, señorita."

"There was no battle?"

"None, señorita."

"No blood spilt, no bones broken?" she said.

"Not one drop of blood, not one single bone," José assured her.

"Señor Rawlings did not get hurt?"

"He owns not a scratch, señorita. He is in fine cheer, drinking wine."

"Indeed. We may expect him back, then, quite soon?"

"As soon as the bottle is finished, señorita, or Señora López has fallen asleep."

"Thank you, José."

However, while she was wondering what dress she should wear for supper that evening, Isabella began to worry. Hours had gone by, and there was no sign of Jason, or the two vaqueros with him. He was not so in love with old Señora López, was he, that he would fall asleep with her? He would return in time for supper, surely.

She paced about in a way that aroused Luisa's curiosity. She fixed her mind on gowns again. Perhaps she would wear the deep warm red one, with its black horizontal hem stripes. Luisa said she looked beautiful in it. What was she doing? She was not thinking about dressing to please herself but to impress Jason. She had not done such a thing, dressed to impress a man, since she had been an infatuated girl of sixteen. Resolutely she decided she would ask her maid Rosa simply to select the first gown that came to hand.

Evening came, supper was almost ready to be served, and still Jason was not back. Isabella carried her worry to Luisa, who had just finished dressing and was about to go down.

"Luisa—"

"Why, Isabella, how magnificent!" Luisa thought her sister had never looked lovelier. Isabella was wearing her gown of deep warm red, after all, the wide skirt embracing the layered petticoats, her bare shoulders gliding into rounded planes. An oleander bloom adorned her clustered curls. "Isabella, you are simply breathtaking. Are you in love?"

"Am I in love because I put a gown on? And who should I be in love with? You may discount Philip—"

"Ah, poor Philip," smiled Luisa, "he is out of the reckoning because there's someone else."

"There's no one else. Luisa, I am worried. I'm sure something must have happened to Jason. Colonel Hendriks is perhaps more dangerous than we thought. He's a cannibal, that one. He's so hungry for land and power he will swallow everything and everyone."

"I don't think Jason will allow himself to be swallowed," said Luisa.

"But I dislike it intensely that he still isn't back," said Isabella. "Colonel Hendriks has all the Americans in his pocket, and Jason is the only man who has stood up to him. Who is to say that Colonel Hendriks won't arrange for some Americans to beat him to death?"

"Isabella, that is too dramatic for words," said Luisa. "Nobody would do that. And Jason has two good vaqueros with him."

"Well, I am going to take ten more and see what has happened to him."

"I'm sure it isn't necessary," said Luisa, "but go if you must or you'll bite your nails off. You are suffering from natural concern, of course—"

"I am going!"

Isabella handled the buggy herself, José by her side. She frequently drove the Cordova vehicles, and with enjoyment, although José did not approve at all. Ladies should be driven, especially Cordova ladies. Isabella ignored his mutters and whipped the horse to the kind of gallop that had the buggy swaying, rocking, and jolting over the dirt road. A dozen vaqueros followed close behind, wondering what all the fuss was about.

"Señorita, such a pace is not advisable," said José, "it—"

"Do you wish to get off and walk, José?"

"It's not what I'd choose, señorita."

"Then please be quiet."

The buggy rattled through Westboro and the few folks out at this evening hour turned to stare as the dust rose around vehicle and horsemen.

Jason and the two vaqueros who had stayed with him lifted their heads at the sudden arrival of noise outside. One vaquero got up and opened the door of the room. His action coincided with the tempestuous entrance of Isabella, black cloak over her gown, dust scarf over her head. Señora López smiled. For all that her eyes were sleepy and wine-dreamy, they gleamed. There was more than one empty bottle. The wine had been smooth, the conversation good, as conversation should be. Unfortunately too many people nowadays preferred to let muskets or swords do their talking for them. And here was Señorita Isabella, a young woman of great standing, who from the look on her face was about to fire every weapon she had.

Isabella was beset by anger and chagrin. She had come at breakneck speed for fear that Jason and the vaqueros were at the mercy of hostile Americans. Instead they were indulging intemperance. There must have been eight or nine bottles on the table, all empty or nearly so. Her vaqueros had foolish grins on their faces, Jason the enigmatic smile of a man in his cups, and old Señora López the expression of a black-clad Mexican matriarch to whom all things were unimportant except God.

The second vaquero got to his feet. He and his comrade bowed gallantly to their patroness.

"Señorita—"

"How dare you! Go outside, both of you!"

The wine-happy vaqueros smiled apologetically and sidled out, keeping cautious eyes on the whip in Isabella's gloved hand. She would not use it, of course, but it was quivering as if she might.

Jason rose from his chair. Isabella's cloak and skirts flounced as she rounded on him. She looked magnificently furious.

"Oh, this is too much!" she cried.

"Isabella?" he said, his blue eyes sleepy.

"Everyone has been frantic with worry!" She did not care to advise him that Luisa and José had not shared her concern. "It was thought that anything might have happened to you. Instead you have been sitting here drinking wine with not a care in your head. This is terrible, almost unforgivable."

"I'd just begun to think—" Jason stopped and carefully collected his thoughts. He felt mellow and peaceful. The conviviality of the last few hours—the wine, companionship, and laughter— had drawn him back into the pleasanter realms of life. Isabella's sudden tempestuous arrival signalled that protracted conviviality might have to be paid for. Jason elucidated carefully. "I'd just begun to think it was time I returned to Cordova, not wishing to delay supper—"

"Had you? Supper, señor, is already long delayed." Isabella drew a deep breath to let her fire cool, for the sleepy eyes of Señora López were turned on her, a glimmer in them, as if she knew why a woman could be more angry with one more than all others. And there was an omitted courtesy to be given. "I am sorry, Señora López, in intruding like this. Forgive me, please."

"It is understandable, señorita," said María López.

"I thought Señor Rawlings in trouble, you see."

"Ah, that is what comes with the *Inglés*—trouble. If not for themselves, then for others, and mostly for others. Señor Rawlings has made trouble for me with Colonel Hendriks. But I am not complaining. It is better to offer wine to a man like Señor Rawlings than to beat him over the head."

Jason laughed. It came from his sense of warm well-being and his appreciation of Señora López. Isabella stared at him. He was so relaxed, suspiciously so.

"Señor, are you drunk?" she asked.

"God's life, I hope not," said Jason. "My horse will never allow me on his back if I am."

He was impossible. His horse—how ridiculous. Suddenly she wanted to laugh. But she remained scolding.

"If your horse refuses to carry you, señor," she said, "my vaqueros will do so instead. Señora López, do you wish us to take him off your hands?"

"I am sorry to have detained him so long, señorita," said the old lady. "Señor, go with her and make your peace with her. Señorita, you were generous with Sancho. Five thousand dollars was above the figure he asked."

Jason raised an eyebrow and Isabella looked quite flustered.

"Oh, it was agreeable to both of us, five thousand," she said.

"A woman's gesture, señora?" said Jason to María López.

"A woman's gesture, señor," she agreed. She gave him her hand. He kissed it—with the care of a man who knew himself mellow. "*Adiós*, señor," she said, "I am glad you came."

Outside, Isabella said, "You may drive me home, please."

"Five thousand, señorita?" said Jason enquiringly.

"You wished me to be gracious and I was. That is all. Please drive me home."

"There's my horse—"

"You will fall off of him. José will look after Napoleon for you." The sun was dying and its purple light flooded the land. It touched old San Carlos with fire. "You will drive the buggy for me, señor? Thank you. José dislikes my taking the reins. In his opinion it is not right for a lady when she has a gentleman with her. You will be able to sit fairly upright?"

Jason laughed again. She had never seen him in such good humour.

"I'm not drunk, you know," he said. The vaqueros looked on, grinning.

"No, you are only rather happy, and I like you like that—" She coloured. "That is, you are sometimes inclined to be very sober, and it is always better to hear a man laugh than to listen to him being heavily silent."

So he drove her back to Cordova in the buggy, with his cavalry mount trotting haughtily behind and José up with a vaquero. Napoleon had allowed the Mexican to mount, but had refused to budge a single hoof. The cavalcade of buggy and vaqueros passed through Westboro as Sam Purdy's saloon doors were swinging to the entry of evening customers. Black were the outlines of buildings against the purple and indigo sky. Far in the west the horizon was a retreating blaze. The mesquite glowed and Jason was singing the song of the Fighting 7th. His voice carried, and the vaqueros riding in escort soon picked up the tune, even if they could make nothing of the words, and began to whistle an accompaniment. Isabella warmed to the magic of the evening, to its atmosphere. Her vaqueros liked Jason. He was a cavalryman, a horseman, *un hombre bravo*, and wise in his healthy respect for mustangs. He had said quite frankly that he would as soon attempt to ride a tiger, and that was wisdom indeed.

To remember times similar to this one it was necessary for Isabella to think back to the days when she was perched on her grandfather's horse in company with his vaqueros, many of them grizzled men of the ranges. There had never been any difficulty in finding something to sing about.

The buggy ran for home, the greased hubs turning freely and the shod wheels smoothly grinding the dirt surface. Isabella's cloaked shoulder touched Jason's. She glanced at him. He was still so relaxed, a man of warmth and good comradeship. The vaqueros were singing a song of their own now, and he was humming it. Wine was good for him. It was not good for some men: they let it take possession of their senses and became idiots. It made Jason very agreeable indeed.

"Are we late?" he asked suddenly.

"Late?"

"For supper?"

"I think it fair to say you are later than I am," she said, "but as you saved your loved one—"

"My loved one?" The horizon was a flame-tipped inkiness.

"Señora López. You saved her and Sancho from angry Americans, so my vaqueros told me, so what does a little lateness matter?"

They heard a shot then, and another, well away on their right in the purpling dusk. The cavalcade stopped and listened. An owl hooted, mournfully and complainingly, as if for a meal missed.

"Someone is after a steer, perhaps," said Isabella, "and my night vaqueros are discouraging him. Or they have shot a coyote."

"Shall we go and look?" asked Jason.

"It isn't necessary, thank you, Jason. My vaqueros will be awake. Go on, please."

They went on, the vaqueros with their sombreros hanging around their necks, until at last they reached the house. Luisa greeted the return of her sister and Jason in the easy way of a young lady who knew there had been no need to fuss. At the same time she did confess herself famished and begged for supper to be served at once. Jason begged for a little extra delay in order to freshen himself. Isabella took the opportunity offered by this to repair the ravages of rushing and racing, emotions and upsets, and presented herself, when supper was finally served, as a rich and striking picture of how incomparable Castile had blossomed in the fertile bounty of Texas.

Jason was so impressed that he kept his eyes off her during the meal, though he conversed pleasantly enough. Damned, he thought, if it wasn't going to become all too much too soon. He frowned.

"What is wrong, has something displeased you?" asked Luisa.

"We are not, perhaps, as enchanting to be with as Señora López?" said Isabella.

"Colonel Hendriks," said Jason, "is a man of ambition."

"He is making you frown?" said Isabella. "Jason, every American in Texas is a man of ambition. Are you a man of no ambition yourself?"

"Yes, why do you not buy land and settle here?" said Luisa. "You would make a fine Texan and a good neighbour."

Isabella willed him to consider it, but he said, "Texas is for the Americans. They'll reap, sow, and harvest. They are that kind of people." He paused, smiling faintly. "After supper, shall we sing? I can manage a song better than I can conquer mountains."

So they had music and song. Isabella became so warmly committed to the enjoyment of it that Luisa cast her artful smiles. Jason sailed along like a man in spirited company, and if one or two of his quips seemed to poke a cryptic tongue at himself, neither sister questioned why. It was enough to have him entertain and amuse them. Once, when Isabella turned two pages of music together, he said, "Isabella, it is supposed to be better to hang the maestro than to cut the song in half."

"Well, we are not going to hang you," laughed Isabella, glowing, "and there are plenty of other songs."

Eventually, at her most demure, Luisa said, "I am suddenly asleep on my feet. You will let me say good night, you two?"

She had no sooner retired than Jason closed the harpsichord and stood up.

"I must let you retire too, Isabella," he said. "Your duenna will be in as soon as she realises we're alone."

Isabella's smile was overbright.

"Oh, I am sure she knows I am safe with you."

"Indeed, you are," he said, "though I don't care for my dullness to be as obvious as that." He did not look a dull man to her. She felt composure teetering on the brink. Her blood was beating erratically. She dropped her eyes and began an inspection of the wide revers of his coat. "And I ought to point out," he said, "that in that gown you're hardly safe from any man."

He had not meant to say anything as personal as that, but it was out, it was said.

Isabella was assailed by weakness.

"But I am safe from you?" she said.

"Of course, though the gown is beautiful." He became crisp. "I must say good night. Thank you for coming to my rescue. It may not have been necessary, but neither was it unappreciated."

Why did he always have to speak so generally, so precisely. Isabella made a little face.

"Tomorrow, perhaps we can escape alarms," she said.

"Tomorrow," said Jason carefully, "I ought to make peace with Lisbet Hendriks. I was a little bad-tempered with her when we last met. And making peace with her might help to make peace with her father too."

"You are free, of course, to do as you wish," said Isabella stiffly.

"It's a small problem, but of my own making."

"It's for you to decide how important such a small problem is."

"Yes," he said. "Good night, Isabella."

"Good night, señor."

She sat down as the door closed behind him. She felt things were not making sense. She did not really desire anything except ownership of Cordova; she had that and needed nothing else. If Jason preferred spending tomorrow with the daughter of Colonel Hendriks, what did that matter to the owner of Cordova?

Nothing. Except that she was hot with jealousy.

Colonel Hendriks called at Cordova early the next morning. With him was Ed Braddock, who took his cue from the Colonel much of the time. This morning, since the Colonel was brusque, Braddock was dour.

"What is it you want, señores?" Isabella, dressed for riding, was not in her warmest mood. Jason had gone off a while ago to call on Lisbet Hendriks, and his defection hurt.

"I'm here to tell you, señorita," said the Colonel grimly, "that I want that Navaho of yours. I want him under lock and key. Mr. Braddock is here to take him."

Isabella, quite unreceptive, said, "I do not recognise Señor Braddock's right to take any servant of mine. He is not a law officer, Colonel Hendriks, he is only a man who acts for you."

"I shoulder the responsibility of the law in Westboro until we get a full-time officer appointed," said the Colonel, "and I'm warranted by Marshal Stokes of Raikes Ford to nominate representatives. Your Navaho ambushed my two boundary riders last night, as they'll testify. I want him, señorita."

"They will testify to Apulca ambushing them?" Isabella laughed in scorn. "They are not dead, then?"

"Fortunately, although they were fired on, I'm glad to say they escaped, but that—"

"Escaped? From an Indian ambush? Apulca hardly covered himself with credit, allowing ambushed men to escape to testify against him. I have never heard of such carelessness in an Indian. Are they badly wounded, the men?"

"No, they ain't," said Braddock touchily, "but no thanks to the Navaho."

"Are they wounded at all?" asked Isabella.

"No, they ain't," admitted Braddock, "but you go git him for me, Miss Cordova, or—"

"That's not the point," interrupted the Colonel. "It makes no difference whether my men were hit or not. That redskin tried to blast their heads off."

"Colonel Hendriks," said Isabella coldly, "no Indian as intelligent as Apulca would ambush two white men, fire at them, miss them, let them escape, and show himself at the same time. You have made a mistake. But thank you for calling."

"There's no mistake," said the Colonel. "My men escaped, circled back, and saw your redskin running away. I understand you've been warned before about letting him carry a musket. Mr. Braddock is here to take him in, and I'm here to see that he does."

"I am not impressed," said Isabella, "particularly as your men were on my land last night."

"My men—"

"Were on my land. I heard those shots last night, as did others with me. It was almost dark. Your men have remarkable eyesight, Colonel, if they are able to clearly identify a running man at that hour. Cordova has been losing stock for a year, did you know that? Well, it is true. Naturally, you yourself are an honest man. But I suggest you speak to your two riders again, and ask them what they were doing on my land. My vaqueros, in defence of my stock, will often fire before they ask questions, and the law supports them in this."

"By God," Hendricks said, "you'd turn the story upside down, would you? It's not going to work. I'm telling you here and now to hand over that Navaho. He'll get a fair trial."

"I am not handing over any of my Indians for trial by Americans."

"He'll get a jury trial," said Braddock. "Ain't nothing fairer'n that."

"Jury trial?" Isabella did not want to lose her temper, but she could not contain her contempt. It showed in her expression, and gave a biting edge to her voice.

"For attempted murder," said Braddock. "It ain't no laughin' matter." He stood his ground solidly. "You go call him, Miss Cordova."

"Call him? I am to run around calling him. I am not accustomed to doing that. When I next see him I will talk to him. That is all I will do."

"No, you gotta bring him," insisted Braddock. "I'll do the talkin'. He'll get his rights. I'll let him know why I'm arrestin' him."

"Whenever the Mexican authorities had a reason for arresting someone," said Isabella, "they produced an official notice of arrest. Do you have such a notice, Señor Braddock?"

"I'm warranted—"

"I wish to see written authority."

"How you gonna like it if I get Marshal Stokes to come here himself?"

"Arrange it, by all means," said Isabella.

"Señorita," said the Colonel, "you refuse to hand over the Navaho?"

"Yes. And you have only yourself to blame, señor, for being so unconvincing. However, I will make one concession. I will consult my lawyer and be advised by him."

"I'm in great restraint, señorita," breathed the Colonel. "I've been tolerably sensitive of your feelings, but I swear I could act out of all reason if I get stepped on again by that filibustering lawyer. My man here, Mr. Braddock, will settle things. I'll have him ride to Raikes Ford and either bring back Marshal Stokes or an arrest warrant."

"You seem in great worry, señor, over one harmless Indian," said Isabella.

"My worry is for my men," said the Colonel, "and by my reckoning there's no such thing as a harmless Indian."

"*Adiós*, señores," said Isabella with polite finality.

As he rode back to Westboro with the Colonel, Braddock said,

"She's a mighty tough woman, that one. She ain't gonna give you that redskin."

"I know that, I guessed it," said the Colonel, "so we'll leave it to simmer a while."

"Colonel, you reckon your riders' story will hold up?"

"Maybe it won't have to. It's Isabella Cordova I want, not her Navaho. She's just put one foot into the net by defying the law."

"She ain't rightly compelled to hand the Injun over, is she?"

"She is if I say so."

"Them steers she claimed she's losin'. You reckon maybe the homesteaders are rustlin' them?"

"She has no fences," said the Colonel, "and stray steers don't lack a welcome from anybody. She seems to forget she's no longer the only landowner around these parts. She doesn't seem to realise she's got people living right on top of her north and east borders. Any steer that strays into a family's backyard is invited to stay. I figure she could be losing cattle right enough, but they're not being rustled."

"Just welcomed in an' eaten, eh?" grinned Braddock.

"And will be until she realises times are changing. Texas doesn't belong to Cordova."

# 19

Esmeralda, bobbing in flustered respect to Jason, said, "Miss Lisbet, she ain't home, Mist' Rawlings. She gone ridin' like she often do this time of day. And the Colonel, he ain't home neither. He gone early, then come back, then he go again, with Miz Purdy. She been here with recipes an' all, and he 'scortin' her back to town."

"Recipes?" Jason smiled. "I'd have thought that was more the province of Mary Lou."

"Oh, Miz Purdy, she know all ways with dishes, Mist' Rawlings."

"Should I have passed the Colonel?" asked Jason. He had taken his time to reach the plantation, stopping off in town to drink coffee at Mary Lou's and to renew acquaintance with Sam Purdy, whom he liked.

"More'n one way to town," said Esmeralda. "I declare, it ain't right there ain't no one to receive you, Mist' Rawlings. But all the same I don't know if they was expecting you."

"No one was," said Jason. "I'm only making a courtesy call. I left rather abruptly last time I was here."

"As sho' as the good Lawd's my saviour, sir, I put that right out of my mind," said Esmeralda fervently.

"My manners shocked you?" said Jason.

"I don't remember nothin'," she said. "I done went deaf an' blind."

"Well, I'm sure Miss Lisbet didn't."

"Mist' Rawlings, would you step in an' wait?" offered Esmeralda.

"I think not. Please tell her I called, and give her my compliments."

"She's going to scratch holes in me," said Esmeralda.

"For talking to me?"

"For not havin' you step in an' wait."

He smiled, took his leave, and rode back down the gravelled drive between lines of pine trees. It wasn't important. It was all one whether Lisbet Hendriks was home or not. He was simply getting away from Cordova for a while—from Isabella. It was a matter for damnation that she had stirred in him an awareness that he could not go through life without a woman. But she was the last one he could look at. Setting aside all other factors, one could hardly contemplate killing her father one day and asking her hand the next. To fall in love with her meant that reason was committing suicide. He must cut short his stay at Cordova. He should never have entered the place as a guest. He had let things happen, perhaps meeting Antoinette had cracked the ice, and perhaps because he had subconsciously relaxed—knowing he had caught up with his man at last and only needed to wait.

That thought brought back some of his obsessive resolution. He turned off the long drive, entered the pines, dismounted, and tethered Napoleon. He walked slowly through the trees, thinking to take a close look at the Hendriks cotton, and to ponder a while on things. There was a fascination about the plants and their floating fluffy whiteness. He ambled towards the fields, through trees and bright flowering bushes, then stopped. Ahead of him he saw two figures. He was startled, but they were oblivious of his presence. They lay shielded but visible, Colonel Hendriks and Mrs. Purdy, she with her bodice in a state of disarray, her plump white breasts spilling free. Jason took one look, turned very quietly, and walked silently back to Napoleon. He glimpsed what in his abstraction he had missed before, a trap standing within the seclusion of pines some twenty yards away. He resumed his ride along the drive and wondered if Sam Purdy was allowing Colonel Hendriks the favours of his wife in return for benefits such as the managership and part ownership of an hotel. He decided not.

At this moment Lisbet burst into his cynical musings, musings that came out of his disillusionment with women. The Colonel's daughter came like a hellfire camp follower, her short whip whistling, her skirts flying, her booted legs astride a masculine saddle. Petticoats swirled and the lacy frills of short pantaloons flirted around her knees. Jason pulled Napoleon close to the verge to give the Virginian girl room to pass. She saw him. Giving an involuntary little scream, she pulled up in crimson mortification, spurred boots grinding in the stirrups and tight reins making her horse stand up. As it plunged down she shook astride the saddle.

"You are a peeping fiend of darkness!" she cried.

Jason raised his hat and made her a little bow.

"Pass, friend," he said. "Headquarters lie straight ahead. But I advise adjustment of your uniform before reporting to your Colonel. You're carrying despatches of enormous urgency?"

"Sir, your eyes!" She was flaming.

"I assure you, on the word of a gentleman—"

"You're no gentleman, sir! If you were, you would not be staring at my petticoats!"

"More than petticoats, and quite delectable." He was in the mood to be a little cruel. Lisbet, no prude, quivered as he went on, "Am I deceived in what is before my eyes? Pantaloons? Limbs? Great heavens and good gad, madam, is it true, then, that young ladies have legs?"

Lisbet gave another little yelp. It was not that she minded his discovery of her legs, which she knew, without conceit, were shapely. What she did mind was being put at such a disadvantage by the unexpectedness of the encounter, caught with everything flying. And those searching eyes of his. This man of all men. Why had she not simply galloped past him? Why did she not ride away from him now? The cynical look on his face and the sheer impertinence of his every word made her vibrate like a plucked violin.

"Oh, I declare with all my bones, sir, you are an ogling cad!"

"Cover yourself up, madam."

"How dare you!"

"Legs, madam, legs," he said sternly. " 'Pon my soul, what are young ladies coming to?"

What a fury and a flame he was in her blood and eyes. A man after her own outrageous heart, so full of provocations that life with him would be a turmoil of kicks and screams, interspersed with moments of such excitement that she did not dare lay thought to them. She covered her knees as best she could, her masculine posture not being of the greatest help.

"I'm sorry to have shocked you, sir," she said, drawling her words in the most cutting of ways. "I did not know you were so sensitive. I'd have thought you old enough to have acquired a little worldliness, or at least a wife. A wife would have helped you overcome your tender susceptibilities."

"I must look around for one," said Jason.

"I surely do recommend you try Austin. You might find a lady clerk there."

"A man might do far worse. I called, by the way, to apologise for my bad behaviour the other night."

Lisbet eyed him with suspicion, so that she sat her horse looking like a brooding Richmond belle who had lost her way to the ball of the year.

"I'm downright mad with you, Mr. Rawlings."

"Still?" said Jason.

"You are the meanest man I've ever set eyes on—helping those high and mighty Cordovas to cheat my father the way you did."

"Come now, child," he said, "that was a matter of legal ifs and buts, declared so by Judge Conner himself."

"Detestable beast," she breathed, "it was you who introduced every if and but. And I do declare it was you who whispered in the ear of old María López and had her sell to the Cordovas, after all."

"Ah, well, that's dead and done for now."

"Is it?" Lisbet tossed her head. The fires that slumbered close to the surface kindled in her eyes. "You'll see otherwise, sir. Pa isn't the man to lie down in the face of sneaky deviousness. You've only frustrated him; you haven't beaten him."

There, he observed, spoke the father's committed daughter. Next, he supposed, would come the image of tantalising woman. They all protested a degree of helplessness—but ye gods, the power they had, and knew they had. For a year he had danced to the tune set by Edwina. It did not take a prophet of great divinity to pronounce that no matter how many men Lisbet Hendriks took a full-blooded fancy to, she would make puppets of them all.

"Madam?" he said, inviting the play.

"You've called to apologise, you say?" Lisbet lifted eyes that were like those of a cat who could both see and smell the proffered dish of warm milk. "Well, Mr. Rawlings, you all get right down off that horse, sir, and bend your knee. Then maybe I'll hear what you can make of a suitable apology."

Jason got down. He did not bend his knee, for he knew that wasn't an important part of the game. He held up his arms to her. He had time to dally and was calculatingly willing to play with this silky Virginian baggage. She saw his smile, read in it the possibility of flirtatious dalliance with Esmeralda nowhere in sight, and brought her left leg over the saddle. She descended in a foam of petticoats and landed in his arms. As her feet touched ground he kissed her, imprisoning her startled lips without compromise. She had not expected him to engage like this as quickly as this, and for a moment her every limb stiffened, then yielded. Their warm mouths melted into each other. All the same, when he released her she struck at him with her whip. He took the blow on an uplifted arm.

"Oh, I surely never have been so taken advantage of!" she cried. "You are a deplorable cad, sir, do you hear?"

"At least I'm forgiven for my behaviour during our previous meeting," he said.

"You are not." She was flushed, her eyes challenging and defiant.

"I judged I was, since you kissed me so warmly."

"That is a lie, sir, I did not!"

"A lie?" He raised an eyebrow. "But it happened, madam."

"It wasn't of my initiative," she cried. "You took advantage of me!"

"I? A travelling lawyer? I avoid all such lawless acts. They're a danger to my calling, quite against all the ethics. Madam, you set upon me. Could I hold you off? Not I. However, whatever the risk to my calling, I'll set the matter right for you and turn the coin upwards."

She gasped as she found herself in his arms again. She opened her mouth to scream. Too late—the new imprisonment of her lips cut off her breath. I must swoon, she thought, it is expected of me. She shuddered with delight. How the fiend could kiss. She felt him tormenting her, making her lips part and devour. Such torment she accepted as his way of stimulating her; it was not yet in her consciousness of men to sense or realise that he was in cynical discovery of her willingness to play the frivolous baggage. Her knees began to shake and her bones to melt. He freed her. She held on to him out of necessity for a moment.

"There," he said, "we're at evens now."

Blushing, she put a hand to her breast.

"Sir, I—oh, I am assaulted," she gasped.

"Grievously?" he said. "But, madam, I did not complain when you leapt from your horse and fell upon me as amorously as Venus in her cups."

"A fiendish fabrication!"

He laughed. She retreated, but was spellbound. Wild, burgeoning Texas had unearthed a man who neither chewed tobacco nor talked only about Texas. This was a country of great striving adventurers. In Westboro County her father was the only one who had the additional asset of brains: he ran rings around the rest. And most of those were in his pocket. She doubted if Jason Rawlings would prove one of the herd. Her lips were still warm from his kisses, still tender. She shivered with excitement.

"Do you prefer kissing to argument, madam?" asked Jason.

"Oh, you're not a man of honour, sir."

"Well, we're both guilty," he said.

"We are not!"

"Yet you're very accomplished."

"At what sir?" she asked.

"At kissing."

Lisbet sought to blush, but failed.

"Oh, you all!" she cried. "Do you think it an occupation of mine, kissing every man who helps me from a horse?"

"I fancy, Miss Hendriks, you show such excellent promise that though kissing may not be your occupation now, you'll come to it very naturally in time."

Lisbet's white teeth showed.

"Oh, you've spent your time in low dance halls, in saloons, sir! Stand back—or declare yourself."

"Declare myself?"

"If you wish to kiss me again, Mr. Rawlings, your intentions must be honourable and must be declared."

"Ah, that's it, is it?" Jason smiled. "Well, frankly, I can't afford such intentions. But a kiss or two—I'm game enough to oblige you in that recreation."

"Recreation?" Lisbet looked ready to spring. "How dare you, sir. You've compromised me and insulted me. My father shall hear of this."

"Your father is a man of honour, no doubt," said Jason.

"Yes, he is, sir."

"But you've hardly been compromised. Only the horses bore witness. It was a sweet diversion, no more, as you well know, little baggage."

"Baggage? *Baggage?*" Lisbet's smouldering eyes took fire. "I shall scream the sky down!"

"You'll disturb your honourable father if you do," said Jason, and remounted Napoleon. A trap pulled out of the trees some way down the drive, turning towards them. It contained the Colonel and Mrs. Purdy. Jason watched it. Lisbet heard it and turned.

"There is my father, sir," she said.

"I know," said Jason, and cantered away.

"Oh, you are a disgrace and a coward!" she cried, left with the infuriating suspicion that he had been trifling with her. She kicked at the gravel in rage.

Sam Houston, large, blunt, industrious, listened in his office to his colleague, Hamilton Winstanley.

"This friend of mine," Winstanley said, "we served together in the Virginian Rifles, and I'd like to oblige him."

"But damn it," said Houston, "you don't expect me to go personally, do you?"

"I'd just like your signature."

"It's a Land Commission matter," said Houston, "so why d'you want my signature?"

"To make it talk," said Winstanley.

"It's a big spread, is it?"

"None bigger, and a long-established one. They could have pushed their boundaries every which way in the time they've had it. If you'd sign this accompanying letter, the authorisation to check the validity of the original grant, and the present holding, would be given weight. They'd have to cooperate."

"They're Spanish, you said?"

"They are," said Winstanley.

Sam Houston tugged his moustache.

"They all hang every Spanish right and principle round my neck," he said. "And if we act the way they talk, Texas is going to march steadily backwards. They make a year's meal of every debate. You promise them a free people's republic, which they asked for. You win it for them, and there's not one of them wants it. They treat their servants like peasants, and complain about our way with niggers. Well, I'll sign since the spread is that big and the family that self-important. Who's after any land they aren't entitled to be holding?"

"I told you, Sam, my friend, Colonel John Hendriks."

"What's he want it for?" asked Houston.

"Cotton."

Sam Houston looked more interested.

"Cotton, eh? What's the Cordova industry?"

"A few cows," said Winstanley.

"Well, cotton's the better bet for our economy," said Houston, signing the letter. "We're not exporting cows. Those damn Spanishers. With their way of standing still, they're a growing liability to Texas."

Isabella swooped down the stairs just in time to catch Jason as he entered.

"Jason! Where have you been?" She was palpably at odds with the day.

"I rode over to see Lisbet," he said.

"Lisbet?" she said, unreceptive to the point of haughtiness.

"I did tell you."

"You mentioned you wished to see Señorita Hendriks; I do not know her as Lisbet."

"Nevertheless, that's her name."

Sensitive, she said, "Why are you so cool? Have I offended you?"

"Now that's a silly question," said Jason, who had made up his mind to get no closer to her.

Her chin went up.

"Señor, I will not be spoken to like that," she said indignantly. "It was bad enough having Colonel Hendriks bully me this morning. I had no one to stand up for me, no one—"

"You can stand up very well for yourself."

"You are supposed to be my lawyer—"

"I'm not."

"But you are supposed to be," she insisted. "And it was very upsetting to have you go casually off, leaving me at the mercies of that man."

"Isabella, this lawyer game is over."

"It's not a game, nor is it over," she cried, his lack of sympathy bringing on the now all too familiar feeling of confused emotions. "It is quite legal to appoint a friend to look after one's affairs, whether he's a lawyer or not. It's being a friend that matters. Oh, now you are looking very cool—"

"This, I swear, is my patient look."

"Oh, I am very grateful for such a patient look as that," she said, trying a little sarcasm. "But that greedy American is trying to intimidate me. It was hardly the nicest thing to happen to me, having the father call to shout at me while you were away making peace with the daughter."

"It was an uneasy peace," said Jason, "though we parted on a kiss."

Isabella, badly hurt, paled and said numbly, "A kiss?"

Jason reasoned that a man who had gotten himself into deep water should get out the best way he could. That entailed making a lifeline of a flippant observation that flighty Virginian baggage weren't all that difficult to kiss. The look on Isabella's face stopped him, however.

"I was only teasing," he said. "But you were taking your turn to bully."

Her relief was immediate, her belief in his implied retraction without question—but she stood up to his accusation.

"I was not bullying," she said. "I was only upset. And, of course, señor, it is none of my business even if you kiss all the American girls you meet."

"I rarely kiss any of them," said Jason, "nor any Spanish girls either."

Isabella, much to her embarrassment, turned a dusky red.

"Señor," she said as calmly as she could, "this is not a subject I often discuss."

Jason coughed a little and said, "I'm glad to hear it, señorita. It's a flighty subject, señorita. It's not on the same level, señorita, as Cordova cattle."

"Oh!" Isabella shook both fists at him. "What is this señorita, señorita? You are gaming me."

"A little," said Jason.

Her lush curls sprang and danced as she laughed wholeheartedly, filling her eyes with brightness and delight.

"I am not señorita, I am Isabella," she said.

"I was merely implying," said Jason, "that I seem to be señor more often than anything else."

"That is different."

"Tell me about Colonel Hendriks."

She told him, warmly pouring herself out to him. Isabella became worried as she realised how much she had come to rely on him. It was so ridiculous—she was the Cordova, rich and powerful. She should not rely on anyone but herself. Nevertheless, here she was telling him everything, and asking what was to be done.

Jason, thoughtful, said, "Colonel Hendriks seems to have had a busy morning, the business slightly mixed."

"Yes?" she said, puzzled.

"What has Apulca said?"

"Nothing."

"What have you asked him?"

"Everything."

"And all his answers have been nothing?"

"Yes," said Isabella, "which means he is in contempt of all the questions. Which means he did not ambush those men, as I knew he would not. Apulca is a fatalist. He lets things happen and accepts all happenings. That is not to say he would not avoid a rattlesnake or refuse to defend Cordova; he would fight for Luisa and me. But he would not be the cause of any attack on us. He lives with the glories of Navaho history in his mind, but does not think about making history himself; he has accepted the fact of the white man's power and presence."

"Is that typical of most Indians?"

"Of some," said Isabella. "Not all of them are killers of white children. If they are wronged, they can be cruel in their vengeance —the Apaches and Comanches mercilessly so. But consider what has been done to them, by us, by the British, by the Americans. Señor—"

"Señorita?"

Isabella smiled and shook her head.

"Jason, that is our way, the way we are brought up. Sometimes my mother would call my father señor, my grandmother the same with my grandfather. Perhaps we are a little too formal sometimes, but you must not think that whenever I call you señor I have stopped liking you, even if—"

"Even if I am a descendant of pirates like Drake?"

"Oh, that robber!" She was off at once. "England should have hanged him for what he did to *Nombre de Dios!*"

"Isabella, calm yourself."

"I am calm," said Isabella proudly, "I am nearly always calm. Well, perhaps not as calm as your English women. I have heard they are so contained that they will continue to read a book during moments of love."

"Really?" said Jason. "How interesting."

And Isabella, born into a world which regarded the sexual issues of love as intensely and prohibitively private, was shot with crimson at her involuntary incursion into forbidden realms. Wishing Cordova would gape open and swallow her, she nevertheless stood bravely up to her public burning. Jason began to laugh.

"Oh," she gasped, "I did not mean—" She stopped, seeing that explanation posed the danger of further embarrassment.

To see a woman of such vitality and beauty plunged into confusion by what was only an amusing little reference to a subject which frequently took possession of the minds of most people, had the strange effect of making Jason want to kiss her and laugh it all away with her.

"You need not explain," he smiled, "for whatever you meant, and whether it's true or not, it's still very amusing. I fancy we don't have to pursue it. But there's still the boring question of Colonel Hendriks to consider." Inwardly he began to damn himself again. Yet he was trapped, as much now by the ridiculous but endearing nature of her confusion as by the woman she was. He jerked his thoughts back to the Colonel. "There's a way, I think, of turning our American friend into a more amenable neighbour. He's fired an opening shot in a new campaign against you. Well, we might be able to stop him bringing his heavier cannon up."

"How?" she asked, loving him because he had not tormented her into making her explain herself.

"Leave it with me."

"I am not to know what you intend?"

"I intend," said Jason, "to ride into Westboro this afternoon."

"I shall come with you," she said.

"No, you will stay here."

"Oh?" She put her chin up again, making herself look regally lovely. "You are giving me orders now?"

"No, advice. I'm supposed to be your lawyer."


"Luisa, do you think that Hendriks girl good-looking?" asked Isabella that day, in a seemingly casual, offhand way.

"In a way," said Luisa.

"Myself," said Isabella carelessly, "I'd not have considered her outstanding."

"But she's quite pretty with her eyes and her complexion."

"Oh, pooh, she has no complexion at all, compared with yours."

"Thank you, Isabella," said Luisa, feeling she was fairly sure she knew what this was all about. "Jason has told me that too. Well, actually he said my complexion is remarkably fine considering Texas is so savage to the skin."

Isabella bit her lip. No one had told her how fine her own complexion was. That is, he had not. She shook her head and hustled him out of her mind.


"Good afternoon, Sam," said Jason.

"Howdy," said Sam Purdy. "Shot?"

"Small one."

"It ain't your best likin'?"

"I still have a stomach," said Jason, "I'd like to keep it."

"You gotta lick that sorta stomach," said Sam. "If whisky don't lick it, nothing will."

"All the same, just a small shot," said Jason. Sam poured a tot and Jason took it down. "Mrs. Purdy in?"

"Yup."

"May I say hello to her?"

"You can go through."

"I'm obliged," said Jason.

"Welcome," said Sam.

Mrs. Purdy hastily disengaged herself from her apron and her kitchen and received Jason in her little parlour. She was pleased to have him call, for she considered him a gentleman of handsome friendliness. She exchanged cordial openings with him, then Jason said, "I really wanted to mention that Colonel Hendriks is setting up a case against Apulca, the Cordova Navaho."

"Oh, yes, I was real sorry to hear about the trouble," she said. "But them Injuns, Mr. Rawlings, you have no idea."

"Ah, so you know about it? The Colonel told you?"

Her sudden pink confusion had its suggestion of guiltiness. He felt sorry for her, but sorrier for Sam. Sam would take cuckolding pretty hard.

"I—yes, he did kind of mention it," she said.

"Mrs. Purdy, I want you to tell him to forget it," said Jason, like a man imparting a confidence. "Apulca is innocent, but the Colonel still might have him brought to trial. Be so good, my dear Mrs. Purdy, as to prevail on your patron not to. As an Indian, Apulca may not get the fairest hearing. It would be better for the whole thing to be dropped. I'll leave it to you to speak to the Colonel."

Mrs. Purdy began to tremble.

"Mr. Rawlings," she said faintly, "I can't do that. What notice would he take of me? You'd have to ask someone like his daughter, Miss Lisbet."

"Mrs. Purdy, I'm asking you."

"But, Mr. Rawlings, the very idea." Unable to meet his eyes, she picked up a cushion and agitatedly smoothed it. "I'm nobody. The Colonel wouldn't listen to me."

"I'm sure he would, Mrs. Purdy," said Jason evenly. "I'm sure he thinks a great deal of you. I've every good reason to believe he would listen very carefully to you. I'd go and see him myself, but I'm not as well thought of by him as you are. Do you know what I mean?"

All that Mrs. Purdy knew was that somehow Jason Rawlings had discovered she was being unfaithful to Sam. It was there, in his eyes and his smile, and it was like a cold and deadly exposure of her indiscretions.

"Mr. Rawlings," she gasped, trembling, "I—how you just figure out I can talk to Colonel Hendriks about that Injun—"

"Oh, I have it nicely figured out, Mrs. Purdy." Jason's urbanity was icy indeed, for he felt a common bond with Sam. If Mrs. Purdy's conscience had teeth which bit her more painfully now, she had done the sharpening herself. And there was Apulca, who deserved something better than that which, for reasons of his own, her paramour had in mind for him.

Mrs. Purdy, in agitation and panic, whispered, "I'll—I'll see what I can do, Mr. Rawlings, though I'm real doubtful—I can't hardly think how to go about it—"

"Believe me, I've great confidence in you, Mrs. Purdy," said Jason. "Especially as Colonel Hendriks, being a gallant Virginian, will always listen to a lady as pretty as you. Talk to him, won't you?"

"Oh, I will, I surely will," she said, and there was anguished plea in her eyes.

"Naturally, this is purely between you and me," he said, but his smile told her she was out on a limb.

Colonel Hendriks was surprised to see his ladylove. She never came to the plantation except by arrangement. When she did come she was always shy and nervous. This time she confessed she was downright worried. He listened to her as she sat perched on the very edge of a leather couch, her face pale and every word an anxious one. The Colonel began to glower.

"Rubbish," he said, brusquely interrupting. "How can he know?"

"I just feel he does, it was the way he talked—oh, it was wrong what we did this morning out there." A little moan broke from her. "I'll just die, I surely will."

~ 223 ~

"Now don't fret," he said. "There was nobody out there except you and me, and you won't die, Laura, you're too healthy."

"I mean I'll surely curl up," she gasped, "Mr. Rawlings knowing and all. Oh, I'm ashamed to death."

He knew it was no good being rough with her. That would only make the alarm bells ring more discordantly in her frightened ears. She was not a woman who would respond to being browbeaten. It was his way of charming her, cajoling her and caressing her that had brought her into his arms—as well as what he could do for her and Sam. At thirty-three she was a beguiling armful and satisfyingly ardent once love had conquered her qualms.

"Now see here, Laura," he said, "that smooth-talking little islander is only guessing. I'll concede he's shrewd enough to guess a thing or two—but he lacks all proof. Hold your pretty chin up. I'm not falling for a new bluff, nor should you. You are imagining things."

"No, I ain't—no, I'm not." Mrs. Purdy was racked with apprehension. "And Sam looked real suspicious when I said I was going out again. I said I was seeing some church ladies. I'm scared about Mr. Rawlings. He knows. Could he—?" She shuddered at the thought. "Could he have seen us this morning?"

The Colonel, about to exorcise the shaking devil in her for raising such an unthinkable spectre, drew a sharp breath. Rawlings had been there this morning, had talked with Lisbet, and had ridden off when he and Laura appeared in the trap. Had that damned cold-nose Englishman been prowling about?

"By God," he said. His expression increased his love's agitation. She was a warm woman in a man's arms, but not the coolest in an emergency. She made a blushing mistress. But as a guilty wife she was liable to blush once too often. If she thought anyone witnessed her in amorous dalliance, she would shake night and day—and go to pieces at the first question a suspicious husband might put to her.

"Oh, I remember!" she gasped in fright. "Mr. Rawlings was here this morning—we saw him."

"Calling on Lisbet. Lisbet fancied she could make something of him, but I suspect she's changed her mind." The Colonel's handsome smile was full of charming reassurance. "Calm yourself. It's Lisbet his eye was on. But I don't aim to hand my daughter over to an impecunious lawyer, whether she's changed her mind or not.

I don't know what devious game he's playing with you and me over that Cordova redskin, but I won't have it worrying your pretty head."

His smile and his air of confidence soothed her worst fears. He took her hands and drew her to her feet. He tenderly embraced her. Shyly she came to rest against his protective chest. But her nervousness was still acute.

"You'll—you'll let that Injun go?" she pleaded.

"I haven't got him."

"I mean—"

"I'll do it for you, Laura," he said, her curving warmth arousing ardour.

"Oh, it surely would take a worry off my mind," she said gratefully.

"I'll accept benefit in kind," he smiled.

She blushed and trembled.

"Oh, I couldn't—not again—not here—"

"No, not here. Upstairs. Lisbet's in town."

"Colonel Hendriks—oh—"

Her shaking knees sagged. He lifted her. Her spirit was grateful and her flesh weak as she let him carry her from the room and up the stairs.

# 20

The stage, which called once a week at Westboro, pulled up outside Hanchuck's, agents for everything from passenger conveyance to Indian affairs. When the land commissioner alighted, with his capacious bag, he thought little of the place. A one-eyed street and dust. He thought even less of it when he discovered there was no hotel. He was directed to Sam Purdy's. Neither Sam nor Mrs. Purdy impressed him. Neither did the room he was offered. As a government official, he was used to slightly more prestigious accommodations. He was an upgraded clerk, and accordingly his attitude reflected his sense of elevation. Environmentally, however, he was adaptable, for his investigatory work took him into the outlandish wilds of Texas among all kinds of people. All kinds of people included many who had enlarged their holdings well beyond the limits laid down in their original land grants. The chief culprits were the old Spanish families, now citizens of Houston's hard-won Republic. They seemed to regard themselves as the elite of Texas, which further offended land commissioner William Hoskins. If any elite class could exist at all in a democratic republic, it could only be made up of people who represented the strength and incorruptibility of its administration—people like himself.

What a place of pioneers Westboro was. He stood outside the saloon, calculating what people were beginning to make of the town. Well, he had to give them their due, these Americans who came West, to work and sweat and build. But why they had to make Westboro look like a cattle town he did not know. As far as his information went, only one family raised cows—the Cordova family. And he imagined their reception of him would be no more cordial than that of others of their kind.

He went back into the saloon and asked Sam Purdy where a trap could be hired.

"Ain't none," said Sam. "Everyone got their own."

"What about visitors?"

"Hardly get visitors."

"I'm not surprised."

"You goin' somewhere?"

"I've a call to make, yes. I'll need a trap—and later on I'll need a horse."

"Only sell liquor here. You can get a horse from the livery. Down the street." It was quite a speech for Sam, but he was just as helpful as he was laconic.

"Señorita?"

"Yes, Manuel?" Isabella looked up from poring over her accounts—her conscientious weekly task.

"A visitor, señorita, a gentleman from Houston."

"An interesting gentleman?"

"An Americano, señorita."

~ 226 ~

"Oh, even some Americanos are interesting. What does he want?"

"He said, señorita, that his business is official."

Isabella chewed the end of her quill. Official? Was it to do with Apulca? She got up and went into the hall, her concern covered by a cloak of resolution. A thin man awaited her, his hands behind his back, his attention focussed on a painting of the Madonna. He looked as if he was pricing it. He turned, his black coat a sober companion to his dark grey trousers. He viewed Isabella with the detachment of incorruptibility.

"Madam—"

"I am Señorita Cordova."

"I wish to see the head of the house. Your father, perhaps?"

"I am the head of the house, in that I own Cordova. What is your business, señor?"

"My business is with you, then, señorita," he said politely. "I am William Hoskins of the Land Commission in Houston, and am one of its commissioners. I'm authorised to examine your title to this estate and to check it against your physical holding. Your grant, no doubt, originated from the imperialist government of Spain. Our republican government has agreed not to contest such grants, but reserves its right to check the validity of relevant deeds. Perhaps you'll be good enough—"

"A moment, señor." Isabella held up her hand to stem the clinical outpouring. "I should like it, señor, if you would not address me as if I were a class of infants. I confess myself delighted to learn that the Americans of Houston have magnanimously agreed to recognise the sovereignty of old Spain, while at the same time reserving the right to be suspicious. Tell me, what are their feelings concerning land grants made to Americans by the deposed Mexican authorities? Is the validity of these grants to be checked too, or is it only the holdings of Spanish families which are suspect?"

William Hoskins pursed his lips. His not unhandsome features were as well ordered as one of his own filing systems, for which he was noted.

"Naturally, señorita, you are free to express opinions—"

"Naturally."

"But there is no discrimination. May I see your deeds, please?"

Isabella considered his look of quiet authority. He was not an overbearing man, such as she might have expected. She was young, but not so young that she could not detect an anonymous hand had stirred the pot.

"You are—?" she enquired.

William Hoskins let a slight frown mar the smooth forehead beneath his standing mop of stiff brown hair.

"I've told you, madam."

"Señorita, if you please. I am not a madam."

He would have liked to tell her she was as much a madam as many of them, but he rarely shed his mask of imperviousness.

"I am William Hoskins of the Land Commission—"

"Where is your uniform?"

"We don't wear uniforms." Really, he thought. "We aren't soldiers."

"Where is your authority?"

He produced his papers. One was signed by Sam Houston himself. Isabella glanced at them without taking them, then waved them aside.

"I can do nothing, señor, without first consulting my lawyer."

"You aren't required to do anything, Miss Cordova, except produce your deeds."

"That is what I mean," said Isabella, "I never produce my deeds except when my lawyer is present. Fortunately, he happens to be here, otherwise you might have had to call again. We have saved you that."

"I'm afraid you—"

"Please enter, señor, and take a seat," said Isabella, and ushered him into the spacious room full of cool shadows. Then she went in search of Jason. She found him out on the patio, absorbed in a game of backgammon with Luisa. "Jason, will you please come?" Isabella arrived at his elbow in a swirl of silks. "A poky-nosed official from the Land Commission is here, asking to inspect the Cordova land grant. I wish you to come and put him in his place."

Luisa regarded her sister with a little dismay. Isabella sometimes sounded as if she owned Jason—or would like to own him.

"Isabella," he said, "you're much better at dealing with your own government officials than I am."

"Oh, I have received him very calmly, yes," she said. "But I know I shall become angry. You will remain calm. So please come.

The man is rather like a polite piece of wood. You will know how to saw him in half."

"You cannot resist that, Jason," smiled Luisa.

"I can," said Jason.

"Oh, you would not be as mean as that," said Isabella. He had his elbow on the table, his head bent over the board, and would not look up at her. He had been very reserved with her lately, giving most of his time to Luisa. "Jason, he has come to investigate Cordova. Do you not see how I am being harassed? First one thing, then another. The business over Apulca—"

"That was days ago," said Jason, "and I think you'll find it's finished with."

"Oh, I expect you dealt with it very cleverly," she said. "But this investigation, it's a plot. Please come."

Luisa looked hard at her sister. Isabella was quite capable of standing up to officials, as Jason had said. Why did she want him to stand up with her so often? She had always been like her grandfather in self-reliance. She was in love. She had to be.

Jason got up. With something of a sigh, Luisa thought. Isabella smiled.

"I'm making a mistake," he said.

"No, you are going to be a help to me again," she said. "And that is not a mistake."

He followed her back into the house. She turned to him in the hall, wishing he would be more agreeable instead of being so remote. She hesitated, wanting to ask him if anything was wrong.

"Come along," he said. "Let's see what we can do with your unwelcome visitor. We're keeping him waiting."

They entered the room to find Mr. Hoskins standing with his back to the fireplace, his hands clasped behind him. He did not look impatient. Indeed, he had come up against this kind of treatment before. Keeping him waiting was an attempt to ignore him, in the hope he would go away. But the better representatives of the new Republic were not as poor-spirited as that.

"Señor Hoskins," said Isabella, "forgive me for being so long, but here is Señor Rawlings, my—"

"I am the señorita's adviser," said Jason, who did not want to be named lawyer too often.

"Your servant, sir," said Mr. Hoskins, "but it's of no consequence."

"You're of no consequence?" said Jason.

So, he was at it already, put up to it no doubt by the woman, who had been quick to play the game of confusion herself. The land commissioner smiled thinly.

"I was referring to your standing as Miss Cordova's adviser, sir. The Spanish Queen herself, if she claimed a holding in Texas, wouldn't be entitled to a single acre of it if it wasn't properly documented and registered."

Jason looked enquiringly at the well-kept gentleman.

"What has the Spanish Queen to do with it?" he asked. "Señorita Isabella Cordova is a Texan, and has been since birth. We're not going to be faced with irrelevancies and confusions, are we? I'd not want to think you've come here in a spirit of careless partiality."

Ah, they were going to be meticulously difficult. That was no novelty either. It was the basis of procrastination.

"Mr. Rawlings, as the servant of my government and its people, I exercise no partiality."

"Even so, señor," said Isabella, "you have not arrived at Cordova by careless chance, have you?"

"If Cordova were selected out of a hat for investigation," said Mr. Hoskins frankly, "it would mean nothing personal. The Land Commission has the authority to investigate the validity of all land grants. There are question marks against the ownership of large amounts of Texas."

"I am not surprised," said Isabella, "for most of us would admit it all really belongs to the Texas Indians."

"They have notions of legality, only notions," said Mr. Hoskins.

"You're authorised to inform Señorita Cordova why her holding is under investigation?" said Jason.

"No, sir. I don't have to give reasons. Nor are such reasons necessarily obligatory on the part of Miss Cordova to produce the deeds."

"Of course," said Jason. "Señorita, you may allow Mr. Hoskins to see them."

"I shall require, when my assistant arrives tomorrow," said Mr. Hoskins, "to have possession of them for the time it takes me to check the boundaries."

"In that case," said Jason, "please let us see your authorisation." Neatly Mr. Hoskins produced his papers. Jason studied them, saw that the authorisation was backed up by a letter signed by the President himself. He handed the papers back. "You're not a man to exceed your terms of reference, Mr. Hoskins?"

"I am not, sir," said Mr. Hoskins.

"You'll notice, then, that although you're authorised to inspect the land grant and check the holding, you aren't authorised to take unlimited possession of the deeds. Nowhere does it say so."

"It's allowed for," said Mr. Hoskins patiently. "Please refer to the wording '. . . and to take all other steps deemed necessary,' etc., etc."

"Come, man," said Jason, "such a specific point can't be covered by a vague generality. It would never stand up in a court of law. I'll tell you why. In the first place, no court would allow you to take possession of someone else's property and wander off with it. Señorita Cordova's deeds are as much her property as her house, and even more valuable. Secondly, you'll take days to ride and check the boundaries of Cordova. Hence my reference to wandering off. Watch out for the Comanches, by the way. Now suppose you lose her deeds, or the Comanches eat them? Where would Señorita Cordova stand then in the eyes of the Land Commission? She would have a holding, but no title to it."

For once Mr. Hoskins lost his impervious look. His very eyes seemed to gnash together in his sharp irritation. Isabella, however, regarded Jason with delight. She really had no worries that the official would find anything wrong, but how delicious to have Jason stand the man on his head.

"Mr. Rawlings," said Mr. Hoskins snappishly, "that sounds, sir, as if you intend to be obstructive."

"I disagree, señor," said Isabella. "So you say that if you lose my deeds, if they are blown away by the wind, you will claim that a protest about such a happening was obstructive? You will have to make a copy."

"I'm not a clerk," said Mr. Hoskins, "and surely a copy exists?"

"Yes, in Mexico City," said Isabella sweetly. She knew no department of the Houston government could expect assistance from that quarter.

"You understand the grant is in Spanish?" said Jason.

"Most of us, sir, are fully equipped in that language."

Isabella went away to get the deeds. She returned with them, and Mr. Hoskins inspected them. The original grant, written out on parchment, was a maze of florid Spanish script, the signature of a Spanish king a flowery flourish. He could not dispute that signature, or the date or the import of the grant.

"You are satisfied, señor?" said Isabella.

"This document, Miss Cordova, seems quite in order. I shall return tomorrow with my assistant, who will be arriving from Austin."

"Is he a clerk?" she asked.

"A surveyor," said Mr. Hoskins. "As to my—ah—wandering off with your deeds, you may accompany us, Miss Cordova. Many owners insist, and they have a right to. And we appreciate any help we receive from them."

"It is suggested, señor, that I wander for days with you?" said Isabella in astonishment at so outrageous a proposition.

"A slip of my tongue, for which I apologise," said Mr. Hoskins, admitting his gaffe without quibble. "It's the first time I've dealt with a lady owner."

"A copy of the grant must be made," said Isabella, "and you will need horses."

"I know. They can be hired from the livery in Westboro."

"You are welcome, señor, to use horses from my stables," said Isabella generously. She had had her moment. With Jason, she had shown him Cordova mettle. And as she had nothing to fear, she did not wish to torment the commissioner further. Mr. Hoskins, however, was determined when he left not to concede her a square yard. Nor would he use her horses. To do so might be to accept a small dose of palliative bribery.

"Jason, that was rather naughty of us," said Isabella when they had seen the commissioner out. "The poor man arrived so sure of himself, and has departed quite shaken."

"Did you enjoy it?" asked Jason.

She laughed.

"Oh, yes. His face. Did you see it crack? But these Americans from Houston, they think they discovered Texas, peopled it, and made it."

"I think they'll make more of it than other people before them."

"Sometimes I believe you like them," she said.

"I only believe it's better to take people as you find them, whether they're Americans or Spanish or Mexicans or whatever."

"Perhaps you are right. You would make a good Texan. Yes?" She spoke lightly.

"No," said Jason, "I'm a man for the four full seasons. I like spring and summer, autumn and winter. I like grass to be green and sometimes wet, and sun that doesn't take the skin off your back."

"It has not taken the skin off mine." She moved closer to him as he stood by the fireplace. Her silks whispered.

"You were born to it," he said, "you couldn't exist without it."

She looked at the fireplace. She could have told him there were times in Texas when the huge fire had to blaze and roar.

"Jason, have I done something to displease you? You have been very cool lately."

"You're mistaken."

"There, that is very cool. 'You're mistaken,' you say." Her features became momentarily prim as she mouthed his words.

"That's nonsense," he said brusquely.

"Please don't quarrel with me," she said unsteadily.

"I don't intend to. I'm in your house, and I appreciate all your kindnesses. But I have a house of my own in England. It's heavily mortgaged, and how the devil I'm going to redeem that mortgage I don't know. I can't leave my sister with all the worries on her shoulders for much longer. I must think of going back. But first I have to meet your father. I have business with him."

"Then you do know him," said Isabella, speaking through muffling little shock waves of dismay. How could he talk like that about going?

"No. But I do have business with him. It's nothing to do with Cordova, or Texas. That's all I can say. Have you been in touch with him?" He had asked her the same question some days ago, feeling she might have written to her father and mentioned that Cordova had a guest, a gentleman from England who was waiting to see him. Isabella had said she had not written; her father was not a prolific correspondent and had given her no address.

"No," she said. "Jason, I told you, I have no idea where he is staying. But he should be back in a few days, and you will see him then. Is there a risk you might lose your house in England?"

"I hope not," he said.

But if it did happen, she thought, there would be less reason for him to go home and more reason for him to stay here. However, because he had done so much for her she had to say, "If you aren't too proud, Jason, I would—"

"For God's sake, don't offer to save my home for me," he said abruptly, and left the room.

Horrified, Isabella wondered what she had done that made him keep such a distance from her.

"Now, *ma petite bonbon*," said Antoinette, kneeling in front of Clare, the child sitting on a stool. "But no. *Anglais*. English. My little sweet." Clare smiled. "So now, say, 'Papa, I love you.' That is for when he comes, your papa. He is so high." She raised her hand to its farthest. "When you say it, he will love you too, then."

"Love Papa," said Clare. She dimpled, and her green eyes gazed fascinatedly at Antoinette, who was so warm and nice. "Love you," said Clare.

Antoinette hugged her. Each day she called at the Blazeys' house and Mrs. Blazey released Clare to her, for Antoinette to take to her lodgings. In the early evening Antoinette took her back. Her lodgings were clean and comfortable. She had two rooms and so much money she felt rich. She was in a constant state of wonder. Providing she was careful, dressed simply, wore gloves and a shady bonnet, no one bothered her or looked questioningly at her. Maryland was not a wholly committed slave-owning state. But she needed to be careful, and was. No one stopped her in the streets of Baltimore to take her into custody and return her to New Orleans. She was free, and was still trying to accustom herself to the headiness of freedom. Sometimes she felt as if she had drunk too much wine. There was no establishment wherein she was inspected for her graces and her promise, no conversations by which her suitability as a mistress could be judged. She did not have to endure a single moment's shame or humiliation. She was free. Jason Rawlings had delivered her. Without fuss or trouble, without even a single knife being drawn. Edwina, his wife, who had been so good to her, had said he would come one day, and he had. She thought he would be a man of fierce, outraged pride—a man who had not made a good husband. Instead she could only wonder why Edwina had left him. The answer was not in him, of course, it was in Edwina herself, a woman born to be an exciting mistress, not a faithful wife.

Baltimore was very American, and not at all like New Orleans. Seamen came ashore, great tanned sailors. They looked at her, many of them, and after weeks fighting seas grey with death were stunned by the magnificence of her eyes. She looked like a cousin at least to a royal house of Europe, so peerless were her features and so elegant her walk. The Blazeys were most impressed, and Mrs. Blazey never failed to offer her tea. Antoinette, much to her credit, never failed to accept. She hid her astonishment at Mrs. Blazey's apparently unquenchable thirst for the undrinkable. Antoinette's courage in sharing the pot, her impeccable behaviour, and her quite devastating charm mellowed the prim and pious lady and won the fussy heart of Mr. Blazey. More definite became the indication that they would relinquish Clare permanently when her adoptive father arrived to claim her.

When he did. Antoinette had long begun to count the days.

Little Clare was a jewel, a gem. The moment she left the house of quiet and fervent piety each day, she changed from a well-moulded statue of painful goodness to a lively child of joy. Edwina had not departed the world without giving it something. She had given it Clare. Monsieur Rawlings would fully forgive his wife, so brave at the last, for she had bequeathed him a most precious gift.

"Clare? That is a sweet name, isn't it?" said Antoinette. "I have not heard it before. Oh, in New Orleans everyone is Antoinette or Marie or Fifi. Fifi. Isn't that a silly name?"

"Fifi?" said Clare. She was almost three years old now, and the fascination Antoinette had for her swam in her green eyes.

"Yes, Fifi. Now, let us count. When your papa comes he will find you a clever girl. One." She held up a finger. "One."

"One," said Clare.

"*Deux.*" Two fingers showed.

"*Deux*," said Clare.

Antoinette smacked herself on the forehead.

"I am confusing," she said, "it is two. Two. *Anglais*. Your papa is *Anglais*. English. They are everywhere, the English, all over. They live on a small island, you see, *chérie*, and so they are always jumping into boats and going on long journeys to see if other countries are bigger and better. If a country pleases them they stay, and if the people tell them to go home again they hit them on the head. Bonk. Like so. Bonk." Antoinette gave her head a smart little rap. Clare giggled and her eyes shone. "Your papa, he is very *Anglais*, with such long legs and so handsome. He has crossed enormous seas and is not afraid of anyone. Not anyone. But he does not go bonk on people's heads. He looks at them and says do this or do that. And they say, 'Yes, m'sieu, at once, m'sieu.'"

"I like Papa," said Clare, but just a little dubiously.

"Oh, everyone who is nice likes your papa—and you are very nice. He is going to take us to England. Shall I tell you about England?" Antoinette rose from her knees and carried Clare to a chair. She sat down with the child perched happily on her lap. She drew on her imagination and what she remembered from books she had read. "Now, it is so big." She spread her hands a little. "Only so big, you see? Now, how do so many people live on so small an island without falling off?"

Clare thought and said, "Poor Papa fell off?"

Antoinette laughed.

"Oh, no. People only fall off if they are pushed, and the English are so polite that they never push. Do you see? That is, they never push each other. Sometimes they are a little naughty and push other people—"

A knock sounded. Antoinette put Clare down and answered it. Mr. Dillman Farquhar beamed at her as she pulled open the door.

"Oh, m'sieu, how nice." Antoinette smiled happily. Mr. Farquhar had been a source of great help and a tower of strength, assisting her to find her lodgings and to locate the Blazeys. He called frequently. Entering, he took her hand and gallantly applied his lips to her fingers. His complete acceptance of her as a young lady without inferiorities gave her intense pleasure.

"You're blooming," he said.

"You too, m'sieu, seem in the best of health."

"I don't resist all temptations," grinned Mr. Farquhar, "but I figure to fight the worst. An' how's our smaller lady, Miss Pickle?" He picked Clare up and swung her. She shrieked with delight.

"Oh, m'sieu, be careful with her," said Antoinette.

"Pickle," said Mr. Farquhar, and set Clare down. She held up her arms for more. He swung her again. She burst into new delight. He bundled her playfully into Antoinette's arms, the one who had made her a child of laughter. Antoinette cuddled her. "No problems?" he said.

"Oh, everything is most satisfactory," said Antoinette. "But more than that. I did not know I could be so happy."

He understood that. Here was one who had not let freedom confuse her. He knew scores of blacks who had escaped to the North, most of whom spent many months in childlike wonder because the meaning of freedom was so incomprehensible at first. To put them into domestic service to families, to put them into any kind of paid work, was part of that incomprehensibility—for if one had to work, to do what one was told to, then one was not free, after all. Only a change of masters had taken place. To try to explain the meaning of giving service and being paid for it—as a necessary rule of existence—was, in some cases, to attempt the impossible.

Mr. Farquhar knew he would not have to explain the complexities of a free social order to Antoinette. One of her parents, or perhaps both, had gifted her with a high degree of intelligence and adaptability. He heaped silent blessings on Jason Rawlings for having delivered this sweet creature from degradation.

Obviously Jason Rawlings had remarked the unusual intelligence and deep sensitivity of Antoinette. His was an action compounded of compassion and common sense. There was the girl, destined for carnal enslavement, and there was the child, unwanted from the moment of conception. What was more natural and more sensible than to free one from the unbearable, the other from charity, and bring them together?

"Ah, that *Anglais*," said Mr. Farquhar in his hearty way, a heartiness that disguised his shrewdness, "there's a man who knows what he's doing, huh?"

That was how Antoinette referred to him sometimes. Her

*Anglais*. She smiled at the remark, but she also coloured a little. He understood. Grateful octoroons could develop passionate attachments. He himself kept such a woman in Boston. She looked after a small house he had there. And whenever he was home she looked after him. He himself would have married her, for he had a completely unprejudiced and healthy outlook somewhat in advance of the charitable outlook of colleagues. But Boston would have recoiled in shock and outrage, and his colleagues would have damned him for carrying freedom to lengths as explosive as that. He had spoken to this woman about marriage and she, eyes very tender, had said, "No. If you marry me they will throw stones at you, don't you know that?"

The matrons of Boston suspected that his relationship with his coloured wench was not of the purest, but he offered no confession and she gave no offence. He was a man hearty for life and wished peace and understanding on people. His undercover work for the abolitionists was a vocation, and he went at it full of cheerful faith and confidence, laying his tongue heavily only on those who demeaned themselves by enslaving others.

"Yes, that *Anglais* knows where he's going, all right," added Mr. Farquhar, with a nod of his head.

"M'sieu," said Antoinette, "you mean Clare's papa?"

"Is he that? Well, I guess he is, and a stouter feller I never—"

"Oh, that is not true," said Antoinette indignantly, "you know it isn't. You will confuse Clare, make her think her papa is fat."

"Dear lady, dear young lady," said Mr. Farquhar, "stout also means brave and reliable. You have my word. No, no, not fat, certainly not."

"That is so?" Antoinette's little smile charmed him. "The significant difference is noted, m'sieu." She put Clare down, and Clare circled around Antoinette's skirt of watered silk. "M'sieu, you have not heard from him?"

"I don't expect to," said Mr. Farquhar. "He and I, two ships passing. But in warm friendship, I figure. I presumed, mademoiselle, that it was you he would be in touch with."

"He has not been in touch yet. M'sieu, will you stay for coffee? I am to make Clare a drink of lemon and quinine, and—"

"Sensible, sensible. Thank you, but I can't stay, blessed angel. My time in Baltimore is up for the moment. I'm a noticeable man, an' time runs out quickly for me in some places. I must run, Antoinette, d'you understand?"

"I think I have read of a saying in English books I have managed to master. Is it he who fights and runs away—"

"Lives to fight another day? That's it." Mr. Farquhar grinned. "I use it as my guiding light. There are some men in town, representing the interests of certain Southerners, that I don't intend to run up against. I called to say goodbye."

"I have a saying of my own," said Antoinette. "I will tell you. One loves friends, one never says goodbye to them."

"You'll do," smiled Mr. Farquhar, "you'll do. Be free, dear young lady, be free. Fly into life. Mr. Rawlings has great faith in you. You're to become the exceptional exception."

"Exceptional exception? What is that, m'sieu?"

"Who knows? Queen of England? Empress of France?" Mr. Farquhar's smile was broad. "Be of joy. *Au revoir*."

"You are a dear man," said Antoinette, and kissed him warmly on the cheek.

"So long, pickle," he said to Clare, and gave her a twist of candy as he departed.

An hour later there was a loud knock on the door, a loud, demanding one. Opening it, Antoinette was confronted by two men in dark hats and black velveteens, the velveteens strongly patched at knees and elbows. They had muskets under their arms. Bushy-browed and hard-eyed, they looked her over, and one barked at her.

"Where is he?"

"Your pardon?"

"Farquhar. He's been here." The man poked a finger into his own eyes, one after the other. "Them's the eyes we wear. We got others. Who are you?"

The other man shouldered his way in. Antoinette felt the onset of a fear so intense that her blood seemed to drain and icy cold came rushing in. She knew what these men were, what they were like, how they could forage, worry, shake, and destroy. They were chasers, bounty hunters, retained by slave owners for the purpose of reclaiming escaped blacks and smelling out abolitionists. They slipped in and out of northern states, infiltrating the pastures on which grazed the rescued lambs of Africa, forcibly snatching back those whom the abolitionists' shepherds left unguarded. They were wolves as well as bloodhounds, despised as much by some Southerners as by Northerners. Many people called them the Aydees, for "Alive or Dead" was their maxim. There was more to be gained by returning an escaped slave alive, but delivery of a dead one did not go unrewarded.

They preyed too on the roving abolitionists—such as Dillman Farquhar—who did their work deep in the heart of the cotton lands and were known to walk off, metaphorically speaking, with a slave under each arm and one clinging to their coattails. The southern bounty hunters gave short shrift to these audacious purloiners of private property. The rewards for disposing of this kind of abolitionist were not made public.

Who am I? Antoinette's very bones were ice. Not a New Orleans citizen, no. These men would know the mulatto girls, their characteristics and their Creole patois. French, they would think, what is she doing in Baltimore? The hostile, suspicious eyes were basilisk-like. She must speak her best English.

"I am Edwina Rawlings."

The man inside the room was peering and poking, ignoring Clare, who stood with the immobility of a child who sensed she had to be very good. The man in the doorway glanced at her, then fixed his eyes again on Antoinette. They seemed to growl at her.

"Where's that damn 'bolitionist?"

Antoinette tried hard, saying, "Gone, mister, gone to Memphis." Memphis was the only place that came to her dry tongue, and she prayed immediately that Monsieur Farquhar had gone anywhere but there.

The man glared. She was pale, her lambent skin white in her fear. Here was a man who had only to look at her fingernails. They had only the faintest tint, she had so little Negro blood in her, but it would be enough for those eyes. The man inside looked her over in deadly scrutiny, then at Clare. And Antoinette realised that if the man thought Clare was her child, then Clare could save her—for she was without doubt a child of white parents.

"She yours?" said the man at the door.

"Yes," said Antoinette, and managed to add for good measure, "Yes, mister."

"Well, damned if that don't beat all, that cantin', prayin' 'bolitionist settin' up with this fancy an' callin' hellfire down on decent folks who got fancies of their own." He peeled off a lurid grin. "He landed you with that li'l chicken?"

"Yes."

"She ain't no size," said the other man. "Where's your tongue?" he asked Clare.

"I'm good," said Clare, and Antoinette's thumping heart tightened.

"Well, she sure is purty," said the man at the door. He entered, and with a belligerence that disturbed the air. His colleague was irritably losing interest. The bird had obviously flown. But they were still suspicious. He looked at Clare, weighed her up, and then again searched the pale face of Antoinette.

"He married you?"

"No," said Antoinette. "He said he had a wife."

The second man scowled in disgust.

"He ain't got no wife. He ain't got nothing but cant. Where you from? You ain't no Marylander."

Where was she from? What place was there that would be safe to mention? She knew her English and her accent were not those of an Anglo-Saxon American of any state she could think of.

"From England," she said, and frenziedly prayed.

The eyes seemed to calculate: England was a good cotton customer, had good kinship with the Southerners. And the child was pretty—looked English.

"England, huh? Well, you shoulda stayed there. You ain't gonna get nothing from that belly-aching 'bolitionist. Where'd you say he's gone?"

"Memphis."

"You sure that's where?"

"So he said, mister." Antoinette moved and tucked Clare's face into her skirts, caressing her hair. The child was trembling.

"So you say he said." They prowled around, in and out of both rooms. "He live here 'times?"

"No, he only visits."

"You 'bolitionist?"

Antoinette remembered how some whites spoke.

"It don't bother me none, mister." But that was almost a mistake, such a departure from her delicate, precise English as might have screamed at some ears.

However, it brought only a cursory response. "You ain't got much more tongue than your brat."

"Cat tied it, I reckon," said the other man. "But we'll get the joker." He stabbed a hard finger at Antoinette. "Only not in Memphis. If he said Memphis, that's where he ain't gone for sure."

"We're wasting time," said his colleague. They left as belligerently as they had arrived, but without saying a word more. Antoinette drew a deep breath, sank to her knees, and embraced Clare.

"There, they are gone, the funny men," she said. "They were so funny, yes?" And she dipped into her reservoir of courage and drew up a bright, reassuring smile.

"Two," said Clare.

"Yes, two funny men. Two, sweet one."

Why didn't Monsieur Rawlings come? Clare was waiting for him; they were both waiting.

# 22

Jason presented the clerkly Mr. Hoskins and his assistant with a copy of the Cordova land grant.

"I thought there wasn't a copy," said Mr. Hoskins.

"There wasn't," said Jason. "I made one."

"I'm obliged, sir," said Mr. Hoskins, "but I must see the original again."

"Quite so," said Jason, "I might have made a mistake or two."

The commissioner diligently checked the copy against the original and professed himself satisfied.

"And thank you," he said.

"I'll remind you to watch out for Indians."

"The Comanches, Mr. Rawlings, keep to the mountains."

"Don't rely on that, Mr. Hoskins."

Isabella came out as the commissioner and the surveyor were riding away.

"They are wasting their time," she said.

"But someone wants it done."

"Of course. Colonel Hendriks has been at work again. He is wasting his time too." She was in her riding habit, her hat in her hand. She looked warm and lovely in the sunshine. "Jason, Luisa and I are going to gallop. Will you come with us? Please do."

He had thought he could wait patiently for his man. But because of other things now, he could not.

"Will you let me cry off? I must go to Austin."

"Where my father is? Why must you? It is easier, isn't it, to wait here for him?"

"I can't wait forever."

"Jason," she said, turning her hat with her hands, "I should like you to tell me. Are you going to leave us? You may stay, you know, as long as you wish."

He looked at the white wall, at the climbing plants that splashed the colour of blooms on the white.

"Isabella, you must be a little tired of my face by now. The welcome guest should always depart a day too early, rather than a day too late."

Hurt, she espoused the wound with a rush of protest.

"You are not a welcome guest, you are a friend! Why do you say such things? I would have thought better of you than that, and so would Luisa. Cordova is not an hotel, it is a place, a home, and people who share it with us are our friends."

"Isabella, what is the difference? Welcome guests and friends are much the same."

"Señor," she said, up on her high horse, "a stranger, weary and with a long way still to go, is a welcome guest for a night. But he is not a friend, only a traveller in need. And am I to be left to be bullied and harassed by the Americans? You know they want Cordova, you have seen that for yourself very well, and you cannot simply ride off and leave us to be trampled by them."

"What nonsense is this? You are not a woman to be bullied or harassed by anyone—you are powerful, you have vaqueros—"

"But I am not a soldier, a general!"

"Neither am I."

Her deep brown eyes were hot, her hands clenching her hat. The sky was washed by pale blue and in the distance the Cerro Jorobado glittered.

"How would you like it if, while you were away in Austin, Cordova was attacked and burned by Colonel Hendriks and his Americans?" she asked.

"That's more nonsense."

"It is not! You know what is happening to Texas, it is being Americanised. It is being taken over by people who want land, the best land—and they will take it from Indians, our Mexicans, and us. Colonel Hendriks is a land pirate—he is no gentleman—and will use guns and fire to take what he wants if we do not give it to him."

"I can't believe that, and I don't believe you do," said Jason.

"I have only just begun to realise that Colonel Hendriks is a frightening desperado," said Isabella. "That commissioner with a twitching nose and the surveyor, they are his agents in some way, and will cut Cordova in half if they can see a way to."

"I thought you said you had nothing to worry about there, that they were wasting their time."

"Oh, you are being miserably diffcult," said Isabella.

"I must go to Austin."

She looked defeated.

"You are going to say goodbye," she said in a strained voice.

"Austin isn't far. I'll be back in a few days."

She put all pride aside and said, "I will make no fuss, nor will Luisa, we will both behave very well about your going—as long as we know you have promised to return."

"A few days might mean a few more, that's all."

"Please be frank," she said. "If you mean to leave Texas and go back to England, I would rather you say so."

"I only said I might be a little longer than a few days."

"Yes." She twisted her hat about. "Please come back, won't you? You have been such a help to us. I am not too afraid of Colonel Hendriks, I confess it. But until he has given up wanting our land, I shall be a little worried."

"Then I must get back as soon as possible," said Jason, and damned himself again for his weakness. He retrieved his position a little by adding, "But I must also get back to England some time or other."

"I cannot complain," she said quietly.

He did not find his man in Austin. He searched hard enough, for he knew it would be better now to kill him in Austin rather than at Cordova. The man was lodged at no hotel. If he was in Austin at all, he was probably in the house of friends. Jason felt he might have found him had he pursued the search with a thoroughness that took no account of time. But he had promised Isabella that he would be back. And also, hadn't Isabella always been sure her father would return, though he was now well outside the mentioned fortnight. That brought the thought that he might be on his way now. The fact of being Isabella's father gave him no dispensation in Jason's book, though it did cast a dark shadow of tragic incredulity over the inevitable.

Jason knew he had brought that particular consequence on himself. He had accepted the challenge of ironic fate when he should have left it alone. He had discounted the effect a woman like Isabella might have on him. She was so damnably and unmistakeably a woman, with a vitality that made Edwina's sparkle seem thin in memory. He did not want another Edwina. Isabella was a healthy bewitchment, with creamy curves that shone and a skin that gleamed in the light of evening lamps. Black gowns, white gowns, red gowns, all bodiced to enhance the promise of her warm body. But what was any of that when set against the theft of a soldier's wife? He thought of Edwina, a brief burst of brilliance in life.

He could not draw back.

He could not do other than return to Cordova and resume his wait for his man.

"You're Colonel Hendriks?" William Hoskins was polite, though faintly disapproving.

"I am. You'll take a drink, Mr. Hoskins?" The Colonel had hopes of the commissioner.

"I don't touch liquor, sir, and I'm pressed for time. This is very unusual, but the order from my superior was to report to you before returning to Houston, and therefore I'm here."

The Colonel smiled in the handsome way that slipped a few years from him.

"We're all subject to the unusual at times," he said. "You've finished your survey of Cordova?"

"We have, sir."

"Well?" said the Colonel.

"There are no discrepancies," announced Mr. Hoskins. "The land grant made under the authority of the Spanish king at the time is in order, and being so is accepted as valid by the republican government of Texas. And the deeds held by the present owner, Isabella Cordova, coincide with the marked boundaries. I've found no fault. She holds no land she isn't entitled to."

The Colonel's smiled slipped badly. The man was a bureaucrat from the feet up if he didn't understand either flexibility or possibility.

"With a spread ten times bigger than anyone else's this side of the Colorado, you can't fault the damn size of it?"

"Are you suggesting, sir, that I should?" asked Mr. Hoskins with dangerous quiet.

The Colonel evaded that by saying, "Isn't there a limit on the size of land grants?"

"There is now. It has no retrospective aspect. It's not a principle of any good government to legislate retrospectively, Colonel."

"It's criminal," said the Colonel, "she doesn't work more than thirty percent of her holding. You can legislate on that, can't you?"

"I can't, sir," said Mr. Hoskins with precise nicety. "You should address that appeal to the President. I regret I can't stay longer, I must catch the stage. Good morning."

The Colonel was left in a savage mood. He was being frustrated at every turn. That damned Isabella Cordova. She was blocking his path to power. When he had first seen her, before her grandfather died, the look of her, the undiluted warm-blooded picture of Spanish beauty that had come to his eyes, had put into his mind the thought of divorcing his wife. When her grandfather died, there was another thought, that of uniting the great hacienda of Cordova with the Hendriks estate. By marriage. But he soon came to realise Isabella Cordova had a Spanish insularity he could never breach. She also had no idea how to use her vast holding. She had all that fine river land which had never known the single bite of a spade or the briefest turn of a plough. And now she'd virtually showed him the door in respect to Sancho's grant and over the case of that Navaho. That last case rested on the word of his two boundary riders against the word of the redskin. His men would say what he had told them to. But Isabella Cordova's negative reaction had suited him, for it gave him just the excuse he was looking for. The excuse to have Braddock burn the place down and see the Cordovas off in order to get the Navaho. If redskins were good for nothing else, they made useful pawns. Only Jason Rawlings had caused him to hold back on that action, with his unspoken threat to Laura Purdy.

Well, Jason Rawlings had since left Cordova.

"What are you doing?" Laura Purdy spoke from the bed, in which she lay naked. Colonel Hendriks, having dressed, was buckling a cartridge belt around his waist.

"Don't fret," he said. He had spent an entirely pleasant half hour with Sam's blushing but yielding wife. He was equipping himself now for different action.

"Colonel—you're not—oh, you're not going after Sam?" It was her first thought, that her self-assured lover was going to put Sam out of the way, for Sam had become a mite suspicious, looking hard at her today when she said she was going to Hendriks again, to mix another new recipe for the Colonel's cook. The Colonel wished to set a more varied table for friends and guests, and since his cook's talent was confined to Virginian dishes she was rightly pleased, she said, to go and help with new recipes now and then. She hadn't liked Sam's look too much, she told the Colonel. But she hadn't expected he would go after Sam.

The Colonel, buttoning his coat, said, "Sam? Why should I go after Sam?"

"I thought—well, I told you he acted kind of suspicious."

"That pretty head of yours, Laura," said the Colonel, "lets the bees get inside it and set to buzzing. Sam lacks the imagination to see you in my arms."

She blushed. Her clothes were piled on a chair, snowy petticoats heaped.

"Oh, I don't rightly know what he might think," she said, "except he's never been jealous. But then I ain't never given him cause before."

He looked at himself in the mirror. No doubt about it, he was still a well-set-up figure. He still had the class and air of old Virginia. He came of handsome stock, and there were few better than the Virginian. There wasn't a man of his age to touch him in Westboro County, Texas. His contemporaries and younger men were too rawboned, too close to the earth. He glanced over his shoulder at his mistress. She was always a surprising pleasure. She was also a clean woman, her every undergarment was spotless. She had no great intellect, but he thought now that her instinct for survival, strong in most women, was superior to her weakness. He had suspected previously that she might crumple if Sam began to ask questions. But she knew Sam had no proof and she could deal with him. Probably in a prettily hurt way. If she couldn't, he would, and in no pretty way.

"Laura," he said, "you'd prefer it if we didn't see each other for a while?"

A deeply infatuated woman now, she said, "Oh, no."

He crossed to the bed. She blushed again and drew the sheets closer to her chin. He still had a little time to linger.

"Get up, my pretty puss," he said, "and I'll dress you."

"Colonel Hendriks, oh, it surely was terrible enough letting you undress me—you must go out—I just can't get up while you're here."

The Colonel's smile was full of wicked charm.

"Sam's never dressed you?" he said.

"Oh, how can you embarrass me so? Sam would never dream of doing such a thing."

"I said he had no imagination. I reckon it would be mighty sweet to deck you out—"

"Oh," she gasped, her very ears tingling, "how you can be so shameless, it's just not nice—I never heard such embarrassing talk."

"I'll make amends, then," smiled the Colonel. "I'll leave you to your pretty blushes and your clothes."

"But where are you going? Why did you put that belt on?"

"It's a declaration of war, Laura," he said. "I aim to collect one musket-toting redskin now that Mr. Rawlings has shaken his dust —and I aim to persuade Isabella Cordova to sue for peace on my terms. The Cordovas have been running this part of Texas long enough. It's time we took over. That land has got to be brought to life—it's got to grow cotton."

She had some idea then of his ruthless strength of purpose. Virginia and a spendthrift wife had reduced him almost to penury. He meant now, with the wealth of his plantation behind him, to scale the heights of power.

"Them Spanishers and Mexicans aren't like us," she said, "but it don't seem hardly right to run them off their land."

"I'll handle them," he said, "you handle Sam."

He left her. Outside the house he met Lisbet, just back from visiting neighbours. Mrs. Purdy's buggy stood nearby, her black driver idling around, waiting. Lisbet greeted her father with a knowing smile.

"Miz Purdy feeling relaxed, Pa?" she asked.

"Mind your business, minx," he said.

"Poor Sam," she said, but she had no objections to her father's ways with women, as long as he didn't think about marrying one of them. "Where are you going with that?" She pointed to the musket under his arm; usually he wore a holstered pistol.

"We're picking up that Cordova Navaho," said her father. A stable hand arrived with his horse. "And I daresay we might find cause and time to settle with Isabella Cordova."

"You'll have to settle with Jason Rawlings first," she said a little spitefully. "He's her guard dog, isn't he?"

"He's gone."

"Gone?" Lisbet looked disgusted.

"He took off from Cordova a week ago."

"You never said."

"He's not a subject I've wished to discuss with you."

"Pa, you've got your interests, I've got mine. I don't interfere with yours, and I'll thank you not to decide about mine. I'm for you, Pa, you know that, but I had a score to settle with Mr. Rawlings. If he's gone I'm bereft of my right to scratch him into bits."

The Colonel's eyes glinted.

"You couldn't get the ring through his nose, missy, eh?" he said. "Well, he's gone and he's taken a slight problem of mine with him, the only favour he did me while he was here."

"What problem?" she asked.

"Don't ask questions."

Lisbet's smile was impudent.

"Pa, he surely did plant a mote in your eye."

"And I'm not sure he didn't plant one in yours, miss."

Impudence turned into vixenish frustration.

"Why didn't you hire him, Pa?"

"I might have, but he's a Mex lover," said her father. "Don't wait supper for me. And remember there are better men than Jason Rawlings."

"Then find one for me."

"To marry?"

"To play with," she said, and at once he saw her libidinous mother in her. He mounted his horse and looked down at her.

"I've told you," he said thickly, "I'll allow you some games, but I'll not allow those. You hear me?"

"I hear you, Pa. Have you all done with Miz Purdy for today?"

He scowled at her. She smiled in turn. He grinned at her impudence, and then laughed as he rode away to collect Ed Braddock in Westboro, where his overseer was busy doing some collecting of his own. As the Colonel reached the end of his long, leafy drive, a man stepped out from the pines not far from the house. He eyed the retreating figure of the Colonel, then made his way to the house, leaving his horse tethered among the pines.

Laura Purdy heard a sudden fuss and commotion on the landing outside the Colonel's bedroom. Joe's voice was raised in protest, so was Lisbet's. It made no difference. The door banged open, Sam barged in and slammed it shut. He looked at her. She was numbed, horrified, and in her underclothes. She stood in palsied shock, trembling with fear and guilt. A moan broke from her, and her face drained of colour. Sam was grey, his eyes livid. It took him long seconds to find his voice.

"Finish dressin', Laura, and go home."

"Sam—"

"Where's Hendriks gone?"

"I don't know—Sam—oh—" She swayed and sat heavily down on a chair.

"Where's he gone?"

She did not dare to say. She knew murder would be done. Gulping, she moaned with shame and despair.

"I don't know, I only—oh, Sam, I'm sorry—"

"Shut up! Get dressed. Go home."

After rounding up men willing to help the Colonel settle the score with Cordova, Ed Braddock finally reached the saloon. He wanted Sam Purdy in. Sam was a regular can-buster with a musket or flintlock. It wouldn't do no harm for him to shut up the saloon for a while.

But the saloon was already shut. Which meant it wasn't open when it should have been. Braddock reckoned the Colonel wouldn't like that, Sam pleasing himself about what time he unbarred his doors. There were several drifters lounging around, waiting for the opening. These were mainly loners, wandering from one area to the next, staying a while and looking, considering the prospects, doing a bit of work here and a bit there, then telling themselves it would be better elsewhere. It would never be better anywhere for such men; they were the West's gypsies.

Braddock went down the side alley to the rear door, and banged on it. There was no answer. Sam and his missus were both out, it seemed, and their darkie wasn't around either. Braddock returned to the boardwalk.

"Hey," said one drifter, "this the saloon or ain't it?"

"You got it right, mister," said Braddock, "but I ain't its keeper."

The Colonel had said get forty men. Braddock went across the street, buttonholing a tall, stringy man called Eli Hansen on the way.

"Friend?" said Eli, a powerful prayer.

"Eli, the Mex on the Cordova spread've shot up some of the boys. Colonel Hendriks had sent 'em up to get that Injun, Apulca, and the Mex peppered 'em. I'm collectin' a posse to go up and settle it."

"It's not my quarrel, nor the Lord's," said Eli, who had a homestead ten miles north of the town.

"When Mex shoot up our folks," said Braddock, "that makes it our quarrel."

"Not for me it don't," said Eli. "I'm peaceable, 'cept when I'm personally aggravated. Aside from that, I only fight the Lord's battles, not the Colonel's."

"The Colonel ain't goin' to like that, Eli."

"Well, even he don't come higher than the Lord," said Eli.

"You ain't gonna carry a musket for us?" said Braddock.

"I'm peaceable," said Eli. "And so's that Injun, to my reckoning. I never seen any Injun more so. Friend, he who carries the fiery sword against his neighbours shall end up with the devil on his doorstep. Good day to you."

"Cantin' yellerbelly," muttered Braddock to himself as he went on. He entered Mary Lou's eating place. She had four customers, all dining on hot beef hash and beans, with their hats respectably off. Mary Lou, seeing Braddock, put her large plump hands on her large plump hips and let a frown crease her round homely face.

Knowing what he was after, she said, "Now, Ed, you get outa here."

Braddock, ignoring her, addressed the eaters. The story was as he had told Eli and others, that Colonel Hendriks had sent some men up to flush out the Cordova Navaho, that they'd been shot up by Isabella Cordova's vaqueros, and that the Navaho was still there, getting illegal protection from Isabella. So the Colonel wanted it settled now, right now. The Cordovas had asked for war, and they were going to get it.

One man forked the last mouthful of hash into his mouth. Then he stood up, retrieved his hat, and said, "I'll go get my horse."

"The Colonel'll be right obliged," said Braddock cheerfully. Just as cheerfully he said to the other three man, "What's holding you back?"

"I'm eatin'," said one.

"I'm eatin' too," said another, "but I still ain't goin'."

"Nor me," said the third. "I ain't got no quarrel with the Cordovas, or their Mex."

"So now you get, Ed, you hear?" said Mary Lou.

"I'm gittin' my horse," said the obliging man, and left.

"Colonel needs men," said Braddock. "Them Cordova spitfires have spit once too often."

"Them Cordovas is ladies, an' you know it," said Mary Lou. "So maybe they're a bit fancy, that ain't no crime. I ain't havin' you yank my customers off to help the Colonel fight 'em. They don't bother me none, an' I don't hold us botherin' them any."

"They set their Mex on the Colonel's deputed men," said Braddock.

"Who said?" jeered Mary Lou.

"Mary Lou, you goin' against the Colonel?" said Braddock.

"I ain't goin' against anyone," said Mary Lou resolutely, "an' certainly not them young Cordova ladies. I'm keepin' the peace an' feedin' faces, and I don't owe the Colonel nothing, not while I pay my rent and dues regular. Now you listen, Ed, folks are beginnin' to wonder about the Colonel, and I don't reckon you're doin' yourself any good carryin' out all his errands without askin' questions—"

"Shut up," said Braddock, but he grinned. He liked Mary Lou, though he couldn't take her seriously. "You don't know the half of it, Mary Lou, so keep out of it. I'm only askin' for these boys to help us teach them Mex a lesson."

"I've done my share of that," said one man. "I ain't fightin' private wars for Colonel Hendriks. If he wants Cordova, let him get it legal."

"You'll be sorry," said Braddock, "you'll all be sorry."

He stalked out, and rode from the town to call on some homesteaders. The results were mixed. As Mary Lou said, not everyone liked what they thought Colonel Hendriks was up to. But there were some willing to earn the Colonel's dollars, and Braddock, when he returned to town, had some thirty hirelings. After some thought he spoke to the drifters. They were frankly willing to do almost anything for fifty dollars apiece.

The Colonel arrived. He had picked up some men himself, men as roughriding as the drifters, and was satisfied with the combined muster. He had his strategy worked out, and had already made his opening move by inducing Braddock to spread the word that Westboro men had been attacked by Cordova's Mexican riders.

Those willing to help the Colonel settle the issue asked no questions concerning the identities of the attacked men, or even whether any of them had suffered the common and fatal complaint of too much hot lead. For a promised consideration, questions weren't necessary. In any case, most knew that the answers lay in the Colonel's ambitions.

Coming from her room, Isabella heard voices in the hall. She stopped, put a hand to her mouth, and sped down the stairs, skirts hitched and petticoats swinging. She came floating in a rush of dark silk and peeping white lace over the tiled floor of the hall. Luisa turned at the open door.

"Isabella, look who is here."

"A man to buy beef?" said Isabella in light containment of her gladness.

"I've only the price of half a steer," said Jason.

Isabella looked at him, her colour warm, her eyes bright.

"Jason, I am so pleased," she said, and gave him her hand. "Luisa, aren't we pleased?"

"One of us is quite overcome," said Luisa, happy for her sister, who had spent days in restless search of one thing after another, and apparently finding nothing that relaxed her.

"I'm back too soon?" said Jason, his smile wry.

"Too soon? Oh," said Isabella, "how can that be, when you have been away for weeks?"

"Nine days," said Jason.

"Are you sure?" Isabella was glowing, pleasure enriching her vividness. Jason looked so good to her eyes. She had not expected him. She had been depressingly sure he would not come back. Her pulse beat quite riotously. Jason's smile seemed a little rueful for some reason, but it was a smile, and for her.

Luisa, watching her sister, saw the light in her eyes. Yes, Isabella was in love. Isabella, who had said she would never be in desperate need of a husband while she had Cordova. Undoubtedly smitten, she was looking at Jason as if she could eat him. That was said to be the most intense kind of love, that which made you want to consume your heart's desire.

Luisa laughed and flitted away, leaving them to each other.

"Jason, I am so glad you are back," said Isabella. "My declaration means I have forgiven you for going. You are lucky. There has been no trouble—"

"How does that make me lucky?" asked Jason.

"Well, if you had found us in terrible misfortune your conscience would have given you a dreadful time," said Isabella. "But we are quite without mishap, thank you. Even Señor Hoskins went away satisfied. He said Texas was full of benighted land grabbers, but that we did not seem to be among them. What is benighted?"

"Something to do with moral darkness."

"There now," said Isabella as she closed the door and stood in the hall with him, "you are such a knowing man that I shall accept your interpretation." She lightly touched her curls and smiled at him. "I am not as competent as I like to believe I am, and Cordova is so big. Luisa and I cannot handle its responsibilities in the same way as a man."

"Yes, you can." Jason, out of necessity, was in a sober mood. "Luisa is quick and intelligent—"

"But she will not be here long. She will marry Fernando Alba very soon."

"My felicitations, then, go to Fernando Alba. But it will make no difference, for you yourself are courageous and sensible—"

"Sensible?" Isabella hated the word.

"—and you're also naturally managerial. Added to that, you have your vaqueros."

"What have my vaqueros to do with running Cordova? And what is managerial?" Isabella felt it sounded as unflattering as sensible.

"You have an aptitude for management," said Jason.

"That is managerial?" Isabella made an expressive gesture of rejection. "Well, I am not that—and I hope never will be. It sounds dreadful, like something to do with a sugar factory. It is men who are managerial. That is natural, not dreadful." She smiled again, drew a necessary breath, and went on. "Jason do you think you could be managerial for me? For Luisa and me?"

"Manage Cordova?" His expression was strange.

"Yes." Her smile hid her nervousness. "You have such a cool head."

"I know nothing about running a hacienda, nothing."

"Oh, it would take you no time at all to learn," she assured him. "Even José says you are a man with a head, which is a great compliment, because José thinks the number of men who manage to exist with no heads is unbelievable. He says their survival can only be due to the benign paternalism of God. I will have papers drawn up, if you wish, so that your position would be protected. It would not do if Luisa or I had the power to dismiss you whenever you put us into one of our tempers."

"Really? Upon my soul," said Jason, "I had no idea Luisa was addicted to tempers."

"She isn't really. Neither of us is. It is just that some men can be very provoking." Again Isabella smiled very brightly. "It is agreed, then? You will stay and manage Cordova for us?"

"Come now, Isabella," he said, "you know very well that nothing would frustrate you more than having to give way to someone who was trying to run the place for you—especially someone without experience. In any event, I've a heavy debt around my neck, my mortgaged house in England. You're being very generous, but—"

"No, I am being very serious," said Isabella, and she was. She had endured nine terribly restless days and one or two sleepless nights. And she didn't know any other way to keep him at Cordova, unless he himself suggested the only possible alternative: marriage. She would give him half of Cordova then, as well as herself.

But Jason was set on avoiding the trap into which fate seemed determined to lead him. After the briefest of pauses, he said, "I'd be completely out of my depth." At which point, their conversation was interrupted by a hammering at the door behind them. Jason opened it. Colonel Hendriks was standing there, and from the look in his eyes it was obvious that this was no social call. Isabella came forward. The Colonel, seeing Jason, drew his eyebrows together. Without preliminary, he addressed himself to Isabella.

"By God," he said, "are you people out of your senses? I met Braddock in Westboro. He was intending to ride here with the warrant and pick up your Navaho. I was greeted with the news that some of your vaqueros attacked several Westboro men a while ago. It's a mighty provocative bunch of hands you hire, señorita, and coming so soon after your Navaho ambushed my men makes it look like war."

"Colonel Hendriks," said Isabella fiercely, "my vaqueros will always defend Cordova and Cordova stock. But they will not attack any man without good cause. Therefore, I know your Americans must have fired first, though I have heard nothing about any fight myself."

"I tell you," said the Colonel angrily, brandishing his riding crop. "I tell you—"

"Señor," interrupted Isabella coldly, "your loud voice and waving fists do not impress me. A loud voice, señor, comes from an unquiet mind."

"Damn my bones," said the Colonel, "I've come to the end of my patience. First I have my two boundary riders fired on by your Navaho—"

"Not so, Colonel," said Jason crisply. "Apulca has witnesses who will be able to show any court he was elsewhere at the time."

Isabella recognised that as an expedient arrow. Apulca very possibly could produce such witnesses, but had never said so.

"You keep out of this, Rawlings," snapped the Colonel, and turned back to Isabella. "You hear this, señorita. I've come not only to see Ed Braddock rightly take that redskin, I've also come to tell you to hand over your Mexican riders as well. I've come alone to say this, but you should know that Braddock and other men are outside your gates. Either you hand over that Navaho and the Mexicans or Braddock and his men will come and get them, and anyone else who tries to stand in the way of the law."

Jason looked the Colonel in the eye.

"It's no law, Colonel Hendriks, to charge men on the evidence of one party alone," said Jason slowly and evenly. "I'd hardly have thought it necessary to tell you that both parties must first be questioned. What would you think of any law which allowed you to be arrested on my demand, and disallowed you the right to say anything before you got to court? Is arrest automatic in Texas when one man accuses another? That's how the reign of terror began in the French Revolution. Bring Braddock here by all means, and let him ask questions. Señorita Cordova will, I'm sure, arrange to have her vaqueros ride in and answer them. But don't talk of taking Apulca and the vaqueros by force, because that looks as if you and Braddock have already found them guilty. A most dangerous way of administering the law."

The Colonel, an ugly mottle darkening his face, said, "I'm not here to bandy the fine points of law with you. I'm here with an ultimatum: hand over the Navaho or Braddock and his men will come and get him. Then they'll ride out and pick up those drunken vaqueros who attacked some of the Westboro men near town this morning. I could have brought Braddock and the others to this door, but I told them to hold off so that I could come to offer Señorita Cordova the chance to cooperate."

"You would not dare to attack Cordova," said Isabella.

"The law has the right—"

"That man is the law? Señor Braddock? Then I am sorry for Texas."

The Colonel turned his back and strode to his horse. He mounted.

"I've given you fair warning," he said.

"Then I give you one too," said Jason. "Don't do it, Colonel."

"Braddock will decide. He's the arresting officer."

Since everyone knew Braddock only did what the Colonel told him to, this was a hard one to swallow. Isabella's eyes were angrily contemptuous.

"You'll make the decision, Colonel, you know that," said Jason.

"All I can do," said the Colonel, "is to suggest to Braddock that he give you thirty minutes to hand over the Navaho and to go round up those drunken vaqueros, but I can't guarantee you'll get it."

"Tell him yes," murmured Jason to Isabella, at which she flashed him an angry look.

"No," she said to the Colonel. He rode away, through the arched gateway and down the long winding drive to the road, where Braddock and his men were waiting.

"You should have said yes." Jason was emphatic.

"Well, I have said no," retorted Isabella.

"Braddock could have done nothing except lock them up and wait for a judge."

"He would have hanged them!"

"With your men locked up, the Colonel would have no excuse for attacking Cordova."

"He would not dare to!"

"He will now. I suggest you get your vaqueros here as quickly as possible."

"You are out of sympathy with me," she said.

"Don't be foolish," said Jason.

Isabella, plainly hurt, turned away.

"Yes, I will bring in my vaqueros," she said, "but you must leave. It is going to be different now. It is not going to be an argument about the law, it is going to be a fight. We can ask you to speak for us, and you have, more than once, but we cannot ask you to risk your life for us, especially as Cordova means so little to you."

"That's just as foolish," said Jason, "and I shall stay."

"I will not permit you to," she said emotionally.

"I'm staying," said Jason.

"Thank you," she said, and put a hand on his arm. "Please, you give the orders. You have been a soldier."

"I can make suggestions. Who will you send to bring in your vaqueros?"

"José," she replied. "He has endurance and brains, that one." She called for José. When he came, she gave him his orders and off he went, taking Apulca with him, saying that two heads were always better than one.

Isabella had a servant round up several vaqueros who were within easy reach, and there were also the stable hands and menservants willing to help defend the house.

"It should be a costly business for the Colonel, taking the house," said Jason, "costly enough to discourage him, I fancy. You've thick walls and a tiled roof. I'd concentrate your men on its defence. You should be able to hold it until José gets back with the vaqueros. How many can he expect to bring?"

"Twenty or more," said Isabella. "There are others, but the largest number are out there herding cattle into the San Pedro Valley. José should reach them in twenty minutes or so."

"Good," said Jason, "that should do us nicely. I'd get the horses out of the stables if I were you. We may need them."

"We are to fight on horseback?"

"Not in defence of the house, no. But you'll have to let the stables, the storehouse, and other outbuildings go—so bring the horses out here. Myself, I prefer to have a horse available in most fights."

~ 259 ~

"Yes, I see." Isabella felt intensely glad that he had elected to stay and give her his help. "I am very happy you are with us."

"What's your armoury? Muskets, flintlocks, pistols, what? Smoothbore muskets or rifled ones?"

"Come and see." She took him through the house. In the armoury, a clean dry room next to the study, were a collection of swords and sabres and a large number of muskets, flintlocks, and pistols, ancient and modern. Jason ignored the older ones. He was also disinterested in the smoothbore weapons. He set aside rifled firearms. Isabella opened a drawer, taking from it a revolver of glinting newness.

"What's that?" asked Jason.

"My father brought it with him when he returned here several weeks ago. He said only a few had been made so far, and that was one of them."

Jason examined it. He had heard of the weapon. It was a six-chamber revolver made by Samuel Colt. The rotating breech could be turned, locked, and unlocked by the one simple action of cocking. No manual rotation was necessary. He thought it extremely novel. Generally, he did not have a high opinion of pistols or revolvers. Their accuracy was suspect, and also limited. One might hit a target at a distance of ten yards. Outside of that, success could not be guaranteed. A man could be shot in the chest if he was obliging enough to bring his chest within range, but if he kept his distance and on the move, the shot was fired in hope rather than certainty. Nevertheless, the shining Colt, with a .45 calibre, looked handsome and deadly. He loaded it and put it inside his belt.

"Jason," said Isabella, "to use a pistol you need to be close to the enemy. Please do not consider it necessary on this occasion. This house is a fortress. It was built as one in the days when it had to be so. With our vaqueros and servants we can hold it. No one is to put himself at unnecessary risk, least of all you. Luisa and I can both use firearms."

"Well, who would ask you not to defend your own house?" Jason was concentrating on the weapons he had unracked. "You know which of your servants can handle a gun, so supply them from these here. Where's the ammunition?"

"You will find some in those drawers. The rest and other things

Manuel will get for you. We keep only a little ammunition in here. Jason, will you give out the weapons, please, and tell everyone what to do? You are to be in command, it is better so."

"Very well." He did not want to argue her out of her insistence. He felt he had enough problems already. When a man let complacency create a singular problem for himself, others were bound to result, one after another. "Thirty minutes, the Colonel said. I wonder."

"We shall be ready, whenever he comes," said Isabella. "Our vaqueros will be watching for him now, and you may be sure Manuel has all the servants and children inside the house. The women and children he will send down to the cellars. I am going up to see Luisa and change my clothes. Manuel will bring to you those who will handle firearms."

She liked it that although there was an atmosphere of urgency, Jason seemed very collected. She left him to it, and he handed out flintlocks and muskets. There were ten able-bodied servants and stable hands happy to fight for Cordova, as well as eight vaqueros. Before Isabella and Luisa came down with their dresses changed for more practical wear, Jason had disposed the servants and vaqueros around the house, most of them in rooms on the upper floors. From the upper floors the fields of fire were highly satisfactory to Jason. He himself took up a position in a guest room. From there he could see the main arched entrance gate, as well as ground beyond the high white wall. The drive itself was not visible due to the profusion of shrubs and trees which thickly lined it. Isabella and Luisa joined him, Luisa apprehensive but courageous, and Isabella determined to remain as cool as Jason seemed to be.

The afternoon sun passed from its zenith to descend slowly westwards. The yellow grasses that swarmed over the land well beyond the environs of the house began to take on a golden tint. A scattering of wild geese fluttered coastwards in the high heaven of blue. The quietness that always seemed like the voiceless herald of any conflict settled over Cordova. To Jason it had a worrying quality. The thirty minutes of grace had gone by. The Americans had not shown one hand, one boot, one horse, or one musket. Only the grasses had stirred.

"Colonel Hendriks has thought better of it," said Luisa, "and I am glad. It is a bad thing to make war on people, it is worse to make war on one's neighbours."

"I do not believe he has thought better of it," said Isabella, a musket across her knees as she sat at the window. "He had blood in his eyes. What do you think, Jason?"

"I'd like to think they've all returned home," said Jason, "but my bones won't let me. The Colonel has concocted two reasons for attacking Cordova, and I don't fancy he's going to waste them."

"He means, of course, to make everything so uncomfortable for me that I will either give up Cordova and go elsewhere or sell him part of it," said Isabella.

"Yes, precisely so," said Jason. Hell, God's life, he thought, the saints themselves could not say that when he had settled his score with Isabella's father he would owe anything to Cordova.

They saw José then. He came riding from the west, cutting across country and heading at a sweating gallop for the house. Jason went out to the landing and shouted for someone below to open up the gate. Isabella saw Manuel dart across the paved court to unlock and unbar the gate. He swung it back and a minute later José rode through. Jason went down with the sisters.

José burst into the hall.

"Señorita! The gringos. They're riding for San Pedro Valley!"

He told his story. The main herds of Cordova were moving through San Pedro Valley, miles to the west, and eating it up as they did at this time of the year. There were a score or so of vaqueros looking after them. José and Apulca, having been despatched to bring the vaqueros to the house, rode hard for the valley. It was not long, however, before they realised there were men in pursuit, almost thirty of them. Americans. Where José and Apulca rode, the Americans followed—some at a pace that began to close the distance. José told Apulca to continue, for the Navaho had the faster mustang. It was necessary too for the Indian to avoid being taken, since it might be supposed that he was the one the Americans were chasing. He needed the protection the vaqueros would give him if he could reach them before the Americans did. Only a simpleton, however, would conclude that so formidable a body of gringos were after one Indian alone. José, accordingly, made his own conclusion, which was that the Americans meant to prevent the vaqueros riding to the help of their patroness. He turned south at a moment when he was out of sight, hid himself and his horse, watched the gringos ride by in pursuit of Apulca, then doubled back to the house. So here he was, and what did the señorita intend to do?

There was only one thing Isabella felt she could do. Go after the Americans and take them in the rear while they were attacking the vaqueros.

Jason realised the Colonel, an old soldier himself, had stolen a march on them. He would have guessed, of course, that Isabella would send for her vaqueros. As the Colonel himself did not know where they were, what was better than to be led to them? His offer of thirty minutes' grace had come from a very neat turn of mind. It lulled the opposition. He had waited, no doubt, until lookouts signalled the emergence of José and Apulca, and then gone after them. He was not going to attack the house until he had disposed of Isabella's nearest Mexican riders. Possibly, too, he reasoned that the noise of such an attack might easily reach the ears of a wandering vaquero or two, and that it would not be enough, therefore, merely to catch José and Apulca before they were able to alert the fiery Mexicans of Cordova.

Urgent, insistent, Isabella said, "Jason, we must go at once."

Jason hesitated.

"I confess I'd like to have two men ride down to the road first and do some scouting—"

"There's no time," she said. "All the Americans have gone. They are after the men Colonel Hendriks accused, and since we are sure his accusation was made only to give him a false excuse for a fight, he will attack all my vaqueros at San Pedro. And if my vaqueros are taken by surprise, most of them will be massacred. I am going at once, with the men we have here. My vaqueros would always ride to help me. I must help them."

She was right. Yet he wasn't sure she was wholly right. But he had José, six vaqueros, and four stable hands mounted in minutes, leaving the rest of the men behind just in case. He insisted on that. As an afterthought, he also had sabres from the armoury put into the hands of each member of his party. There was a brief argument with Isabella, but she was determined to ride too, though it left them with the responsibility of keeping her out of the way of flying shot when the moment arrived. Luisa, very quiet, stood and watched them go.

They rode fast into the light of the late-afternoon sun, which was showering the Texas landscape with gold. They raced through whispering grasses, along the tracks and over the ranges. They galloped hard down descents while the sun drew them into its blazing embrace. It took them all of thirty pounding minutes before they heard the sound of rifles cracking in San Pedro Valley ahead. They dropped down into a long, rolling hollow and came slowly out of it. Napoleon's nose was sniffing and twitching at the scent of battle. Musket fire rattled and echoed. Peering over the top of the rise, they saw the Americans. Their force was split. They had men at the entrance to the valley and others forming a barrier some six hundred yards farther on, bottling up the vaqueros, who with their mustangs were holed up at various points. The valley wall was a lush pasture of grass. On its high, sloping sides mesquite vied with grass. Jason guessed that the farther group of Americans, born in the adventurous mould of their kind, had made their way down those slopes to cut off any retreat by the vaqueros.

He could clearly see the foremost Americans, spread across the head of the valley, a dozen or more of them. Those farther down were not so clear. Every man was dug in, but the smoke of their musket fire hung visibly in the air. The trapped vaqueros, flat in the grass in the folds of the ground, were returning the fire. Jason supposed the Colonel had combed Westboro for hirelings, probably promising them a small piece of Cordova cake. He could not see the man himself, but he could see what he was up to—the crippling of Isabella's main strength, her vaqueros. The Americans, their horses tethered near the head of the valley, were taking care and pains to achieve this.

"There, look what is happening," said Isabella bitterly. "They mean to kill all my friends, and to swear afterwards that the vaqueros attacked first."

"Damned if I don't feel uneasy about things," said Jason as they withdrew.

"Are we going to attack them?" Isabella, black hat shading her angry face, was aggressive. "We are not going to spend the time talking, are we?"

"For a moment we are," said Jason. "We might form a front against that first line of Americans, taking some of the pressure off the vaqueros—but I don't myself fancy a hard slogging match with muskets, not against Americans."

"You are afraid?" She was aghast.

"Cautious," said Jason. "In respect of offering ourselves for target practice, that is. Outside of that, I favour all or nothing. José, how many muskets do we have?"

There were fifteen in all—Isabella having one, and two men each having a pair. Jason let Isabella keep hers, and had the two men take the rest. One man was to circle round until he was on the left flank of the foremost Americans, the other to come round opposite their right flank.

"But what are the rest of us to do?" asked Isabella, wincing at the continuous sounds of fire.

"You'll stay here, please," said Jason, "while we run in, pick up your trapped vaqueros, and run out again. Have you ever seen a cavalry charge?" Isabella shook her head. "Well, you'll see an amateurish one in a moment," he said, wondering at the same time how the devil he had become as inextricably involved as this. "As well as amateurish, it'll be of minor proportions too. But it may still be a little unnerving to the opposition. José?"

"Señor?"

Jason, speaking in Spanish for the benefit of all, said, "We're sending the two vaqueros with the muskets to pepper the Americans on each flank. With seven muskets each, all loaded, they should be able to make satisfactory nuisances of themselves during the time the rest of us will be running at the Americans. As we have no muskets ourselves, we'll use the sabres. Is it agreed?"

"We shall not stay behind, señor. We will run at them with you," said José.

To the two vaqueros, Jason said, "As soon as we see you in position, we shall go in. And you will open fire the moment you see us break cover. We mean to run at them, break through them, pick up your comrades, and break through again to return here. Does everyone understand that?"

"Everyone, señor," said José, while the Mexicans grinned, pulled on their moustaches, and shut their ears to the sounds of their comrades under fire.

"You are going to run at the Americans in the open?" asked Isabella, while with a nod from Jason the two vaqueros went their separate ways.

"We're going to surprise them, I hope," said Jason. He knew the Americans' reputation as sharpshooters. He had to bring himself and the Mexicans down on them before they could lay on a concentrated fire. "No one is to be less than six metres from his neighbour. In that way you will give each other room and make only single targets for the Americans. Do you understand, *hombres?*"

"Everyone is listening with both ears, señor," said José.

"The Americans may not be as quick as usual when reloading," said Jason. "They're grounded, and charging horses and naked swords can unsettle men. Pick the man immediately in front of you. Go for his arms. Don't try to take his head off. Cut, don't thrust. You will likely leave your sabre behind if you stick it into a man. Ride through them to your comrades. If they have the brains to see what is happening, they might also have the sense to take to their horses at once and ride back with us, which is what we want them to do. In that event, we should have no trouble in breaking through a second time. The señorita will stay here. If any of you are wounded, ride back to her. Don't sit and nurse yourselves."

The Mexicans grinned again, pushed their sombreros hard down over their foreheads to shield their eyes from the sun, gripped their sabres, and waited for Jason to give the word. He edged Napoleon cautiously forward until he could see over the rise. The Americans ahead had their backs to him. They were flat in the grass, not moving except to keep up a steady rate of fire. They were the cork in the bottle. The trapped vaqueros were being squeezed, for farther down the other line of Americans had advanced. That did mean more than mere containment. Jason watched, waiting for the two men he had sent to arrive in position.

Isabella appeared at his elbow. Heart pounding at what was about to happen, she said, "Why did you not find a sabre for me?"

"Because I don't fancy there's much point in trying to save Cordova if the Cordova herself is shot from her horse."

"But what if you are killed?" she said in a low voice. "Do you think Cordova is worth as much as that to me?"

"Stay here," he said.

"It is wrong," she protested. "You should not be fighting my battles." She was taut with emotion. "Oh, sweet Santa María, please don't get killed, Jason."

"I assure you, I mean to avoid that. I've another engagement to keep, one important to me."

He detected the slightest movement to the right of the grounded Americans. One vaquero had arrived. A moment later, the other was in position on the Americans' left.

"Now, José. Now, *hombres*." Jason cleared the rise and rode forward a short distance. Napoleon stepped perkily, head up. The Mexicans, nine of them, followed, dispersing at intervals on either side of him, sabres drawn. The Americans were a hundred and fifty yards ahead, give or take a little. A good distance, that. The charge would be at a flying peak by then, and if the vaqueros in the valley were sharp enough to realise what was happening and the advantage it gave them, they could leave their holes and gallop back with the rescue party, braving the American muskets at their rear. The success of the manoeuvre would depend on how well the two flanking vaqueros used their firearms, and how many Americans could turn to present loaded muskets.

Jason lifted his sabre, pointed it into the sun, put Napoleon to the trot, the run, and the gallop. The old cavalry mount went at his work as if the scent of battle was heady. José and his friends galloped with Jason. The grounded Americans began to lift their heads. Shots from the two vaqueros began to whistle. Americans spun in the grass, swivelling to take on the flank attackers, or to gape at the oncoming rush of the horsemen. They began to ram home cartridges. The charging vaqueros yelled, bending low in their saddles and swinging their sabres. Isabella's stable hands yelled with them. The fiery sun flashed along shining blades. On they came, ten from Cordova, thundering in concert, Jason giving Napoleon his head. The horse pricked up his ears and attacked the earth with flying, gouging hooves. The clarion call of the Fighting 7th came out of the sun and the wind.

The trapped vaqueros sat up. An American on one knee sighted his musket on a charging Mexican, but jerked and fell sideways as a shot from a flanking vaquero took him in a shoulder.

The charge accelerated. In the valley the vaqueros yelled encouragement. A flintlock roared. The ball sank on its fiery course to singe Napoleon's left foreleg, and the horse drew its lips back until huge teeth showed in a vicious gleam. They swept on while Isabella watched with her blood in tumult and her heart hammering. The flanking vaqueros kept the Americans at odds with the situation as the Cordova men pounded in on them. Some came to their knees, others kept their heads down. Musket balls flew wildly, and a stable hand pitched from his flying horse. Jason and the rest went on, the galloping horses looming massively, the fiery mustangs running pell-mell and the flashing sabres looking wickedly sharp. Under knee and spur, Napoleon and the Mexican horses hit the Americans. The sabres swung and slashed and cut, blades reflecting the golden fire of the sun, and to Isabella it seemed as if bright flashing light was scything the men of Westboro. Jason's sabre took from a man his hat and the best part of his right ear. Kneeling Americans pitched. Muskets dropped and hands clutched at gashed flesh. The Cordova nine split the hirelings apart and ran on.

The vaqueros were up, calling and whistling their horses. The farther line of Americans showed itself as their men came to their feet. Jason and his Mexicans galloped on, the Mexicans waving their sabres at their comrades.

"Come! Come! *Pronto, pronto!*"

They circled and one by one the vaqueros rode out of their holes, some showing bloody bandages. Jason roared at them, and he and José led the way back. They charged again, flying at the surprised and somewhat shattered Americans. Braddock was there, his arm gashed, his face expressive of black, growling fury. He picked out Jason, rammed home a cartridge, and sighted. His musket wavered, his gashed arm on fire. He jerked on the trigger. Jason came on and Braddock grinned with sour frustration. He rolled in the grass, flattening himself, and Jason thundered by him, his sabre picking Braddock's hat from his head. José reeled in his saddle as a ball plunged into his arm. Jason bawled at him, "Go on, go on!" José went on, back to Isabella.

They came, the vaqueros, riding hell for leather. Jason knew that Isabella did not want a battle, only for her vaqueros to be rescued. They broke through and the Americans let them go. They rode up to Isabella, and her face was alight with relief and exultation, for Jason was with them. Then he shocked her. As soon as they had all arrived, Jason rode back towards the Americans. Braddock, on his feet, looked up at him.

"Mr. Braddock," said Jason, while the other Americans looked on, "you're guilty of an unprovoked war, you know that."

Braddock's grin had something of a glare to it.

"We had our rights to come after the Navaho," he said, "and it ain't over yet, fancy mouth."

"It's over for you," said Jason. "Do I understand that almost thirty of you rode to take one Indian? A gentleman like Judge Conner might consider that a little suspect. And if the law requires you to make war on women, Mr. Braddock, it's no improvement on the law of Mexico."

"Hold it," said one American. "We ain't here to make war on no women. We was told some uppity Mex had been shootin' up Westboro men."

"Find me Westboro men with holes in them," said Jason, "and I might begin to take you seriously. Where's Colonel Hendriks?"

"Ain't here, is he?" said Braddock, and Jason looked hard at him.

"You didn't lick us, mister," said a thin-faced man. "You was lucky, that's all."

"Conceded," said Jason. They had been lucky, he knew that, to find the Americans off their horses. But then, that was how they themselves had chosen to fight off the vaqueros, taking their time and keeping their losses to a minimum. "All the same, I suggest you find out exactly why you were brought into all this by Colonel Hendriks. If it was for payment of a few dollars—"

"Not for me, mister, it wasn't," said the thin-faced man. "Just on account of them drunk Mex."

"Then you've a receptive ear for a deceptive tongue, my friend," said Jason, and at that he turned and rode back to Isabella. There he found the vaqueros in fine fettle, clapping shoulders and declaring themselves and Jason to be the best of *hombres bravos*. Isabella was doing what she could for José and the wounded stable hand, the latter with a bullet in his thigh. José had a ball lodged in the muscle of his left arm. He was not too pleased with himself, claiming that any man on a charging horse who got in the way of a musket ball when the sun was at his back was either very stupid or unpardonably clumsy. A vaquero drew a knife, ran a finger over its sharp point, and offered surgery to both José and the stable hand.

"No," said Isabella, who was emotionally proud of everyone, "wait until we get back. Then José and Pedro can be taken to the doctor in Westboro. They will manage until then." She turned swimming eyes on Jason. "Thank you," she said. "Apulca is here, and he thanks you too."

"Thank your vaqueros and your servants," he said. "And if you're ever in similar trouble, give them sabres and turn them into cavalrymen again. They're horsemen, your vaqueros, and none better. Colonel Hendriks is conspicuously absent, I find. I think we should ride back at once."

Braddock watched them depart as the other Americans came up.

"Let's get after them," he said. "The Colonel should've finished his work by now, seein' the place was left wide open for him. But he just might still need us."

"What work?" asked a man.

"That Cordova house," said Braddock, the pain of his arm making his grin savage.

The man spat.

"Count me out," he said. "I ain't never averse to puttin' down uppity Mex, but I ain't helpin' to run them Cordova sisters off their land by burnin' their house down. I don't even like the sound of it."

"Nor me," said another, "and I ain't sure I like the sound of other things. Ed, you said them Cordova Mex was lyin' in wait for the boys who came up to take the Navaho. So how'd they know the boys was comin'?"

"How do I know?" said Braddock belligerently.

"Well, I tell you, Ed, I'm quittin'."

They argued. Braddock fumed. But most of them quit, for all his fuming.

Isabella, Jason, and the Mexicans had not ridden far before a glow appeared in the sky ahead. The sun, edging towards the horizon at their backs, flushed the land and the heavens with colour, but the glow to the east of them was not one which nature was painting.

"The house!" gasped Isabella.

They went on a wild urgent gallop then—and as they went the glow spread to give an alarming redness to the evening sky. The grasses became tinted with flame. Cordova was burning. They galloped out of the red light of the dying sun and into the rim of hot lights cast by the flaring, roaring inferno of the house. Bathed in that light were Luisa and women and children, with some men-servants. Manuel and others lay dead inside the inferno. A number of things had been brought out, salvaged because they had not been too difficult to get at or carry. Jewel boxes, deed chests, and other small but valuable effects lay in a heap on the ground. The tears were streaming down Luisa's face, and the women stood in shock, terror, and helplessness. Luisa wept out the story.

Ten minutes after Jason and Isabella had gone with their little force, Colonel Hendriks struck, with yet more hirelings, and of the worst kind. They surrounded the place, broke down the gates, climbed the wall at the rear, shot their way in front and back, and took the house. Manuel and other men had defended bravely and died bravely. Luisa, the remaining menservants, the women and children were bundled out and the house set on fire. When Hendriks and his hirelings had gone, Luisa and two servants ran in to bring out what they could while they could. Then there was nothing else to do but stand and watch as the house went up in smoke and flame.

And as Isabella watched now, eyes fierce and mouth set, the heavy tiled roof sagged, flames shot upwards like gigantic tongues of roaring yellow, and smoke billowed blackly. The roof crashed inwards, a million sparks flew, and the house perished.

Isabella stood numbed.

And Jason knew the Colonel had outfoxed him. But it was not that which filled him with savage anger, it was the burning of the house and the murder of the servants. He spoke to the vaqueros.

"Willingly, señor, willingly," they said in response.

He went to Isabella.

"We are going to the Hendriks place," he said.

Isabella said nothing. She put her arms around her weeping sister.

They raced towards Westboro. The vaqueros were silent, following Jason as dusk began to mask the town. They rode through it and on towards the Hendriks plantation. They clattered down the long straight drive between the brooding pines. They turned and came up to the sprawling house. The lights were on, flickering in the hanging candelabras. Jason and six vaqueros dismounted. Jason stood aside and the vaqueros kicked and battered the door down. Across the way, in their quarters, the Negroes were singing as timber shattered and fell.

Colonel Hendriks, Lisbet, and their butler rushed into the hall as the men of Cordova broke in. The Mexicans showed their teeth. Jason, stony-faced, confronted the livid Colonel. Fury and surprise distorted the Colonel's features. He knew Jason and Isabella had ridden off with a small party of Mexicans, but he had thought they would make little difference to the outcome in San Pedro Valley. Braddock had known that in one way or another Rawlings was to be disposed of before the evening was out. Braddock, obviously, had failed.

"Damn your eyes," he shouted, "you've kicked my door in!"

"That's a small price to pay," said Jason, "too small." He turned to the vaqueros. "Fire the house," he said.

"By God—" the Colonel choked.

"Colonel Hendriks, get yourself out, and your daughter and your servants."

Lisbet stared in mesmerised horror. Jason Rawlings looked like a man ready to pull the devil out of hell itself. Joe ran to the kitchen to get the servants out through the back way. The Colonel turned and pounded into his study. The vaqueros swarmed after Joe into the kitchens, where fire was always available. The Colonel reappeared, carrying a pistol, but found himself looking

~ 272 ~

into the shining blue snout of a Colt .45. Jason kicked the pistol from the Colonel's hand. Screams sounded from the kitchen. And Lisbet screamed too then, for fire appeared.

Out came the vaqueros, carrying blazing kindling, and began to swarm everywhere. Esmeralda appeared, her eyes rolling.

"Get out of my house!" shouted the maddened Colonel.

"Get out yourself," said Jason, "and as fast as you can."

"My niggers, I'll get my niggers and have them tear you to pieces!" roared the Colonel, and ran from the house into a solid wall of horsed vaqueros.

Lisbet flung up her head, looked at Jason with eyes of hate, and said, "When they hang you, Mr. Rawlings, when you are all dancing, I'll be there playing my fiddle."

"Go outside," said Jason.

She went, accompanied by Joe and Esmeralda, Esmeralda moaning.

The vaqueros fired the house. Timber-built in the main, it torched into flame. In ten minutes it was crackling and burning fast. They fired the cotton and the vast fields of white ran with red sheeting light. They fired the stables, the storehouse, the smokehouse, and the granary. All they left alone were the Negroes' quarters.

Hendriks burned and cindered. When it was all well and truly done, Jason spoke to the demented Colonel.

"When a man makes war on women, sir, when he burns their house and murders their servants, he forfeits his right to a house of his own. Come again to Cordova, and I shall kill you."

"Devil out of hell!" screamed Lisbet.

Jason mounted and took the vaqueros away. On the road into town, a man passed them, driving a buggy. He did not stop, nor did they. Not long after, Colonel Hendriks, viewing the charred house and burned plantation with eyes that were still lividly bulging, turned at the sound of a voice. The dying flames gave light to the darkness.

"Nasty mess, Colonel."

It was Sam Purdy, and he held a levelled flintlock.

"Get out of here." The Colonel's voice was unsteady. "You refused to join me."

"You didn't ask me personal, you just sent a feller." Sam's voice was as level as his flintlock. "I been lookin' for you, Colonel. You been real busy, I hear. But I've still been lookin' for you, on account of Laura. You ain't a fittin' man to live with decent folks. Time you was gone, I reckon."

The flintlock exploded.

Lisbet screamed again.

Sam walked away.


The sweating vaqueros were clearing the debris and the ashes, uncovering the foundations and making ready for Cordova to rise again. Fernando Alba had come, with some of his own vaqueros, and he gave to Luisa the kind of comfort she so badly needed. Everyone was living in the outbuildings. Isabella, watching the work, was in deep sadness for her dead servants, but still had a fierce belief in Cordova. Days ago it had perished, her beautiful house, but she would build a new one.

No one had called in law officers, neither Westboro citizens nor Hendriks, neither Isabella nor Jason. The law could not put right what had been done. It was a not uncommon incident in Texas and the western territories of the United States.

Colonel Hendriks, with Sam Purdy's lead lodged in his spine, would never walk again. Lisbet was arranging to take him back to Virginia. The saloonkeeper had disappeared with his wife.

Isabella looked around. Jason was talking to José, who had his arm in a sling. She went across. She detached Jason, desperate to talk to him. He must stay now, and surely he would.

"It will not take long to rebuild, Jason," she said, "and it will be an even finer and stronger house."

"I'm sure it will," he said. He was dark with thoughts of the greed of men, a greed for other people's possessions, for other men's wives, for power and for riches. He could leave Cordova now if he had a mind to, for the peace and greenness of Dorset called—but there was still another covetous man to deal with, and deal with him he must. It would be better now not to wait for him, but to go to Austin again and there search in earnest.

"I am so sad for my servants," said Isabella.

"We were outwitted," said Jason, and brooded on the fact.

"But not outfought," she said. She looked, he thought, enchanting in the sunshine. Too much so. "Jason, you are going to stay now, yes?"

"Isabella, you don't need me to stay and watch your new house go up. I've got my own house in England. I may lose it, for I've no idea how to save it unless I come into a legacy. But I must go back and try. I owe it to my sister."

Her mouth trembled. Did he not realise what it would do to her, if after losing her house, she lost him too? He must know she had feelings for him.

"Jason, I will buy your house for you, your mortgage. That will take all worries from your sister, and leave you free to stay here. You are part of Texas now, part of Cordova too. You have been so strong for us, you cannot leave us now, surely." She was really quite desperate and, faltering, added, "I am not disposed to let you go too easily."

"Isabella, you—" He stopped, seeing her looking beyond him, her eyes widening.

"There," she said breathlessly, "now you can stay, for here is my father, whom you have been wanting to meet for so long."

Jason turned. He saw a man approaching, approaching on a grey horse.

"That is your father?" he said, as Don Esteban Sylvestre y Cordova came riding up to the ruins.

"He has heard about Cordova, of course," said Isabella. "Everyone has. That has made him come. He will be wondering whether we are ruined or not, but he is my father for all his faults."

She did not run to him. She waited. It was Jason who possessed her mind, not her father. Jason watched as his man dismounted and tethered his horse to the shattered archway gate. Although the icy resolution which had driven him on for three years had not, because of certain events, been so obsessive recently, it was still there, and touched at this moment by a little dart of fire.

Don Esteban walked towards Isabella. He was dark and slender, and handsome in a way that defied his forty-nine years. His deep blue coat, though a little dusty, was fashionably set off by his lighter blue trousers. He took off his hat to reveal hair that was thick, well ordered, and with no trace of grey. His moustache was a luxuriance, and his black lashes as long as a woman's. He sighed as he kissed Isabella.

"Isabella, you have been struck by the devil and his fiery hordes. Oh, the saints, not a stick left. I came as soon as I heard. Is all gone?"

"The worst is that we lost valuable lives, good men," said Isabella. She felt little emotion at seeing her father, though affection was not absent. It was Jason who was in her blood. He was so difficult to understand, sometimes very companionable, sometimes strangely reserved. Whatever he had come to Texas for, he hadn't found in Cordova. He was going to leave. Her father was a lovable gallant, made for the card tables, for social inconsequentialities. He would bring lightness and a little laughter if he stayed. But she would a thousand times rather have Jason stay. With shock, she found herself asking what point there was in rebuilding if Jason were to leave.

Her father gazed at the ruins, at the chaos and at walls that still partly stood.

"So much waste, so much gone," he said, "and my heart is sad for you, Isabella. *Cara mía*, it has always meant so much more to you than to me." He looked at Jason, drawn by the feel of the introspective blue eyes. "Are you an architect, señor, come to consider what can rise out of these ashes?"

"I am no architect, I am just a friend," said Jason, clinically working out a solution.

"There's a long story to tell you, Father," said Isabella, so concerned with her own desperation that she had forgotten to introduce Jason. What was it about a man to make him so blind that he could not see a woman's love for him?

"Ah, stories," her father was saying, "the fantasies of life and the reasons for our dreams."

Isabella, coming to, said, "Oh, I have not introduced you—"

"Where is Luisa?" asked Don Esteban.

"She is in town, at the store with Fernando Alba, buying things to make one of the outbuildings more comfortable. Father, here is a gentleman who has been wanting—"

"Pardon me," said Jason, who did not want to be introduced yet.

"Señor?" The dark eyes between the long lashes were questioning. There was the touch of the sophisticate in the manners and the already perceptible air of faint boredom. He had come, thought Jason, only because he could not have failed to, and would be away as soon as he had discovered that Isabella was not ruined. Well, there was no point in delaying the confrontation. And it was a deep satisfaction to know, as Jason looked into the inquisitive eyes and the slender, well-cared-for countenance, that there was still the fierce resolve to render the account and extract the payment.

"Don Esteban, a word in your ear, if I may?" he said politely, "I have a little business I'd like to discuss with you."

"He has been waiting to see you, Father," said Isabella.

"To discuss business? With me?" Don Esteban's smile had the amused superciliousness of the grandee. "Señor, I never discuss business with anyone. It is a cross some people have to bear, and a drudgery others thoughtlessly take upon themselves. It is a thing, señor, invented by some men to plague the rest of us."

"Mine is not of the plaguing kind," said Jason, "and if you would be so kind as to draw aside with me for five minutes—?"

The fine dark eyes flickered.

"I came here to console my daughters, señor, to lighten their desolation. But I suppose that even in these circumstances a total of five minutes does not seem much to ask, much less to concede."

"It will be to your advantage, señor."

"Ah. You have discovered a weakness of mine. I am incurably addicted to capitalising on advantage, possibly because I am so often beset by disadvantages." Here Don Esteban's faint smile was a little at odds with the light of wariness in his eyes. "However, your business must wait, I regret. It cannot be more important than tragedy. And I do not even know your name."

Jason could not stop Isabella a second time.

"Father," she said, "this is Jason Rawlings, who reached us from England and is set on leaving us to return there."

"Ah," sighed her father, and his urbane view of life sharpened.

"There's a familiar ring?" suggested Jason. "We've met before, perhaps?"

The long lashes narrowed. Each man was in knowledge of the other.

"I cannot recall it," murmured Don Esteban almost lazily, "but, naturally, if you are Isabella's friend I am happy to be acquainted with you now."

The cuckoo, long out of the other's nest, smiled sleepily. The cuckold, a hawk, was poised to strike. The onlooker, oblivious, was in the grip of hot, impossible thoughts. Her vaqueros, if she asked them to, would detain Jason forcibly, for all that he was *un hombre bravo* to them. And José, a man of wisdom, would help her to contrive a situation whereby Jason would seem to have incontestably compromised her. The English might have heretical leanings but were reputed never to shirk the honourable course attendant on the compromising of a lady, and Jason was a Catholic. If she had to bind him to Cordova that way, then why not? He came of a race of pirates. Well, she would turn pirate herself.

"Don Esteban," said Jason, "I repeat: it would be to your advantage to give me a few minutes in private."

Don Esteban permitted himself a smile of resignation. Perhaps the emphasis on advantage caused it.

"You are pressing me, señor?"

"A little," conceded Jason, and the ice was beginning to freeze his burdened soul. But he smiled. The sun beat down. The vaqueros sweated. Yet Don Esteban merely looked as cool as if summer had not quite ousted temperate spring.

"Oh, I will draw aside," said Isabella, "and leave you two to be as mysterious and as private as you wish."

She turned and walked away. Her going eased Don Esteban's disquiet. He had felt that this unpleasantly persistent person was going to be even more unpleasant by speaking in front of her. Isabella's generosity might not always go in advance of what she expected in a man, particularly her own father.

"Well, you have my ear, señor," he said.

"Walk with me to your horse, if you would," said Jason. Don Esteban sighed again, but walked nonetheless. Jason whistled up Napoleon, and Napoleon began to walk too, converging on the men. Reaching his grey, which had been tethered by the archway, Isabella's father looked coolly at Jason.

"In the light of what has befallen my cherished daughters," he said, "what is it that you seem to consider more important, señor?"

With his back to the ruined house, Jason produced the Colt.

"This is not unimportant," he said. "Is it yours?"

"Indeed it is." The dark eyes narrowed again, but no one could have said that the bird's feathers looked ruffled. "Why is it in your possession?"

"In my possession, Señor Sylvestre, as you sometimes call yourself, it's a means of persuasion. In yours, it would be a temptation. I want you to get on your horse and ride a little way with me.

~ 278 ~

Quietly and without fuss. If not, I shall blow your head off. That's a relatively minor happening in Texas."

"It would not be a minor happening to me." Don Esteban ran a hand over his thick moustache. "I would only point out that as I feel you are going to do it in any case, I could hardly be concerned whether it takes place here or elsewhere."

"If you ride with me, you have my word that nothing of the kind will happen at all," said Jason. "I think you know that what I have to say to you is best said far from the ears of your daughter, or anyone else here. You'd not wish her too much distress, would you?"

"I am a considerate man, señor, where the feelings of both of my daughters are concerned," said Don Esteban. "Though I cannot agree that I know what it is you wish to say to me. I am quite in the dark. However, as you are pointing that Colt at me, I am not in the best position to argue."

"I shall not shoot you if you come with me," said Jason.

"I have your word?" said Don Esteban, with a smile that was almost winning.

"You have my word as a gentleman, sir," said Jason. "Oblige me by mounting."

Don Esteban mounted the grey. Jason swung himself up on Napoleon.

Jason, riding off with his man, turned to call to Isabella, who was watching in curiosity.

"We shall not be long."

What did that matter, she thought, if when he returned with her father he began a much longer journey back to England? Was it possible to detain him and force him to marry her, when he had never declared any love for her? It was possible, perhaps, but she knew it would be farcical and disastrous. She was the Cordova. She commanded a fortune; she commanded her servants, her vaqueros, her family. It did not seem so very much to command a man.

They rode until they were half a mile from the house, Jason and his man, until they could not be seen. The earth had the yielding richness of land close to a river. The corncrakes rustled, and in the distance the Cerro Jorobado was the colour of shining blue smoke.

"This will do," said Jason. He had ridden behind Don Esteban all the way. Don Esteban halted, wheeled round, and faced Jason.

"Well, señor?"

"Tell me about my wife," said Jason.

"Your wife? Señor, your wife?" Don Esteban gave the impression of a man sincerely attempting the impossible in the way of recollections. "I really have no idea what to say about the lady, for the simple reason that I have never met her."

"You've met her," said Jason, "and your position is precarious."

"May I remind you," said Don Esteban, sitting his horse finely, "that you said our conversation was to be to my advantage."

"I lied," said Jason. "Tell me about my wife."

A most painful sigh came from Don Esteban. Undoubtedly, the unpleasant person had a bourgeois outlook. Such a fellow had no right to wear a sword. Swords were for gentlemen.

"Señor, I do not talk about other men's wives."

"There are always exceptional occasions," said Jason. "This is one. Get down, Señor Sylvestre."

They both dismounted. Don Esteban stood in well-tailored aloofness, hands behind his back. Jason, the revolver in his belt, watched him.

"And now, señor?" The man was still cool. It was not difficult to imagine the appeal he would have had for Edwina.

"Tell me about my wife," said Jason again.

Don Esteban shrugged.

"A wayward creature, Señor Rawlings, who insisted on attaching herself to me. What could I do?" He sighed, at the same moment withdrawing his hands from under the tail of his dark blue coat. In his right hand was a small pistol with an inlaid ivory butt. "And now, señor," he began.

But Jason, knowing his man, knowing he would make his move, reacted instantly. With a quick movement, he kicked the slender right shin of Don Esteban with the toe of his boot. Don Esteban staggered, hissing with pain. Jason knocked the pistol from his hand and put a foot on it.

"I've spent three years looking for you, Señor Sylvestre. I've also spent many hours wondering what moves you might make to kill me before I could kill you. You sold my wife to a man called Johnson, who took her to New Orleans and hired her out to other men. She took her own life not long ago, because she had the

French sickness. A man, when he takes another man's wife, must, whatever else obtains, accept an honourable responsibility for her. To discard that responsibility by handing her over to a procurer is not a commendable action, nor a pretty one."

Don Esteban stood with the pain of a bruised shinbone raising a slight film of sweat on his face, but his air of disdain was like a delicately armoured shield.

"You are mistaken, señor," he said. "I was introduced to Señor Johnson, a gentleman of independent means, by other gentlemen. Your wife and I, alas, no longer shared a mutual affection. She was attracted to Señor Johnson—"

"And you were low on finances."

"Be careful, señor. The statement is one thing, the implication another." Don Esteban shrugged again. "But I can see you have a tiresome desire to avenge your honour. If you will be so good as to return my pistol to me, we can settle the matter as gentlemen should. Though I must admit, I do not consider firing pistols at each other the most civilised of gestures."

Jackson picked up the pistol and tossed it away. He remounted Napoleon, leaned sideways, and cuffed the grey. She reared up, emitted a shrill whinny, and galloped away, tail streaming and head pointing in the direction of the livery stables in Westboro.

"You must start running, Señor Sylvestre," said Jason, and rode past the man, turning and pulling up forty yards away. He drew his sabre and Don Esteban saw bright light run sharply along the shining blade. The Texan sucked in breath and ran for the pistol. But Jason came at the gallop and was on his man before he sighted the weapon. The whistling sabre sliced the dark blue with such neat precision that Don Esteban read the chilling message. Jason turned and came again as the Texan scrabbled in the long grass, searching for the pistol. Napoleon was pounding, noisy, the sabre a flash in the sunlight, and a scarlet weal ran wet over Don Esteban's fine forehead. His hat flew and blood flowed into his eyes. On his knees he turned and turned again, ravaging the grass with tearing hands, searching. The gallop of the horse was a thunder in his ears. He threw himself sideways, the bright sword hissed, and sleeve and arm were slashed.

"Assassin! Barbarian!" he screamed. He came to his feet. Jason rode in on him again, the teeth of his horse as frightening as the flash of his sabre. Don Esteban, paralysed, felt sharpness savage his cheek, horse and rider momentarily blotting out the blue of sweet heaven. The blood ran from his slashed forehead and cheek. "Assassin!" he screamed again. He turned and through eyes that blinked away blood saw the glint of the pistol in the grass. He swooped for it. Jason galloped in, standing in the stirrups, the sabre lifted high and drawn back. Don Esteban levelled the pistol with shaking hands. Jason hurled the sabre. The Texan saw the flash of flying blade and flung himself sideways, firing wildly as he did so. The shot spat into the grass. Don Esteban, his shoulder buffeted by Napoleon, spun, staggered, and fell. Jason leapt down, retrieved the sabre, remounted, rode on, and rode back. Don Esteban got up and ran. He ran without direction, screaming. Sweat and blood blinded him. The sabre whistled, hissed, and slashed as Jason came at his man again and again.

Isabella, sitting on a piled heap of stones, looked up as Jason returned. He ducked in under the arched gateway and rode up to her. She had never seen his face as she saw it now. It was ravaged by darkness.

"Go to your father," he said. "You'll find him not far from the track leading to the river. He's cut to pieces. He won't die, but his wounds will scar him for life. He took my wife and my wife poisoned herself. I meant to kill him, but didn't, because he's your father. That saved his life for him. Goodbye, señorita."

He rode away, turning his back on Isabella's anguished eyes and stricken face.

Clare chattered. Antoinette smiled, hiding her growing unhappiness. All that she had told the child about her papa was likely, it seemed, to sound a foolishness in the end. Mrs. Blazey was beginning to ask questions and make comments, to look both dubious and suspicious. And freedom was no longer exhilarating but uneasy. If those men came back, there would be a new cruelty in their eyes and words. She must change her lodgings, or think about going north—to Boston, perhaps. But how could she leave Baltimore and Clare? Yet she could not stay indefinitely in Maryland. Some people in Maryland knew too much about the characteristics of even the fairest mulatto women; one day someone would point at her. Only in the northern states could a freed slave walk freely.

Obviously something terrible must have happened to her *Anglais*. The thought caused her anguish, pain, and heartache. He would surely have come by now if he had survived his meeting with the man who had robbed him of Edwina. He was a brave man and an understanding one, but it was possible that men like him, for all their qualities, might not always be able to survive in wild Texas.

A sudden knock, firm and decisive, startled her. She paled. She had paid for bolts to be fixed to her door since the frightening visit of the two bounty hunters. She stood up, calming herself because of Clare, and called, "Who is there, please?"

The answer came very clearly through the bolted door.

"Aren't you expecting me?"

Her colour rushed back, her feet rushed forward, and her hands rushed to the bolts. Joyously she pulled them back. She opened the door and trembled in her bliss. There he was, his buckskin shirt and breeches dreadfully worn and shabby, but an ecstasy to her eyes. He had a quizzical look on his face, so dark from the Texas sun and wind.

"M'sieu! Oh, m'sieu!" She could not help herself. She hugged him.

"Mademoiselle?"

She blushed and drew back, her huge eyes melting with joy. The sun had lined his eyes and taken the moisture from his flesh. His teeth were white, his eyes very blue. Antoinette muttered a prayer of thanks to herself.

"Oh, m'sieu!" She could find no other words.

"May I come in?"

"I am dreaming, dreaming." She stood aside, closing the door as he entered. She felt swamped by waves of hot, giddy happiness. He commanded the small room. Clare, small, pretty, and shy, got up from her stool and peered at him. The wide pink sash around her dress showed a huge bow. Jason smiled down at her, and a dimple made its soft mark on her cheek. Her green eyes, her mother's eyes, tugged at him. He bowed.

"Shall we meet, little cherub?"

"Clare!" Antoinette intervened in swooping delight, picking the child up and bringing her close to Jason. "Oh, here he is at last, your papa."

"Papa?" said Jason.

Antoinette flashed him a look of entreaty. He must not deny the child.

"Yes, your papa, Clare. Did I not say he was—" She checked herself. "There, I told you he was nice. You see?"

Clare, in wonder at all the excitement, decided to be good and smiled at Jason. As he stared at her, Jason found himself ruminating on exactly what kind of woman Edwina had been, and what was the full extent of her lover's disdain for life, that they could have given up a child like this.

"You have a very pretty nose," he said.

Antoinette laughed, and Clare giggled.

"Oh, m'sieu, we are overjoyed to see you. We have worried so much."

"One so little as Clare has worried?" he said.

"In sympathy with me," said Antoinette.

"Bring her to the window."

Antoinette carried Clare to the gabled window, sitting her on the wide ledge. The light touched the faces of the woman and the child. There was shy curiosity in the eyes of the child, and the reflection of rapturous relief in the eyes of the woman. Jason smiled at them both, his lean features relaxing. Antoinette's colour climbed. He was so close, almost touching her. She had thought these last few days that he would never arrive, never; and suddenly here he was, alive and strong and within inches of her. Clare gazed in a little awe now. Jason winked at her.

"You're a young lady," he said.

"I'm nice," said Clare.

"Yes, that's possible," he said, "you look a cherub to me."

Clare giggled, and Antoinette's exhilarating sense of freedom returned.

" 'Toinette is nice?" said Clare.

"That's also possible," said Jason.

"Four," said Clare, and held up three fingers.

"There's one missing," said Jason, and pulled up her little finger. "That's four."

"I'm good," said Clare.

"I should be surprised if you weren't."

" 'Toinette is good?"

"I think we can allow that she is extremely good," said Jason.

Clare smiled, looked very shy, and said, "Papa good?"

He laughed. He shed his darkness, and shut out the anguished eyes of Isabella.

"Shall we go to England, little girl?" he said. Clare could not think why not, especially as Antoinette mentioned it often. She nodded. "Antoinette?" he said.

"M'sieu, you will really take me too?"

"We will go, all three." He knew he owed her a great deal for her care of the child. "On the first available boat. Though France might suit you better, particularly the South of France—"

"M'sieu, you said nothing about France before. If I am not being impertinent, may I say that I cannot be governess to Clare if she is in England and I am in France?"

"You may say that, indeed you may," said Jason, "and you have done. So, then, we'll go, all three, to England."

Antoinette looked misty.

"M'sieu, you are—that is, I wish to say—"

"You've already said it, in New Orleans. Antoinette, you need not say it again. You have proved yourself with Clare, and it is I who am in debt to you now. Do we have any money left?"

"Money?" Walking on air for the moment, she was a little uncomprehending.

"I am without funds," he replied as he ruffled Clare's ringlets. "I spent my last few cents on a bath and a shave an hour ago, after I'd been told at the shipping office where you were. I have only what I stand in." He had lost his last few possessions in the Cordova fire. His worn shirt and breeches would sigh to their weary end and drop from him in another week.

"Oh, we are embarrassed with riches, m'sieu! Wait, hold Clare, please, and I will show you."

Clare accepted his protective arm, and Antoinette hurried into the bedroom. She was so glad of this opportunity to be alone. She put a hand tightly to her mouth, and the warm flood of surging emotions broke and the hot tears spilled. He had come back, without wounds, or scars, to take her and Clare to England, as he had promised, lacking only money. Oh, sweet Mary, how glad she was she had so much to give him.

She returned when she had composed herself, and showed him a small inlaid rosewood casket. She opened it. Crammed inside was a thousand dollars in greenbacks.

"You see?" she smiled. "A thousand dollars. We are rich."

"That's yours," said Jason with Clare's arms around his neck. "I meant, was there anything left of the money I gave you?"

"Oh, yes. Yes. But, m'sieu, all the money we have is our money, everything. There is your passage to pay for, and new clothes for you. M'sieu, will you please take this and look after it for all of us?"

"Yes, but we'll spend the other money first."

"Oh, m'sieu, you cannot know how pleased Clare and I are to see you, to know nothing happened to you."

"No, nothing happened to me," he said. It was only Isabella's stricken look that haunted him.

Antoinette did not ask questions. Perhaps he would tell her sometime if he had met the man, and what had happened.

"Tomorrow, when you have new clothes and are very handsome and imposing," she said, "we must go to see Madame Blazey. She will be happy then for Clare to go with us."

"Well, let us put our heads together and decide the colour of the new coat I must buy," said Jason, and he put one arm around Clare's waist as she sat still perched on his leg and the other around Antoinette. They all dipped their heads to confer solemnly on the subject, while Antoinette shivered within the embrace of his arm, and drowned in happiness.

# BOOK TWO

# WARWICK PLACE

# 1

The August sky was a canopy of deep blue, the air warm, balmy, and soft. The wheat stood golden and the fields shimmered. The road from Bath was dry, and its dust powdered the green verges and wild hedgerows. From the coach Antoinette gazed at the rich lushness of summer, and on her lap Clare prattled. The golden flowers of the western gorse decked the bushes with bright colour, upon which danced clusters of parasitical epithymum, palely pink. A mile farther and the coach was running between sloping heathlands, where the heather carpeted the undulating rises with purple.

Faintly she caught the scent of a proliferation of wild thyme. With wonder, her eyes traversed the hazy lines of green-clad chalk hills and dipped to meadows dappled with white and gold.

"Clare, is it not beautiful?" she whispered. She was a little self-conscious because of the other passengers, though it did not occur to her that their smiles meant they found her and Clare much more fascinating than vistas. Clare reached for Jason's old hunter watch. He let her have it. She put it to her ear to hear its sombre tick, and smiled up at him in delight. He winked at her. The stage lumbered on in jolting, ponderous progress over the rutted road, and only Antoinette was absorbed in the rustic tranquility of her new environment. So many different trees, trees of every kind. Great spreading oaks, bunched and twisted yews, and soaring poplars. And the air. When one breathed in so much of the polluted air of New Orleans, this was heaven's own.

The meadows called. She wished the coach would stop, so that she might jump out and dance over those dappled surfaces of green, so that she might run and fly through the soft clean air.

They caught up with a piled farm cart. Her nose twitched.

"Oh," she said, and looked tragic. Jason agreed the aroma was acidly pungent, but pointed out that what Nature gave had to be returned to her in some form or other, or she would become barren. Antoinette held her nose all the same. The cart gave way, trundling on to the verge, and the team of six horses pulled the coach past. "Mmm," she breathed sufferingly.

"You can let go now," said Jason, but she was careful and only freed her nose hesitantly.

"It was a moment of disillusionment, m'sieu," she whispered to him. But a mass of scented yellow honeysuckle, climbing a passing hedgerow, soon restored her sense of enchantment. For the sake of long-nosed people who ventured to enquire, she was travelling as Clare's nursemaid and governess, and as Jason's ward, and it did not discountenance Jason if any of them raised a sceptical eyebrow. Antoinette came to realise that while he observed some conventions, he did not give a fig for others.

She had been sick on the lurching, tossing sailing ship in which they had crossed the Atlantic. When Jason came to the tiny cabin she shared with Clare, she shuddered with shame that he should find her so dreadfully down and ugly. He gave her brandy, which so outraged her suffering stomach that she brought up everything still in it. He returned later and gave her more. She shuddered anew, only to fall asleep as heavily as a drunk, and when she awoke next morning she was free of suffering. At the end of the voyage, he looked at her with a smile as they stepped ashore amid the crowded masts of Bristol.

He said, "I was told, Antoinette, that you would reach England an old woman. Upon the soul of every roaring sailor, you've flourished."

"At one time, m'sieu, I wished to die," she said.

"Not so now?"

"Oh, no!"

Nor now. The coach ran on, swaying and creaking through a village, the post horn announcing their passage. Behind the coach, linked to it, trotted Napoleon, in disgust as always at this mode of progress. The cottages of pale stone rubbed shoulders with each other, tiny latticed windows glinting in the sun. A woman in a brown dress and straw bonnet looked up from sweeping her kerb and returned the salute of the coachman with a wave of her broom.

Thirty minutes later they pulled up in bustling Blandford, and the passengers alighted. Jason got off with Clare in his arms. When he set her down, she was still more interested in his watch than anything else. To her, one place was very much like another. It was people and things which engaged most of her curiosity. She adored Antoinette, and was shyly fond of Jason.

Antoinette gazed around while the ostlers attended to the change of horses, and the coachman and postilion disappeared into the inn. The passengers, after stretching their legs, followed.

"M'sieu, we are here?" she asked, looking up and down the sunny market street. "This is where you live?"

"Not precisely," said Jason. "Our house is a few miles away. Come, let me see you and Clare tucked into some comfortable chairs, while I discover what can be done about hiring a carriage."

"Oh, but I should not mind walking," she said. "The day is so lovely, and I have sat for so long that I am tender."

"Everywhere?"

"No, m'sieu," she smiled, "only in one place. I am quite able to walk."

"I can't have it so," said Jason. "It's too far. And there's the luggage. We can afford a comfortable four-wheeler, and won't settle for less than a spanking trap. It will depend on what is available."

He took her and Clare into the inn, where a private room was put at their disposal, and Antoinette's eyes grew wider as she tried to assimilate every variation of her new environment. Jason saw to it that refreshment was served to them, drank a large tankard of ale himself, then went to see that the luggage was being properly unloaded and set aside. That done, he sought the hire of a carriage. The best that was available was a trap. So it was that in this frisky vehicle Antoinette and Clare were carried to Jason's home, Warwick Place, whilst he himself rode alongside on Napoleon, who was blowing and snorting with satisfaction at the smell and feel of old familiar things.

Warwick Place was built of rose-red brick faced with stone. It resembled a small Elizabethan manor house, though in fact it had only been erected in 1720. The architect had favoured Elizabethan styles, and could not be divorced from his preferences. His finished work, however, was not a disappointment, for he had created a house of character.

Antoinette caught her first glance of Warwick Place as the hired trap entered the drive leading directly to the front entrance, which was centrally situated between the outer gables. Its warm colour and its mullioned windows beckoned the travellers. Wide lawns on either side of the drive gave the effect of a splendidly spacious approach, and the house itself stood grandly isolated from everything except the bounty of nature.

"M'sieu," she gasped to Jason, "that is your house?"

"I was born in it, brought up in it, and was left it by my father. But whether it remains mine or not is a matter of touch and go."

She was not quite sure what he meant by that, she was only sure that the house was beautiful. And everything was so peaceful and quiet. She remembered that his wife had talked about it once, saying it was a place of so much peace that one longed for war to arrive at the door.

"M'sieu, such a house. It will overcome me."

"Only if it falls down."

The trap turned into the circular forecourt and wheeled round to a halt outside the double-doored entrance. Jason dismounted, gave Napoleon a friendly slap, and the horse trotted away to the stables at the rear of the house as if he had never been away. The trap driver helped Antoinette and Clare to alight, then began to unload the luggage, most of it Antoinette's. Jason drew her aside.

"Now remember, Antoinette, before we let ourselves in, that your parents are dead. They were New Orleans French and left you financially distressed, which is why you've come to be Clare's governess. This doesn't mean you're a servant. A companion, rather. You are white, you look white, and indeed you have little enough of any blood that isn't white. And your manners, sweet child, are better than those of a duchess. Although penniless, you come of Creole aristocracy, and accordingly may conduct yourself in style. You understand? I don't want you to be hurt. Nor shall you be. You must forget everything that obtained in New Orleans. You must come to realise you can give to life just as much as any other person, and are therefore entitled to what life can give you."

"I understand, m'sieu," she said, feeling breathless. "But what I shall never understand is why your wife—why she—" She did not finish.

"Why my wife left me?" He smiled. Edwina was a regret, a memory now, not a bitterness. "Well, some wives, you know, are quick to discover that husbands are dull."

"M'sieu," she said in her soft earnest way, "you are far from dull."

"Ah," said Jason, "but you aren't married to me, and don't therefore have the knowing and critical eye of a wife."

"I am still not convinced, m'sieu."

A face showed at a window, and a few moments later the oak doors opened and a woman in a dress of summer eau de nile emerged to stand on the stone step. Eyes as blue as Jason's opened wide at the sight of Antoinette, Clare, and Jason himself.

"Oh, you dreadful wretch!" she cried. "Not a word from you about this, not a line!" She came off the step, met Jason, and received his warm kiss. Antoinette knew this must be his sister. He talked about her on the voyage home, though he had said nothing about the man who robbed him of his wife. Constance Rawlings, putting her arms around her brother, kissed him back. She was extremely fond of Jason, with whom she had shared the scampering mischievous frolics of growing up. What she thought of Edwina she could not put into words, and contented herself with referring to her as a poor silly woman. She eyed Jason fondly but severely. "Horrid man, why did you not write that you were coming? And who is the young lady, who is the child?"

"The child is Clare," said Jason, and called the little girl. She came at once, smiling and healthy, the shyness there as she gazed up at Constance. Constance was not a beautiful woman—her face was too thin—but neither was she a plain one. When she smiled, when the light ran into her blue eyes and sparkled between her wide red lips, the beholder forgot her face was rather thin and found himself looking. She smiled now at Clare. The luggage thumped on to the step, and the trap driver began to scrape his feet. Jason paid him off and tipped him.

"Thank 'ee mighty, sur," he said, and off he went.

"Cherub," said Jason to Clare, while Antoinette hovered a little nervously in the background, "here we have my sister Constance, who will be your aunt."

"Aunt?" said Constance.

"Quite so. I'll explain later. Clare is somewhat on the way to three. She's also somewhat small, but that's a natural characteristic of any child of her age—"

"Hold," said Constance, "not so fast, I pray."

"In slower time, then," said Jason, "here too is Antoinette Giraud, also of tender years, though a little more advanced than Clare."

"I am nineteen," put in Antoinette, a little indignantly.

"Wait, wait, I beg," said Constance, then shook her head and laughed, for there was a happiness among these three people which told her neither sin nor dubiety obtained. She looked in curiosity at Antoinette, and remarked her melting-eyed, flawless beauty. "Great good heavens," she said, "what sweet bloom is this you've plucked from the Americas?"

"Antoinette, this is my sister Constance," said Jason, and Antoinette dropped a curtsey so graceful that Constance was touched and enchanted. "My sister," smiled Jason, "has a gift of dramatising the arrival of the morning sun or the first drop of afternoon rain. She has done quite well by your arrival, I think, Antoinette, so gently kiss her cheek and make known to her you are to be her friend and companion as well as governess to Clare."

Constance accepted the light touch of soft lips on her cheek, looked into the amber-brown eyes that were so earnest, and saw in them a desperate wish to be accepted and liked. She smiled; and Antoinette, reading kindness and warmth, felt pleasure and relief.

"Why are we standing here, pray tell?" asked Constance.

"I fancy we rather feel you haven't yet lowered the draw-bridge," said Jason.

"The doors are open," said Constance. "Come, Antoinette, come, child, let us learn more about each other, for I confess myself agog. Let us with a chatter of confidences put to shame a brother who has sent only two letters in over three years. Jason, please call Masters to arrange for your bags to be brought in."

Intrigued beyond measure, she swept Clare and Antoinette into the house and through the hall at a speed which gave Antoinette no time to appreciate the oak-panelled walls or three gilt-framed paintings, which merely flashed by. Constance ushered them into the west drawing room, spacious and bright. Covering most of the square floor was a pale red carpet with a woodland pattern. On the walls hung a host of framed canvases. Above the pink marble fireplace was a huge mirror, made up of several reflecting shapes inset within gilt surrounds. Upholstered armchairs invested the room with an air of welcoming comfort, and a huge settee faced the fireplace. In the hearth stood a tapestried screen. Antoinette drew her breath. It was all so lovely, the room full of colour and light.

When Jason joined them a few minutes later, some part of the saga had already unfolded. Antoinette was answering more questions, and Clare was sitting watching and being extremely good.

"Constance, what are you thinking of?" asked Jason.

"I am not thinking of anything," said Constance, "I am engaged in extracting everything I can while I can. You will only give me the bare bones, and even then miss out a few. Men reduce the body of every good story to a skeleton. So far I've discovered there's a place waiting you in heaven by reason of your saintly rescue of our mademoiselle from the distress of penury. But I still don't understand how you came to be in New Orleans—"

"Constance, be a sweet creature now," said Jason, "and save your curiosity for later. Show Antoinette and Clare to a room which they may share until Clare is disposed to have her own. They're considerably fatigued, and also in need of sustenance. Be careful, however, not to serve tea to Antoinette, for she has told me she can't look favourably on it."

"Oh, m'sieu, that is not fair," cried Antoinette.

"What isn't?" asked Constance, wishful to hear every word and every reason. She was parched for news of all that had happened to Jason, all that pertained to Edwina, and all that had moved her brother to return home with Antoinette and Clare in tow. The extraordinary materialisation of the delicious child and the beautiful young French lady called for a prolonged and stimulating explanation that must be a story in itself.

"Mademoiselle," said Antoinette, "I was not to know Monsieur Rawlings likes tea and was miserably trapped into declaring it— mademoiselle, do you like tea?"

"My dear," said Constance, rising, "it isn't music that soothes the savage breast of civilisation, it's tea. But come, Jason is right, I am selfishly detaining you. And the child looks as if she would like to close her eyes for a while. So come."

Antoinette, excited rather than tired, nevertheless welcomed a chance to repair the effects of travel. She carried the sleepy Clare in her arms as Constance led the way up a broad oak staircase.

Constance was down again in ten minutes, having left a maid to see that everything was comfortable for Antoinette and the child in a guest room. She could not bear to wait any longer to hear what Jason had to tell her. But first of all he asked about his father's death.

"He's in his grave these many months, my dear," she said. "And I was used to wearing black until quite recently. But it doesn't suit me. I am plain enough as it is."

"That," said Jason, "is nonsense."

She told him how his father had died about a year ago, falling from a window in a London club. Rumour said that in an excess of drink and in despair at his debts he did not fall at all. But the verdict was accidental death. Jason must now understand that there was no money to speak of, only debts. She was at her wit's end, and only too pleased to hand over all worries to him. She herself intended to retire to a small cottage on the modest legacy left to her by her mother.

Jason's father, Gervase Rawlings, had been the third son of Sir Peter Rawlings, and Warwick Place with its acres of farmlands had been the baronet's wedding gift to Gervase. The farms brought in an income, but needed sound management—something which proved outside any natural bent of Gervase, who had a great liking for his charming wife, and an even greater liking for London. After his wife died, three years before Jason married Edwina, he spent most of his time in the metropolis, as well as most of his income.

Jason, after a moment's regret that any man, particularly his likeable father, should die so foolishly, said, "We're orphans, you and I, Constance."

"Well, we still have each other," she replied, in similarly wry vein. "You've lost Edwina, I presume, since you've not brought her back with you. I vow myself very intrigued by what you did bring, your quite delightful Miss Giraud. She is hardly designed to be a governess. And how came you not to provide her with a chaperone? Or was it your intention to compromise her?"

"Under the circumstances, I counted myself her chaperone. She was satisfied with the arrangement, and so was I. She too is an orphan. But I'd better tell you about Edwina."

He gave Constance the full story, not only of Edwina but of his eventual confrontation with her lover at Cordova. He held back only the truth about Antoinette, for he did not intend at any time to depart from what he had agreed with the octoroon girl. Not even Constance, a woman of understanding, was to know that Antoinette had a small amount of coloured blood in her. So of course Constance accepted the story that the young lady was the daughter of New Orleans Creoles who had left her penniless.

"You have had an Odyssey, not a journey," said Constance. She remarked a change in him. His features had always been handsomely pleasing to her, and characteristic of a man of engaging humour and good will. They were leaner and harder now, and he himself, she felt, was harder too. "Why did you decide to spoil that man's prettiness instead of shooting him? I vow I had one impression only when you left, that you meant to put him into his coffin. I thought it a waste, not of life but your time. You have lost three years. So why did you only cut him about?"

"Constance, there are twists in every man's thoughts, and perverse turns in many of his intentions."

Constance looked thoughtfully at him.

"Was it his daughters who made you spare him?"

"The thought of them, perhaps," said Jason. "Also the thought that death, after all, was a lighter sentence than scarring him."

"So," said Constance, "Edwina lies in New Orleans, then, and her daughter rests upstairs. Jason, you're as forgiving as our father was soft. I am sorry for Edwina, poor foolish woman. In looking for ever brighter candlelight she fell into the darkness of a miserable death. Well, perhaps life will show you a little charity now, for I swear you're in need of it. There's only a small amount of money available, and everything is mortgaged, everything, the house and the furniture, the farms and the livestock. We possess nothing, Jason, and you've brought home a child and a French girl. Well-deserving as they are, they're two more liabilities. Perhaps instead of spending all this time searching for a man whom you spared in the end, you should have stayed here and kept Father out of debt and the house out of the hands of a moneylender."

Jason eyed the lawns through the sunlit windows. Their com-

pact velvet green made up for some things, though not for Isabella.

"Constance, how much does your legacy bring in?"

"Oh, no," said his sister, "oh, no. I am under no obligation
whatever and will not be coerced into foolishness."

"My sweet and most dear sister—"

"Stand off," said Constance as he turned and took her hand.
She knew he was aware of her affection for him. At twenty-seven
she was three years younger than he and during their growing
years he had been her champion, happily blacking the eyes or
bloodying the noses of boys who had a tendency to pull her long
brown hair.

"Naturally," said Jason, "whatever you contributed towards expenses would be repaid in full."

"I have contributed already," said Constance, "and am not to
be persuaded into contributing more. You must remember that as
I'm destined to be an old maid—"

"More nonsense."

"—I need to provide for myself. Desperately in debt as we are,
we shall almost certainly lose Warwick Place—and I refuse even
to contemplate the shame and horror of throwing myself on par-
ish relief. You are a man, and may find ways of earning a living."

"Are things as desperate as that?" Jason sat down, frowning.

"They are. Father had no head on him at all. How you will pay
that French girl, if she's to be Clare's governess, heaven knows.
Even our servants, who have been so good about everything, are
only receiving half their pay—and have been for some time. I was
used to a clear, untroubled conscience about our servants. Now I
cannot look any of them in the face. But I could dismiss none,
even though I should have done so for economy's sake. You must
take on the woe of that responsibility, for I vow that as a weak
and tender woman it is too much for me."

"I shall do nothing so drastic until I've fully investigated all our
woes," said Jason. "And let me tell you, I've not come home, in
any event, to preside over our liquidation."

"You have my best wishes," said Constance. "On top of which,
it's time fortune turned in your favour. You've given an undeserv-
ing woman and her lover three years of your life, but you are still
a young man. I daresay it doesn't signify to you, for you were
never one to go about with a mirror in your hand, but I confess

I'd like to see a little more flesh on your bones. You are very thin."

"It's not a fatal condition," he said. "What's happened to Antoinette and Clare?"

"I fancy they're both napping. The young lady was wearier than she thought. So I ordered no refreshment."

"It's been an exhausting journey. As to Antoinette, I look to you, Constance, to give her kindness."

"La, man," she said, "are my sentiments to be compelled from me? If she's as sweet as she seems, then I'll need no compulsion. I shall respond with every kindness. If she is not what she seems, I shall say so and ask for a new arrangement. At the moment, I find her a charming creature. She may be penniless, but so beautiful a young lady should not suffer our charity too long. I vow she'll be able to take her pick of the richest men in the county."

"She has earned my regard, not my charity, in what she has done for me in respect of Clare," said Jason crisply. "She has no one but us. I intend to make her my ward until she's twenty-five, so that until then or until she elects to marry, she shall be protected."

"That's almost unreasonably softhearted," said Constance, "yet very practical. But I'm not sure she wouldn't rather be your wife than your ward. She cannot speak your name without those eyes of hers betraying her regard for you."

"I've an affection for Antoinette, I admit. But she, I fancy, goes about in clouds of emotional gratitude. That's not a basis for marriage."

"Perhaps you're right. I'm a simple woman myself, with little understanding of the deeper or more intimate feelings of my fellow beings." Constance spoke indeed in the modest way of a simple woman, and took no heed of her brother's smile. "I shall probably never come to a sophisticated turn in life, knowing, as I do, that an unmarried woman cannot experience—"

"Constance, married or unmarried, you will always entertain people, so enough of your simplicities, which I fancy escape most of us."

"Very well." She smiled. "Let me order tea, and while we have it you shall tell me more of the Americas. You need not mention Edwina again. No woman could have been more unfortunate in her choice of a lover, nor more foolish. It is an unhappy fact, is it not, that few women prefer a good man to a bad one, and that women who make fools of themselves do so over villains, never over heroes. It would be better for all women like Edwina to be endowed with a little less beauty and a great deal more sense."

"Coming from so simple a woman as you, Constance, those observations are really quite remarkable."

Antoinette awoke. She sat up, embarrassed. She had committed the unpardonable sin of falling asleep when she had been left by her hostess to merely take a brief rest. The clock told her that her brief rest had lasted three hours. She had drifted off on wings of dreamy, sleepy happiness. Now the windows of the large bedroom were flushed with evening light. She got up. How quiet the house was, how soft that light. The room was flooded with it, so that it felt like a fragrantly delicate caress. Because of the many windows, almost every room she had seen so far drew in the day's brightness from dawn till dusk. She had not imagined such a sense of captured light in any private house, for in New Orleans shuttered windows held most of nature's light at bay.

A pastel blue paper patterned with faded roses covered the bedroom walls. A square, framed mirror occupied the space above the mantelshelf and reflected the warm light. The walnut furniture was charming, though it did not have the exquisite elegance of the Louis XV pieces collected by Monsieur Johnson for his house in New Orleans.

New Orleans. Her little shudder was immediately followed by a sense of blessed relief. She crossed to the window. The sun was gilding the western sky, and a thin flotilla of clouds sailed through seas of gold and red and blue. The parkland that spread outwards and away from the back gardens lay in lambent green under the evening sun. A giant oak, brilliantly glossy, soared above a cluster of silver-barked birch trees. To the east a church spire reached upwards from a mass of sycamores, their palmate leaves coming to her eyes as a conglomeration of bright emerald foliage.

Shadows moved across a distant meadow, shadows which resolved into the shapes of slowly trudging beasts. A herd of cows was going home. A blackbird swooped from auburn light and landed on the stone ledge of the window. It saw the eyes that flashed between long sooty lashes, and was off again like a small whirring projectile. The church clock chimed the hour, the sound faint but sweet. She counted the seven chimes.

About to move away, she was held by the figure of a horseman. The horse was black and the coat of the rider was brown. His dark head was bare. He came at a trot across the parkland, shoulders drooping a little as he rode in his relaxed way. Down below, a child emerged from the shadows cast by the house, a child who scampered to meet him, calling, "Papa! Papa!" Behind followed a lady gowned in blue silk taffeta. Clare and Constance. Antoinette heard the little girl call again.

" 'Poleon! 'Poleon!"

Jason leaned down, took her up, and in high excitement she chattered and giggled. Constance, drawn by the indefinable, looked up and saw Antoinette at the window. Antoinette opened it and leaned out.

"My dear," called Constance, "if you are rested we sup in half an hour."

"Oh, calamity dreadful," gasped Antoinette, and withdrew her head. There was so much to do, to undress, to see to her toilet, and to dress again—and what to wear? And Clare to put to bed. Oh, how wonderful life was.

Constance took on the task of putting Clare to bed, and this enabled Antoinette to go down on the stroke of seven-thirty. She wore a gown of softest yellow, and looked like Louisiana's rarest and loveliest flower. At least she had been allowed to bring away the superb gowns which had formed her extensive wardrobe in that house in New Orleans. Common sense had triumphed over any feelings of aversion. One might despise the traditions, one could not fault the clothes.

The dining room looked out on to the back gardens and the parklands, and the colours were of the kind that came only with a descending summer sun. Every colour softly glowed. Red streaks of light shot the yellow-brown carpet. The long refectory table was of polished oak, the oak chairs padded in yellow-brown. Two crystal chandeliers hung above the table, the candles not yet lit. On the panelled walls were pictures, the subjects being children, adults, and landscapes. Antoinette supposed the portraits were ancestral. She also supposed Jason was of the aristocratic class, though she had never thought of him as an elegant gentleman, rather more as one who had made Monsieur Johnson quake a little.

She and Constance supped alone, attended by Masters the factotum, and Emily, a rosy-faced Dorset girl, always quick to respond with a smile if caught by an eye and always quick to avoid the smile being caught by Masters, who was a glutton for sobriety among servants in the dining room.

Captain Rawlings, Constance informed Antoinette, would not appear. He was snacking in the steward's room. With the steward, Mr. Harris.

"Captain Rawlings?" said Antoinette.

"Did you not know my brother was a captain with the Queen's 7th Lancers?" Constance spoke with just a little pride. She had an affection for Britain's cavalry regiments, and a greater understanding of the soldier's lot than most people.

"He is a soldier," said Antoinette.

"He was," said Constance, "but we need not discuss why he left the Army. You know it all, my dear, having befriended that poor foolish woman who was his wife, and it doesn't matter any more. It's all a closed book now. Is the mutton to your liking?"

The mutton, which was lamb carved at the sideboard by Masters, had arrived on a piping-hot plate and lay simmering in its juices. It was so tender that it was a melting succulence in the mouth; Antoinette had never eaten meat like it.

"Mademoiselle, it is excellent."

"But do you like it?" There was a glimmer of amusement in Constance's smile. She knew the gastronomic fancies of the French, the finesse they applied to their cuisine and the distaste they had for other people's menus.

"Oh, yes, mademoiselle." Antoinette's eyes were pools of assurance. "Without question. It is so tender, so famishing."

"Famishing?"

"Yes? Famishing is to make one feel hungry for more, isn't it?"

"One could say so." Constance found the girl charming. "Your English is remarkably good, Antoinette. Where did you learn to speak it so well?"

Antoinette knew there might always be questions of a disconcerting quality, and care had to be taken with all her answers. Truth could be given with this one.

"I was educated at a convent, and was taught English there," she said. "Also I read many English books later, and of course even in New Orleans almost everyone speaks English now. It is America which owns Louisiana these days."

"A sale and a purchase arranged over the heads of the people," said Constance. "Quite outrageous, especially as America looks down her nose at our possessions."

"Oh, the Creoles are still most unhappy, mademoiselle." Antoinette drew back as Masters brought fresh slices of the lamb on a hot platter. "Thank you," she said as he began to transfer them, then lifted an agitated hand. "Oh, too much, too much."

"You are sure, miss?" Masters was kind but lugubrious.

"Well, I will see. It all looks *delicieux*. I cannot think why Monsieur Rawlings should wish to miss it."

"He's peering into the accounts of the estate," said Constance, "and with a frowning brow, I fancy."

"Ah, he is giving them a look," said Antoinette, "that will bring them to order if there is anything wrong with them."

Constance laughed. The girl was enchanting, obviously aristocratic but absolutely without airs, though very full of graces. Her beauty was almost disturbing. A pity, thought Constance, that a little of it could not be passed to me.

"Antoinette, I think you should know—"

Jason came in then. Constance, about to tell Antoinette what everyone else at Warwick Place knew, that times were highly critical, decided Jason must tell her himself. The girl's colour, she noticed, heightened the moment he entered the room. Now exactly how does the land lie with her? Is she in love with my brother, or simply excessively grateful to him? New Orleans, so I've heard, is a decadent city, where defenceless virtue is at daily risk and an orphan girl with beauty such as hers must have felt herself parlously exposed. Yet I confess I cannot understand why her position should have been so parlous when there must have been family friends of some kind, and certainly a gentleman or two willing to court her in an honourable way. In any event, Jason could no more afford a new wife than a new horse. And after Edwina, I doubt he'll ever want to marry again. But this French girl should have no trouble finding a husband among the nicer gentlemen of Dorset, not with those looks. Perhaps I might help her to look around for the richest as well as the nicest. Such a girl should go through life with her beauty enhanced by adornment.

Jason, nodding at his sister and Antoinette, went to the sideboard.

"Masters, would you give me a glass, please?" he said as he picked up the carving knife. Masters filled a glass with wine, and Emily carried it to him. He drank half of it, put the glass down, carved himself a slice of hot mutton, and ate it with relish. Emily caught his eye and smiled. Antoinette watched him simply because she always found it difficult not to.

"Jason," protested Constance as he carved and demolished a second slice, "I vow your manners are an embarrassment." Jason emptied his glass. "Sweet heaven, sir," said Constance, "do you imagine that all we wish to see in you after three years is an ability to guzzle and gobble?" This gave Emily a fit of the giggles, and Masters put her out of the room. "Why don't you sit down with us and dine in a civilised way?" finished Constance.

"Beg your forgiveness, no time," said Jason, and to his sister's disgust cut a large piece of cheese, which, with a refilled glass, he began to carry away with him. He turned at the open door. "Your servant, ladies," he said, and disappeared.

Antoinette put her napkin to her mouth. Constance eyed her suspiciously. "I should not care to have you to think such behaviour less than disgraceful," she said. "I must apologise for the wretch."

"Oh, mademoiselle, I scarcely noticed a thing," said Antoinette. All the same, and despite the help of the napkin, she burst into laughter. Constance smiled.

"Sir?" Ralph Harris, the middle-aged steward, entered the room. "Have you been up all night?"

Jason, sitting at the steward's desk, closed one more neatly kept book.

"Not quite," he said. "It was good of you to stay up with me as you did, but I went to bed not long after you retired yourself."

"I was only too pleased to be of assistance." Ralph Harris was pleasant-faced, pleasant-mannered, and had been steward at Warwick Place for twenty years.

"We're in a pretty fix, Ralph."

"We've been perilously close to the edge for years."

"I fancy we're about to fall over it," said Jason.

"The outgoings are depressingly heavy."

"Depressingly."

"That's the dairy farm book," said Harris, nodding at the one Jason had just closed. "Have you seen them all now, sir?"

"No, there are one or two more. But I must let you have your desk back now. I must take a ride and look at things other than figures. I'm beginning to find them indigestible." He got up, stuffing into his coat pocket some notes he had made. Ralph Harris's smile was rueful. Obviously the new owner meant not so much a ride around as a keen inspection. Well, that would do no harm. The previous squire, Jason's father, had not ridden around the estate on an inspection for a dozen or more years.

"It's a fine day for it," he said.

"Yes," said Jason. "By the way, though not a keeper of books myself, I know a little about figures and can recognise well-kept accounts. I'm obliged to you, Ralph, very much so, from the look of these." He had his hand on the pile of ledgers.

"Oh, accounts represent one more part of my occupation," said Harris. "And it's a part which I don't find difficult. Mr. Rawlings, whatever I can do to help—"

"Thank you. It goes without saying that I depend on you. Incidentally," said Jason, "according to one set of figures I've seen, you've only been drawing half your salary for the last six months."

"A bearable exigency of the moment," smiled Harris, "and I'd like to see it through until we turn the corner. Mrs. Harris and I have the cottage, remember, and free board. We're neither in want nor down to our last change of clothing."

"Well, we'll sink or swim soon enough, I fancy," said Jason.

"If I may say so," said Harris, "you're a new broom with a difference."

"I'm very new," said Jason, "but I don't know how different I am."

He was very new when it came to being squire of Warwick Place and the nearby village of Dunniford. He wasn't helped by the fault of neglect, family neglect. He had spent his most energetic years in the Army, and his father had spent the better part of many years in London. Neither he nor his father had kept a caring eye on the estate. Both deserved what neglect had reaped— impending bankruptcy.

But, damn it, the place was his now. He was not going to part with it too easily. For all that he had enjoyed his time in the cavalry, he had a love for his home and the beauty that was all around it. He had lost Edwina. He had, because of the obsession of vengeance, also lost Isabella. He must make some effort to see that he did not lose his inheritance.

He walked frowning through the hall.

"M'sieu?" Antoinette appeared, looking hesitant.

"Well now, by all the saints, here is summer," he said, for she was in pale blue. "Is summer settled in?"

"I am summer, m'sieu?" She smiled. "If I am, then summer is most settled in. I am overcome by so much kindness, but I am also alarmed."

"The house is on fire?"

"It is not a comical matter," she said. "M'sieu, I beg you, you cannot possibly think I am to be paid for being governess to Clare."

"It isn't to be thought you should receive nothing. What's brought the matter up?"

"Mademoiselle Rawlings spoke to me last night. She said you should have done so, but as you had not, she must herself."

"My sister doesn't like people being kept in the dark," said Jason. "So I suppose she told you, did she, that we could not afford to pay you?"

"She said there was no money, none at all." Antoinette was plainly distressed.

"It's not as bad as that," he said.

"But I do not want to be paid. How could you think so? I want nothing, no, not a cent, and there is all the money I still have."

"Antoinette, you have what is left of your thousand dollars, and what we spent is owed to you. It's one more debt, I'm afraid, young lady, but you shall be repaid in time."

"No, no," said Antoinette. "What was spent was for all of us, did we not agree so? And what is left you must have. I do not need it. M'sieu, I have everything, freedom, happiness, and kindness, and you have given me all of these things. I do not need money as well. Oh, please take it."

"Very well." He smiled and lightly squeezed her hand. "When I need it, I'll ask for it. Will that do?"

"Yes, m'sieu, though I would rather you had it now. May I ask, are the portraits in the house of your family and ancestors?"

"Upon my soul, no," he said. "We only came into possession of Warwick Place when it was acquired for my father, by my grandfather. I can lay no claim to being a descendant of the illustrious ladies and gentlemen of the Warwick family, whose line died out years ago."

"Ah," she said, and smiled. "Do you see, m'sieu, I was a little puzzled. Although illustrious, they are not remarkable for their beauty."

"Neither am I," said Jason.

Antoinette might have said that to her he was one of God's own men, that he looked so, but she knew that would be an immodest declaration of the love she had for him. So she just said, "But you do not look like—that is—"

"Not like him?" Jason pointed to the hall portrait of a man with a startlingly rubicund face under a white-powdered wig.

She had a smile in her eyes as she said, "M'sieu, I think you can say we are agreed on that."

"It seems to me, Antoinette, that you and I are destined to be friends for life, for we come to agreement over so many things. Where's Clare?"

"With Mademoiselle," said Antoinette, "who is already attached to her. I am on my way to join them."

"Good. You can tell my sister, if you will, that I expect to be out most of the morning. I have to look around at cows and things. By the way, do you ride?"

"I was never taught to sit a horse, m'sieu."

"Then someone must teach you."

"Oh, m'sieu," she said in alarm, "I should fall off."

"Only a few times," he said.

Jason was out not just for the morning, as it happened, but for most of the day. He took in the whole of the estate, reacquainting himself with gardeners, agricultural labourers, dairy farm hands, and the ancient shepherd. These were employees he had not laid eyes on since last being home with Edwina. They saw in him a more incisive and involved squire than his father, more inquisitive about what was what, and more interested. He told them, among other things, that he was now a widower, and they sighed that so pretty a lady as Mrs. Rawlings had passed away while still young. He rode to the wheat and barley fields, he watched the roving sheep, he inspected the dairy farm and saw the lively young bullocks and heifers. He asked questions about crops, milk yields, cattle sales, and lambing, and he checked his notes.

Everything was in order. Ralph Harris had handled the management of the estate like a man born to it. The fields and the farms were models of good husbandry.

He returned very late in the day, and went to the steward's room. Ralph Harris was still there and looked, from his welcoming smile, as if he had known he might as well wait for this new discussion. He got up, brought a chair forward, and they sat down together. Jason talked about the excellent yields.

"Well, in all modesty," said Ralph, "they have been very satisfactory when averaged out over several years."

"You've a first-class management ability," said Jason, "and we've been lucky that you've stayed with us. I'm damned if I fully understand why we're so much in debt."

"Mr. Rawlings," said Ralph, "I think we agreed you hadn't seen all the books."

"Not all, no, but enough, I thought."

"You haven't seen this very private journal." Ralph extracted a small accounts book from a drawer, and pushed it forward over the desk. "I didn't want to thrust anything under your nose. I wanted to let you decide for yourself exactly how you wished to check everything. You've seen the dairy and noted it to be a going concern, you've looked at the crops and decided they couldn't be more promising. So you're puzzled, I suggest, because with the estate so healthy even the mortgage should be comfortably manageable as far as the payment of interest is concerned. But some liabilities can be invisible, Mr. Rawlings."

"So?" said Jason.

"That book will tell you why your finances are so parlous. I didn't want to brandish it immediately as if it represented my flag of honour. It might have looked as if I had an eagerness to camouflage incompetence. However, you've now seen the general accounts and you've seen the estate. But that is our albatross, that book, sir."

Jason opened the small book. It dealt with London creditors. There were neatly inscribed names and addresses, and neatly inscribed amounts.

"Damnation," he said, "a whole pack of them."

"I regret," said Ralph, "that your father amassed far more debts in London than he did wise friends. The book was his idea, I assure you. He passed the debts on to the estate, but didn't want them shown in the accounts. He had ideas at one time of selling the place, and they'd have made the accounts look extremely sick. They were a charge on the estate. When your father died, there were other creditors who came dunning us, and these I had to add to the others. I managed to persuade them all to accept repayment by instalments, showing them that we could do so. Failing that, Warwick Place would have been liquidated. Fortunately, most of the creditors represent reputable people like—um—tailors, wine merchants, and so on. They make no demands as long as we make punctual repayments. Again fortunately, the mortgage holder has been very reasonable. Your father was at least able to raise the mortgage from a good friend, Sir Richard Davenport. Sir Richard has held off dunning us for the sake of friendship, and out of respect for Miss Constance. But he isn't disposed to hold off indefinitely. And the fact is, he hasn't had a groat in the way of interest for twelve months. Every penny we've had to spare has gone to the creditors in London."

"God's justice," said Jason wryly, "here I am, come prying and poking around after years of disinterest and giving the impression, I daresay, that I'd only to scan a few figures before pronouncing on cause, effect, and remedy. Well, I'm not of that turn of mind, Ralph, I simply had to start somewhere. I'm damned sorry the family hasn't made proper capital of all your efforts. What's the sum total of debts still outstanding to the London creditors?"

"A little in excess of three thousand pounds."

"Oh, the devil, a small fortune, and that on top of a mortgage of five thousand due for settlement."

"Plus unpaid interest, sir."

"D'you know it, Ralph, I fancy I can't even afford a pair of new boots."

"I fancy you're not disposed to sink with or without new boots," said Ralph. "It would be of some help if we could get quicker payment for our produce and livestock. Merchants, millers, and farmers all keep us waiting. Credit is what everyone wants."

"That," said Jason, "seems to be what we can least afford to give."

Wanting to go further into this particular facet, Jason advised Constance that she and Antoinette should commence supper without waiting for him. He looked in on Clare, who had just been put to bed. She was sleepy from a long, full day in the gardens and the sunshine, but shyly asked to be kissed good night. He bent and kissed her, and she put warm arms around his neck and murmured, "Love you, Papa."

Constance waylaid him as he came out of the bedroom.

"I've decided to refuse your request," she said. "We shall wait for you, and you'll dine with us. I'm not to be aggravated more about it. I've scarcely seen you since your reappearance, and your charming young lady from New Orleans has seen even less. Much as we are beginning to like each other, we won't accept deprivation of masculine company. We are adamant about this—"

"Both of you?"

"I, sir, am very much adamant. So it's no use your muttering about it. Please make yourself ready, and come down as soon as possible. I'll ask Masters to delay the meal for you. Make haste, for Antoinette is already waiting. Incidentally, I'm quite unable to understand how you came to think of turning her into a governess. It must be the most unimaginative thought you have ever had. You would not ask a swan to quack, would you? You must help her to come out—"

"Come out?"

"Certainly," said Constance, whisking her fan. "It would be deplorable, sir, to hide such a superb creature in the schoolroom with Clare. I can see to Clare, much of the time. You must see to Antoinette and help her to meet the county. Inside a few months, she'll have received a hundred proposals. The penury of her thriftless parents doesn't signify, she herself—"

"Am I to change for supper, Constance, or stand here listening to how I'm to order Antoinette's life for her?"

"Go and change, please."

At supper Constance was handsomely dressed in deep green, Antoinette in captivating black and gold. Jason was well turned out in a coat of Oxford blue and trousers of light grey. His cravat was a splash of light blue. Antoinette felt herself carried along on a tide of warm content, though quite how it had all come about she could not really describe. She had been transported on clouds from a New Orleans slave market to a house of quiet beauty. No, she had not been transported. Jason Rawlings had built a bridge for her, told her to cross it, and she had. It had led her to an oasis of peace and security, and New Orleans seemed a hundred years away. She had even found that the tea served at Warwick Place was not at all like the tea served by good Mrs. Sarah Blazey. Constance Rawlings pronounced it the nectar of all truly civilised people, and advised her to take only a slice of lemon with it. While Antoinette could not honestly equate it with nectar, she was at least now willing to persevere with it.

Where, Constance was asking, had her brother been all day? Over the chink of cutlery, Jason replied that he had been out and about, here and there on the estate.

"Oh, I vow, men are either the closest of creatures or the most unsatisfactory," declared Constance. "Give a man wit, and he shares the best of it with his mirror. Give a man an estate, and he dismisses a whole day in a single sentence. Out and about, sir, here and there, what does that mean, pray?"

"It means," said Jason, "that I've been looking everything over, and have found nothing to complain about."

"But did you meet people, dear man, people? Did you meet Tom Clarke, for instance? If so, how is his pretty wife and their new baby?"

"Tom Clarke." Jason was cautious. Antoinette watched him, saw his caution, and let a smile creep into her eyes. "Ah, yes. The dairy farm foreman."

"Eyes, dear brother, eyes. Ears, sir, ears." Constance always enjoyed taking a conversation along and introducing her own kind of words. Tom Clarke is your new woodman. Poor Zeth Albright died two years ago."

"The dairy farm foreman—"

"Is Jeff Clarke. People and names go together and very often fit."

Antoinette laughed. Constance looked at her, and the lashes of one eye came together in a slow wink. And Antoinette knew she could love Constance too.

"Let me confess," said Jason, "that, their rumps aside, cows were more on my mind today than the woodman's new baby. Antoinette, how was today for you?"

"Oh, quite lovely," said Antoinette. "Clare was so good, and Mademoiselle Rawlings so helpful. We took tea in the gardens—"

"Tea?" said Jason.

"Oh, I am encountering the pot bravely," said Antoinette earnestly, "and will triumph in the end. I am allowed to say that what is poured from the pot here is superior?"

"Yes, that is allowed," said Jason, "and will please Emily."

"Thank you, m'sieu. One does not need courage to sip from a superior pot—only determination."

"Dear me," said Constance.

"It is the custom in this country to take tea," said Antoinette. "Therefore, I am determined, oh, I am resolute, m'sieu and mademoiselle, to adopt this custom myself and become intrepidly *anglaise*."

"There," smiled Constance, "who could have faced up to it better?"

"I have spoken correctly concerning tea?" enquired Antoinette.

"I've heard no one quite so correct," said Jason. "Antoinette, you're to come out, I believe."

"Come out?"

"Enter the social life of the county."

"That is so," said Constance kindly. "Otherwise people will discover we are keeping you to ourselves and will descend on us in creeping hordes. Pop-eyed young gentlemen will search you out for themselves. I was not used myself to being kept hidden when I was a young lady."

"God's life, you're not an old woman yet," said Jason. "And I thought, last time I was home, that Ned Tranter was—"

"I am not aware of the gentleman, sir," interrupted Constance. "Now, Antoinette, concerning your coming out."

"Mademoiselle," said Antoinette, "I am very happy, there is no need—"

"My dear young lady," said Constance, "it's not to be thought for a moment that after giving Jason so much invaluable help with Clare you should become a governess or nursemaid. I won't have it, I really won't. Jason shall have the pleasure of arranging a reception in your honour. He'll achieve well for you, he has a way of prevailing on people."

"Oh, I am sure he could make the angels dance for him, if he desired," said Antoinette.

"Do you think so?" said Constance.

"It was not said seriously, mademoiselle."

"My dear girl, I'm aware of that," said Constance, "and am sharing the joke with you."

"You permit me a little joke or two?" said Antoinette.

"Oh, we are all permitted the occasional one," said Constance.

"That is a custom too?"

"It's a habit with some," said Jason, "and an omission in others."

Antoinette turned the conversation back, as she said, "M'sieu, I am not urgently disposed to come out. I am happily committed to my duties with Clare."

"Heavens, sweet child," said Constance, "you aren't committed at all. My brother has absolutely no right to deny our friends sight of you. Indeed, I vow it our bounden duty to bring you out, and I daresay in only a little while you'll fly into the arms of a most loving beau."

Constance did not want this enchanting belle from New Orleans to be denied her rightful prospects. Whether she married or not, she was entitled at this bright time of her life to enjoy having beaux skirmishing around her. Constance herself had enjoyed those all too brief years of delicious flirtations, though no young man had ended up proposing to her. She came in the end to accept that she was no great beauty. She did not mope too much about it, but there were times when she felt life was a little incomplete.

Antoinette cast perturbed glances at Jason.

"Constance is right," he said. Masters, a bottle of Burgundy in his hand, bent and whispered. The bottle was almost the last of its like left in the cellar. Jason grimaced at the news. "I doubt we can afford to restock yet," he said plainly. Masters, accepting what could not be helped, said, "Very good, sir."

~ 313 ~

Antoinette's mouth was compressed. After supper, when Constance had gone up to peep in on Clare, she confronted Jason.

"M'sieu," she said unhappily, "I am not free, after all?"

Jason, regarding the brandy decanter with a resigned look for its meagre contents, said, "What is this about, Antoinette?"

"M'sieu," she said, "if I am to be disposed of, if I am to be handed over to a man I may not care for, then I am not free, am I?"

"I agree," said Jason, "you aren't."

She turned pale, and her elegant splendour seemed to fade and shrink.

"M'sieu," she whispered, "I am to believe you would dispose of me?"

"You are to believe I'd do no such thing," he said. "You're as free, sweet girl, as you want to be—as you're entitled to be. I'd only remind you that you're in a country foreign to you, and I brought you to it and accordingly consider you my responsibility. Which means that if I thought you contemplated doing something foolish I should draw you aside and try to dissuade you as firmly as I could. That is the only way you aren't free. You are still vulnerable, Antoinette, and I mean to become your official guardian, to give you what protection may be necessary, until you're twenty-five. In every other way your life is your own, so be assured you've nothing to worry about."

"Oh, I can never repay your kindness and care," she said breathlessly. "But it is permitted that I kiss you?"

"Kissing," said Jason with gravity suitable to the moment, "is as much a custom here as elsewhere, though it isn't compulsory."

"This, m'sieu, is in gratitude," she said, and put her hands on his shoulders, came up on tiptoe, and kissed his mouth with warm, passionate lips.

The next day, Jason took Napoleon and made some calls. His first was on a miller, several miles away. A warm breeze blew in Jason's face. It played over the packed wheat standing tall in the fields, and the fields rippled with changing shades of gold. Old Napoleon seemed in a mellow mood, for he made no fuss about being turned into a hack. The summer breeze ran over them, soft and quick. For anyone who might have missed the Texas sun, thought Jason, there was compensation in a landscape whose infinite variety of greens was rich throughout the four seasons. The scent of Dorset pines induced headiness in Napoleon, who executed a few frisky sidesteps as they approached the village of Dunniford.

A river ran gurgling through the village, wound to pass under the stone bridge, and rushed from there on its descent to Wivels-combe Mill. The huge wheel ground out its crushing revolutions, and inside the mill the chute spilled light brown flour from last season's grain. Wesley Chater, the miller, large and dusty, eyed his visitor and blinked away a covering or two from his eyelids.

"Good morning to you, Mr. Chater," said Jason.

"Well, I be fair 'mazed," said the miller, "it be years since I seen 'ee, Cap'n Rawlings."

"A few," said Jason.

"All that sold'ering, it be killin' on some folks."

"More mortal than milling, perhaps," said Jason.

"Millin' ain't drackly mortal," said Mr. Chater, with a grin that stretched his floury features. "You be squire now, I reckon."

"It seems so."

"Ar," said the miller, and nodded. "Well, you be a good cut for it."

"We'll see. How is Mrs. Chater?"

"She be middlin' to diddlin' to lively, thank 'ee. Her's a rare old 'ooman."

"And the children?"

"Growed up an' gone preachin', both. Mrs. Rawlings, Cap'n, she be well?"

"My wife passed away some months ago."

"Ar," said Mr. Chater, and shook his head. "I be sorry."

"Whose grain is that?" asked Jason amid the vibrations. The great cogged wheels made the stout oak beams and uprights shudder as they turned.

"That be Partridge grain, Cap'n. Warwick grain be there." Mr. Chater indicated some stacked sacks.

"It's good?" said Jason, taking a pinch of the flour. He tasted it. The wheaten flour was rich.

"Good enough," said the miller. "Yours be just as good."

"I wonder," said Jason with a smile, "is it possible you could pay the balance still owing to us?"

"Be there a balance?" Mr. Chater thought, blinked, and came

out of it with an embarrassed grin. "Step down, Cap'n, an' we'll have a tiddly look at the book. Will 'ee take a mug of ale?"

"With pleasure, Mr. Chater."

"Ar," said the miller genially, "you be cut out for squire right enough."

He supplied the ale and the dusty, stiff-bound book which showed, indeed, that there were still monies owing. He squared up without cavil, though he did count the money out very slowly, as if reluctant to see it depart from his possession. Jason thanked him, and drank the ale. Afterwards he asked him to be accommodating by settling up as quickly as possible when making his purchase of this year's grain. He received the miller's assurance, said a few words to Mrs. Chater to make her smile rosily, wished them both a cordial good day, and went to make other calls of a similar nature on all merchants, millers, and farmers who bought from Warwick Place.

He was able to take back a not inconsiderable amount of money to Ralph Harris, who was impressed and calculated that the new squire was actually going to be a help instead of another liability.

Three days later, Jason rode over to see Sir Richard Davenport, who lived on the other side of Blandford. Sir Richard was a retired merchant, knighted for his contributions to the purse of the Whigs. He received Jason courteously, listened to what he had to say, and then said, "True, Warwick Place is mortgaged to me. True again, I have held off in the matter of unpaid interest since the death of your father, for I knew you to be out of the country, and I knew that Miss Constance had the devil's own book tossed into her lap. It don't make easy reading and analysis for anyone."

"You're speaking of the financial mess my father got himself into?"

"I am. I suspect my visit only added to her worries—I did see your sister a few months ago, when I passed by to enquire after the state of things—though I assured her I wouldn't press the estate for the moment. You should know I committed myself to this mortgage out of friendship for your father, since I'd no wish to see him in the hands of avaricious moneylenders, and I happened to have capital available at the time. Nor would I say Warwick Place doesn't make for a good investment. However, aware of your father's predilection for amassing new debts on top of old ones, I knew the time might come when, if the mortgage couldn't be redeemed, friendship would have to be set aside. It never was my intention to tie up the capital indefinitely, y'know, and the fact is, I'm at the stage when I wish my two daughters to benefit to some extent during my lifetime. That doesn't mean I want Warwick Place for them and their husbands, but it's a saleable property, sir. Very much so. The mortgage is due for redemption on the last day of September, as I advised Miss Constance, and it ain't making for hard words, I hope, when I tell you I'd favour prompt settlement. Nor does it signify outside of simple truth in reminding you no interest has been paid these last twelve months and more. I might have foreclosed a year ago, but am not in want and have reached a fairly philosophical turn in a hard life."

Jason said, "I'm able here and now, Sir Richard, to settle the outstanding interest, with apologies for not having done so before and with a great many thanks for your indulgence."

"Are ye so able, by heaven?" Sir Richard spoke approvingly. He liked a man to be honourably cognisant of his debts.

"I am. I have the money with me. We managed to collect something from debtors of our own. I'll be frank and tell you I made the due amount up by sinking my pride and securing a loan yesterday from an uncle of mine. The terms were generous, and our straits accordingly not so dire as they were."

"Then, sir," said Sir Richard briskly, "I'll scribble a receipt. But I must ask, how d'ye look to deal with me on the last day of September?"

"Candidly, I don't anticipate being able to do anything except ask for an extension or renewal."

"Straightforward, sir, straightforward. But I hope it won't come to that. My own position is that I desire the return of the capital, and if you're unable to oblige, it's possible that either the mortgage or the estate would have to be sold. It don't follow this would be required immediately, and if necessary I may be persuaded to give you grace until December quarter day."

"That's a further kindness," said Jason, "which I appreciate."

"It ain't precisely promised," said Sir Richard. "It don't at the moment go beyond a suggestion. I may offer grace, I may not."

"Either way," said Jason with a faint smile, "I've one foot in the quicksands."

"You're disposed to sell Warwick Place?"

"I'm not."

"Stay and smoke a pipe with me, and take a glass of Madeira."

"Thank you," said Jason.

Temporarily, Jason was able to breathe. Immediate pressures were off him. He had not only settled with Sir Richard Davenport in respect of the mortgage interest, he had also paid the servants what was owing to them. His gesture bound them to him in gratitude. And there was also the promise of a bumper harvest. The ears on the wheat were fat, the barley and other crops ripening fast. But he knew he was still up against it, and no mistake. There was little chance of being able to find more than a modest percentage of the amount necessary to redeem the mortgage. The only relative who had been financially competent to help him, his father's brother Percival, had somewhat made up for the lack of funds in other relatives by generally waving aside settlement of the loan until such time as Jason was in better straits.

There was nothing that could be sold. Sir Richard Davenport and London creditors had first claim on every brick, every stone, every piece of furniture, every blade of grass, and all stock. But Jason kept his worries to himself. But there was also Antoinette, and, as Constance emphasised, it was their human duty to see to her welfare and her prospects. She must meet the county. The county had known Jason as a boy and a young man, a boy who had been at public school and a young man who had entered the Army from university. Neighbouring farmers, landowners, gentry, and dowagers all wished to see what he was like as a widower at the age of thirty. They also wished to take a look at Antoinette, having heard he was harbouring a ward of tantalising beauty.

On the day Jason became Antoinette's legal guardian, when she and Jason and Constance returned from the magistrate's court, she flew up to her room too full of words. There she allowed herself some tears.

A week later she was presented to the county. Jason dug into his strained pocket and Constance made a generous contribution from her own purse, with the result that from five o'clock in the evening of the day in question Warwick Place looked as if prosperity had returned. Antoinette swam into being in a gown of sheerest white, her natural elegance foiling all the effects of her shyness and nervousness. She had never worn a white gown, and she could not tell Constance, who helped her choose one in Blandford, that she was too imperfect to wear the colour of purity on formal occasions. She did, however, hesitantly ask Jason what he thought.

Jason smiled and said, "I fancy few of the company will be able to match their purity with yours, so white it shall be—especially as Constance declares it will suit you famously for the occasion."

So she wore white, and looked like a fragrant bloom of summer. The farmers, the gentry, the dowagers, and their sons alike were either enchanted or smitten. Daughters of the gentry, however, while conceding her charm, were far more taken with her widowed guardian. And it somewhat disconcerted Antoinette when, engaged herself by a garrulous dowager or smitten son, she saw how he was contending with the peaches and cream of Dorset maidens. As to complexions, Antoinette's was pale honey, setting the quality of perfection in an era when even in rural Dorset young ladies did not offer their faces unshaded to the sun. Huge were the bonnets worn to keep the skin natural in colour and texture. Flawless was Antoinette's colour, and melting her eyes in the light of that summer evening, when late August was still warm enough for the company to be presented to her out of doors and for people to saunter. She received the dowagers and the gentlemen and the young men and young ladies in the gardens, each of them introduced to her by Jason and Constance. She made a floating progress on her guardian's arm, Constance in smiling attendance and looking gently amused at the reactions of sundry gentlemen, whose eyes either popped or dizzily blinked when they alighted on Antoinette. Constance, in green silk, her figure undeniably shapely, might have made a dignified chaperone for her brother's ward on this occasion, had it not been for the fact that her acute sense of humour always kept stiff dignity at bay.

So gracefully did Antoinette move that there was no doubt in anyone's mind concerning her background and antecedents. They were accepted as unquestionably aristocratic. She was the quintessence of elegance and charm. Cousins of Jason were there. But Antoinette, breathless and high-strung, was unable to take clear notice of any one person introduced to her. She was in a whirl. Faces, figures, and names came and went. There were ladies and there were gentlemen: the ladies were dressed in every imaginable colour, the gentlemen were clad in their country best or in fashionable extravagance. Some were gallant with rustic simplicity, others larded their compliments with many a bon mot. Guests needed no specific qualification to be on the list except that of being a friend, a neighbour, or a relative. The sophisticated rubbed shoulders with ruddy-faced farmers, the daughters of rich dowagers with the apple-cheeked daughters of the farmers, although it did mean that those who liked witty repartee rather than rural exchanges had to be selective when looking for conversation.

A cousin of Jason's approached as Antoinette disengaged from a tongue-tied farmer's son. Jason introduced him as Noel Rawlings. He had the Rawlings blue eyes, was a cheerful and engaging young man, and knew some of the loveliest young ladies in Dorset. When he came face to face with Antoinette, however, the images of all other beauties sank without a trace. Antoinette curtseyed. Noel reached for her hand as she straightened up, brought her fingers to his lips, and said very distinctly, "Oh, ye gods." Antoinette, still in her own kind of trance, could only murmur politely, "Thank you."

"Thank you?" said Noel. "But I only made an exclamation. Dear young lady, I'm charmed, dashed if I ain't, and considerably so. Jason, you've brought a stunner to Warwick Place. May I monopolise her?"

"You may not," said Jason, "for I'll not risk others setting on you and hammering you."

"Well, I shall follow her about and hang the consequences," said Noel, handsome in a dark brown coat and cream trousers. "And at least I'm promised a turn with her when the fiddles begin to warble, ain't I?"

"That," said Jason, "I leave to Antoinette."

"Well, I shall be at you, sweet young lady, you may rely on that," said Noel, and Antoinette murmured politely, though such was her state of wonder that she remained no more aware of him than of any of the others. Noel's eyes followed her as she floated away on Jason's arm to meet more people. A stunner, by heaven, a regular stunner.

One guest arrived late, as was characteristic of him, for he was a person who avoided the herd in favour of being noticed. Gerald Morecombe had never been renowned for his modesty, but he did own an experienced and discriminating eye, plus an aptitude for affecting a pallid languor much in vogue in London twenty years earlier and come a little late to Dorset. A dandy from the crown of his hat to the toes of his polished boots, he could not look into a mirror without feeling that its reflection showed a *ton* and an elegance unlikely to be seen ever again in Dorset. He had spent a few seasons in London years ago, but such was the pace set, so plentiful the *ton* and elegance, and so negligible the impression he made that he wisely decided to give up being a minnow in a well-stocked lake and become the outstanding fish in a placid backwater. There he indulged in the pleasantness of swimming lazily around in search of the outstanding female of the species. He had not yet found this paragon, but had alighted on some near ones and left a few of them slightly tarnished. As he pointed out very reasonably to an unreasonable widow, whose ethics he found shockingly and surprisingly strict, mere inspection and touch were not enough. How could they be? One must go deeper than that when selecting a lifelong partner. It was time he was married. He was forty, and any Dorset woman would have to look far to get herself a better catch. He was a man of the world, had travelled Europe, been to the South Seas and to America. He was thin, long-nosed, and had a languid smile that appealed to some ladies.

He had heard that Jason Rawlings' ward was out of the ordinary, but doubted if she was more so than other young ladies whose beauty had gone before them and in his eyes proved exaggerated. So when he finally appeared and was introduced to Antoinette, his glance fell unconcernedly on her. Remarkably, at that moment something that was almost a warm gleam appeared in his eyes. Here was a paragon, in physical form at least. Her colouring was matchless, her eyes had the soft lambency he had come across

~ 321 ~

in the South Seas, and her figure was quite superb. In short, this time all the reports had not been exaggerated, but lamentably inadequate.

Antoinette, the evening sky warm above her, was vaguely aware of his hand retaining its limp clasp of hers. She looked up into one more face among many. Despite her confusing excitements, she was able for once to take note. And she noted an exquisitely elegant gentleman, smoothly pale of face and with an enormous, many-folded cravat that kept his pointed chin high. He seemed modishly relaxed, but with a gleam in his eye for all that. She had seen his like before, and that same gleam, in New Orleans. A little shiver came over her, and at once she found herself disliking him intensely. Gently, she extracted her hand.

"'Pon my dear soul," averred Mr. Morecombe, purringly pleased, "if it ain't the damnedest thing, meetin' with Elysian fragrance in a field full of milkmaids. I take it, Rawlings, you're not disposed to release her into my care for an hour or two?"

"To what purpose?" asked Jason.

"I'm without purpose, sir. I'm faint for lack of any," said Mr. Morecombe. "The idyllic moves me, and I vow to induct her into the delights of the muse. It's the evening for poetry, and I've some delicate compositions of my own that will come sweetly to her ears. A sunset, a tree, and a simple seat will suit us very well." He cast Antoinette his favour in the shape of a delicately winning smile. "Miss Giraud, do you care to dispense with tediousness and disport with the muse?"

"You will forgive me, m'sieu?" said Antoinette as the colour and chatter of ladies and gentlemen graced the gardens around her.

"Only very reluctantly," said Mr. Morecombe, "and do I remark France in you?"

"I am from New Orleans, m'sieu," said Antoinette, wishing Jason would remove her from what to her were staring fishy eyes.

"Ah, a city of quaint eccentricities and exotic blooms—"

"You will forgive me?" said Antoinette again.

Mr. Morecombe's sigh was plaintive. Lightly he touched and arranged a lock that fell carefully over his alabaster forehead. It drew attention not only to his stylishly coiffed hair, but also to his high intellectual brow and his fine, pale hand.

"I'm not too forgivin' when I'm rebuffed," he complained, "but—"

"Put up with it for the moment, won't you?" said Jason, and to Antoinette's relief took her off to circulate among the guests. As they passed on the way, Constance gave Mr. Morecombe the merest of brief polite smiles. Anything more, and he might have detained her and captured her ear. Constance had nothing against the gentleman, except his conversation; for Mr. Morecombe's conversation was all about Mr. Morecombe.

The gleam in Mr. Morecombe's eye faded as Antoinette sailed away. His teeth bit on his lip. He had been accorded no more than a minute with her, and felt this to be only as much as she had accorded others. Since he considered most of the others to be rustics, he also felt the enchanting creature had dealt disproportionately with him. That would have to be put right, for he was frankly enamoured.

The evening changed from clear warm light to glowing gold. With the advent of dusk, the fiddlers began to move their bows and the company danced on the lawns, which were illuminated by lamps. It was a breathless fairyland for Antoinette. She was the belle of the evening, the flickering lights of the lamps playing over her flushed face, and she was so besieged by gentlemen wishful to stand up with her that Constance came to her help and roundly declared them to be a rabble.

"Come, you aren't bidding for corn, sirs, but for the favours of a young lady. If you wish to stand with her, please approach in an orderly way. Pushing, gentlemen, is highly improper. I won't have it!"

Antoinette laughed, for Constance was so firmly commanding that the gentlemen began to fall sheepishly back. Noel, who had been standing off watching the elderly vie with the young, approached as they fell back, breached the discomfited ranks, and presented himself to Antoinette with a cheerful flourish and gallant bow. So she stood up with him in the first square dance, and he was delighted with her as she quickly fell in with his calling.

Soon she began to lose her nervousness and danced with one gentleman after another. Nor could she escape the languid but persistent Mr. Morecombe, who although declaring that country dancing was exerting rather than stimulating, announced he would commit himself for once if she would care to stand up with

~ 323 ~

him. Which, in all conscience, she could not refuse to do. Though by the end of it she liked him no better, finding him ostentatious, pretentious, scented, and affected. Nor did she like his pale white hands.

And he, looking into her remarkable eyes, wondered what it was about her that for the moment struck an indefinable chord.

She escaped to freshen herself while the guests were having supper from tables on the garden terrace. She was quite dizzy. The evening was hers, it had been set aside for her so that she could formally meet the friends and neighbours and relatives of Jason Rawlings and his sister. She was not hungry, and ate nothing except a slice of mutton carved from a carcase roasted on a spit. But she thirstily drank a glass of wine. She returned amid guests to the lawn when the infectious fiddles began their music again. She saw Jason standing at one end of the terrace talking to his neighbour Ned Tranter, a pleasant and likeable gentleman farmer, whom she had already met a few days ago. Mr. Tranter moved away at that moment, travelling rather hesitantly in the footsteps of Constance, who for some strange reason affected not to know him or even see him when he ventured to catch her up, but immediately engaged with another gentleman in the first cotillion after supper.

Antoinette detached herself from descending guests and approached Jason, who seemed to be deep in sombre reflections. He almost looked sad. It distressed her. She reached him and said softly, "M'sieu?"

He turned and gave her a smile.

"Are you enjoying yourself?" he asked.

"Oh, I am still dizzy," she said, "so many people and I have met them all. But, m'sieu, why are you sad?"

"Am I so? Well, if I am," he said, "it's probably for my lost youth, which an evening like this brings back to me." But it was not his youth he had been thinking about. It was Isabella.

"Is it a custom in England for guardians to stand up with their wards in dances?" asked Antoinette.

"It's not a custom I've ever heard of."

"Then, dear m'sieu," she said, colouring a little, "is it permitted for me to ask that you stand up with me?"

"I hadn't so arranged the evening, sweet one," he smiled, "that I was going to miss the pleasure of doing exactly that. Therefore, may I?"

As she stood up with him in a roundelay, whilst they made their steps and their passing movements, she was at her dizziest and happiest.

It came to an end, as it had to, sometime after midnight, and most the guests departed, each saying goodbye to her. Mr. Morecombe's goodbye was a sighing one. He declared to Jason that his ward had a charm remindful of unspoiled maidens of the South Seas.

Some guests with long journeys in front of them stayed overnight and departed in the morning. Noel Rawlings was one of them. Constance and Antoinette were allowed the indulgence of taking a light breakfast in bed, but Noel, having eaten his with Jason, would not go until Antoinette had come down. When she did, she looked as fresh as springtime. Noel met her in the west drawing room. Antoinette, entering, wondered what his name was, for she was sure it would be the impolitest thing to admit she could not remember.

"My dear young lady," said Noel, "I could not go until I'd laid eyes on you again. And I ain't so sure, after such a wine-filled night, you don't come more dizzily to them than you did last evening."

"M'sieu?" she said, trying earnestly to recall his name.

Noel laughed and shook his head.

"Damn me," he said, "if I don't believe you were so up in the clouds that you don't remember whether I was there or not."

He was very pleasant, much more to her liking than Mr. Morecombe.

"Oh, but of course I remember you," she said.

"Am I Henry Fitt or George Marsh?" he asked.

"M'sieu," she said, avoiding that, "surely we danced, yes?"

"Oh, egad, we did," he laughed. "I remember that very well myself." His blue eyes teased her. "But I doubt you remember it at all. That's a wounding blow."

Antoinette dug into her confused images of the previous night. She had stood up with him, she recalled that, try though she might she could not fit a name to him. The only guest she could place clearly in name and form was the insidious Mr. Morecombe.

"M'sieu, you did stand up with me," she said.

"Like so many others?"

She smiled. He had his air of regret that she could not separate him from all those others, but showed no sulks.

"I am sure your name will come to me," she said in soft apology for being so remiss. She would ask Jason who he was, and would remember his name from then on.

"It had better," said Noel severely, "for I shall call again, you may be sure of that. And when I do, woe betide you if I'm no more than Mr. Nobody to you."

"Mr. Nobody?" She didn't remember that name.

"A mere nobody. Nobody at all to you," laughed Noel, and kissed her hand and departed.

Gentlemen contrived to call, so did dowagers with their sons. Antoinette began to feel a little alarmed as young men made known their feelings in ardent prose or tongue-tied stammers. She did not want to be courted, for it posed the threat of divorcing her from Warwick Place, of removing her from a house and people she loved. She must impress on her guardian that the gentlemen were wasting their time.

"You must know," she said to him when they were alone one day, "that as well as not wishing to marry any of them, I simply cannot."

"Cannot?" said Jason, who thought her delicious to have around.

"Must not, m'sieu, and you yourself know why."

"We've agreed, Antoinette, that you're white."

"But if I marry and have children," she said, "who can say they will not be black."

"I can say, and do." He put his hands lightly on her shoulders. His touch thrilled her body. "That's what we call an old wives' tale. There's not enough coloured blood in you to put even the tiniest smudge into any children you may have."

"In New Orleans they say—"

"I know what they say. In New Orleans they would. It's to try to keep you in what they think is your destined place, to discourage you, should you ever be free, from marrying a white man."

"M'sieu, I will always believe you before other people. But the truth is, I am not desperately inclined to marry anyone."

"Well, let me say once again, you alone may decide this. There's no one, no one at all, who can compel you to accept a proposal. You may receive a hundred, as Constance says, and you are free to turn all of them down."

"But is it true, if I did marry I should not have coloured children?" asked Antoinette.

"In my book, quite true."

"So if I did receive a proposal from a man I loved, I should be doing him no wrong in marrying him?"

"You'd be doing him a great favour, God's life you would," said Jason. "For it's unlikely he'd get a sweeter wife or a lovelier one."

Her eyes glowed.

"M'sieu, do you really think that of me?"

He laughed.

"Do you suppose I see less with my eyes than others do with theirs?" he said.

"Oh, I am very happy to know you have such an opinion of me, m'sieu," she said, "and I am more than happy that I may decide so much for myself, that I can remain here if I wish and watch Clare grow up—oh, I must tell you I am so in love with everything here."

"And see how well you do with Clare." He smiled. "She dotes on you."

"And on you now," she said. "She loves her papa, as others do." At which she kissed him on the cheek.

"A tender salute," said Jason.

"One may kiss one's guardian or father?"

"It's not forbidden."

"Then I am most happy," said Antoinette, and smiled as she floated away.

Jason knew she was still grateful to him. Yet someone might cure her of gratitude's emotional quality, someone intelligent enough to know how to make her responsive and not uneasy.

Mr. Gerald Morecombe was not to be put off. Firstly, because he was enamoured. And secondly because he could not conceive any young lady finding anything to dislike in him. He was among other gentlemen who called at Warwick Place from time to time, except that he called more often. He was not to know that Antoinette found him disturbingly remindful of the elegant dandies of New Orleans. His nearness made her shudder. The captivated gentleman, however, was persistent. She felt constrained by politeness to accompany him when he asked her to walk with him in the gardens. At such times, the better part of his habitual languor was replaced by a chemical activity that almost produced a bead or two of perspiration. He was referred to by Jason as that vapid wet-nose looking for a lost handkerchief.

As for himself, Mr. Morecombe constantly declared to Jason that Antoinette was the personification of all that was best about the glorious-eyed maidens of the Pacific, who undoubtedly had orbs of such soft brilliance as to be unequalled anywhere else in the world.

"And her colourin', Rawlings. I vow to you, sir, you'll not find it in any country in Europe. Damned if I don't sometimes think I've seen her like in some exotic garden—"

"Are you declaring an interest, Mr. Morecombe?"

"Damn me, sir, I'm considerin' buildin' a love nest, an Eden, an Arcadia, and offerin' a ring. I ain't given to dallyin' lightly with so sweet a gal."

"I'm glad to hear it," said Jason, but he knew Morecombe had as much hope of winning Antoinette as a limp stick of licorice.

Mr. Morecombe, however, had a vanity that made him myopic. He could never see very far beyond the end of his long pale nose. The gold of summer had begun to retreat from the advance of russet autumn on a day when he contrived to isolate himself in the gardens with Antoinette. His lukewarm blood growing hot, he permitted himself the indiscreet liberty of placing an arm around her waist and attempting to kiss her. It never occurred to him that any young lady, buried in the wilds of Dorset, would refuse her lips to such a worthy fellow as himself. But Antoinette's eyes took fire, and stingingly she slapped his face. He, seething, saw the fire, the rushing angry blood, and heard the singing intonation of her furious voice.

"*Canaille!*"

That struck the chord which had eluded him up till now. New Orleans was her birthplace. New Orleans, which he had visited, and which was famous for its mulatto girls, beautiful beyond compare. He seized her arms, looked into her lambent eyes, and his face distorted with spite and malice. He knew what they called her kind in New Orleans.

"Damn me if you ain't a nigra," he hissed.

Antoinette paled, tore herself free, and ran into the house. Mr.

Morecombe composed himself, and in further spite requested a private word with the owner of Warwick Place. Jason received him in the east drawing room ten minutes later.

"A word or two with you, Rawlings," said Mr. Morecombe, and Jason took that icily.

"You may speak first, Morecombe," he said. "I'll take my turn when you've done."

"That wench of yours, sir. Egad, that damn wench."

"Wench, you say?" Jason was icier. "Take care of your nose, man, for your tongue may be its undoing."

"Softly, Rawlings, softly, else I'll carry my news elsewhere. The girl comes from New Orleans, I understand." Mr. Morecombe delicately wiped his mouth, then tucked his silk square into his sleeve, from where it dangled with limp *ton*. Quietly malicious, he described how he had come across white-skinned mulatto girls of rare looks in the West Indies and the Americas. New Orleans had a reputation for producing the best of them, and it was his frank opinion that Antoinette was a deceiving creature, for undoubtedly she was no Creole but a fair-skinned quadroon or octoroon. Her eyes and her fingernails—

"You, sir," interrupted Jason bitingly, "shall be taken by the ear to Paris and invited to address the Duc d'Amiens, the cousin of her late father. If that isn't to your liking or convenience, you shall write him a letter, telling him what you have just told me. I'll witness your signature and you'll stand upon your declared charge. Indeed, I'll insist on a second witness of your own choosing. You're a travelled man, I believe, and may have met the Duc d'Amiens. In which case you'll know his mettle concerning his family's honour. Shall I have paper brought, Morecombe, and a quill?"

Mr. Morecombe stared uneasily into the cold, dark face. As a dilettante and not a brawler, he objected very much to being invited to commit suicide. But was the fellow bluffing? The cold blue eyes said not. An air of delicate repugnance invested Mr. Morecombe.

"I vow to you, sir, it was my sincere belief—"

"A pox on you," said Jason. "You shall write that letter now and take the consequence."

"Damn my eyes," said Mr. Morecombe petulantly, "you seem determined to press incivility on me, which, considering the dues of friendship, is a little ungracious, to say the least. I do protest there ain't nothing in the air but a small misunderstanding."

"Is it your misunderstanding, or mine?"

"But d'you see, sir, I wasn't informed that the young lady was a niece of the Duc d'Amiens. You can't deny this lack disadvantaged me, and I ain't inclined to write any letter which might result in physical unpleasantness. I assure you, Rawlings, there's no need of such a letter. Naturally, I withdraw."

"Morecombe," said Jason, "it's now my turn to speak. I'll be brief. You distressed my ward, and reduced her to tears. Consequently, I'm now going to kick you all the way to your carriage and see you depart standing up in it."

"Sir," said Morecombe indignantly, "I was not used in your father's time to seeing ruffians in this house."

"Times have changed," said Jason. "You may depart, sir, but on the understanding that you do need to write a letter. To me. In it you will apologise for your conduct, and unreservedly withdraw all you said about my ward. Or I'll have you in court for slander of a most objectionable and damaging kind."

Mr. Morecombe almost became red in the face.

"You've no witnesses, sir, none," he said.

"Behind that door, which leads to the library," said Jason, pointing, "is my neighbour Ned Tranter, whom you know. His ear is at the keyhole. Do you wish to see him?"

"I wish only to depart. You shall have the damned letter." And Mr. Morecombe went off in a pettish sulk, disgusted at the manners and intemperance of the new owner of Warwick Place.

Antoinette, seeing him go, went running to Jason.

"Oh, m'sieu, what did he say?" She was in distress and agitation. "He knows what I am, he—"

"What are you?"

"I am discovered—"

"You are Antoinette Giraud. And Mr. Morecombe is going to write a letter of abject apology. I fancy he has a flea and a half in his ear." Jason told her what he had said to the gentleman. Antoinette's anxiety slipped away. She laughed.

"Oh, m'sieu, the Duc d'Amiens? Who is he, pray?"

"God's life," said Jason, "I've really no more idea than you."

Antoinette stared at him, then laughed again. Impulsively she hugged him.

"Oh, out of a thousand men you are the best and most clever," she said.

"Go and take tea with Constance," he said. "I must see friend Ned."

He went into the library. Ned Tranter, who had a farm adjacent to Warwick Place, looked up from his inspection of a book.

"I'm sorry about the interruption," said Jason. "Let's take a glass." Inside a cabinet stood decanters of sherry. Ned Tranter poured a pale dry blend for both of them. They stood at the window and sipped. Ned Tranter was a broad-shouldered man of thirty-three, healthy and rugged of countenance, his coat and breeches quiet in colour and neat in fit.

"If we can continue our conversation?" said Ned.

"Yes. But Antoinette suffered a disillusionment, and I had to suffer Gerald Morecombe."

"I'd sooner suffer a colic than that prize popinjay," said Ned. "Jason, the matter you raised, I've thought hard on it these last few minutes, but swear to you the better part of my finances is tied up in stock and seed, which is the way of it among farmers. I could, however, find you five hundred pounds—providing you'll restore my credit with your sister."

"You were my last chance," said Jason. "Aside from a usurer, who'd bleed me to death. Five hundred pounds is a friendly gesture, but only a tenth of what I need."

"Five thousand, that's the sum?" Ned whistled. "Egad, that's more of a mountain than a debt."

"As to Constance, why are you out of credit with her?"

"You've been away years," said Ned with a sigh. "You've not noticed since you've come back?"

"I've noticed she affects not to notice you. Why?"

Ned looked sheepish.

"I called her a quack-nosed nuisance," he said.

"Hardly likely to endear you to any woman," said Jason.

"And a pigeon-toed monkey."

"Hardly an improvement."

"All of twelve years ago," said Ned, "and she was a monkey."

"Twelve? Twelve?" Jason looked sceptical. "You mean she still holds it against you?"

"Been like an iceberg ever since," said Ned. "Never knew a cooler woman, or a handsomer."

"What can I do with her that you can't do better?" asked Jason.

"Get her to receive me," said Ned.

"She does receive you."

"Damned if she does," said Ned. "She only looks as if I ain't there."

"Ned, are you set on Constance?" asked Jason.

"Best intentions, I assure you," said Ned.

"Then go and speak to her."

"Easier said than done," said Ned gloomily. "I tell you, at fifteen she was a chattering monkey. Then suddenly at twenty she was a handsome gal, and I made an effort when she was twenty-one. Floored me, I swear, with just a look. Been trying ever since. She reduces me to a mumble within seconds."

"Take her by the ear," advised Jason, "and pour yourself clearly into it. Constance can't be wooed by mumbles. She equates mumbles with old women and doddering men."

"Take the ear of so tender a woman?" said Ned.

"Not literally, man."

"Literally or otherwise, I lack the courage. I'm not renowned for being a social lion."

"Nor Constance for being a lioness. She'll not eat you."

"You might think not," said Ned. "I'm not so sure."

That evening Jason spoke to Constance just before supper.

"Why are you so cool to Ned Tranter these days?" he enquired.

Constance raised a fine eyebrow.

"Ned Tranter?"

"Our neighbour whom you cut so often."

"A hey and a ho to you, sir," said Constance. "I'm a woman of sympathy towards all deserving creatures."

"With the exception of Ned, who's also likeable."

"Likeable?" Constance was not impressed. "I think him excessively shifty."

"Shifty? Ned?" Jason was not impressed himself.

"His eyes are so close I wonder he's able to separate one from the other at times."

"His eyes are as wide apart as yours."

"He's also uncouth," said Constance.

"Ned?"

"And a miserable mumbler."

"I've never noticed it."

"Well, how should you," said Constance, "seeing you've spent so little time here these several years? The man has become a chronic mumbler. One could have a more stimulating conversation with a parrot."

"I fancy you'd find it very repetitive. However," said Jason, moving away, "if those are your feelings—"

"A moment," said Constance. "What interest do you have in Mr. Tranter?"

"I did hope he'd be able to advance me a tidy loan."

Constance quizzed him suspiciously.

"Are you suggesting—? Fie, sir, and shame on you. Do you think you can inveigle me into being sweet to the man to help you get your loan? Before I'd even begin to treat civilly with him, Ned Tranter must—" Constance stopped.

"Must what?" asked Jason.

"Never mind," said Constance, "it's of no consequence."

# 4

The harvest was gathered before the leaves fell, and it turned out not a poor one. But set against the enormity of liabilities, the return for what had been gathered, though added to by livestock sales and rents, rang almost hollowly in the coffers. Jason could find no one, no friend or relative or neighbour, prepared to take over the mortgage. On the other hand, there were usurers. But he avoided them as if they were plague-ridden.

Autumn came at last, in russet hues dying under the starkly bare branches of the deciduous trees. Antoinette entered the damp of early winter and then the cold, crisp exhilaration of a dry December. Jason began to teach her to ride. She was excited, but nervous and novice-like, and in a borrowed habit of Constance's slid inexorably from the saddle as soon as the horse moved. So

Jason put her on Napoleon. The old warrior horse turned his head, looked at her out of astonished eyes, rolled them, and showed his teeth. Antoinette begged him to be calm and kind. Napoleon snorted and Jason stood by, hiding his smile. Antoinette bravely patted the beast. Napoleon rumbled.

"Relax young lady," said Jason, hatted and warmly coated, "you're as stiff as a board."

"I am stiff with fright," confessed Antoinette. "I shall fall and the monster will devour me. Oh, heavens, I am so far off the ground."

"You'll make a tempting morsel for any monster," said Jason. "Relax now. Talk lovingly to the brute."

"Ah, *je m'appelle Antoinette, mon Napoléon. Comment allez-vous?*"

"Ye gods," murmured Jason.

Napoleon began to walk. Antoinette emitted a little shriek. Jason gave her a stern look. She swayed. Napoleon stopped. She righted her seat. Napoleon resumed his walk.

"Oh, *mon Dieu*," she breathed. Napoleon executed a slow circle. She swayed again, but stayed on. Napoleon completed the circle and stopped. "There," she gasped, "I have done it."

"You mean that by the grace of Holy Mary you haven't fallen off."

"By extraordinary skill, m'sieu, that is what I mean. I shall stop now, or success will go to my head."

"Stop? We hardly have you mounted, my girl. You'll perform for an hour."

"An hour? Oh, merciful angels," cried Antoinette. "I am in the hands of two monsters."

But at the end of the hour she was flushed and triumphant, even if aching. By the end of the week she could ride. Her nose turned pink in the frosts of December, but her eyes glowed with love of life and her blood rushed tingling through her veins. The cold weather shocked her when she put her feet out of bed first thing in the mornings, but never did it reduce her. She and Clare ran together over the frosted carpet of the parklands in coats, muffs, and boots. And there were always such huge crackling blazes in the fireplace that it was a rapture to come in from winter's chill and enter the warmth and comfort of home, Clare to hug and kiss her papa, and Antoinette to lightly salute him. Kissing, Antoinette realised, was as permissible for a ward as for a daughter.

Christmas was magic. Constance took her into Blandford so that she could make purchases which would enable her to engage in the exchange of presents on Christmas Day. And on Christmas Day, when the fire in the west drawing room was at its highest and warmest, the presents were exchanged, and Antoinette wondered where she could go to hide her tears of love and happiness. In the dining room the servants sat down to dine with the family, and Jason carved an enormous joint of roast beef. Clare was in delight because there was so much laughter.

A score of Dorset gentlemen declared themselves in love with Antoinette. But this was no longer a worrying matter. She was not to be disposed of, she could please herself as to her wants and desires. She so came to terms with freedom that when Jason and Constance took her to a county ball she danced quadrilles and polkas with all the gentlemen who begged the favour. Only once during the long evening did her eyes lose their light of happiness. That was when Jason was partnered by a beautiful, fair-haired woman for a third time. A little flame leapt then and flared for a brief moment into hot fire.

Jason had received his quarter's grace from Sir Richard Davenport. In January he was given a further but final reprieve, until March quarter day. That set him at his wit's end.

During the last week of January a Mr. Thomas Fox of Gray's Inn Road, London, received by appointment a visitor. Mr. Fox was a solicitor to whom honest men repaired when in need of sound legal advice, and shadier characters when in need of conscientious representation. Mr. Fox's visitor, an extroverted, self-confident gentleman of darkly tanned visage, needed neither. He merely required Mr. Fox to act for him in a matter that was quite straightforward but extremely confidential. In accented English he explained what it was.

"In Dorset, sir, Dorset?" said Mr. Fox. Which provoked the healthy-looking gentleman into saying at once that expenses were of no importance and would all be taken care of. "Quite so, quite so. But a solicitor in Bridport or Dorchester might serve you just as well, and certainly more economically. And there's the time involved, sir. I'd be away from my practice for a week, I fear."

The gentleman produced his card and also mentioned the name of the distinguished personage who had recommended him to Mr. Fox. At which Mr. Fox became deferential. His visitor assured him he could name his own fee, and requested that he be obliging, for he himself was not disposed to travel to Dorset.

"Constance—er—Miss Rawlings—?"

"Whence did you spring?" asked Constance of the figure hovering at the door.

"From a word or two with Jason," said Ned Tranter.

Constance, seated beside the fire with her embroidery, continued with her intricate work.

"Please close the door as you leave," she said.

"I'm hardly in yet," said Ned.

"You are more in than out," said Constance, resolute in her concentration on the silk thread, "but you're quite free to be wholly out."

"Now look here," said Ned.

"Look here? Do you command me, sir?"

"I ain't said a word," he protested.

"Look here, look here—they are words," said Constance, "and not ones I am used to."

"My oath in it," muttered Ned, "contrary women are the devil."

"What's that you say, sir?" Constance lifted her head, her face slightly flushed—due no doubt to her nearness to the fire.

"Nothing," said Ned, still muttering.

"You are mumbling, Mr. Tranter."

"Oh, damn my eyes," said Ned recklessly.

Constance rose very handsomely, extended a stiff arm, and pointed a proud finger.

"Go, sir. Depart. There is the door."

"I shan't," said Ned, "and that I stand on."

"Then I'll have the servants throw you out," she said. "We were never used to oafs, sir."

Ned looked at her. What a Tartar she was, what a rare piece. What a fine figure of a woman she made, what a wife she could be.

"Constance—"

"You are staring, sir."

"Oh, look here—"

"Am I a freak, sir?"

Ned mumbled, "I ain't ever said so, I—"

"Remove yourself," said Constance.

"Oh, damnation," said Ned, and removed himself.

Constance regarded the closed door and said to herself. "I shall never forgive the wretch, never." She put a hand to her nose and felt its delicate contours. It really did not seem too bad a nose to her.

When Sir Richard Davenport arrived in a closed carriage towards the end of March, it spelt doom to Jason. Grimly he reflected on his fate. Jason had satisfied his need for revenge, but was now burdened with a new obsession, a fierce desire to hold on to Warwick Place. He loved the house and estate. How to retain his inheritance was something that occupied his mind and his time day in and day out, which at least kept him from brooding on what might have been in other directions. Constance sometimes suggested that if he was still thinking about Edwina he was doing no good at all.

Sir Richard Davenport was in an amiable mood, but in any mood he never beat about the bush. Consequently, he came almost at once to the purpose of his visit.

"I'd not have wanted to agree to the matter without first consulting you," he said, comfortably square to the fire as he spread his coattails to warm his seat. A glass of sherry came into his hand, and he inspected its clarity with appreciation.

"What matter?" asked Jason.

"Someone is interested in acquiring the mortgage," said Sir Richard, "and for a sum which I'm not disposed to refuse. You've no objections? I understand the interest you pay now will be reduced—"

"Reduced? But you've implied, I think, that the capital outlay will be higher."

"So it will be, but all the same there's a promise of reduced interest rates. The term will be for five years. You can't quibble about that, eh? Another five years to raise the money to redeem the mortgage. I'm on my way to visit my elder daughter. Considered it convenient and right to call on you and acquaint you with the news. Ye'll welcome the arrangement?"

"May I ask you who my new creditor will be?"

"As I understand it, nominally a London solicitor," said Sir Richard. "Name of Thomas Fox. Acting for an interested client, of course, though he hadn't said who yet. I imagine you may have a friend generously inclined to do you a good turn on the quiet. The fellow Fox came to see me in January to discuss the matter. I've no idea how he knew I held the mortgage, and he was as close as his kind are, b'gad. But he seemed an upright man, even if he did cut his teeth on plum stones. I've since had a communication from him. I've a feeling you're not going to be pressed, not until the new term is up, when I rather fancy his client might want to retire to Warwick Place if you can't redeem."

"Five years?" Jason mused. "It's still a good investment for any man, and what my position will be by then I don't know. But at the moment I'm running with the devil on my tail, and can't afford to balk your sale of the mortgage. I'll have to accept a new creditor. However, my thanks to you, Sir Richard, for having been a generous one."

"I'm not generous," said Sir Richard, "I'm mellowed. I'll have my solicitor see to things. Your health, Captain Rawlings."

# 5

Spring burst on the first day of May. It had advanced erratically in April, showering the flower beds with the yellow of daffodils and the glistening wetness of rain. Clouds capped the hills one day and the sun fought through the next, and sometimes the wind still blew chill. But in May, as the month opened, there came the warmth that made spring burst. Wildflowers peeped in a more wanton profusion, and the primroses smiled. The trees brought forth their first tints of green, and new lambs trotted on black feet. Antoinette rode with Jason into the suddenly teeming growth, their horses throwing up the damp soil of the downs and the leaves in the woods.

Outside the house a hired trap from town drew up. In it was a woman dressed in black, her face heavily veiled. The driver turned in his seat.

"Go and ring the bell, please," she said, her voice firm and resonant, "and then return."

He got down, went to the double-doored entrance, and pulled the bell. Then he returned to the trap as directed. One of the doors opened, and Masters stood there. He looked enquiringly and politely at the lady, came from the step, and opened the trap door.

Isabella alighted with a dignified rustle, and very deliberately.

"Madam?" said Masters.

"I am not expected." She refrained from lifting the veil. "Is Mr. Jason Rawlings at home?"

"Not at the moment, madam," said Masters, as curious as the devil. The woman, despite her sombre attire, brought an air of the exotic. Beneath her hat and through the veil shone the visible richness of raven hair. The eyes were a glorious brown.

"No matter," said Isabella, immensely cool in spite of pounding nerves. "When do you expect him back?"

"By teatime, madam."

"Teatime?" The warm voice was faintly satirical. "What time is teatime?"

"Four o'clock, madam."

"That is almost two hours."

"I'm sorry—"

"It is not important. I will call again." The deep brown eyes glimmered behind the veil. "At teatime. Meanwhile I will inspect the house and the land."

"Madam?" Masters lifted an eyebrow.

"Your name, please?"

"Masters, madam. The butler."

"Masters?" enquired Isabella.

"Henry Masters, madam."

"And you are addressed as Masters? That would not do where I come from." Her accent was a lilt in the butler's ears. "My servants are my friends. We would not say Masters." She thought for a moment. "Very well, you may show me the house. It seems, from the outside, not to be too indifferent."

In truth she thought it beautiful, she thought it mellow with colour and age, but was not going to say so. She would not depart from being polite to the servants and merciless with him. With him, the man who thought he owned this house, she had a score to settle.

Masters, completely at a loss, demurred in a confused way. Isabella, so outwardly cool as to be quite majestic, waved his confusion aside. He took her on a tour of the house. Constance was out, visiting neighbours, Clare with her. Isabella inspected every room. The tour was a leisurely one. She made it so, her survey deliberate. It quickened into warm interest, but she did not show it.

"Whose room is this?" she asked as she looked around a bedroom.

"Captain Rawlings', madam."

Captain? Of course, he had been a soldier. She was sure the room was his the moment the butler opened the door for her. Comfortable but plain and practical. Frills and prettiness would not appeal to him, or to any man with a soul as barren as his. Such a man had no right to own a house as warm and lovely as this one. It was a wonder he had not destroyed its warmth by putting a plain and practical aspect on every room. Here it was that he slept—with his conscience untroubled, no doubt. He had scarred a man for life, scarred him cruelly. And he had scarred her too.

"What is this room?" she asked, looking in on another.

"A nursery, madam."

It was enchanting, a room to delight a child and made so, surely, by a woman's hand. But what child, whose child?

She turned to Masters and said, her voice vibrating. "There is a child?"

"A little girl, madam."

"But Mrs. Rawlings—?"

"Alas, she is dead," said Masters sorrowfully. Neither he nor any other servant knew the true story of Edwina. Constance, in order to dispel any whispers, had casually put it about ages ago that her brother and his wife were travelling abroad, which indeed had been true.

"Captain Rawlings married again?" said Isabella, and Masters thought there was a little fire behind the veil.

"No, madam. The child was born sometime before his wife died."

She left the nursery abruptly. Down in the hall she advised Masters she would inspect the land. He had been most helpful, but she did not think she would need him further, she said.

"As you wish, madam," said Masters, refraining from telling her that his duties, in any case, lay inside the house, not outside. Who she was and what she was about he had no idea—except that she was, from her accent, a foreigner, and foreigners had odd ways.

Isabella returned to the waiting trap.

"I wish to ride over this," she said to the driver, and gestured with her gloved hand. It took in all he could see, and he grimaced.

"I ain't drackly reckonin' to go gallivantin'," he said.

Isabella, not understanding a word of so localised a dialect, said imperiously, "Proceed please. In that direction." Again she gestured.

The man mumbled a little, but obeyed. The soft vistas opened up for Isabella. She saw the hills, the sweep of the bright spring sky, and the changing contours of green, greens uncommon to Texas. She went this way and that way, out beyond the parklands, skirting woodlands, and since nothing of what the driver said made any sense to her, so incomprehensible was his Dorset burr, she ignored it and communicated directions to him in a way that told him it was no use arguing. He grumbled and muttered and grinned and scratched his ear, and the trap rolled and swayed over high ground and low, leaving wheel marks where the ground was yielding.

Since she saw no fences or boundary stones, only the extensive vistas, it seemed to her that Jason had a holding of considerable proportions. As far as those hills, perhaps? How soft everything was. The air, the colours, and the sun itself. Could that be the same sun which burned the great plains of Texas?

She came up against a low stone wall.

"Why is that there?" she asked.

"Sheep, I reckon," said the driver.

"Is there a way through?"

"No, ma'm, there aren't. Wouldn't keep um in if there was."

"Go that way, then," she said, having translated that answer fairly well.

They went on over soft ground and came across rolling pastures on which a herd of cows grazed. They were splendidly fat animals. But there could not have been more than a hundred or so. Beyond the pastures men were sowing fields. Isabella, fascinated by what looked like rich, furrowed earth, watched as the men walked the furrows and tossed the seed.

"You may take me back now," she said at last.

"Tidy old time be had by summun, not by me," said the trap driver.

"Proceed, if you please," commanded Isabella, and looked with interest as they passed the stone cottages of farm labourers. The pale stone was soft too. The land itself seemed tranquil, though it had none of the awesome grandeur of Texas. It could be devoured by Texas without a single earthly hiccough. However, much as it was, it belonged to her now. Almost.

She steeled herself when the trap arrived back at the house. She alighted, told the driver to wait, and walked to the entrance with calm deliberation, though a pulse beat in her throat. About to ring, she heard the sound of galloping horses. She turned and saw them, and their riders. They were coming from the east of the spacious front lawns, over a great sward of spreading parkland and riding past a huge oak. She waited, her eyes on the man. Her limbs trembled, then stiffened, and she stood in icy resolution.

Jason pulled up beside the trap. Antoinette clattered over the forecourt, spied the figure in black on the stone step, and wheeled her horse around. Isabella saw the face of beauty and eyes as big and wide as Spanish gold crowns. Her mouth compressed. Jason was staring. Isabella put her veil up. Creamy and vivid she looked, as if she had just stepped out of the Texas sun—but on the day Cordova died, so unyielding and bitter was her expression.

"I wish to see you, Captain Rawlings," she said, "and am sure you will spare me the time."

"Oh, my God," said Jason. She saw pain on his face, and dark memories in his eyes. "Oh, my God," he said again.

The door opened. Masters appeared. He inclined his head as Isabella swept past him and entered the house. Antoinette, agitated, rode up to Jason. His expression, that of a man in shock, frightened her.

"Who is that woman?" she asked.

"Someone I met in Texas."

"Send her back there!" Antoinette was fierce. "Send her back!"

"Don't be foolish."

"M'sieu, I beg you! She is a black angel of the devil. She looked at you as if she already had you roasting in his fires."

"Oh, the devil and I are old adversaries," said Jason, and got off his horse.

"Sweet m'sieu, please send her away."

"She's only paying a visit. She's come a long way, so I must see her and find out why. Then she'll be gone, I fancy."

"She will not," said Antoinette. "She is a woman who has come to possess you. Did you not see her eyes?"

"Take Napoleon for me," said Jason.

"Yes. But, m'sieu, do not look into her eyes. Command her to lower her veil, I beg you."

He smiled at her. Antoinette shook her head in anxiety.

"There's nothing to worry about," he said.

He went into the house. Isabella had come in mourning. It made him wonder if he had killed her father, after all. She was waiting for him, for Masters had shown her into the west drawing room. She seemed to stand in possession of it. As he entered and closed the door, her mouth tightened.

"Please sit down," he said.

"I do not require a chair," she said. He looked brown and healthy. The deep hollows in his face had filled out a little. She wished he might have grown ugly. It would have been easier then.

"It's a long way from Texas, Isabella. At least, I found it so. Did you?"

"I was in no hurry, señor. My way was mapped for me, and I came without haste."

Her rich beauty was darkly haloed by her black.

"Are you in mourning?" he asked.

"Yes." Her voice was cold, bitter.

"For your father?"

"For Cordova. As to my father, you did him no honour by not killing him. He hides himself from the light of day."

"I see," he said. He was as polite as she was cold. "If you don't understand why I did what I did, it's of no use trying to explain."

"I understand very well, Señor Capitán," said Isabella icily. "I understand you were in honour bound to put a pistol into his hand and let him stand up against you. That is how gentlemen usually settle such things."

"I don't count myself the same kind of gentleman as your father. In any event, he had his pistol. He would not have hesitated to use it. Indeed, he did use it. I'll not discuss it, nor excuse myself. You may defend him as you wish—"

"I do not defend him!" Isabella was swift in her bitter retort. "But if he offended God in what he did, so did you in what you did. To use him like that, to cut his face to ribbons!" She became passionate. "That was the work of a sadist, a devil! And to enter our house as you did, posing as a friend while only waiting for my father to return, that was contemptible!"

There was a little sadness in his eyes, but he was still disinclined to give her reasons and excuses.

"You haven't come all the way from Texas to talk about your father," he said.

"No."

"Or to show me you're in mourning for Cordova."

"Yes, I am in mourning," she said, "not only for Cordova but for my murdered servants, and a man I thought fine but whose soul was dead."

"Will you take some tea? It's about to be served and will refresh you."

"You are a devil, yes," she said, "and a cold and calculating one."

"And you are far more Spanish than Texan. Come now," said Jason calmly, "we agree on how we stand. You've suffered tragedy at Cordova, and I've lost a wife. You'll not forgive me for what I did to your father, and I'll not forgive him for what he did to her. So there's nothing either of us can do to help the other. Accordingly, shall we accept that you feel a sense of grievance, and I feel I've settled a score? You'll find tea just the thing for you now, and over it you can tell me why you're here. Shall I ring for the pot?"

Oh, she thought, he is far colder than I could ever be. He is taking the ground from under me. Courage, Isabella, courage. Deal your deathblow with a smile on your face.

"Yes, please ring," she said.

Jason rang, and when Emily came he asked for tea to be

brought. Antoinette passed through the hall, went upstairs, and paced her room like a caged tigress.

Jason said, "Isabella—"

"I think," she interrupted, "you have not the right to call me Isabella."

"We've had these little arguments before," he said, and wondered why she had not come to terms with her true role in life, which was to be a woman and a man's warm, cherished joy.

"I am Isabella to all my friends, Captain Rawlings, and do not think myself different from other people in what I expect of any friend."

"You're young," said Jason, "and have yet to discover that even friends can be imperfect. At my age I'm saddled with disillusionment."

Her chin went up in the familiar way. Emily brought tea. Jason nodded, and she poured. He thanked her, Emily bobbed, cast an intrigued glance at the striking visitor in black, and blushed as Isabella met her eye. She edged out in confused haste.

"She be a rare beauty, t'other woman," she told the kitchen staff.

"That be two on um in the house," said the cook. "Makes for a tiddly old heap of mischief, that do."

Jason urged Isabella to sit down. A little light glimmered in her eyes then. "Indeed, why not?" she said. It was her house, almost. She sat beside the fire. Jason handed her a cup of tea. She sipped it. She looked into the flames, flames that were of a darting transparency because of the afternoon sunshine pouring into the room. Her hatred of him mingled with other emotions. She had come halfway across the world to strike at him, for he himself had not let distance discourage him from striking at her father. And there he was, obviously curious about why she was here, but devoid of the engaging human weakness that beset other people. He had ordered tea, indeed, as if she had merely dropped in just for that. She had seen the house and the land. The house was not Cordova, the land not Texas, but together they represented the sum of her revenge. She was not sure what had happened to her concerning Cordova. She would always have it deep in her heart, but her need of it had burned away in the fire of a desire to make a man suffer for what he had done to her father—and to her. Well, it was only a few seconds away, the moment of fierce satisfaction.

"Begin," said Jason, and she hated that in him too, that almost arrogant touch of masculine carelessness. It indicated that her presence was no more important to him than the arrival of everyday things.

"Begin?" she said coldly.

"Yes. You still haven't told me why you're here. But first may I say that while you're quite impressive in black, I prefer you in richer colours?"

She returned her cup and saucer to him. She had drunk only a little of the tea.

"We will not discuss your tastes, señor, or my clothes," she said. "I will only tell you my practical reasons for wearing black. When I am travelling long distances by myself, it is wiser to look like a widow than an unchaperoned and helpless woman."

"Helpless? Helpless?" Jason laughed. Isabella shot him the fiercest of glances.

"You are amused?" she said.

"Señorita, I'm at death's door with it."

"Then I shall be pleased to help you on your way, señor, by telling you I have posed as a widow all the way from Texas and received constant help and sympathy, where I might otherwise have been subjected to the most unwelcome kind of attentions."

"I hope this continues for you while you're in England," said Jason.

"I too have hopes of meeting with kindness," she said, looking composed, "for I intend to stay, perhaps for a while, perhaps for a year, perhaps even longer. Who knows?" Her shrug was graceful, cryptic.

"Stay?" he said.

"I imagine there are people in England who can show kindness."

"I'd be obliged," said Jason, "if you'd explain."

"It's quite simple," she said. "I expect to come into possession of some property here, and may therefore take up residence."

"Which property?" He was suddenly alert.

"Ah, which now? Let me see." She savoured the moment, letting it linger. "The name, what is it? Yes, I have it. Warwick Place, I think. Yes, that is it, Warwick Place."

Jason's face grew so dark that apprehension laid cold fingers on her sense of triumph.

"Impossible," he said.

"Quite the contrary, señor."

"Then you're mad."

"Not at all," she said. "I am very calm, very decided, and very calculating. It is a leaf I have taken from your book. I like the property, yes. Tomorrow, perhaps, you will be kind enough to accompany me and show me just how much land there is. I saw some excellent cattle a little while ago, but the herd was very small. I shall increase it."

Jason moved to the fireplace and turned logs with a long iron fork. The burning wood crackled, sparks flew and flames leapt. He was so close she could have touched him. Her body trembled.

"I hope you aren't serious," he said.

"I am very serious," said Isabella, a fixed little smile on her face. "I have control of a mortgage which should have been redeemed last September. It has not been. I am informed that foreclosure can be effected."

"Your information doesn't tally with mine," said Jason. He rammed the fork back into the iron cradle.

"That is probably because you have been misled. All is fair in war, señor."

"You're at war with me?" said Jason incredulously.

"You, señor, were first at war with me. You turned my father into a pitiful thing, you used Luisa and me—"

"There was another side to the coin," he said angrily.

"But you would not deny you came to Cordova to wait for my father, that you gave me false friendship—"

"God's justice," he said, "have you come all the way from Texas to trick me, madam?"

"You came all the way from England to trick me and disfigure my father."

She had eyes that were hot, but a poise that was controlled. He showed disgust and anger.

"I came to Texas to settle my score with him," he said, "and he may count himself lucky I didn't take his head off."

"Well, I am here to settle my score with you," said Isabella. "The Cordovas are a proud people, señor."

"Your pride, madam, is enough for all the Cordovas, dead and living." He looked hard at her, his expression a scowl. "You've control of the mortgage, you say? How was this done?"

Calmly, with her little demons of triumph executing a jig, she painted the canvas for him. A week or so after he left Cordova, her friend Philip de Ravero called to give her comfort, cheer, and sympathy. Also a loving hug from his strong right arm, though she did not include this in her picture. Philip was going to Europe again. It came to her then what she should do. She asked him to go first to England, to find out what he could about Jason Rawlings, whom he had met, who had a house in Dorset and who had served with the cavalry in the British Army. Philip was to discover where Jason Rawlings resided in Dorset, and if he still had a heavy mortgage round his neck. If so, Philip was to investigate the possibilities of acquiring that mortgage without bringing her name into it or his own. Philip professed himself happy to undertake the task, and asked only for a sweet kiss or two, which she gave him without suffering any emotional disturbance, although this too she excluded from her exposition. She placed into Philip's hands a letter which, consequent upon her instructing her bank, empowered him to make use of unlimited funds. She herself would travel to England later, probably arriving in April. That would give him time to do all that was necessary. If he found that the mortgage had been paid off, then he need do nothing more.

"Had you arrived and received exactly that news from your obliging friend," said Jason, "what would you have done?"

"I should have had to think about settling with you in another way," she said. However, Philip had found everything as they both hoped it would be, he being one with her in the way she intended to avenge her father. He handled the whole matter with breezy competence, reaching the point where he was able to commission a lawyer to act on her behalf. He had had few difficulties in obtaining all the information necessary, for her money did all that was required to persuade people to extract such information from other people. The lawyer negotiated with a Sir Richard Davenport, discovered to be the holder of the mortgage, and subsequently acquired it. This same lawyer now held the documents in trust for her, and when he received her instructions to foreclose would do so.

Jason only said then, "How much did you pay?"

"Much more than the original sum. But it is of no matter—I am a rich woman."

"I took no cognisance of the amount, for I'm only committed to the original sum of five thousand pounds."

"Which is still beyond your means to pay?" she said.

"Well beyond all my means at the moment. To be rich is to be fortunate, señorita. To use your money in this way is to be sadly misguided."

"But I was determined to see you as low in life as my father is," said Isabella. "And, indeed, I think I am kinder to you than you were to him."

"Or he was to me?"

"You judged my father as if you were God," she said. "You are not God, as I shall show you. There—"

"You are a spoiled brat," said Jason.

The colour rushed furiously into her face.

"Oh, you will be sorry for that!" she breathed.

"From the way you have behaved so far, I don't doubt that."

She waited until she could speak calmly, then said, "There are affairs, señor, between many faithless wives and many erring men. I am not a woman who has refused to see the weaknesses of people. But such affairs are matters of honourable revenge when the moment comes, not of brutality. There are duelling pistols. My father would have accepted the outcome of a duel."

"I shouldn't," said Jason. "Having made off with my wife, he wasn't going to be given the chance of blowing my head off. You may not have sheltered yourself from the weaknesses of people, but you still have a very naïve view of life, and little idea of the kind of man your father is."

"My father—"

"Your father, madam, can go to hell," said Jason. "I've made my own gesture by sending him part of the way."

Isabella's eyes blazed.

"Have you no shame, no remorse?" she cried.

"Not where your father is concerned," said Jason. "Now let's talk sensibly. I understood from Sir Richard that I was to be offered a five-year extension. That was agreed, I think."

"I lied," said Isabella, fighting an anger which threatened to destroy the pleasure of her triumph. "That is, my lawyer lied for me, though he was unaware of it. I believe you lied yourself once, to my father, and told him so. So we are quits on deception, I think.

Yet mine was not quite a lie, for Sir Richard Davenport was told that an extension of five years would be favourably considered. He accepted that this meant he could advise you an extension would certainly be granted, especially as my lawyer promised the rate of interest would be lowered. That promise, Señor Rawlings, naturally seemed to be the guarantee of an extension. It concluded the matter. Everyone signed. You were only too pleased, of course, for you felt you could breathe again. But there will be no extension, for I have considered it as favourably as I can, as agreed, and decided against it. My lawyer in London will foreclose when I instruct him to."

Jason, dark and grim, was quite unable to understand her. Except that she had Spanish blood and was a woman as well, which made for the unreasonable as well as the inexplicable. Damned if he would ever trust any woman wholly again. This one had been on his mind since he rode away from Cordova. How was it possible that a woman he had found all too easy to love could turn on him like this? There was her father, yes, and a vengeance that had shocked her—but there were so many other things she might have weighed against this. She herself knew he had not spent his time at Cordova merely waiting for her father. That meant nothing, it seemed, possibly because she was a woman whose pride and power made her feel all her family were sacrosanct.

Isabella, watching him, seeing him dark and brooding, realised her knees were trembling, even though she was securely seated.

"Well," he said eventually, "you'll do very nicely out of it, even if you have paid a high price. The house is in good shape, so is the estate. Though what you'll do with it when you return to Cordova, I don't know. Compared with Cordova, Warwick Place can't amount to much more than a whim."

"I am not returning to Cordova," she said. "I have sold it."

He eyed her in pity for her lunacy.

"Yes, you're quite mad," he said.

"Luisa married Fernando in December and—"

"I'm very happy for Luisa. Luisa is sweet."

"Do you think I could not have been sweet?" she flashed. "Do you—" She checked herself. She must go about her vengeance as coldly as he had gone about his. "My father has shut himself up in a dark room in Austin. I could not live by myself in a new house that had never known my family. So I sold Cordova to Americans, all of it, everything. They have it at last."

"I thought Cordova was your whole life," he said.

"It was once," she said. "It is gone now, as other things have gone. I am disillusioned too, señor. I am staying at an inn in your little town. I hope you will give me the courtesy of Warwick Place, so that tomorrow I may move from the inn and stay here for a while. You accept this, señor, my staying here?"

"I've little option. After all," he said bitterly, "the place is virtually your own."

"Yes." Precisely she said, "I would like to see all there is to see, to find out exactly what land goes with the property. Perhaps you will be good enough to show me all this. I will arrive in the morning." She rose to her feet. "Will you be so kind as to see me out, señor?"

He saw her out and watched her go off in the trap, her veil drawn over her face, her back straight, her air one of calm satisfaction and triumph. He was not close enough to see that behind her veil her face was very pale, as if unimaginable effort had drained her.

# 6

Antoinette appeared the moment Isabella had gone. She flew into the drawing room. Jason was sitting beside the fire, frowning.

"What did she want?"

"Oh, to renew a strange friendship," he said. "I'm damned if it's possible for most women to understand themselves, let alone other people. Well, there it is, an odd friendship renewed." He let it go at that. He did not want this gentle, sensitive girl to know he was saddled with a problem that was insurmountable.

"M'sieu, what have you in common with black witches?" she asked.

"Not enough to make me want to seek them out and consort with them."

"You are sad," said Antoinette. "She has put darkness in your face. If she comes again, no matter what her reason, put a knife into my hand and I will kill her for you."

Jason looked up at her. An intense little light glowed in her eyes. He shook his head.

"I think not, Antoinette. The consequences would be disastrous for both of us. We should likely have our necks stretched. And that can be disastrous enough to be fatal."

Antoinette sank to her knees beside him.

"M'sieu?" she whispered.

"Well?" he said, reflecting on the necessity of rejoining the Army.

"I adore you always. You must know that." Her voice was soft, murmurous. "When you are troubled, I will help you. When you are hurt, I will share your pain. And when you are lonely, I will comfort you."

"All that is for my old age," said Jason.

She folded her arms over his knees and rested her head there.

Constance returned with Clare. The child ran into Jason's arms, was picked up, tossed about, shrieked with joy, was set down and sent to have her hands washed by Antoinette, for Jason said they were indescribably grubby. Left alone with his sister, he broke the bad news to her. Constance listened without saying a word, her bonnet shading her face, her eyes watching him as he stood before the windows, looking at what he was going to lose.

Having heard everything, Constance finally said, "The woman is mad."

"Quite out of her senses."

"So much so it is most intriguing."

"Intriguing?" said Jason.

"Some women suffer emotional problems in the wildest way. She has come thousands of miles, even across the Atlantic, to repay you for what you did to her father? Oh, most intriguing, I vow it so."

"Do you?" said Jason grimly.

"For the moment, yes. Tell me, is she beautiful?"

"As a sunset."

"Jason, dear man, did you pay court to her in Texas?"

"I did not. That would have been a trifle macabre, I fancy."

"Ah," said Constance.

"Upon my damned soul," said Jason irritably.

"My dear," said Constance, "you're faced with disaster. If I have to look for my little cottage sooner than I thought, that isn't too serious. But you, with Clare and Antoinette to consider, you are in very troubled waters. However, if I were you, I'd not be too gloomy. The ship may never sink. I shall look forward to meeting this mad young lady from Texas tomorrow."

"Be a good soul and keep this all to yourself for the moment," said Jason. He did not want to talk more about it. He had had to tell his sister, but he did not want to discuss it further. He changed the subject, saying, "By the way, poor Ned Tranter is likely to join the circus of lunatics himself pretty soon. I've a feeling you're putting him towards Bedlam."

"I?" Constance was wide-eyed with innocence under her bonnet. "What have I to do with Mr. Tranter's state of mind?"

"Come out of your innocence, miss, it's wasted on me. Aren't you aware of his feelings for you?"

"I have very little to do with Mr. Tranter or his feelings, except that I know he doesn't like the shape of my nose or the point of my feet."

"Good God," said Jason, "you've seethed about that all these years?"

Constance flushed.

"What do you know about all these years?" she said. "Oh, the tittle-tattling beast, he's been talking to you. I shall never speak to him again."

"That won't set him down too much, for you rarely speak to him now."

Constance turned her back. Outside, the clouds of April were coming back to intrude into May. A light scattering of rain fell.

"Jason, in your pity for me you should not try to be a match-maker."

"Fiddlesticks," said Jason, "I'm not pitying you. You're a very self-sufficient woman."

"Indeed I'm not," said Constance. "It's a brave front I put up."

"You're a woman, you can endure very well. That's the strength of women. But if you've no wish to be married, I'd not want to harass you. All the same, it's a great waste."

"I'm quite reconciled to the fact that no one will ask me," said Constance. "I'm plainly featured—"

"I don't see you like that," said Jason, "nor does Ned. Damned if he don't like your shape excessively."

Constance blushed to her roots.

"Do you say, sir, do you dare to say that that low haymaker has had the vulgar effrontery to discuss my person without you dealing him a single blow?"

"Well, you have a shape, Constance, and it's my belief Ned would very much like to get his arms around it."

"Oh, you are low, sir, as low as he is," declared Constance, stifling the laughter that was ready to burst.

"Constance, we both have our troubles, you and I," said Jason, "but Ned doesn't come out of the same stable as Isabella Cordova. He represents far less trouble to you than she does to me."

Constance touched his arm.

"Jason," she said, "are you trying to say that Ned—that Mr. Tranter of his own accord has a fancy for paying court to me, and that you aren't pushing the man?"

"Any man who can't do his own pushing won't get you," said Jason. "I can only tell you that Ned asked me to see if you'd receive him more favourably than you do."

"He has intentions towards me?" she said with slight disbelief.

"Ask him."

"Ask him? Ask him? You absurd man, that is not the role of any woman. A man does little enough, therefore let him conduct the wooing. That is a generalisation, it isn't a message directed at Mr. Tranter. Nor, in my father's time, was I expected to look seriously at a farmer."

"Ned's no straw-sucker or turnip-head, you know that."

"Dear me, is he not?" said Constance with a smile.

"It really would be a waste, you know, if you became an old maid," said Jason.

"Some old maids are very contented women," said Constance. "They have escaped the turbulent strains that come from having to live with the vexations of men. However, perhaps I haven't been precisely gracious to Ned. I shall watch how he comes about. As for your own particular problem, you must deal with her as best you can. It really is intriguing, my dear. All the way from Texas just to buy up a mortgage? I wonder."

Isabella arrived the next morning, with a huge amount of luggage. A room had been aired and prepared for her. She took possession graciously, thanking all concerned for their trouble. She was not dressed in black this time, but in bright colours. A light green feathered bonnet of satin caressed her dark head. An embroidered spencer jacket of the same green, with puffed shoulders and long velour sleeves, pinched her slender waist and moulded her round breasts. Her skirt of darker green billowed and the flounced hem flirted around a starched petticoat. She looked devastatingly beautiful, and made Constance think that she must have spent an immeasurable amount of time on garnishing herself in such inspired fashion. Her ensemble was perfection. More and more intriguing, thought Constance. When one arrived to ruin a man, was it necessary to look as beautiful as this?

Constance received Isabella in the east drawing room, which was mainly reserved for feminine gatherings. Jason in earlier days had called it the chatter box. He, having now made the introduction, without looking as much as he might at the vision of Texas beauty so delectably adorned, took himself off, going to the stables with Antoinette and Clare. Clare loved horses.

"You are kind to receive me, señorita," said Isabella, drawing off her gloves, "and I shall not take up too much of your time, I hope."

"Myself, I hope there will be time to sit. Good." They seated themselves. Isabella was polite, Constance as pleasant as always. "I'm usually known within the house as Miss Constance. Incidentally, from all I've been told, I'm not sure if I'm receiving you or you're receiving me."

"Please do not put me at a disadvantage," said Isabella with a smile. "The situation is delicate enough, yes? I wish you to know I have no intention of being impossibly difficult. I desire only to acquaint myself fully with the house and the holding—"

"Holding?" said Constance.

"The land?"

"Oh, the estate, you mean."

"Yes. I would like to discover all about everything," said Isabella, "so that I can decide whether to take up permanent residence eventually."

"Surely," said Constance sweetly, "you must have decided that already? You have virtually bought the place. You can't mean to sell it. My opinion won't count for much, for I'm an ignoramus concerning values, but if you did sell you might not get as much as you laid out, which I believe was considerable."

"It is not important, the money, or the possibility of selling at a loss."

"What a happy and fortunate position to be in," said Constance.

"Satisfying at least, señorita," conceded Isabella, envying Jason's sister her tranquility. She knew she herself had a more fiery spirit. It had not been a help of late, it had not assisted her to fall asleep easily.

"For my part," said Constance, "I can't deny it's all very upsetting, though not as much for me as for my brother. Life has dealt him some hard blows these last few years. But then, if it had not been you it would have been someone else."

"Someone else?" Isabella opened her eyes wide, then veiled them.

"Taking possession of Warwick Place. He's been in no position to raise the necessary money, though he has been in a state of hope. However, it's done now."

"What is done?" asked Isabella.

"He has lost Warwick Place."

"I have not foreclosed yet."

"Come," smiled Constance, "you mean to, so there's an end to it."

"Señorita," said Isabella, with just a touch of resonant firmness, "I will say when there's an end to it."

"Oh, Jason is quite resigned," said Constance. "Sad but resigned. You need not hold back out of kindness. He means to enquire, I think, into the possibility of resuming his Army career. There's little else for a gentleman to do."

Isabella bit her lip.

"You think me hard, señorita?" she said.

"I think you extraordinary," said Constance.

"There's a saying, isn't there, an eye for an eye?"

"But it wasn't your eye," said Constance. "However, it's of no use for us to quarrel, and I am sure, if we did, that you would get the better of it. I'm aware, of course, of the unhappy circumstances. Although I can't say if they were less unhappy for Jason than for you. And when we've said that, Miss Cordova, we've really said everything, have we not?"

"I am not used to having words put into my mouth, señorita."

"It's all one, though, isn't it?" said Constance amicably.

"I have not said I am taking possession," declared Isabella, "only that I may consider it. I have not said I will place your brother in a position where he will have to become a soldier again. Nor have I said that things were unhappier for me than for him. How do you know I may not offer to let your brother manage Warwick Place for me when I return to Texas?"

"I'd not offer him that if I were you," said Constance.

"Why not?"

"In his present mood, he would not be above tossing you into the pond."

"That is not very amusing, señorita."

"But, my dear Miss Cordova," said Constance, "surely you have not come all the way from Texas to make Jason a steward?"

Isabella committed herself to a wry smile.

"You conduct a very sharp conversation," she said.

"Do you think so?" Constance looked doubtful. "I am hardly renowned for my wit. Heigh-ho, no matter. For the time you're here, I feel you and I will get along very well and not come to a single blow. Certainly, it isn't for me to intervene in the quarrel you have with my brother. And perhaps it does a man good to know that a woman can be a formidable foe—"

"Señorita, you are tipping both ends of the scales."

"Oh, I assure you," said Constance, "I desire only to sit peacefully on the fence. I'm quite able to, for I've a little money of my own and can live modestly as my own independent self whenever it's necessary. I'm not demanding of life, Miss Cordova, only grateful that God has given me the opportunity to observe it. I could never, I vow, do what you have done—"

Isabella, interrupting decisively, said, "I thought everything had been said about what I have done and why."

"I meant," smiled Constance, "that never should I have had the courage or the strength to undertake a journey from Texas to here. I should have palpitated all the way. You are a remarkable young lady—and yes, very formidable."

"I really do not like that word," said Isabella. "Señorita, it is kind of you to sit and talk with me, even—" Out of impulse came a little smile which Constance rather liked. "Even if you are pinching me a trifle at times. I know I am an intruder here, not a guest—but I hope I shall not be too much of an inconvenience or too much of an embarrassment. If you will be gracious enough to allow me to dine with you, I shall be happy with that and will keep to myself at other times, except when I am inspecting things."

"You are naturally expected to dine with us," said Constance in her very pleasantest way, "especially as no one can deny that much of the produce you'll find on the table is really yours. As to the other times, do you cry off from joining us because you wish to spare me the sight of you and Jason throwing things at each other?"

"Whatever his behaviour is like, señorita, I do not behave like a child myself."

"Oh, you've advanced well beyond that, well beyond," said Constance. "But you are right, I'm not sure I could trust Jason. His mood is extremely dark and scowling."

"He is not resigned, then?" said Isabella.

"Oh, yes. But still capable of smashing a few ornaments. You've bested him, and he knows it. Being a man, he naturally scowls. What man would not at being bested by a woman? May I compliment you on looking so ravishing? You have arrived like a summer morning. I vow those are the prettiest greens. Pray declare their origin; I'm quite smitten."

"I bought them in London, with other things."

Even more intriguing, thought Constance. Why should a woman concerned only with revenge wish to deck herself out so irresistibly?

"Well, you are ravishing in them. I'm in wonder at you."

"Why?" Isabella felt the need to tread with caution.

"Oh, because I'm a mouse myself, you know."

"That is not an answer, señorita, nor do I think it true."

"But it is," said Constance. She smiled very agreeably. "Miss Cordova, I've a feeling we may get to like each other."

Isabella rose. Constance followed suit. Isabella stood in colourful array, Constance in a simple morning dress of brown silk with bishop sleeves.

"I must change," said Isabella, "for your brother is to show me how much land there is."

"You're riding out together?"

"We have agreed to maintain a mutual civility."

"Mutual civility?" said Constance to herself, when Isabella had left the room. "That won't mean anything but a painful social strain. But she is not as mad as I thought she must be, only determined. Now that means something."

# 7

Isabella wore a riding habit lustrously black in its newness, her top hat trailing its long filmy blue veil. The little jacket trimly enclosed her waist, and around the neck of the white shirtfront she wore a soft blue cravat. Jason looked briefly at her when, as a superb picture of equestrian elegance, she presented herself at the stables. But he made no comment. He had a horse ready for her, a horse she found almost uninterestingly gentle compared with any Texas mustang.

They rode out of the environs of the house and gardens, over the parklands, and headed towards the farms. Napoleon trotted with a characteristic air of disdain, as if he considered Isabella's mount a mere half a horse. Such disdain, thought Isabella, went very well with his rider's taciturn mood.

But Isabella was not going to let herself be drawn into commenting on it. She said politely after a while that everything looked very well ordered.

"Tidy husbandry is always the most economical," said Jason.

"The scenery too is pretty," she said.

"Pretty? Pretty? Good God," he said in disgust.

"I am used, of course, to much more spacious horizons."

"You favour quantity?"

"I am a lover of all nature, señor," she said. In truth she was enchanted by the landscape of the hills, the many shades of green, and the variety of different trees. Oaks, yews, larches, pines, chestnuts, sycamores, and many more. So many little woodlands dotted the estate.

"You took a risk, buying this place without looking at it," he said. "Now see what you've got. A pretty little something."

"I did not take over that mortgage for any reason but one."

"Well, we've had that reason thrown severally at us. Now let it lie."

"You are not to speak to me like that, please," she said.

He cast her an icy glance. She put her chin up.

"There's the dairy herd," he said, and pointed to the pastures where the cows grazed. Beyond in other pastures bullocks skipped.

"That is hardly a herd," she said.

"It's all you've got."

"I must point out, señor, that all I have so far is a piece of paper. I have taken possession of nothing yet. However, when I do we must increase the cattle stock tenfold."

"We? What does that mean," he asked as Napoleon ambled over a soft, rutted track, "that you are installing a husband as well?"

Momentarily Isabella looked startled.

"I meant Warwick Place," she said.

They rode down a slope. Rabbits skipped in panic, white tails whisking. A crow flew up, cawing in bad temper at being disturbed. Wildflowers flecked the turf with colour, with gold and white and pink and blue. Isabella revelled in the soft air. The day was fresh, but she was not cold. It was really quite beautiful here, though the clouds were racing overhead and the sun was only a lukewarm cousin to the ball of fire that gave Texas such brilliant light. And Texas seemed a million miles way. Was it really possible that she could dispense with the wild, awesome majesty of her native land, turn her back on its life-giving rivers and its vast plains? Philip had said that in Dorset one was buried long before one was dead.

You will find it lamentably dull, he said.

But then Philip was not engaged, as she was, in a contest of wills with such an opponent as Jason—a contest that made every moment pluck at her nerves in a way that was both racking and exhilarating.

Nothing of those sensitive nerves was apparent as she said, "I spoke to your sister this morning." She knew he would probably not converse unless she did.

"You held your own?" he said.

"Barely," she said, "but I like her."

"Everyone likes Constance."

"Who is that other woman?" she asked carelessly. She had seen his riding companion of yesterday leaving the house with a child that morning. The child had stared in curiosity, the young woman had looked through her.

"She's my ward, Antoinette."

"Your ward?"

"She had no one else. There, that's as far as the estate goes on this side." He pointed to a stone wall.

"There? But that is nothing. I thought as far as those hills at least."

"Those hills are many miles away," said Jason. "Your holding here is two thousand acres. That's not regarded as inconsiderable. It will bring you a return."

She saw the sweep of green farmlands to the west.

"Is that ours?" she asked.

"Yours, you mean? No. It belongs to a neighbour, Ned Tranter."

"He will sell?" said Isabella. "If so, we must buy."

He gave her a look of dark curiosity.

"Ned won't sell," he said. "He'd be no more willing than you were with Colonel Hendriks. Let me give you a little advice, for what it's worth. You'll not be able to turn Dorset into another Texas, however much land you buy. If that's your ambition, to make a vast estate of Warwick Place and fill it with cattle and horses, it won't be even a good imitation of Texas. It will only be a way of spending money, and a way of amusing yourself for a while. You're a Texan. You were born there. Born Texans can't escape their country. Dorset isn't for a woman like you. It will bore you."

"I do not mind being given advice," said Isabella. "But do mind being given a lecture."

"Not only can't you escape Texas," said Jason, "you can't escape your pride."

Her blood rose heatedly. She used her switch on the flank of her horse. Amazed, the gentle beast stood up. Isabella, angry though she was, adjusted adroitly, cuffed it, brought it down, gave it a kick, and sent it running. Jason watched her go, and let Napoleon amble after her. The placid old hack would be winded in a couple of furlongs. He caught up with her as she skirted a wood of pines. Her mount was dawdling and puffing.

"This is not a horse!" she cried.

"Be of good cheer," said Jason, "for though not a horse it will carry you home, if you elect to travel at its pace and not yours."

His attitude, one of sarcasm and sourness, scourged her nerves and emotions. Her face flamed.

"I would not mount any guest of mine on an animal as stupid as this one!" she said furiously.

"Well, you must take it as it is, for it's yours, as everything else is," he said, "saving only our most personal possessions and my Napoleon."

"Oh, take care, señor," she flared, "or I will put you out of this place tomorrow!"

"I believe you," he said. "You have the temper for it."

They clashed, the icy blue eyes and those hot angry brown ones.

"Yes, I have, indeed I have!"

"You're a ridiculous woman," said Jason, "and a plaguey one. I'd rather treat with a Spanish donkey."

Isabella's hand tightened convulsively around the switch, her glove seams straining.

"Oh, I have complained about Americans in my time," she said bitterly, "for they have dealt with me as hard, ambitious men. But they have all at least been men and not one of them, no, not one, would have so forgotten his manhood as to insult me as you have."

Jason received that with a faint smile.

"I confess your respect for Colonel Hendriks as a man escaped me," he said.

"There are always exceptions, señor."

"Believe me," said Jason, "you'd be much happier if you returned to Texas. In which case you might care to sell Warwick

~ 362 ~

Place back to me, though I'd have to beg generous terms from you. I—"

"You, señor," she breathed, "may beg on both knees, and from dawn until sundown, and be availed nothing! Nothing!"

"Come now," said Jason, "I could offer you a thousand pounds down and so much per annum. I should hope our past friendship would count for something."

"Friendship? Oh, Santa María!" she cried.

"Shall we ride back? There's more to see, but we're both in a bad temper today."

"I began this day in a peaceful mood! It is you who have put me into a temper."

His smile was derisive.

"What did you expect of me?" he said. "That I would sing and dance for you?"

She took time to reflect on that. Her temper cooled.

"No. I could not expect that," she said.

They returned to the house, Jason silent, she in cold pride. The clouds, gathering, spread across the sky in huge soft plateaux of grey and white. The sun lay hidden and the light darkened. The first drops of rain caught Isabella as they reached the stables. Jason dismounted. She stayed obstinately in her saddle. He seemed as if he might be unchivalrous enough to ignore her. She was quite capable of reaching the ground by herself. They both knew it. But in proud, seething obstinacy she waited. The raindrops quickly became a heavy shower. Jason slapped Napoleon, who trotted out to frisk in the rain, and then he turned to Isabella. He gave her his hand. She came lightly from the saddle then, picked up her habit, and ran through the shower to the house. Masters let her in. She was never disposed to vent her anger on others, especially not on servants, so she thanked Masters and smiled at him, though there was a glitter in her eyes. But she went very angrily up to her room, where she pulled off her top hat and flung it on to the bed.

That cold devil. He had no feelings at all, no graces. How dared he speak to her as he had? She had bested him. His sister had admitted so. She had evened the score. Was he not man enough to accept that? He had said earlier this morning that they should be civil to each other, and then dared to say he would rather treat with a donkey. A donkey! It was deliberate, done to anger her, to reduce her. It was not turning out as she had planned, for she was to have graced the scene in cool triumph, and he was to have been so much at her mercy that—

She spun round at the knock on her door. She composed herself.

"Come."

The door opened. Jason stood there. He did not enter.

"I must apologise," he said.

"There is no need. As you say, I cannot expect you to sing and dance. But I shall do nothing vindictive. All I wanted to do I have done. We are even. So there is—"

"You must allow me, Señorita Cordova, to express my regrets for my bad behaviour."

She smiled stiffly and said, "I am afraid we both forgot to be civil."

At that he gave her a return smile. It weakened her almost disastrously. She felt her knees were going to shake. She conceded he had his own pride and was entitled to it. She turned away, hiding the colour that began to mantle her.

"Mine was the fault," he said.

"And we are at evens, señor, you agree?"

"I agree that that is what you believe," he said.

"I am not making things easy by being here," she said. She put her hands to her hair, pushing the curls into springy place after their compression under her riding hat. She had already made her mark on the room. It looked warm and feminine. Over the bed was a profusion of white undergarments, placed there when she had changed into her new riding habit and underskirt. Her restless eyes sighted on the heap. At home, in the days when Cordova had been alive, her maid Rosita would have put such things away for her. She assumed that here she would have to ask for such service. She glanced at Jason. He had seen the undergarments too: they had raised a smile.

"A very pretty pile of lace" was his immediate response, and that constituted the only natural moment they had shared since her arrival yesterday. Isabella coloured. She supposed that was how a woman might distinguish a man who had been married from one who had not. A married man would look and comment. An unmarried man would try not to look, and would certainly avoid any comment. Wryly Isabella thought to herself that a man who commented, married or not, was the more interesting.

"Señor?" she said, daring him to comment further. Oh, into what straits were her nerves bringing her, when she cared at this moment only to hear if he had more to say on the prettiness of her petticoat and other—

She hastily put herself between him and the other things, for the other things were simply not what any unmarried lady should display to any man, whether he was married or not.

Jason, well aware of what had made her colour and what had impelled her hasty movement, wondered why a woman with such endearing feminine traits should also own such an unforgivable lack of generosity and understanding. He might, not so long ago, have thrown aside his right to deal with her father, and set about pursuing her, wooing her, kissing and winning her. By sticking to his original objective, he had escaped the disappointments that would have come if he had won her. After Edwina, he knew that while he could not command perfection in a wife, any more than a wife could command perfection in a husband, the last kind of woman he wanted was one whose excess of pride and power would only mean he had made another bad mistake.

"Señorita," he said, "I think that in coming among us you've courted major embarrassments and difficulties. I admire your courage."

"Thank you," said Isabella, whose nerves might have been helped by this quiet compliment, had it not been for the fact that her preferences at the moment did not include wanting to hear what he thought of her courage. "I am sorry I left my room a little untidy—" And she made a gesture relating to the hidden heap of lace. It was a very human effort to return the conversation to a more pleasant subject.

"You may call for a maid whenever you wish," said Jason, and that dismissed her preference of the moment. "Señorita, in regard to your presence here, please make allowances for us. You'll need your courage each time you feel we're not making things easy for you. We can give you hospitality and, yes, civility—leaving aside my sourer moods, that is. But you must understand that to us you have the trappings of a bailiff."

"With big boots, long staff, large teeth, and a moustache?"

"Not quite," said Jason. "However, I'll try not to lose my

temper again. May I ask a favour on behalf of my sister, one I know she'd not ask herself? When you do take possession, would you allow her continued residence until she's bought herself a suitable cottage?"

"Oh," she replied hotly, "you cannot think I'd ever have denied her that gentle consideration!"

"I'm not sure what to think of any woman," said Jason. He gave her a polite bow and departed. She stood there, hot and angry again. He was going to be very difficult. She moved to close the door. Clare appeared. Pretty and warm-cheeked, she gazed into the room. Isabella, feeling at this moment that the heaviest cross women had to bear was the insensibility of men, gave the small girl a sympathetic smile.

"Oh, yes, my pretty one," she said, "it's a cross you too will have to endure in time."

"Papa is here?" said Clare, and took a few shy steps into the room.

"No. What is your name, little one?"

"I'm Clare."

Isabella stooped and looked into the green eyes. Clare smiled. Grown-ups gave her fuss, attention, and affection now, and she never had to stand very quiet and very still or speak only when spoken to.

"Oh, you are delicious," said Isabella, enchanted by prettiness, innocence, and mischief. But there was not enchantment alone. Something else came in a little hot rush. A spasm of jealousy that another woman had had his child. It shocked her. The woman herself, his wife, was dead. He had blamed her father for that. She fought her ungenerous emotion. She smiled again at Clare, and the green eyes sparkled. There was, thought Isabella suddenly, something familiar about the child. It was faint but there. She could not think what it was unless it was to do with a similarity to Jason, who had fathered her. "Do you like your papa?" she asked.

Clare nodded and said, "Love Papa."

"Clare? Clare? Clare?" Antoinette came searching. Isabella straightened up, and for a moment Clare was forgotten. Antoinette visibly stiffened, her eyes shining with hostility. Isabella, never easily discountenanced by a woman—though Constance had pricked her a little—returned the hostility with the politest of smiles. It was to be expected, of course, that everyone in the house should either resent her or dislike her.

"Here is Clare," she said, "and I am Isabella Cordova."

"I am aware," said Antoinette. The grace, elegance, and beauty of the New Orleans girl clashed with the matchless figure and richness of the Texas woman. "Clare, come, you must prepare yourself for your meal."

"I am 'pared," said Clare.

"Your hands must be washed. Come, *chérie*." Antoinette reached and took Clare by the arm. Clare smiled goodbye to Isabella, and went happily away with Antoinette to have her hands washed a second time. ·

Isabella closed the door. That young woman was disturbingly beautiful. And not English. How had she come to be Jason's ward?

The hostility was still apparent when she took her first meal with the family thirty minutes later. But Constance held the table together in her pleasant and facile way, and Jason managed to be reasonably civilised. Antoinette, however, pointedly refused to engage with the unwelcome guest. Cold meats were served and Isabella might have enjoyed the meal more than she did, but she was at a high point of tension and it cost her her appetite to disguise it.

At Jason's suggestion, Isabella rode out again with him during the afternoon. The rain had stopped and everything was moistly bright as the clouds parted to let the sun through. Jason drank in the moistness like a man who had spent too long in the desert. Isabella was aware of how rich the wet meadows looked, how mild the sun was. Jason was polite to her and helpful, showing her exactly how much land there was to the estate. He showed her, too, sheep, which moved and grazed over grassy chalk slopes, and described to her, as they rode past acres of tilled ground, what crops had been sown that year.

He talked, but he kept his eyes for the most part on what lay around them. Only briefly did he glance at what, in the soft light of the sun, was a disturbing agent. That was her wide mouth, with its lips deeply pink. When she spoke, her teeth glistened and made her lips look pinker. He dug into his reserves of resistance.

She could not complain of his attitude this afternoon, nor did she. And as he had found another horse for her—one that was not just a hack—there was even less reason to be critical. She supposed him to be coming around, to acknowledging she had paid him back. Yet she did not feel triumphant or exultant. She did not even feel that she wished him to be humble enough to beg clemency of her. Would she have liked it, in any event, if in a sense he had gone down on his knees to her? She knew that was not her idea of how a man should behave; but it was what she had envisaged, and even planned.

They rode all round the estate. Everything was quite different from Cordova. Cordova opened out limitlessly before the eye. Warwick Place with its two thousand acres was neat and compact by comparison, almost ridiculously so. But it had an appeal she could not deny, and would not be difficult to love.

They reached an area of grazing land empty of either cattle or sheep, and Isabella felt an urge for movement, a need to fly in the face of the soft wind, anything that might release her from the tensions of her tightly strung nerves.

"I am going to run my horse," she said.

"You're welcome to," said Jason, "but watch the dip, it may be spongy."

She had to take the descent that led up to broad acres. She cantered down towards the dip. The wind blew at her and the air tinted her face with damp lustre. The turf was soft and yielding, and clods flew. The dip seemed innocuous enough from the look of it and she did not bother to slow up. But the moment she reached it, the horse bogged to its knees and she sailed from the saddle and squelched into wetness.

Jason and Napoleon sauntered down to her, Napoleon picking his way. She sat up, her boots in soggy turf. In her humiliation, she could have wept.

Jason said, "I've seen others fall not half so positive. I've seen none quite so pretty."

Isabella's humiliation took a new turn. Her habit and underskirt were up around her knees. Crimson, she pulled herself up. Her booted feet sank. She gasped. Jason dismounted.

"I am sinking!" she cried.

"Not more than a few inches," he said. He walked through the spongy layer, and put his hands on her waist. He lifted her, and her boots sucked free. The strong clasp of his hands heated her. He swung her to firmer ground.

"Let go of me!" she demanded as her feet found turf. Confusion, compounded of hurt pride and mortification, ran the sense from her. Jason released her, and to her horror she found her feet were not as safely lodged as she thought. The wet turf seemed to slip away, her feet went too and she tumbled sideways. When she looked up from the ground, he was laughing. He reached to give her a hand. But with her colour flaming she sprang up, and before she had given herself time to think she slapped his face.

At the look he gave her, Isabella paled.

"You must pay for that, madam, and will," he said. He saw her mouth, parted, trembling. He took hold of her arms, and pulled her to him and laid his lips on hers. He kissed her, smotheringly and without mercy. Isabella lost her breath. She had never imagined a kiss could reduce her, seduce her, electrify her, and give her joy, pain, and longing all at the same time. Her blood raced.

She heard his voice as his body withdrew.

"I'm sorry. Forgive me, señorita. I should not have done that."

She opened her eyes and wondered how it was that limbs so weak managed to keep her upright.

"You—" She could not get the words out.

"Yes, I'm sorry. I'm afraid, señorita, I'm not a gentleman."

She wanted to say he had done nothing she did not deserve; but his expression, dark with disgust at himself, discouraged her. She drew a deep breath. A little imp of hysteria danced within the whirlpool of her mind. How might one be kissed like that again? By slapping him a second time?

"Señor," she said unsteadily, "I cannot reproach you. I was at fault. But you were laughing at me."

"Yes, I'm sorry," he said again, "you had every right to be angry."

"No, it was stupid of me," she protested.

"Even so, I should not have done that. If you'll accept my apology, perhaps we can complete our outing?"

She wanted to stay and talk about the incident, to discover perhaps what had made him kiss her like that, instead of simply accepting her slap in a way that would have made her feel small. But his demeanour was a dark discouragement. He took her arm

~ 369 ~

and brought her to her horse, which had backed out of the shallow bog and was standing quietly. He helped her to remount.

"Thank you," she said.

He looked at the dip and said, "Our hazards here are really only small ones, señorita—and there are no Comanches. It's the different conditions you may not like. If you stay long enough you—"

"I will stay," she said firmly, and he was not to know how erratically her heart was still beating.

On their ride back to the house the clouds began to race in again from the west, threatening grey banks buffeting sun-tipped white.

"April in England often stays to keep company with May," said Jason, "and so showers linger somewhat."

"I like the rain," said Isabella, as determined not to be discouraged as he was to send her packing.

"Under a burning sun I at least like the thought of it."

"Señor," she said tentatively as the house appeared in the distance, "you have a child."

"There's Clare, yes," he said with a faint smile, "the prettiest little bundle of mischief."

"You said nothing about her when you were at Cordova," said Isabella. "But at Cordova, of course, you dealt very much in secrecy. Did it never occur to you that if you had confided in me—"

"No, it never occurred to me," he said abruptly, which made her hate him a little, "and it's over and done with now."

"But it isn't, is it? What is happening is a continuation, which perhaps you might have guessed at if you had studied the Cordova family better."

"I wasn't there to study your family, señorita."

"Oh," she said emotionally, "do you find it so easy to hurt people?"

"Come now," he said, "my relationship with you and Luisa—"

"Was a lie!"

"Very well, if that's what you choose to think. But let's avoid quarrelling again, shall we?"

Her chin was up, her mouth set, but she could not bear silences with him. After a little while, she managed to say, "You are fond of Warwick Place?"

"I was born here and grew up here," said Jason, "and we all

have an affection for the playgrounds of our youth. However, I'm going to lose it. Since I suppose I took it all for granted, I can't complain too much."

The horses were walking, the clouds had been driven eastwards, leaving the sky clear, and the soft red of the house looked warm in the sunlight.

"You had your revenge, I am having mine," said Isabella.

"I wish you joy of it," he said in some sarcasm. "My sister, by the way, tells me you don't wish to intrude on us except at mealtimes. But all the courtesies of Warwick Place are yours, I assure you."

"No, I am embarrassment enough," she said.

"Señorita," he said, "you can't possibly see yourself in a role as sensitive as that."

"Señor," she said passionately, "there are times when I dislike you intensely."

"I fancy," said Jason, "you've made that very obvious already."

When they reached the stables, neither was in the best of moods, and the kiss they had shared in a moment of impulse and anger edged the nerves of both. But Isabella was determined to stand her ground. She meant to see things through to a planned conclusion. Jason had entered her house as a false friend and so she continued her residence in his life as a bailiff, albeit a ravishingly beautiful one. She had her meals with him and Constance and Antoinette, and each day civility reigned at the table, except that Antoinette simmered and smouldered. At times the fire burned in her eyes, for although no one had told her Jason was to lose Warwick Place, enough was said on occasion for her to suspect that the woman from Texas was here to take everything and give nothing. Jason told Antoinette not to worry, but she did, and with pain in her heart. To Antoinette, her guardian was a man who could deal with all other men, but not with a woman who had come garbed like a black witch.

The cook was sure one evening that a kitchen knife was missing, but she mentioned it only casually and waited for it to return. There were other knives to take its place.

For a week Isabella spent mornings and afternoons looking into everything. Some things, like the kitchen, scullery, pantry, servants' rooms, and stables, she looked into two or three times, making her beauty and her warm graciousness familiar to the staff. It made Constance lift an eyebrow. Such repetitive poking around prolonged the investigative sojourn, which Constance already thought long enough. She herself would not have taken more than two days at the most to decide whether she liked a property or not. There was, she felt, a lot more to Isabella Cordova's act of revenge than plainly met the eye.

Isabella found the house perfect, its atmosphere of warmth and comfort attaching itself to one on entry. But she insisted that much more could be made of the estate if the acreage could be trebled, or at least doubled. Jason said that was entirely up to her. He had been content himself with what land there was, and she would understand, surely, that he could hardly be expected to interest himself in plans or ambitions which were not going to concern him.

"All the same, I am trying to interest you," said Isabella.

"You are beating a dead horse, señorita."

He could not understand what she was about. But he did understand that there was a presence disturbing both to his eye and to his senses. She used a very delicate scent and left the faintest hint of it around. She had not, even in the exotic Spanish atmosphere of Cordova, dressed as beautifully as she did every day at Warwick Place.

He supposed she was drawing out her triumph. For his part, he had to consider what to do about himself, Antoinette, and Clare. Army pay would not keep them in great comfort. But the Army it would have to be. He could not see what else there was.

"Do you think," said Isabella at the end of a week, "do you think I might talk to your neighbour, who owns the land directly west of ours?"

She would keep saying "we" and "ours." It was beginning to get his goat.

"I'll see what I can do," he said.

It was no problem to arrange for Ned Tranter to call. Ned came up the very next day after receiving a note from Jason. Isabella requested he should meet her with Jason present. Jason politely asked to be excused. Politeness was one of the more constant factors at Warwick Place these days. He would make the introduction, he said, after which his presence would be superfluous. Isabella, her state of nerves no better each day, had a terrible feeling that any moment he would make her weep tears in front of him. But when she received Ned she was at her loveliest and most irresistible. Ned was impressed by the rich beauty of the woman who, so Jason briefly said, was to be the next owner of Warwick Place. But he could not be persuaded into considering for a moment the sale of his farm. Nor did he mumble about this, but spoke so decisively that Isabella saw in him the same kind of determination with which she had faced up to Colonel Hendriks. They parted on a note of mutual respect.

Leaving the house, Ned saw Constance. She was giving last year's apples to his horse. She turned as he came up, and he might have wondered at the fact that she was wearing her favourite eau de nile and her best summer bonnet, except that he was not aware of her preferences.

"Why, Mr. Tranter," she said with a smile, "here is your poor horse so famished it's eating wrinkled apples. Shame on you."

Ned gave her a severe look. Constance smiled again. Her fine eyes and handsome mouth made Ned think her a far better bargain than round-faced, pursed-lip simperers. But she had the devil's own way of setting a man down.

"That poor horse just likes apples, madam."

"Madam? madam? I am advanced to the status of a customer for your hay, Mr. Tranter?"

"Now look here—"

"Yes?" said Constance.

"Oh, the devil," muttered Ned. Having just departed undefeated from his encounter with dark beauty from Texas, he

~ 373 ~

judged himself a loser before he had scarcely engaged with the rural craft of Constance. He glowered at his munching horse.

"Your nose is put out?" smiled Constance. "Our resident sword of Damocles has tickled you with her point and pricked you into selling your land?"

"She has not."

"You stood up to her?"

"I ain't selling," said Ned, "and that's flat."

"My goodness, you did stand up to her," Constance murmured. It was like an approving purr. "And she so healthily ravishing and finely determined."

"I own she's a rare creature—"

"Oh? You have an eye for such specimens, Mr. Tranter?"

"Not enough to make me give up my land," said Ned.

"Bravo," said Constance.

"I bid you good day, Miss Constance," he said. With luck he could get away before she had him shifting and mumbling. But he was unable to reach the stirrup, for Constance, somehow, was suddenly in the way. "Miss Constance, kindly stand aside."

"Shan't," said Constance.

"Oh, the devil," said Ned again.

"If you dare to lay hands on me, sir—"

"You know I wouldn't. So stand away."

"Shan't," repeated Constance, "and that's flat too."

"My oath," muttered Ned, "I'm fuzzed if you don't beat all."

"You old muffle-head," said Constance, and stood aside. "There, there's your stirrup. Mount, sir, and run."

"Run?"

"Else I shall box your ears for standing up to Miss Cordova and not to me."

Ned shifted. He realised that she was actually having a conversation with him, such as it was. He stopped shifting.

"Do that, madam," he said, "and I'll put you over my knees."

"You never would," declared Constance.

"No," said Ned, "but braving your scorn for me, I'll be back this afternoon. On my oath I will, and risk all with a question."

"All?" Her eyes were laughing under her bonnet.

"You'll say no, of course," he muttered.

"If, sir, you propose to come back and ask me to jump from my window or into the pond, I'll certainly say no. Mr. Tranter, is

~ 374 ~

your question so critically governed by a small turn of the sun that you cannot ask it now?"

"It's critical to me," said Ned, swinging himself into the saddle, "and I haven't got the courage to risk being set down for good and all while I'm sober. I must first fortify myself."

"If you arrive drunk, sir, I shall box both your ears," said Constance.

"Aye," said Ned gloomily, "I don't doubt it. But I will return, you may rely on that. And damn it, I shan't take no, I'll lay siege, even to your boudoir, damned if I won't." At which exceptional piece of verbal derring-do, he put spurs to his mount for fear that if he delayed his going for a moment Constance would be at his ears and dunning all his senses.

But Constance was smiling as she watched him go. Lay siege to her, even up to her boudoir? He meant to have her then, after all these years? After shattering her girlish infatuation by slighting her as if she had merely been an adolescent nuisance? It was true that in those days she had been at his elbow whenever she could, hiding her devotion to him behind a façade of mischievous teasing; but when he had flung those names at her, he shocked and hurt her beyond all forgiveness. Fifteen years old she had been—and shattered. It injured her sense of pride in later years that though she could not forgive him she still had heartache about him.

Lay siege to her? Did the man realise what he had said? She went into the house, up to her room, and came face to face with her mirror. There, she was plain, there was no avoiding it, and plainer still set beside the other two women in the house.

She could not see, as others could, the appealing clarity of her fine eyes or the kissable quality of her mouth. Nor did she think about how, when in company, people would as soon seek her out to talk to as anyone. In conversation with her, no one thought her plain, only extremely pleasing.

She went downstairs to find a book, a book that would absorb her in the quiet of the gardens and take her mind off an unusually bold Ned. She encountered Isabella in the hall, an Isabella who came stormily out of the west drawing room.

"What is that face for?" asked Constance. For all her curiosity about the strange purpose of a woman who had both beauty and riches, she could not help liking her.

"Am I showing temper?" Isabella was breathing like a hard-pressed tigress. "It's no wonder, when I am so contempted. I do not know how you came to have such a cold-hearted brother. What have I done but even the score?"

"You're taking the roof from his head," said Constance.

"I have not done so yet! Just this moment I offered to let him stay, and for that I am called a child!"

Isabella had been talking to Jason. She had begun by saying, "You are cold to me because of what I have done, but as you acted in pride so did I. Everyone knows that if I had not acquired the mortgage, someone else would. And barring that, then Sir Richard Davenport would have sold Warwick Place over your head. But would someone else do what I am willing to?"

"What is that?" asked Jason.

Her nerves raw because she wanted him far more than Warwick Place, she said with an effort, "I am willing to have you stay and look after everything. No one need go. You know I could not manage by myself."

"You managed Cordova, and that was a mighty estate compared with this."

"But I knew Cordova, I was born there," she said. "You were born here. So stay and manage it for me."

"While you return to Texas?" said Jason.

With her face pale beneath its Spanish tones, she said in a low voice, "May I not stay too?"

"May you?" He wondered what the devil she was up to now, and whether she knew what her continued presence was doing to him. "How might you not? The place is yours."

"Not until I have decided," she said.

"Why not give me a term of five years, and go back to Texas?" he asked, though he knew that the moment she came to her senses he would pursue her and never let her go.

"Oh, you are a hard man," she said bitterly.

"Well, there you have it," said Jason, "a proud woman and a hard man. Two such people could never work together."

"No one has ever found it difficult to work with me. But it is impossible for the gentlest person to work with you! Will you stay or not?"

"Señorita, only a child would think that an offer of sweets could dispel the bitter taste of unreasonable revenge."

"Oh!" She was so miserably angry that she stamped her foot. "You shall go by the week's end! Yes, you and that French ward of yours!"

"And Clare and Constance and the servants?" he said.

"Everyone!" But she was bitten by furious helplessness, for she knew it was not in her to turn anyone out. And the pain was worse because he did not know it too. She stormed from the room and ran into Constance, who after a few words took her into the privacy of the ladies' drawing room.

"Now," said Constance, "there's more to all of this than either you or Jason admit."

"There is nothing except that Jason—that your brother is a man of no understanding and no kindness, no, none at all."

"My dear," said Constance, "you should conduct your little battles with him more coolly and far less extravagantly. You are rampaging about, which may be all very well in Texas—which I understand is just the place for it—but it doesn't do anything but produce uncomfortable echoes in a smaller place like Dorset."

"Señorita, I do not think I should consider the size of a place when I am so unkindly provoked."

"Isabella—I may call you Isabella?"

"Yes." Isabella was rustling about in angry misery. "You are the only one who has been kind to me, who talks to me."

"Well, I am the least affected, of course." Constance smiled at the temperamental Texan. "If I were due to be evicted from my home, however, with not a penny in my pocket, I too might not have been precisely gracious. Perhaps there are reasons why you can't be honest with me—"

"Señorita!" Isabella swung round.

"Can you tell me, for instance," said Constance, "why you really came all the way from Texas to do what you are doing? Jason surely acted no more unreasonably than any husband in revenging himself on your father."

"He brutalised my father," said Isabella passionately. "He inflicted a hundred hideous slashes on his face and body."

"Which quite properly spoiled him for any other man's wife. And that is why you will take the roof from Jason's head?"

Isabella crossed to the window and looked out at burgeoning summer.

"Yes, that is why," she said.

"My poor Isabella," said Constance. Isabella turned.

"That I am not," she said.

"You are rich, you mean?"

"Señorita—"

"Please don't confuse me," said Constance. "If I'm to call you Isabella, you must call me Constance. I can't endure social inconsistencies. It's far too wearing to always be wondering whether one is in favour or out of it. We are to be Isabella and Constance, or not?"

"Oh, I am in too much pride sometimes, I confess," said Isabella. "But, Constance, I am not a poor woman in any way."

"Well, I vow that to me your state seems most unfortunate. Isn't it unfortunate to love my brother as much as you do, when you've put yourself into such an impossible position with him?"

"Never!" Isabella flamed into anguished repudiation. "No woman could love a man who proved such a worthless friend, and so hatefully hard and cold."

"Do you say so?" murmured Constance. "But he's not been so hard that he could not give protection to Antoinette, left destitute in New Orleans by thriftless parents, and provide care and a home for a child unwanted by her mother and her mother's lover."

"Mother and lover?" Isabella paled.

"Jason has surely told you?"

"He has told me nothing!" Isabella was shivering. "The child is his, and his wife's. That is true, isn't it?"

"His wife was her mother, that's true enough," said Constance, "but the father—"

"Oh, leave it unsaid!" gasped Isabella, and put her hands over her ears.

"You don't care to hear that Clare is your father's child? That she's your half sister?"

"No, no, no!" Isabella shuddered.

"Given with money to a couple in Baltimore? You do not know that?"

Constance, out of necessity, was twisting the knife.

Isabella gasped, "Never would my father have—"

"Your father, my dear, is a selfish scoundrel," said Constance, "so let us not hide behind pretty family escutcheons."

"It was an affair," said Isabella desperately, "many men and women have affairs."

"And quickly grow tired of each other, quickly become aware of each other's natural promiscuity, neither being capable of true affection. I am a quiet, dull, rural person and have never attempted to fly the coop. But life is all round us everywhere, it's there to observe, and people are there too. So although one is dull, one is able to observe. I've a feeling that my brother hasn't been too hard on you, but too kind. Did he not even tell you that your father passed his wife on to a procurer from New Orleans?"

Isabella reeled and clutched at a chair. She turned white. She put a hand to her throat and stared at Constance out of dilated eyes.

"That is not true! It could not be true!"

"She died diseased in New Orleans, which is the fate of many procured women," said Constance.

"Oh, sweet heaven, Santa María!" Isabella, stricken, covered her face with her hands and sank to her knees.

"Don't you think it a strange coincidence," said Constance gently but mercilessly, "that in this house, which you have come all the way from Texas to acquire, there lives your father's child, your half sister? Taken into love and care by Jason, on whom you've had your tidy revenge?"

Isabella felt the fires of torment.

"Oh, you are cruel, cruel," she gasped.

"Perhaps I am rather a wretch." Constance smiled. "But it's for your own good. It's better, isn't it, for you to know precisely why Jason did what he did. And it's a kindness to show you, if you do love him, that you haven't inflicted yourself with an affection for a man totally worthless."

"He was wrong in not telling me all this, terribly wrong," cried Isabella. "If only, at Cordova, he had— Constance, help me, what must I do, what can I do?"

"Why not go quietly back to Texas? You have the mortgage. It can be an investment. Jason will give you an honest return on it."

"Go back? But to what?" Isabella lifted eyes of anguish to Constance. "That is no help, to tell me to go back. That is like offering sand to a woman in a desert. Constance, speak to him, explain to him." Isabella rose to her feet, pale with despair. "I did not know any of this, how could I?" At that moment the door opened and Clare peeped in. Isabella stared tragically as the child smiled at her. She knew then what it was she had found faintly familiar. It was a likeness, fragile but perceptible, to her father.

"Clare," said Constance, "run along, sweet, and find Papa. Tell him your Aunt Isabella wishes to see him, that he's not to go out for the moment."

"Yes, find Papa," said Clare, and scampered off in happy search.

"I cannot see him," said Isabella. "Constance, I cannot."

"You prefer to slip away?" asked Constance.

"No. No. But speak to him first for me. Please?"

"Perhaps I'd better," said Constance, "or you'll rush every fence and fall at them all."

Constance found Jason in the library. He was composing a letter, the quill scratching decisively.

"I'm interrupting?" she said.

"Only my letter writing. I'm applying to rejoin the regiment."

"A brave decision," said Constance.

"I have to think of Antoinette and Clare," said Jason. "I can't go wandering off in search of gold."

"Oh, I vow not. No, never." Constance was heartfelt in her agreement. Jason quizzed her, his eyes sharp, for her smile was innocent enough to be thoroughly suspect. "Well, I should tell you, Jason, it will displease Isabella if you go anywhere at all. It will be the second time you've deserted her."

Jason put the quill down and regarded his sister darkly. Her smile became disarming.

"Explain yourself, madam," he said.

"Explain myself? I, sir, am as clear as water undisturbed by the faintest ripple. What mystery there is, both deep and devious, exists only between you and Isabella."

"You may bemuse Ned by such twists and turns, Constance, but not me. Explain yourself."

"Your air of innocence don't signify," said Constance.

"My air of innocence? Mine?"

"It's all put on. I've just discovered that you've been extremely unfair to Isabella. That woman is in misery."

"Do you say so?" he said grimly.

"Scowl as you wish, sir," said Constance. "It don't mean a tinker's kettle. Why didn't you tell her exactly what happened to Edwina? Why didn't you tell her that Clare was the child of the affair, and virtually an abandoned weight? However ashamed Isabella was of her father, she undoubtedly considered him no worse than other philandering men. And goodness knows, many of you make cuckolding an addictive occupation. She isn't so naïve that she isn't aware of this, or so prudish that she doesn't accept it as a regrettable male weakness."

Up to the gills in irony, Jason said, "I hope she also accepts the fact that for every weak man there must also be a correspondingly weak woman."

"Oh, we are poor creatures in our desire to pleasure persuasively unscrupulous men," said Constance.

"That is a personal observation, madam, or an innocent opinion?"

"Fie, sir, do not dishonour your own sister by looking so blackly upon her. I am a mouse of a woman."

"God's death you are," said Jason.

"But it is I, a mere mouse, who has had to tell Isabella the shattering news that Clare is her half sister."

"Then you've let a tigress out of its cage," said Jason. "For she'll now try to claw Clare out of our arms and eat the rest of us in the process."

"Your logic is as thick as your head," said Constance. "She'll do nothing of the kind. She's not likely to add to her mistake by committing another. It's quite obvious to me that in thinking her father no worse than any other man, she decided—or she convinced herself—that you brutalised him. That doesn't mean she excused him, or that she's in favour of wanton women. I've no doubt at all you'd find her a happily faithful wife, and there's much to be said for that in this day and age."

"I would find her so?"

"Oh, tsk, tsk," said Constance. "It's as plain as the nose on your face that she's off her head about you and that it would take very little to turn your tigress into a lamb. Well, perhaps not quite a lamb, she has too much spirit for that. But a little affection is all that would be needed for that change, don't you think? Just a few kind words are all that's required."

"Constance, you're prattling." Jason took up the quill and fiddled with it.

"My dear brother," said Constance, "your myopia verges on mental delinquency. I vow it mystifies me how any of you can distinguish one woman from another, and indeed there are men who look at some women in the same way they look at horses. Can't you see that Isabella didn't embark on her long, trying journey from Texas merely to even a score with you? There was always far more to it than that. You're so blackly taken up with what you feel is her unreasonableness that you haven't stopped to think of what is so obvious. Which is that if she only planned to dispossess you she need never have left Texas at all. She could simply have used an agent to act for her. Has she not looked irresistibly ravishing for you day after day? But what compliments or sweet words have you given the suffering woman? None, I suspect."

"It may seem the oddest thing to you," said Jason, "but when a woman comes to dispossess a man, he's most unlikely to give her sweet words."

"If you had," said Constance, "she might have fallen into your arms."

"To what purpose? Put aside your flights of fancy, Constance, for she's rich and powerful, and I'm virtually a pauper."

"Oh, pride and myopia," sighed Constance, shaking her head. "There never was such a hopeless combination. To own one is enough, to own both is a misery. How can you fail to love so beautiful and spirited a woman when she's just the kind you need after the mistake that was Edwina—"

"Have I said I don't love her?"

"Fie on you, sir, you've said nothing at all. If you do love her, tell her so. She will fall into your arms."

"Are you mad?" asked Jason.

"I'm the only one who isn't," said Constance with sweet equanimity. "Come, dear man, forget you were foolish enough to marry a woman both flighty and selfish. Isabella is quite different. She took you into her house. You helped her. She wanted you to stay. You said so. You shared hazards with her, you made yourself indispensable to her life and emotions. Then with quite callous indifference to her needs, you neatly sliced up her father and rode off. And in doing that you outraged her as much by your desertion of her as by your treatment of her father. Perhaps she is rich and powerful. Such women refuse to let the actions of men govern their lives, however meekly the rest of us submit. Isabella simply decided you weren't going to get away with deserting her. That is my frank opinion. No—my belief."

"You're warming up very nicely," said Jason with the glimmer of a smile, "but this isn't a theatre, and you're not on stage."

"I assure you, my dear," said Constance, "the atmosphere in this house is one of high drama. Isabella is a woman of shattered pride and quite likely, in her misery, to break her neck on a horse that can't jump higher than a farthing. You're a man refusing her what she most needs because you're vexed with her. And Antoinette is hot for battle."

Jason frowned. He was well aware that his enchanting ward was smouldering. He had said nothing, apart from telling her not to worry, for it was not by his advice that Antoinette could prove herself. She alone must show whether she was untainted by the sultry decadence of New Orleans, whether her blood, her mind, and her attitude were uncorrupted.

"Antoinette is angry, no more," he said.

"Perhaps," said Constance. "You must understand that Isabella thought she had good reason for avenging her father since she did not know the extent of his perfidy. That allowed her to present herself at your door as your chief creditor, although she didn't forget to look astonishingly beautiful. She now realises you had every justification for destroying her father's prettiness. But in any event, once she had acquired the mortgage, once she had you helpless, she didn't know how to make her further acquisition. She's been a figure of frustration for days."

"Further acquisition?" said Jason, quite sure all women were creatures of fantasy.

"That further acquisition was you. That was her true purpose. She even sold her own property, didn't she? I vow, Jason, her tempers don't seem half as bad as your myopia. I recommend that you at least make your peace with her. You were unfair not to have told her the full story. It is no good, I suppose, advising you that if you kissed her she would tear the mortgage up? But at least see her and talk to her."

"Who is matchmaking now?" smiled Jason.

~ 383 ~

"I am," said Constance, "which is better than adding to the prevailing woes."

"I'll go and see her," he said.

But Isabella was nowhere to be found.

9

Isabella had left the house and walked feverishly across the spreading swards of green, into and through a pine wood and out on to slopes springy with heather. The May day had a chill to it because there was no sun, only dark clouds. She had put on no coat or cape, she had run from the house as she was, and she wandered in a bright blue dress, her dainty slippers a fragility which softened and yielded to the dampness of the ground. She longed for Texas, for Cordova, for the wildness of the far chaparral, for tall grasses that would hide her and vast spaces that would swallow her. She had sought in anger and pain to make a man so destitute that he would turn to her for clemency, she had sought to show him that neither he nor any other man could lightly discard a woman of Cordova. And if he had turned to her, she would have shown him that she would do anything he wished of her.

The Dorset hills were sombre. The red chimneys of tenants' cottages sent up trails of lazy smoke. She heard the axe of a woodman and the creaking sighs of an old besieged elm. She saw the man, brawny and rough-clad, an empty clay pipe between his teeth, the rhythm of his axe deliberate and tireless. He stopped his work for a moment, and touched his old brown hat to her. She smiled absently, nervously, and went on. Rain began to patter down. She reached a haven of quiet, the branches of trees above her laden with green growth and ferns springing around her feet. The wood was a shelter and hiding place. She sat on a huge fallen branch. The rain stopped after a while. She was hardly aware of its cessation, or of being wet. Her mind was numb and her eyes stared unseeingly.

It took Jason hours to find her. She looked up as the young ferns rustled and his shadow loomed. She was very pale and her beauty was pinched and cold.

"This is foolish," he said. "Come home."

"It is not foolish to think," she said. "And that is all I have been doing, thinking."

"I daresay," he said, "but we've been worried about you."

"I am quite all right. I will come back later."

Jason regarded her silently for a moment. She was stiff from chilled bones.

"You must come now," he said. He stooped and lifted her. Lacking spirit, she neither protested nor resisted. He carried her to Napoleon, and the horse greeted her with pricked ears. Jason set her down. He swung himself up, reached for her, and brought her to a perch in front of him. She said nothing. Napoleon trotted home carrying both of them. The horse did all the talking for the first five minutes, indulging in a variety of pontificating rumbles. Isabella began to shiver.

"Foolishness," said Jason, "and the cure is a hot bath."

"I am cold, yes," she said, "but not in the same way you are."

"Oh, I am the devil himself," he said, and she was not to know what the pressure of her body against his was doing to him.

"I am going back to Texas," she said faintly.

"I thought you might."

His body was warm, hers still cold. She shivered again. It made him mutter. He pulled Napoleon up, took off his coat, and placed it around her. She gathered it.

"Thank you," she said.

"I mean to talk to you later," he said.

"There is no need," she said. "I have learned my lesson. I have learned that the pride of a woman is nothing at all compared with the lack of understanding in a man."

"Very well, I accept all blame," said Jason.

Such a remark, she thought dully, only widened the distance between them. Yet he was in care of her at the moment, taking her home the quickest way and with his coat and one arm around her. She experienced new shivers, and not so much because she was cold this time.

Antoinette, at her window, observed their approach. Fire smouldered and jealousy burned. Everyone had been so happy. She, Clare, Constance, and him. Until that woman had arrived garbed in sinister black.

Jason ordered a hot bath to be prepared as soon as he brought Isabella into the house. Constance took charge of her and felt her shivering from head to foot. The large enamelled hip bath was carried into Isabella's room, and Emily and another maidservant were soon coming and going with kettle and saucepans of hot water.

Isabella stood and looked on vaguely.

Constance said, "Come, this standing about don't make sense at all. You shall bathe, warm yourself, refresh yourself, and be a woman. You shall sail with your head up under Jason's eyes. He don't give a fig for playacting or sighs or silences. But I tell you, he's so bemused by the turn of events he's ready to be pulled down by any woman of mettle. Take those clothes off and drown your miseries in hot water."

"What does it matter? I am to go back to Texas."

"Hm," said Constance, "much good that will do either of you."

A knock sounded. Constance opened the door. Jason looked in. He eyed the steaming bath and the shivering Isabella.

"Why isn't she in that water?" he asked Constance.

"Why? Why? Had she been, do you think, sir, we should have opened the door to your gawking? Go away."

"I'll give her thirty seconds or have her in myself," said Jason, concerned at Isabella's shivers.

"Oh," cried Isabella, "I'll not set one foot in that bath. I had rather freeze to death now than endure another hour in so cold an atmosphere as you make!"

"Very well," said Jason, and advanced into the room. Constance watched with intrigued delight. That these two people were in love was as plain as a house on fire on a dark night. Jason wished to get his hands on Isabella, using any excuse but love, and Isabella obviously wished for all of that, for her eyes dilated and her colour burned. Yet, even so, to be dumped in the bath? She retreated in panic.

"Jason, no—oh, I beg you—I will get in—"

"Immediately," said Jason, and left.

"Come," said Constance, and began to help Isabella undress. Isabella's moment of panic made her feverish in her disrobing.

"Constance, would he dare to come back?" she asked.

"Do you wish him to?" smiled Constance.

"Oh, no! But he would not, would he?"

"He might," said Constance, "he's a man in concern for you."

"Concern? Concern? He has none for me at all."

Undergarments whispered on their journey of departure. Isabella slipped off her pink garters and silk stockings. Naked, she was perfection. Even Venus would have raised a jealous eyebrow.

"Well, should he come back," said Constance, as Isabella lowered herself into the bath, "I dare swear his coldness would take a warm turn."

Isabella, lapped by steaming water, said, "It's no wonder his wife left him."

"Isabella," said Constance in a pleasantly advisory tone, "I should not make any more mistakes if I were you."

After a moment or two Isabella said, "What is the difference? He is determined to have me back to Texas."

"Yes, what is the difference if it's all one to both of you?"

"Constance." Isabella spoke out of mounting soapsuds. "Constance, you—you spoke to him?"

"Indeed I did," said Constance, pinning up the lustrous, blue-black curls of the Texas woman, "and he agreed, I think, that he'd been unfair in not telling you everything."

Isabella sat almost slumbrously in the bath, the warm water foamy with melting soap flakes, the steam rising to cloud the windows. Her knees peeped, glistening smooth and pearly, above the lather, her rounded bosom twin islands in the bubbles.

"Constance," she said, "a woman is a sad spectacle, isn't she, when she sets out to ruin a man and then complains because he will not love her?"

"If you become a sad spectacle," said Constance, "I shall like you far less than I do."

"Did Jason love his wife so much that he cannot forget her? Is that why he dislikes me so, because my father robbed him of her?"

"He was infatuated with her. The poor woman had too much charm and no sense. Jason don't love her memory half as much as he loves the thought of having you in his arms."

"Constance?" Isabella turned in the bath, and the soapy water splashed. "Constance, is that true?"

"I fancy so," said Constance, "but he glooms about his poverty and your riches."

"Oh, that is infamous," cried Isabella, "to deny me for such a little reason! There, you see, he forgives me nothing, not even the small wealth I have."

"Well, you must fight him like a woman," said Constance. "You must weep, shed tears, fall at his feet, threaten suicide, and so on. If you love him, that is."

"Oh, believe me," said Isabella warmly, earnestly, "my dearest wish is to become your sister."

Emily knocked. Constance answered.

"Begging your pardon, Miss Constance," said Emily, "Mr. Tranter is calling, and wishes to see you."

"Oh?" said Constance, a little light in her eyes.

"Yes'm."

"You may tell him," said Constance grandly, "that I'll be down in ten minutes. He may wait in the west drawing room."

Emily delivered the message, but was up again immediately, saying nervously, "Oh, I be all a-quiver, Miss Constance."

"All a-quiver?" Constance hid her smile.

"Mr. Tranter, ma'am," said Emily hesitantly, "oh, I don't hardly know how to tell you, but he says it's to be either now or—or—"

"Or?" said Constance.

"Oh, what's took him I can't tell, Miss Constance. But he downright says it better be either now or—or he'll never dark our door again."

Constance sallied from the room, down the wide staircase, and into the west drawing room. Ned had his watch in his hand, frowning severely at it.

"Mr. Tranter! How dare you present me with ultimatums through one of my servants!"

Ned marked her splendid arrival. He snapped the watch shut and replaced it in his fob pocket.

"So there you are," he said, "just in time. I'd have shaken the dust in another five seconds." Fortified resolution gleamed in his eyes, and the expression on his healthy face was almost Napoleonic. He regarded his love from his battlements, and his love, for all her indignation, felt her knees knock deliciously. But she pointed a regal finger at the door.

"You may shake the dust now, sir," she said, "and at once. I may be a simple mouse of a woman, but never, sir, never of such meekness as to allow any man to order my comings and goings."

"Ah, you're in fine form as usual," said Ned. "But I'm having no more of your nonsense, madam, no more of your trifling. It's all or nothing, yes or no, live or die, wed or not wed."

"Vainglorious twaddle," said Constance.

"Oh, you're a handsome browbeater of a man's tongue, but it don't cut half the ice this time. I'm fortified, madam, I'm resolved, I'm like iron." And Ned stood like a rock, arms folded, brow lowering.

"You're drunk," said the delighted Constance.

"One large glass of brandy, not a drop more," lied Ned, who had thought one would be enough, but had taken a second for good measure. "Now, my good woman—"

"Good woman? Good woman?" Constance vibrated. "Oh, watch your tongue, sir."

"Well, you ain't a bad woman and that's a fact," said Ned. "Give me your hand." He extended his right arm.

"Shan't," said Constance, and put both hands behind her back.

Ned, seeing this rendered her defenceless and gave her, moreover, an arching splendour to her bosom, said, "Then it's all or nothing, do or die." With that he swept her into his arms.

Constance, astonished, gasped, "Swashbuckler!"

"All or nothing," said Ned, and kissed the extremely kissable mouth. It invigorated him no end, such was the warm sweet pleasure. Constance, her lips imprisoned, simulated outrage by closing her eyes tightly. Ned, bold in his feeling of well-being, kissed her again. "There," he said. "Yes or no, wed or not wed. Give me your answer, my beauty."

"Oh, you desperado!" gasped Constance.

"No tarradiddle, madam, no ravings—"

"Ravings? Unhand me, sir!" Constance, thoroughly enjoying every moment, continued. "Do you imagine me a flighty market baggage, willing to be kissed by every man who has just had a glass of brandy? Ask your question tenderly, sir, and then you'll see what good you've done yourself with your cavalier impropriety."

"Oh, hock, buck, and jump, madam, the question is asked," said Ned, feeling that his second glass had been a very imaginative afterthought. "You'll wed me, or I'll carry you up to your boudoir and compromise you beyond repair."

"Beyond repair?" Constance, still in his arms, quivered at the lusty bravado of mumbler turned villain. "Beyond repair, sir?"

"Aye, beyond repair," said Ned, "for I ain't disposed to be chivvied by you a day longer. Not a minute longer. All or nothing, what's it to be?"

"Oh, if I were a man, sir," said Constance, quite unable to resist prolonging such a wooing, "I'd have your head."

"Well, you ain't a man," said Ned, very aware of the heat and roundness of her handsome breasts, "and damned if I'd love you in breeches and a moustache."

"Am I loved, sir, without breeches and moustache?"

"Heartily," said Ned.

Constance smiled, and Ned fell into her blue eyes.

"Then I yield, sir."

"Eh?" said Ned.

"I yield."

"Oh, b'gad," said Ned, "you do?"

"Unequivocally," said Constance.

"You'll marry me?"

"I should like to, if I may," said Constance, "say yes and please and thank you."

"Damned if I ain't going to jump over the moon," said Ned.

Isabella was warm and glowing from her bath. Dressed, she shimmered in deep red. But her warmth was only physical—only in her appearance and her limbs. The stark consciousness of having made the worst mistake of her life in acquiring the mortgage over Jason's head filled her with cold misery. She sat before the mirror and looked into her own unhappy eyes. For all that Constance had said, she knew Jason would never forgive her. At Cordova he had helped her, even fought for her. Here at Warwick Place she had threatened to turn him out. He was not to know she would never have done so, for he had not known all that was in her mind. What had made her act so stupidly? It paralleled the impossible thoughts she had had about using her vaqueros to keep him at Cordova by force. She could have said she had done it out of love. But he would just have looked at her as if she had gone mad.

She would have to leave Warwick Place. She knew that, and must accept it.

A knock on the door made her jump.

"Come, please."

Jason entered. He closed the door. Her little imp of hysteria danced again and she thought: There, Jason, you have put yourself alone in my room with me and compromised me. But he looked as he so often seemed to look, quite remote from the frail emotions that beset others. She felt a bit of resentment about that. She rose to her feet, summoned up her courage, and held her head high, and Jason thought her at her loveliest.

"You look warmer now," he said.

"Yes. Thank you." Despite her resentment, she felt, as always, physical susceptibility because of his nearness. She wished she did not so often want to touch him and to have him touch her.

"The dress is beautiful," he said.

"Thank you."

"I've always wondered," he said musingly, "why a woman as lovely as you has escaped pursuit and conquest."

That almost wrecked her courage. Her eyes clouded over.

"Jason—I—I am sorry I was so silly."

"I was hard on you," he said.

"That is sometimes the only way to deal with foolishness," she said, and he smiled at that.

"But how is it that you haven't been wooed and won?" he asked.

"Oh, I have been courted, if that is what you mean," she said, "but not by anyone I loved. Please do not address me lightly, señor, it is not the moment."

"Isabella, it's time to finish with this señor and señorita business—or we shall have no chance ever to be much more than acquaintances."

"Please," she said unsteadily, "please let me say I am sorry I acted so badly. But you see, I did not know everything that my father had done. His first consideration has always been himself, but I did not think his faults went beyond selfishness and irresponsibility. I wish you had told me everything, I wish you had believed in my understanding."

Jason, studying her, reflected on the warmth of her firm, shapely mouth, the curving line of her figure, and the muted quality of her mood. Isabella saw his eyes dwelling thoughtfully on her décolletage. Thoughtfully? Her face became tinted with pink.

Jason said, "I didn't want to hurt you more than was necessary. I knew you'd be shocked enough by whatever I did to your father." He looked around him, and at the view the windows gave of the gardens. The evening light was soft, the clouds had broken apart. She wanted to go and stand beside him, to feel that what they could see belonged to both of them. But she did not move.

"Why did you want to hurt me?" she asked. "After all, I was a means to an end. That cannot be denied, can it?"

"I made a bad mistake," he said, "and it became a worse one."

"Why?"

"I grew too fond of your father's daughters."

Too fond? That was all? A mere fondness and for both her and Luisa?

"I will leave tomorrow," she said.

"Will you?" He did not seem too pleased.

"Yes. It's the best thing."

"Warwick Place isn't Texas, of course," said Jason.

"But no one could say it isn't beautiful here," said Isabella.

"London people think it dull, but the cows are commendably fat, aren't they?"

He smiled then, his eyes on summer blooms sensitively ready to close against oncoming twilight. "But you would probably find the winters chilly. You're one with your vaqueros and your Texas sun."

"I am not so frail that winter would shrink me," she said, "and my vaqueros ride for Americans now. But I am an intruder here—"

"Constance is very fond of you," said Jason.

"And I of her. I am glad she does not think too badly of me. I did not really even the score, did I? I only made a stupid mistake. But I wish you had told me everything at Cordova, I wish you had."

She was very courageous, he thought. It gave her an endearing regality.

"I wasn't to know you were going to come halfway across the world to dispossess me."

"I did not come just for that," said Isabella.

He saw figures emerge from the shadow of the house below. Constance and Ned. They were walking hand in hand. Constance was laughing.

"You say you'll go tomorrow?" he said. "But how is the business between us to be settled? Do you wish me, perhaps, to sell Warwick Place for you and remit the money. It may not be as much—"

"No! Oh, how can you say that!" Isabella was up in arms. "You know I would never take your home from you. Nor would I ever have done so. How could you think I would?"

"Probably because you said you would."

"Oh, I cannot remember what I said at times." She steadied herself. "You did so much for us at Cordova that you know I could not do less for you here. Warwick Place is yours. There is no debt."

"I can't accept that," said Jason. He turned squarely to her. "Nor can I accept that you'll leave tomorrow."

"My mind is made up," she said.

"So is mine," said Jason. "I shan't let you leave. You're quite alone. You've no friends to come enquiring after you. If necessary, I could lock you in this room. I'm not rich myself. You're very rich. All the same, I doubt I'll let you go. Ever."

She stared at him. His blue eyes were warm, caressing. Her heart raced so wildly she felt she must faint. Hysterically her mind rushed to a moment at Cordova when she had thought to keep him there by any means she could. He intended to keep her here by means of force? Why? Because he was as desperate for her as she was for him? At that heady conclusion, all misery fled, hysteria retreated, and giddy exhilaration arrived. Dizzily she wondered whether she might not do well to swoon. It would place upon Jason the momentous responsibility of deciding what to do next. But—

"You would dare to lock me in?" she said breathlessly.

"I would," said Jason firmly.

"Keep me here by force, compel me to stay, even compromise me?"

"Isabella, you own every brick, stick, and acre of my inheritance, and I've other creditors, but you have my word that I shan't let you go."

~ 393 ~

The exhilaration total, Isabella cried, "Oh, Jason, you are a pirate! Lock me in, then! Do you think I would beat at the door? Or resist being compromised? I would not lift a finger to save myself. Oh, you have no idea— I will be your most willing prisoner."

Jason said, "It was hardly in my mind to put you in chains."

"In chains?" Isabella thrust out her arms and placed her wrists together. "There, even that I will accept."

"Isabella—"

"It is not meant," she said quickly, her breathing erratic, "it's a gesture, that is all, a gesture, to show you how much I wish to belong to you."

"All I meant was that I love you, sweet Texan," said Jason, and he opened his arms. Isabella fell into them. Jason received her warmly. They kissed in a way that might have been known only to the hungriest of lovers, except that Isabella was not so much conscious of participating in a feast as of limbs and body treacherously weak and inclinations unthinkably alarming.

"Oh, you have driven me mad, taking all this time to love me," she gasped. "Jason, it was not Warwick Place I wanted, but I thought if I had it and gave it back to you after a little while it would bring us together again."

"After I'd become suitably chastened?"

"That is not fair! I was rejected and deserted—"

"You were not."

"I loved you and you deserted me," she insisted. "Yet despite that, I gave up Cordova for you, yes, and even Texas."

"I rather fancy you still had the bit between your teeth," said Jason, "but Texas, yes, it was unfortunate in Texas, falling in love with you while waiting for your father."

Realising he had cast his die, Isabella wound her arms around him to let him know he must stand on its fall.

"Jason, why did you not say? I should have been madly happy and would have begged you to forgive my miserable father and let me make up a hundred times for all he had done. But no, you left me, and I thought you had only used me—"

"Some people," observed Jason, "might have said we used each other."

"Oh, how can you hold me like this and say things like that!" Isabella vibrated. "Why don't you kiss me again?"

"First," said Jason, entirely willing to let her linger in his arms, "how rich are you?"

"I am—" She stopped, quizzing him in warm suspicion. "Oh, no, you are not going to make an unfair consideration of that." Swamped by recurring tides of bliss, she was determined not to be pushed back into any sea of misery. She pressed closer and Jason became pleasurably aware of her breasts caressing him. "I am alone with you and compromised. Therefore, you must kiss me and marry me." Her colour rose. "Jason? Please?"

"Will you be happy here?"

"How can you ask? See, did I not sell Cordova and come all this way to make you understand how I loved you? Have I not spent all these months without you? That is misery enough for any woman. I am not going to let you inflict more on me. Jason, please say we will marry."

Jason smiled, his pleasure acute because of her warmth, her shape, and her beguiling eyes.

"Isabella, I don't fancy life without you, though my financial position is precarious. And God's light, you have such a figure that I'm tempted to lock the door and attack every hook and button I can find, for I judge you a beautiful woman in or out of—"

"Oh, stop!" Isabella was rapturous but scarlet.

"Stop? I haven't begun."

"I meant stop saying such things. Once you said I was safe with you. I am not safe now?"

"You're in peril."

Isabella's eyes danced.

"Oh, I am glad to be at such risk. But a moment, before we kiss again." She looked a little serious. "That girl, Antoinette, your ward."

"Yes?"

"She dislikes me."

"Then you must win her round," said Jason.

"It's not just that," said Isabella, wishing in her newfound possessiveness to have him completely to herself. "She eats you with her eyes and kisses you."

"Modest pecks," said Jason.

"But they make me jealous, all the same. She is in love with you."

"Antoinette is only making a religion of gratitude at the moment," he said. "You're aware of the circumstances?"

"Yes," said Isabella. Constance had told her about Antoinette.

"She might, because of her parents, have come to grief in New Orleans."

"Because they left her nothing."

Jason did not answer that, but said, "However, she has sense and so avoided grief. Be patient with her. You've nothing to worry about."

"She is very special?" said Isabella, and asked herself how he could expect her not to be jealous.

"She's my ward. It's you who are very special." He turned her chin up. Her eyes were swimming. "Isabella?"

"Oh, if I am very special to you I am so happy," she said.

"Then shall we make peace, little Texan?"

"May we not kiss first?"

"That was what I meant," he said.

"Oh, then please take your time, please have many kisses," said Isabella. She lifted her mouth. "Please begin. Please?"

# 10

Antoinette sat in her room. She contemplated the wonder of the knife. Its wonder was in what it could do for those she loved. It rested in her lap, its blade edged by years of sharpening. She ran her fingers lightly over it. It had lain in the bottom drawer of her tallboy for several days, hidden among lace and linen. Her eyes were luminous, her resolution a lodged darkness in her mind. Each day she took the knife out, looked at it, thought about it, and lightly stroked it. And each day her resolution strengthened and the dark thoughts became closer to the bright deed.

The woman. She had come to take possession and had succeeded. She wore black no more. She went about plumaged with colour, looking radiant and beautiful. Antoinette had never seen any woman more beautiful and happier. She possessed everyone and everything, she exercised bewitchment. She charmed every person in the house and put her mark on the house itself, and the warm air of summer poured in to enhance her radiance and lay magic upon her.

She possessed Jason. Her eyes followed him and her hands touched him. They were to marry.

There were to be two weddings: Constance was to marry Ned Tranter. And Constance, so pleasant, equable, and sensible, went about as if she too had been bewitched.

Antoinette got up and went to the window, turning the knife caressingly in her hands. The morning was clear. The sun was up, climbing and golden. She could see the deep blue of the heavens and the soft green of the hills. She could hear the murmurous sounds of early summer coming to life. Day after day the late lambs were being born. Her eyes, dreamy, encompassed the bounty of nature and the vistas that were ever-changing; the weather here was never still, and the colours of one moment were not those of the next. The earth was blessed with beauty. Here she had been brought from the New World, whose own wonders she had never been able to view with the eyes of freedom. Here she had been brought by Jason, who had given her his earth, his sky, and his home. And asked for nothing.

All that she could see from the window was accessible to her. She could walk to any part of it. No one would tell her no. And if she met people they would smile, the women would bob and the men touch their hats or their forelocks, because they knew she was the ward of Jason Rawlings, the squire. She could chase through the woods, run through the meadows, climb the slopes, and have the sheep and lambs eyeing her either with placid curiosity or with a nervousness that would have them running the moment she moved. But the lambs could always be caught and held and laughed at. And wherever she went she could stop and spread her arms to the sky and call it her own. She was without chains except those forged by her mixed blood and her sensitive, passionate love for Jason. The chains of her mixed blood she scarcely felt; her passionate love held her in emotional bondage.

And that was hers alone. No woman, even the one who was to

be his wife, could take from her the smallest part of her love. Nor could the woman send her away.

"M'sieu, what is to happen to me when you marry?"

"Nothing is to happen to you, sweet girl. You belong to us. You will gain a sister in Isabella, and she will come to love you as we do."

He had said that yesterday.

The sun ran bright all over the earth, her heart leapt free of its heaviness and her mind cast off its darkness.

She went down to the kitchen.

"I found this knife," she said. "Does it belong here?"

"Oh, Miss 'Tonnit, that be a slicer gone missing," said the cook. "Where be you found um?"

"Oh, outside," said Antoinette, and smiled as she left, which made the cook give out to the kitchen boy that there wasn't a prettier love anywhere. And the kitchen boy got his ears boxed for saying nor wasn't there no love who wore prettier pantaloons.

Antoinette glided through the hall. Isabella appeared.

"Isabella," said Antoinette, "have you seen Clare?"

Isabella, intoxicatedly in love, blinked. Antoinette was smiling at her, the incomparably huge eyes without either hostility or threat.

"Antoinette? Oh, are we to be friends at last?"

"But of course," said Antoinette, "for you are not going to pull the house down now, are you?"

"Nor would I have," declared Isabella warmly.

"Yes, you would."

"Antoinette, so beautiful a house?"

"It is beautiful to those who belong to it," said Antoinette. "To those who cannot belong or enter, it is a place to be pulled down because of envy. You belong to it now, so you must love it and take care of it, and all who are in it."

"Oh, as if I would not," said Isabella.

"There, you are now my sister," said Antoinette, and kissed the astonished Isabella on the cheek. "But be careful."

"Careful?"

"Always. Never put a frown on Jason's face or bring trouble to him. If you ever do I will drown you in the pond."

"Antoinette!"

"So be very careful, dear sister."

"Oh, you are wrong to speak so," protested Isabella. "I came halfway across the world to be his love."

"Halfway?" Antoinette, a poetic elegance, laughed and shook her head. "Only halfway? I know a thousand women in New Orleans who would march twice round the whole world if they knew that in the end it would bring them here."

"You are speaking of those poor Negro slave women," said Isabella.

"Sweet sister," said Antoinette, "I am speaking of many women. But have you seen Clare?"

"She is in the gardens with Constance. Antoinette, a moment." Isabella detained the New Orleans beauty. "You must not misjudge me. I am committed to the happiness of this family, but I think I know what you are trying to tell me." She smiled. "Thank you. I shall be very careful."

Isabella watched Antoinette float away, then entered the library. Jason was there, frowning over figures and calculations. He looked up. Isabella felt a rush of giddy love. She knew indeed what Antoinette had meant.

"You are busy, I know," she said, "but I would just like to say a little something."

"You're a fascinating woman," said Jason, "and if you really can say no more than just a little something, then you're also a remarkable one and quite unlike most other women."

"Thank you."

"Say on, my love," he smiled.

"Oh, that is precious to me," she said.

"What is?"

"Being your love. It's also seriously necessary to my well-being. What are all these figures you are frowning over?"

"They're to do with debts and settlements," said Jason. "Do you see, this is what I owe you—those are the interest payments. And these other calculations, if you can make them out, show how long it will take to repay you. Those are figures relating to other creditors. I'm afraid—"

"Oh, Jason." She had not known about his other creditors until he had told her a few days ago. She took up the notes and would have shredded them had she not stopped to think. She placed them back on the bureau desk and said, "I will accept the figures, they are bound to be true and honest, and I agree to whatever terms you think best. But the other creditors—Jason, you will remember, won't you, that I have some money of my own, and it is only right that I should pay—"

"It's right you should keep your money. It's not right, generous sweetheart, that you should keep me."

"No, I would never attempt to," Isabella assured him. She might have said that in taking her to task often enough because of her pride, he was not entitled to be too proud himself. "But I do not want marriage to make you too poor."

"If you're happy with these figures," said Jason, "it means you're allowing me very generous terms, and so we shan't be in want."

"I am very happy with everything, everything," she said. There were always ways and means of using her money to enrich the estate, to fill the stables with thoroughbreds, to buy more cattle and build more cottages for rent. She dearly wanted to. "Jason?"

"Yes," he said. "I see you are still intent upon saying your little something."

"It is just that I want you to know—oh, that I hope you will never regret our marriage." She hesitated, then went on. "I have been so concerned with my own feelings that I had not thought about how you felt. I have only just realised what you are doing for me in giving marriage another chance."

"I'm only giving you a chance to find out I'll probably make a boring husband."

"No, you are giving me a chance to show you I will never be another Edwina," said Isabella. "There—perhaps I should not have mentioned her, but I have. Do you understand?"

"Yes, and I'm grateful," smiled Jason. "I'm grateful for knowing you, having you, and looking at you."

"Looking at me?" That pleased her immensely.

"Of course. And am I to see what you're setting aside for your trousseau?"

"Oh, willingly I will show you," she said. "Everything, if you wish. Jason, do you wish to see everything?"

"Something would be interesting," said Jason, "everything would be enchanting."

"You do not really mean everything?"

"Yes, I do."

"I should never survive such a display."

"It's quite optional," said Jason.

"Oh, you are a sweet man, it is so good to love you." Isabella stooped and kissed him. "You will see, I shall make up for everything and will leave all decisions to you while I busy myself being your wife."

"I'll be happy for you to be yourself, for I don't fancy any milk and water woman."

"I shall not be that," she assured him. "But yes, you shall decide things. Except, of course, I am perhaps better at dealing with servants and household matters—which you should not have to worry about in any event. And you may happily leave me to see to the furnishing of the room which is to be our own. Also, whenever we go to the cattle market, remember I have a very good eye for horses and steers—"

"Is that how you'll leave all things to me?" Jason laughed, rose to his feet, stooped, and swept her up into his arms. Her dress ballooned, her white petticoats showered, and her lace-trimmed pantaloons emerged into the light. Isabella kicked and gasped as he carried her to the couch in the centre of the library. There he set her down, and she pushed at her billowing clothes. But he caught her hands and she lay there, her face pink, her heart in excited tumult. He sat down on the edge of the couch.

"Jason—oh, heaven above, see how you have uncovered me!"

"Your pantaloons?" He regarded them, with their lace and the pink ribbons that threaded the lace. "Lovely, by the Lord Harry."

"But we aren't married yet," she gasped.

"God's life, married or not, these are extraordinarily delicious. Is the waist tie also of pink?"

"Jason! Oh, remove your eyes! And your hand!"

"Such froth, I swear, is more intoxicating than that which graces a tankard of old ale—"

"Jason! Oh, how can you!"

"All too easily." Jason laughed. Isabella's limbs melted. She received his warm, lingering kiss. She sank into bliss, into love, then stiffness, and gasped. Her toes curled and ecstatic shivers alternated with rapturous burnings.

Oh, the pirate!

Antoinette, unable to locate Clare and Constance for the moment, came round to the front of the house on her way to the stables, for it was to the stables Clare pulled her mentors so often. Outside the house Antoinette halted. The brightness of the day and the shedding of darkness made her breathe deeply and gladly.

A horseman appeared, cantering up from the drive. He reined in, dismounted, and approached. She gazed wonderingly at him for a moment. He was slender. He was also elegant and handsome, as were so many of the Creole dandies of New Orleans, except that he was not one of them. He was taller and had blue eyes like Jason's. His colour was healthy and his smile was that of a young man rediscovering enchantment. He looked into her wondering eyes, doffed his top hat, and uncovered his dark brown hair. He bowed.

"My dear young lady," he said, "are you Warwick's summer princess?"

"M'sieu, I am Antoinette, the ward of the best man in all England, Jason Rawlings," she said.

"Are you, by heaven? And he the best of us all?" His laugh was one of delight. "But who am I?"

"You, m'sieu, are Noel Rawlings."

"So, I'm remembered then. Even though I lack the stature of cousin Jason. Well, I said I'd be back, and so I am. For to tell you the truth, sweet girl of summer, we're always a little duller in my home than they are here."

"Oh, here we dance all day, m'sieu," said Antoinette.

"So should I, in your company," said Noel. "Frankly, I'm here not only to quiz you again, but because I've been roared at by my father, God bless his trumpet. He demands I find something useful to do and I've come, therefore, to discover whether Jason can employ me. Though I ain't precisely the brainiest fellow in Dorset, I can build a rick, shoe a horse, dip a sheep, and play a fine fiddle. So will you take me to my cousin, sweet Antoinette, and give my visit here a rare beginning, even if it don't come to anything better than a hatful of downed skittles?"

Antoinette looked into his laughing eyes, and although nothing and no one could ever lessen her deep and abiding love for Jason, her heart executed a delicious little flip.

"Come, m'sieu," she said gravely, "it is the custom here to welcome most gladly a cousin who can shoe a horse and play a fine fiddle."